Sea
of
Pleasure
&
Pain

J. STŘELOU

Author's note:

This book is a dark romance fantasy set in our world. That being said,
I have taken full creative liberties when creating the fictional town of
Ruadán's Port and the fantastical Kingdom of the Deep, as well as some of
the locations at Santorini. So, if you're a scientist or marine biologist, or
you happen to work for NASA—it's time to suspend your disbelief . . .

After all, none of us truly know what lies in the
deepest, darkest corners of the ocean.

CHECK CONTENT WARNINGS:

Sea of Pleasure and Pain contains depictions of domestic
violence as well as sexual manipulation in a violent domestic relationship (not between main characters).

These scenes were not included for shock value, but as a way to give a voice to
the one in three women globally who have experienced domestic violence.

That being said, your mental health matters, and I understand reliving
this could be triggering. If that's the case, please skip chapter six and eight.
You can find an overview of these chapters at the end of the book after
the acknowledgment, so missing them will not affect your experience.

This book also contains explicit sexual scenes between sea creatures (monster
romance), sexual scenes, sexual coercion, drowning of a child, death, and violence. Readers who may be sensitive to these elements, please read with care.

If you would like a detailed trigger warning, you can
find it on: **juliastrelou.com/content-warnings**

the kingdom
of the deep
neptūnus
uss phantom
wild west of the ocean
port royal
pācificus mer kingdom
blackwater ghost
kaimana sīrēnēs
the lost horizon

veus mer kingdom
nus castle
ruadán's port
luch sírenēs
om
enēs
thálassa mer kingdom
the icarus
sundara sírenēs
okeános mer kingdom
ss midnight gale
er kingdom
krumós mer kingdom
n
w
e
s

cemetery
bayside shopping center
mc
FERRIS WHEEL
samscary st
finn's house
MERROW ROC

RUADÁN'S PORT
ace
morgana's house
bookstore
the port house
cróy st
obivere place
na's jetty
ghthouse

RUNES OF THE OCEAN

Glossary

Aarna (Aar-na) Origin: Sanskrit

Aigéan (Ah-gee-ahn) Origin: Irish

Agápē (Ah-GHAH-peh) Origin: Ancient Greek

Aranare (Ar-ah-nar-ay) Origin: Minoan

Archōn Agorá (Ar-kon A-go-rah) Origin: Ancient Greek

Asherah (Uh-SHEER-uh) Origin: Hebrew and Ugaritic

Ătlanticus (At-lanti-cus) Origin: Latin

Hēracleion (Heh-RAH-klee-on) Origin: Ancient Greek

Iona (eye-OH-na) Origin: Gaelic

Krumós (Kru-mos) Origin: Ancient Greek

Kyano (Ki-a-nos) Origin: Ancient Greek

Lugh (Loo-gh) Origin: Irish

Manannán (Man-nuh-náhn) Origin: Irish

Neptūnus (Nep-tune-us) Origin: Latin

Niveus (Niv-EE-us) Origin: Latin

Okeanós (Oh-KEE-a-nohs) Origin: Ancient Greek

Pācificus (Pa-chif-i-cus) Origin: Latin

Peisinoe (Pee-see-NO-ee) Origin: Ancient Greek

Pháos (FAH-oss) Origin: Ancient Greek

Pisceon (Pies-cee-on) Origin: Latin

Porphura (Por-FOO-rah) Origin: Ancient Greek

Proteus (proh-TAY-yuhs) Origin: Ancient Greek

Ruadán (Roo-ah-dan) Origin: Irish

Selich (Sel-itch) Origin: Scottish

Síocháin (shee-ukh-awn) Origin: Irish

Thálassa (Tha-AH-la-sah) Origin: Ancient Greek

Therme Skótos (ThER-me SKŌ-tos) Origin: Ancient Greek

Sānitātem (Sah-nee-TAH-tem) Origin: Latin

Sundara (Sun-de-ra) Origin: Sanskrit

Prologue

FINN

I'd made a pact with the shadows and my father, and I didn't know which was worse. The freshly healed heart of ink on my chest burned with the reminder of the promises I'd made.

I pressed my palms into the cold stone surface of the war room table, my tail flicking idly as memories of what had happened after Morgana stunned my father and left our castle swirled around me.

I'd done the right thing. No matter how many times I replayed it all in my mind, I always ended up here.

"Cousin." Pisceon was in the doorway, a muscle tightening between his dark brows. "The castle's warding has begun."

I nodded as the beautiful, haunting song of our people filled the space, winding through the currents like a gentle breeze. All around the edges of the kingdom, Mer would be singing in the old tongue of the sea.

My bride-to-be, Glacies, appeared behind Pisceon, pale hair billowing in the current as she crossed her arms over the gleaming Neptūnus breastplate she wore.

I raised a brow in question.

"Pisceon and I will leave today," she said, gesturing toward my cousin. "We'll rally the other Mer and Siren kingdoms, then meet you at Thálassa. From there, we'll travel together to Okeanós for the summit."

"Good." I exhaled, sending a stream of bubbles swirling around me.

Glacies dipped her chin, then she and Pisceon drifted from the room. A small smile tugged at my lips. I was glad to offer her this journey—freedom from our kingdom and the chance to spend time in places more . . . tolerant. Perhaps she and her lover could reunite on the trip.

No sooner had they disappeared into the gloom on the other side of the doorway than my guards Alga and Korul appeared.

"The charts and books that you wanted, sire." Alga inclined his head, his pale tail glowing opalescent in the murky light.

I waved a hand at the table, and Alga dumped them there.

"Thank you. Now leave me," I grunted, sweeping my fringe from my face as I pulled the first map toward me.

A sharp throb at my wrist halted me. I raised my arm, and my breath stuttered for a moment. Dread slithered down my throat and curdled in my gut.

A vein, black and thin as a whisper, snaked beneath my skin, winding like poisoned ivy.

The Shadow.

I curled my webbed fingers into a fist, banging them onto the table with a force that sent the little stone figurines we used for plotting battle strategy rattling.

Fuck.

The world seemed to be caving in on either side of me as my breathing became shallower. How long did I have until I was bedridden, like Glacies's cousin Íss? A year, maybe.

I would end my life before I let them confine me to a bed in the Sānitātem.

Panic clawed through me, each breath growing more ragged until I forced my fists to unclench. I had things I needed to do and promises I needed to keep—*for her.*

Expelling a breath, I riffled through the papers Alga had left until I found the one I was looking for. I pulled the leather strings of the scroll open, hands still trembling. The moon chart was faded brown and hand-painted. Across the top, the word *Luna* was scrawled. A merman with outstretched arms was depicted, surrounded by a ring of painted ovals.

The waning crescent glowed beneath my touch as I traced its curve with my finger. The full moon was positioned at the center of the design. When that moon shone silver, it would be time to meet Morgana at Archōn Agorá.

Something stirred in my chest, tightening around my heart. The silver sickle on the map glowed brighter, reminding me of her. She was the moon, and my thoughts the tide, forever at the mercy of her pull. She looked at me and saw more than darkness, and somehow, that made me want to be . . . better. It reminded me of who I once was, a very long time ago.

The haunting song of the Mer warding the castle drifted into the room, echoing through the chambers in the ancient tongue of the sea.

"Alga. Korul," I called, and the two guards, who had stationed themselves at the door, drifted back into the room.

"Go to the armory and ask them to make me silver bracers that match my breastplate."

They dipped their chins in assent.

"And see if they can make me a cuff in leather as well for when I walk upon the land."

"Yes, Your Highness." The guards left the room.

I lifted my wrist to my face once more. The veins were still faint, delicate, and barely visible, but I knew it wouldn't last. Soon, they'd begin to snake up my arm, and I'd need the cuffs to hide them.

I lowered my fist and cracked my knuckles, exhaling. I had to focus on the task ahead, on the bargains I had struck.

Promises sealed in ink and blood are not to be broken.

The heart-shaped tattoo on my chest throbbed with the weight of that truth, and as it did, shadows slithered from the walls, curling around my wrist and caressing the dark veins that had begun to spread there.

"*You* gave me the Shadow?" I hissed at the swirling darkness, my fingers flexing as it curled up my arms.

Think of it as an extra incentive to keep your promise, little prince.

The voice—ancient, cold as the ocean's deepest trench—coiled through my mind. Then, slowly, the shadows receded, slinking back into the labyrinthine dungeons where they had waited for millennia.

PART ONE

The Sirens

1.

MORGANA

Aranare stood with his back to the ocean, a wooden blade slung across his shoulder, as I trudged across the cliff face, trying to ignore the relentless ache in my muscles.

Louisa had divided my training into three parts: combat with Aranare, mind work and ancient history with her, and magic-wielding, but I wasn't allowed to start that until I had mastered my mind.

I rolled my eyes, thinking of how often I'd failed to quiet my thoughts for more than a few minutes during Louisa's lessons.

The morning wind whipped across the cliffside, tugging at my hair and sweatshirt as waves hissed against the jagged rocks far below. The dark and endless sea stretched beyond the edge of the grassy bluff, its salty scent carrying reminders of what I knew lay deep beneath it. Nearby, weatherworn Celtic gravestones jutted from the earth, cradling strands of early morning mist.

Whenever a storm arose, I wondered if Manannán was gathering more Drowned to swell his ranks, but we hadn't experienced unearthly gales since I'd broken the wheel. Still, I knew he was somewhere beneath the waves, assembling his forces and preparing to strike against the Mer.

The morning wind tousled Aranare's dark hair, his parka zipped up to his chin, but when I reached him, a grin split his face. "Let's see if you're ready to use that wee dagger you love so much."

I'd brought my blade up from the ocean's depths. Like my fur coat, the sea had allowed me to carry it onto land. I'd shown up to our first combat lesson proudly clutching it, only for Aranare to laugh himself hoarse. "You need to learn to walk before you can run, lass," he'd choked out between chuckles.

My dummy sword was nowhere near as fancy as his. I picked up the piece of thick driftwood I now kept up here for training and got into position.

As it turned out, Aranare had a passion for combat and usually spent his mornings working up a sweat in his uncle's gym, making him the perfect sparring partner.

He lunged, and I dodged, tuning out the protests of my sore limbs. He swung again—wood meeting wood—and our gazes locked. Suddenly, I was no longer looking into Aranare's golden eyes; they became onyx as I thought of Finn.

I ducked, pivoted, and struck. My movements had sharpened after weeks of relentless training, with each strike serving as an outlet for my thoughts.

There was an ancient prophecy that could stop the impending war— one tied to me, to my blood. But its second half had been lost.

Finn's father, King Neptūnus, had had my grandmother killed, believing her blood was the key. She'd known it wouldn't work but said nothing. She died to protect me.

Now, Finn and his father had a lead on the missing piece of the prophecy, and I had to go with him—to pretend to trust him—if I wanted to learn the truth.

Aranare repositioned his stance, and I struck again—harder, faster—and again, my thoughts flashing with every blow.

Had Finn killed my grandmother?

Had he done his father's bidding, then set his sights on me?

I circled Aranare on the clifftop, fists clenched around my driftwood stick. Our weapons clashed, and I pushed him back, using my thoughts as my fuel.

Only two weeks remained until the full moon—the night I was to meet Finn beneath the archway of Archōn Agorá and journey to the Kingdom of Thálassa in search of the prophecy.

And for that, I needed to be ready. I needed to be trained.

Thinking about Finn created a boil of rage in my throat. The last time I'd seen him, he'd told me that I was his moon, that he couldn't breathe without me. But that was before, before . . .

I slammed my stick toward Aranare's chest, but he caught the blow with his oak sword, holding it inches from his body. The wood groaned between us as our arms tensed, eyes locking, neither willing to yield.

"Good." He nodded in approval and stepped back, allowing me to catch my breath.

"Let's go again," I said between sharp inhales.

Aranare chuckled as he swung his sword around and lunged, but I sidestepped, morning mist swirling around me like a cloak. Our wooden weapons clashed, and for a moment, he pressed me back.

No. With a twist of my wrist, I hooked my stick under his.

Aranare tried to wrench it back, but I dropped low, sweeping his legs out from under him with a kick. As he stumbled, I struck, knocking the wooden blade from his hand and spinning it down to the grass.

Aranare blinked up at me from one knee, a flicker of surprise crossing his face. I straightened, stick in hand, breathing hard, a satisfied smile curving my lips.

"Wow, great, Morgana," he said breathlessly. "I think that's enough for today. I'll see you here again tomorrow."

I groaned in response, rubbing my shoulder muscles with stiff, cold fingers as I trudged back across the cliff face and down past the bay to the bookstore.

I hadn't seen Finn since I returned to Ruadán's Port. I'd avoided his glassy-eyed clifftop mansion, half expecting to run into him somewhere around town, but he never appeared.

It had been two weeks since I'd burst into the bookstore, telling Aranare and Louisa the Neptūnus family had murdered my grandmother. Louisa had been my grandmother's only friend in this town, so I knew I could trust her. After everything I'd been through, I needed people I could trust. I didn't say what I suspected—that Finn had carried out the killing on his father's orders. I couldn't bring myself to voice it.

Since then, I'd studied daily with Louisa and met Aranare for combat on the cliffs. Rain or shine, we'd trained—even when sleet lashed our faces and I was frozen to the bone. And most nights, I was so exhausted when I fell into bed that I didn't have time to think about Finn and what he might have done.

2.

MORGANA

Louisa waited in the dimly lit back room of the bookstore, her expression unreadable. My chest tightened. I might have been progressing in combat, but my struggle with mind mastery was holding me back, and without that, I couldn't move on to magic-wielding.

"Looks like you had a good lesson." Louisa's thin mouth transformed into a smile as she took in my messy hair and dirty clothes.

I nodded.

"Are you ready for today's session?"

"Sure." I tried to act nonchalant. Still, anxiety clanged through me as I thought about the number of times I had attempted to quiet my mind in this room and instead found myself plagued by thoughts or distracted by Louisa's emotions—usually something between frustration and pity.

"You know what to do." Louisa gestured to the bohemian-style cushion in the corner of the room, which reminded me of something my grandmother would have picked up during her travels. The thought sent a stab of anger through me as I sat down cross-legged on the pillow.

Louisa hit play on the meditation music. I was to sit here for thirty extremely long minutes and focus on clearing my mind. Easier said than done.

I had started to dread this cushion, because every time I sat down, exhaled, and focused on clearing my mind, the thoughts came rushing in. Finn, and the darkness inside of him, that darkness moving within me, the pirates who'd attempted to rape me, the war that was coming, and my father, whom I still hadn't found. I tried to notice these thoughts, release them, and replace them with stillness, but they would tear through my body and rumble up my throat until they consumed me. Then, I would find myself sobbing.

"It's okay," Louisa said each time as she patted my back. "This will get easier. With time, the tears will fade, and the stillness will come as you begin to master your mind."

Today was no different. I closed my eyes and focused on the music. It was beautiful music, Indian in origin, and it wrapped around me with a powerful magic akin to that of the Mer's song. I focused on my breathing as Louisa had taught me, on the patterns of light before my eyelids, but then the first thought made its way in: Finn and what I suspected he'd done. I clenched my fists but dispelled the thought.

What came next wasn't a thought but a feeling. Fear coiled in my gut as I turned inward—I didn't want to be in there. It was too dark, too raw. I needed a distraction. The dread welled up and broke free in a trembling sob.

Louisa walked over with understanding in her eyes. "That's enough for today. Although it doesn't feel like it, you're improving. When you first started, you didn't even make it one minute." She looked at her watch. "Today, you made it twenty."

"I think I prefer combat training," I grumbled.

"I know this might seem stupid, but it is imperative. Mastering your powers takes a disciplined mind and an open heart." Louisa held out her hand to me, and I stood.

"How come you know so much about this stuff anyway?"

"I'm a historian. When I learned that entire species had been reduced to myths and legends in human history books, I made it my life's work to uncover the truths buried within those fables."

"What's next, ancient history?" I dragged my gaze to the table, where the book from yesterday's history lesson still lay open. Its pages were filled with notes on the Minoans, the mysterious people believed to have emerged around 3100 BC in the Mediterranean.

"Let's try something different today. You've already honed your Selkie skills—direction, sensing the ocean's moods, and hunting prey—which is excellent. But if you've inherited the same skills as your grandmother, you should be able to channel that empathic mind magic into more than emotions, and see images. Shall we?" She gestured to the small table and seated herself across from me.

"So what powers do you expect me to have?"

"Your friend Edward was right to think you draw power from the well of peace, but with a Drowned father, you also carry the power of death. That makes your magic unpredictable and dangerous."

I nodded. That was great. So far, my magic had put people into a floating slumber or turned them into dust.

"You ready?" Louisa asked, tucking a strand of silvery hair behind one ear and allowing her gray eyes to meet mine.

I nodded and closed my eyes.

"See if you can see more than my emotions." She slipped her palm into mine.

Taking a deep breath, I squeezed her hand and scanned her emotions:

impatience and unease. She was scared I wouldn't be able to master this in time. I feared she was right.

I exhaled sharply, scrunching my eyes shut as if I could force the self-doubt out of my body. Cautiously, I cracked one open. Darkness. Louisa's steady grip still anchored my hand, but I could no longer see her.

Then the darkness began to fade, replaced by a blinding lightness. Waves were sighing, and sea salt seared my nostrils. My feet were pressed into pale sand, which was dusted with crushed shells and fragments of obsidian that glinted in the sun.

I dragged my eyes to the horizon, the azure ocean glittering in my view. I knew this was not Ruadán's Port; it was too bright, too turquoise.

I spun around. Behind me, a cliff rose in ochre and clay-red stone tiers, its ledges dotted with buildings adorned with painted frescoes. Long wooden boats lined with oars rested on the sand nearby. Beside one of the narrow prows, a dark-haired man, barefoot and bronze-skinned, twisted ropes while humming a melody.

I was suddenly grateful for the history lessons I had taken with Louisa when a realization washed over me: I was standing in ancient Thera, as it had been known before the eruption shattered it into what we now call the Greek island of Santorini. The actual name of this civilization was lost to time, but archaeologists and historians, such as Louisa, referred to them as the Minoans.

My breathing quickened, but the sensation of Louisa's hand in mine remained. This was a vision . . . only a vision. My arm must have been resting on yesterday's open history book, so I'd been led here.

My breath hitched as I realized the scene unfolding before me might have occurred four or five thousand years ago, long before the Battle of the Blue Temple, during what Edward called the Age of Gods.

I swept my gaze around in awe as women in flowing linen strolled across the beach, where strands of wool lay drying after being dyed deep purple. Merchants laughed and called from the docks.

"Manannán," a woman's voice called. I hunched my shoulders and whipped my gaze to her.

She was wearing a colorful dress, her bronzed skin shining in the sun, and her long, black tresses fell down her back. She was holding the hand of a young boy.

"Kitane, my love," another voice answered, and I saw it belonged to the man who had been tending to the boat.

They were not speaking English, but my mind translated what they were saying.

Louisa's hand tightened around mine, grounding me in the moment. A reminder that this was only a vision. A vision of Manannán. But how could this be the God of the Dead?

The young boy let go of his mother's hand and sprinted toward the fisherman, Manannán, who swept him into his strong arms, spinning him around as laughter burst from the child. The man's face was warm and handsome.

I moved closer to the group, taking hesitant steps, but none of them looked my way.

They can't see me.

"Must you go away again so soon?" the woman called Kitane asked, cupping Manannán's cheek.

He blew out a breath and ruffled his son's hair. "We need copper, and I must take supplies of olive oil and wine to Ătlanticus and our men toiling in the Scottish copper mines."

"I want to go with Papa," the child begged, looking between his parents.

Manannán hoisted him up onto his hip. "You are too young, my boy, but one day soon."

The three of them made their way back up the beach, walking straight toward me. My grip tightened on Louisa's hand; surely, they would see me or hear my hammering heart.

They moved closer, and I pulled every part of my body in, but the woman's eyes were fixed on the colorful houses behind me, and the young boy skipped alongside her. Only Manannán turned, his face tilting ever so slightly in my direction, a quizzical expression passing through his olive eyes, but then it was gone. He walked on with his family as the beach dissolved into shadow and the dim back room of the bookstore swam back into view.

I clutched my chest, my breath coming in ragged bursts. There was sweat on my upper lip.

"What did you see?" Louisa's brow was furrowed, her tone grave.

"I saw Manannán, but he wasn't in Taranis's body, and he wasn't the God of the Dead . . . he was just a man." My eyes filled with tears when I thought about the scene I had witnessed, and I didn't know why.

"I think you saw Manannán *before* he became God of the Drowned." Louisa ran a hand through her silvery hair as she surveyed me.

"My elbow—it was on the history book," I gasped as the Minoan frescoes on the page swam into focus, pulling my vision back with them.

"A vision is progress." Louisa blew out a breath. "You still have a long way to go before you're ready to wield even a spark of magic, but with only two weeks until you leave for the Kingdom of Thálassa, we'll begin your magic-wielding tomorrow after combat."

I nodded, sniffing back my tears and stifling a yawn. The vision had exhausted me.

"And Morgana,"—Louisa's gaze burned through me—"if you hurt my son with those wild powers of yours, you will break my heart."

I scrunched my nose in confusion. "Aranare's going to train me in magic-wielding? I thought you were."

"My son is more qualified in that department than I am, you'll see." Louisa smiled.

"I won't hurt him. I promise." I nodded, meeting her gaze, but a cold knot formed in my stomach.

Night had fallen when I arrived back at Granddad's little whitewashed house.

Every day since I'd returned from the depths, I'd followed the same pattern. I'd rise before dawn, pull on gloves and a jacket, and trudge up the hill to meet Aranare. After that, I'd visit Louisa in the bookstore; sometimes I would stay on after the lesson, helping shelve books to earn some money. Then I'd spend whatever time I had left taking care of Granddad. The exhaustion suited me. I welcomed it. Because most days, I was too tired to think about everything that had happened.

Granddad was in the living room reading the paper when I stalked past on my way to the shower. He was better now—not the husk of a man I'd first met—and the thought of that made me smile.

"Your mom called . . . again," he grumbled, rustling the pages with an exasperated sigh.

"I'll call her back tomorrow," I promised, continuing down the hall as my throat tightened.

I hadn't spoken to my mother since learning of my father's death. She'd tried calling countless times, but I avoided her. Between the time difference, my hours beneath the sea, and training, it was easy. Granddad was tired of reassuring her, and I couldn't blame him.

The steaming shower soothed my sore muscles, droplets cascading over my skin as I scrunched my eyes shut and let the heat wash over me. Thoughts of Finn crept in, but I shoved them into the void I'd carved inside myself, refusing to remember the feel of his hands or how they'd made me burn.

After my shower, I padded upstairs and slipped into warm pajamas. Through the small square window, the moon glowed, thin, barely a sliver behind the clouds. Soon it would begin to swell again, growing full. And when it did, it would be time for me to leave. The thought made me wrap my arms around myself.

I meant to head back to the kitchen to have dinner with Granddad, but the moment I collapsed onto the bed, sleep claimed me.

3.

MORGANA

The next day was bitterly cold, and an icy wind tore across the island, making training even more horrible, but we persevered.

We circled each other on the cliff face until my gloved fingers were stiff and my cheeks and nose flushed pink. I hadn't thought my muscles could ache more than they had yesterday, but I'd been wrong.

After hours of clashing dummy swords and drilling new maneuvers, the rain came, frustrating spit-like shards of ice on my skin. Still, Aranare pressed me to continue, even as my teeth chattered and my lips turned blue.

At last, when my body couldn't take another second, he lowered his wooden sword. I collapsed onto the cold grass with a groan, only to spring back up as its chill leached through my sweatpants.

"Mom said you were ready to try wielding today, but I think we'll start with shields, because I don't fancy being turned into dust." Aranare eyed me warily as we stood on the clifftop. Dark clouds hung low overhead, and the sea sighed as it caressed the rocks far below.

I wiped the sweat from my brow as my breathing quickened. The last three occasions I'd tapped into my magic, it had manifested differently each time—turning two Drowned to dust, shattering the Ferris wheel, and sending an entire room of Mer into a stupor. Yes, it had saved me from a few tight spots, but it had felt like pure chance—nothing more than a fluke.

"Not very talkative today, are we?" Aranare folded his arms across his chest and observed me. "So, has Mom had you controlling your mind?"

I nodded, guilt curdling my stomach. I was barely controlling anything.

"Great." Aranare grinned. "Now, I want you to harness that control to shield yourself."

"From what?" I asked, swiping more sweat from my neck with my grass-stained hands.

"From me." His eyes glittered.

"Okay." I furrowed my brow, trying to steady my thoughts as my gaze locked on him. I expected him to reach for his wooden sword again, but he didn't. He just stood there, watching me.

"Are you ready?" he asked, cocking his head to one side.

I held up a shaky hand as panic clawed at my throat. "Give me a minute."

Taking a deep breath, I relaxed my body and then my mind. I let an unwavering belief swell in my heart and glimpsed the flicker of silver power in my subconscious.

"Ready." I swallowed.

"Good, let's see what you've got. Remember, the aim is to protect yourself from me."

I gave him another nod.

Aranare rolled his shoulders, grounding himself as the wind tugged at his track pants. He adjusted his stance but didn't grab his weapon.

I looked inward, reaching for my flickering silver orb of magic, and my power grew, rising beneath my skin until it was humming through every part of me.

It was too much. Too strong. I wouldn't be able to control it.

Terror filled me, and I battled with the magic, shoving the power back until it was a shining speck in my subconscious.

The wind picked up behind Aranare, ruffling his chestnut curls as his scent drifted toward me on the breeze. It was nice, his smell. It was what I imagined heather on the moors smelled like: sweet, and slightly woody, with hints of honey and peat.

My eyes traveled to his arms, which were folded over his chest, and the visible muscles beneath his parka. The speck of silver power I had been suppressing flickered out, and I stepped toward him, wondering how they would feel wrapped around me.

I took another step, gazing into his amber eyes. They were beautiful, his irises flecked with dark browns and greens. Why hadn't I noticed before? And when he smiled, the dimples that appeared in his cheeks pulled my gaze straight to his lips.

I reached out to touch him, but he caught my wrist before my hand made contact.

I blinked through contracting vision, feeling as if a trance had been lifted. "You asshole!" I palmed his chest.

"I told you to shield yourself from me, but you obviously suck at shields." He smirked.

"What *are* you?" I took in Aranare's golden eyes and striking features once more. My manic desire had ebbed, but now I could see it—his otherworldly beauty.

"I told you my family had an invested interest in the feud."

I stared at him, mind whirring. "So you're a merman?"

"No, we are the Lugh Sirens. Our ancestors bred with humans and built a life on land, which protected our race from the Shadow."

The Lugh Sirens. The conversation from the war room swam back into my mind. Pisceon had wanted to call upon them for aid, but King Neptūnus had scorned them as half-breeds. I bit the inside of my cheek. So had Finn, who'd looked right at me when he said it. That's why he'd been so jealous of Aranare.

"I've been training with you for two weeks. You could have told me earlier."

He shrugged. "You could have worked it out."

"Louisa?" I raised my brows.

"No, Mom's human. My dad is half-Siren. You saw him at Iona's funeral."

I thought back to the older man from the beach, who'd had the same brown skin as Aranare and shoulder-length hair.

"But your last name is Williamson."

Aranare let out a raspy laugh. "The Lugh Sirens aren't a royal bloodline like the Neptūnus Mer. We are all over Scotland, Ireland, and Wales. We're named for the Irish god of craftsmanship because we're good with our hands."

"Oh." I threw myself down onto the damp grass. "What was that magic you just used on me?"

"That was my allure." The corner of his mouth turned up as he sat down beside me.

"Finn couldn't use his allure or hypnosis on me. How come you can?"

"The Mer are not as strong in mind magic as the Sirens. They were blessed with other skills. Your mind's magic is strong like ours, but it obviously . . . needs some work."

No shit.

"Are you ready to try wielding your magic now?" Aranare's eyes bounced between mine.

My throat constricted. I wasn't ready, not at all. But we had less than two weeks left until I went to the underwater realm, so I had to at least try.

"Let's start small. Try to harness the power you used on the Mer in the war room and put me into a peaceful sleep. Remember to stay calm. Access the power via your heart, but control it with your mind." He stepped back, tilting his head as he studied me.

Rain struck my face, and the sky became pure gray as I closed my eyes and let my heart pump silvery power through my veins until it filled me. I took a deep breath.

As the power thrummed through my skin, the glow in my subconscious pulsed brighter, drawing closer. My heartbeat fluttered. It was rushing toward me, widening like a great gaping mouth. *No!* I tried to suppress it, to push it down, but it was too late. It was going to consume me.

The magic burst from me in a blinding rush of silver. I fell to my knees on the damp grass, tears blurring my vision as I drew ragged breaths.

Footsteps crunched. Aranare's boots.

I breathed a sigh of relief as he held out his hand to me, but then sucked it back through my teeth. The grass beneath his feet was . . . black. I reached out to touch it, and it left a powdery residue on my fingers. *Dust.*

"It's okay." He gripped my hand, lifting me gently to my feet as tears streamed down my face. "It's my fault. I thought you had made more progress. We'll go back to basics tomorrow."

My legs shook as I stood, and dread slithered through my veins when I dragged my gaze over the cliff face. I'd reduced the grass in a three-foot-wide circle around me to dust.

"Each time I've used my power, I've had no control over what it's done." I blinked hard, trying to steady myself. I held my hands up before me and saw they were trembling. I lowered my gaze, barely breathing. "Louisa's right. I'm not ready, and there's no way I'll be ready in two weeks."

Aranare observed me, the line between his brows etching deeper. His eyes narrowed, then drifted to the gray ocean. He stared so intently that it was as if the waves were answering questions he hadn't voiced.

At last, he turned back to me. "I will accompany you to Thálassa and train you on the journey."

My shoulders sagged, and I let out a relieved sigh. "Thank you."

"I'll see you back here tomorrow." He rubbed a hand over his stubbled jaw before turning and striding across the cliff toward Bayside.

I stomped back down to the bookstore, now darkening with afternoon shades. Mer *and* Sirens walked the streets of Ruadán's Port. Who could know what was real around here anymore?

Allure. That's what Finn used on humans. If I hadn't possessed the Selkies' mind magic, which rivaled the Mer's, I might have found myself in his arms, telling him everything he wanted to know, and then what? He would have made me forget, and I would never have seen him again. I shuddered. I needed to control my magic.

Granddad was in the kitchen when I strode in and began packing away the groceries I'd picked up.

A leaden weight of guilt pressed down on me. Louisa had promised to check in on him while I was gone, but I'd been avoiding the conversation we needed to have: telling him I was heading back to the ocean's depths. And this time, I had no idea when I'd return.

"Did you go fishing today?" I offered him a hot tea with a sheepish smile, then slid into one of the wooden chairs beside him.

"Aye, she was a beauty." His eyes crinkled at the corners.

"Granddad . . ." I toyed with the lacy tablecloth. "I'm going to go away for a while, and I don't want you to worry about me."

He studied me over the rim of his steaming cup. "Does this have something to do with *her*?"

I nodded.

"She wouldn't have wanted you to put yourself in any danger."

"I can't fully explain it," I said, "but I know she spent her life chasing something. All that traveling—it wasn't just a pastime. And now, I have the chance to finish what she started."

"Does this have something to do with that lad who put Barry into a trance? I don't trust him."

My pulse stuttered at Granddad's mention of Finn. This trip had everything to do with him, but I pushed the thought aside.

"Aranare is going to come with me. And my other friend, Edward."

Granddad sighed. "The Williamson boy is a good lad, and I suppose I can't stop you."

I exhaled in relief. "There's one more thing. I need you to tell Mom I've gone to college in Glasgow, because she won't understand."

"Aye." He nodded. "But I'm not going to lie to your mother; you can call her and tell her yourself," he grumbled, stretching for the home phone and holding it out to me.

I dragged my gaze to the big wooden clock on the wall. In Kansas City, it would be morning.

Anxiety pinched my chest. I knew I had to face my mother, to tell her I had learned the truth about my father. Part of me was angry—she'd kept this from me my whole life—but another part felt guilty. This conversation would drag her into a past she'd done everything she could to bury.

I exhaled and dialed her number.

"Hello," she answered sharply.

"Hi, Mom." I toyed with the phone cord, my stomach in knots.

"Morgana, I haven't heard from you in weeks. Every time I call, you're not in. I was getting worried, you know, with your condition and everything . . ." She exhaled.

"I'm going to college, Mom, in Glasgow."

Silence.

"Mom?"

"I want you to share your doctor's number so I can see how you've been doing," came her curt reply.

"Mom," I ground out. "I'm not a child anymore."

"And what about your grandfather? Who will look after him with you in Glasgow? Because I can't, Morgana, I just can't." Her breathing quickened.

"Louisa will check on him, and he's doing better now." I smiled at Granddad.

"Why don't you come home, then?" Mom shot back without hesitation.

"I want to stay here. After all, this is where my *father's* from." I pursed my lips, waiting.

An excruciating silence, followed by a sniff. She was crying.

"Why didn't you tell me, Mom?" Tears spilled silently down my face.

"I c-couldn't open up that piece of my heart. I'm sorry. I knew you would find out soon enough in the port."

All the resentment I'd harbored toward her for her lies and overprotectiveness dissolved the moment I heard her shuddering sobs.

"Mom?"

"Yes?"

"I understand, and I love you."

I handed the phone to Granddad, who nodded and then raised it to his ear.

I stifled a sob of my own as I stepped into the adjacent living room and sank onto the couch. Hearing Mom's voice and her finally speaking of my father sent the weight of everything crashing down on me. I was no longer the sheltered, lost girl who had boarded that plane, rolling her eyes at her overbearing mother. I was a creature of the deep now; I was no longer innocent, but I was no longer lost, either.

"Do you want to see some pictures of them?"

I started at the sound, wiping the tears from beneath my eyes.

Granddad was in the doorway, holding a dusty book.

"May I?" He gestured to the couch, and I hastily moved over. "This was your gran's. There might be some photos of your pa in there." He laid the book, which I now realized was an album, on my lap, groaning as he eased himself down beside me.

My hands trembled as I opened it, revealing pictures of my grandparents' wedding. Turning another page showed my grandmother with Louisa on their travels. They stood at the pyramids of Egypt, both smiling from ear to ear. Then, they visited Stonehenge and Machu Picchu.

After that, my mother was born, and my grandmother cradled her in her arms, walking along the shoreline as she grew from an infant to a toddler. A pang shot through my chest. My grandmother's eyes held that same faraway sorrow I'd seen in the pictures I found in the attic.

As I flicked further through the album, my mother developed into a young woman, and there, near the end of the book, I saw him: Rory Balfour. My father.

By this point, the photos were colored, and I recognized his red hair and kind green eyes from the paper I'd found. He was wearing a sweater that looked like it had seen better days, and a group of kids surrounded him.

"He used to teach the wee lads to fish." Granddad nodded at the picture, and I saw that my father was holding a net.

"The kids loved his lessons. Sometimes, they would wait at his door before the sun rose."

I turned the page and found my mother, sweaty-faced and disheveled, cradling me in what must have been Islay Hospital. She smiled at the camera, my father's arm around her, his gaze fixed on me.

I ran my finger over the photograph of the three of us, and my heart clenched. Seven months from that moment, my father would drown.

"Do you think Mom will ever be able to let go of Dad's death?"

Granddad sighed. "Your ma and pa had one of those rare loves—completely daft about each other. That kind of love never truly leaves you . . . But with time, the weight of it gets easier to carry."

I traced my finger along another photograph: my mother looking at my father with a smile I'd not seen before. She looked carefree and radiant.

She had never remarried and never loved like that again.

4.

MORGANA

For the next two days, Aranare moved our magic sessions to the beach, where sand, already so close to dust, meant I couldn't cause too much damage. He'd given me one job: turn a shell to dust—without obliterating everything around it.

I had not yet succeeded. Either the shell remained untouched, or the sand around me turned ashen as the magic ripped out of me in wild, uncontrolled bursts. I fought the rising terror at my erratic powers and the mounting frustration that came with every failed attempt.

The beach was bitterly cold. Dark clouds sagged over midnight waves while a frigid wind lashed along the coast. I would layer jeans, a hoodie, and my grandmother's fur coat, but by the end of the day, my nose would still be pink and dripping.

Despite the cold, Aranare remained patient. Each time I incinerated a new target and the sand around it, he simply sighed and fetched another shell, placing them before me like a fresh challenge. After two tedious days of staring at shells, my eyes stung and my head throbbed with the effort.

The sun was dipping toward a dark horizon, and my fingers were numb and cold. I hadn't exploded everything around me for the last three hours, but I also hadn't managed to so much as shift a single shell.

Teeth clamped, I glared at the tiny, spiral shell that lay before me in the sand. I held my hand over it, eyes scrunching as I searched for the silver power inside me. A spark flickered, and my pulse stuttered. Panic clogged my mind, and the flare extinguished. I scoured, pleaded, and wrestled with my psyche, trying to find it again. Nothing.

"I can't take it anymore. I need to do something different." I groaned and stood, striding down the beach, sand kicking up beneath my feet.

Aranare blew out a breath as a wrinkle deepened between his brows. "Okay, let's try something new but . . . safer."

"Like what?" I dug my hands into my jacket pockets.

"You must learn to transform into your Selkie body without ending up with the dead." He gestured to the setting sun.

I raised my brows. "And how do you suggest I do that?"

"You need to compartmentalize. Embrace your Selkie side, and lock the Drowned part away."

My throat constricted as I turned to the darkening ocean. The last thing I felt like doing was getting into that water, especially if I might end up on SS *Jones's Lady*, but Aranare was right, and at least Edward was there.

The sun's final rays pierced the inky clouds on the horizon, while the icy wind swept down the beach, tugging my red tresses across my face.

"Unless you'd like to keep working on those shells." Aranare waved a hand at the charred sand around where I'd been sitting.

I flipped him an obscene gesture, pulling my grandmother's old fur coat tighter over my hoodie and jeans, and waded into the water.

Okay, I can do this.

The water was biting cold as it lapped against my ankles, and the wind was turning the swell tumultuous. My mind slipped into memories of my last transformation with Finn. I had almost controlled it then. My fists balled and my heart clenched as I remembered how he'd leaned on the bar and laughed at me afterward.

I can do this.

The salty scent seared my nostrils, and I closed my eyes. The sensation of my magic rolled through my body, as the surf caressed my hips, and then, with a deep breath, I dove.

The water embraced me.

As the power of my transition vibrated through my skin, I focused every ounce of my will on visualizing my Selkie form, free-falling into the open sea, pushing all images of SS *Jones's Lady* from my mind.

It was startlingly cold at first, and for a moment, I heard the voices of the dead.

No! I forced them from my mind, listening instead to the sighing of the sea.

The coat wrapped tighter as the waves rose around me, and there was no resistance this time. No spiraling panic. No abrupt arrival in SS *Jones's Lady*'s rusted underworld. Instead, my limbs lengthened with ease, my fingers webbing. My breath slowed, and my heart calmed. The sleek coat rippled over my skin, smooth and oily like thick velvet as my furry bodysuit appeared.

I kicked downward, cutting through the swirling blue. Then I broke the surface, brushing my dripping hair from my forehead and letting out a whoop.

"Well done. Now shift back, or you will be caught in seal's form for the night," Aranare yelled from the shore, glancing at the last rays of sun on the horizon.

Shit. I took another deep breath.

I can do this.

I visualized my human form, imagining my webs melting away and my fur dispersing. The water rushed around me, and I was again in my grandmother's cumbersome fur jacket.

The sun had set, and I was human.

I stumbled toward the shore, giddy with laughter, and rushed back to Aranare, who gave me a high five.

That night, when I climbed into bed, even though my body ached and my eyes were hooded with exhaustion, I smiled. I might have failed at magic-wielding for two days straight, but mastering this one thing felt damn good.

5.

MORGANA

The knocking started as a patter. I tossed and turned, shrugging it off, but it grew into a steady rapping that was impossible to ignore. I hissed as I sat up, every inch of my body stiff from the days of relentless training. I threw my blanket to the floor, whipping my gaze around my little room. It was still dark.

Had Aranare come to collect me for combat early?

I swung my legs out of bed, and the old springs groaned as I bounced up. Tugging on warm gloves from my dresser, I ran a hand through my tangled bed hair.

The knocking sounded again, dragging me from my thoughts.

"I'm coming!" I muttered as I rushed to the tower window and opened the dark shutters. But it wasn't Aranare standing at my granddad's door dressed for combat as I had expected; it was Skye.

"I'm sorry." She sniffed. "I had nowhere else to go."

"Stay there, I'm coming down."

I took the steps from the attic two at a time, ignoring Granddad's grumble as I ran past his bedroom door.

"Oh, Morgana," Skye wailed as I swung open the front door, throwing her dainty arms around my neck.

She pulled back from me, and I registered her black eye and split lip. This time, they hadn't been covered by a foundation. This time, they were fresh.

Skye was trembling, and her sadness was nauseating as I led her inside and up the stairs to my bedroom.

"I'll make you some tea, then you can tell me everything," I said quietly, shutting the door behind me and padding back to the kitchen.

Skye was taking deep breaths, eyes closed, when I reentered the room. I handed her a hot tea, noticing the mascara streaks running down her cheeks. Her broken heart filled the room, and I wished I had a better grasp on my mind's magic so I could shield myself from her overwhelming emotions.

"I'm sorry this happened to you." I swallowed a huge, guilty lump in my throat. I'd been so caught up in my training, the war of the Kingdom of the Deep, and dwelling on Finn's betrayal that I had only visited Skye at Bayside twice since I'd been back.

"It's not your fault." She smiled sadly and patted the edge of the bed, inviting me to sit.

"What happened?" I breathed as I slid in next to her.

"P-Parker, he—he . . ." She bit her lip as tears cascaded through her long lashes and down her bruised cheeks.

I reached out to touch her matted hair, but pulled my hand back as her sadness consumed me.

"His phone was on the kitchen counter while I was making dinner." Skye sniffed again. "And a message appeared on the screen. 'I miss you, baby,' it said. I confronted him, and he told me I was crazy. He said I 'always make shit up in my head,' and then . . . then he did this to me." She gestured to her lip, and her back heaved. "I snuck out this morning while he was sleeping."

"You're staying with me tonight." I rested my hand over hers, and she lifted her bruised eyes to meet mine.

"I—I can't. It's his thirtieth birthday, and he's having a party on his yacht. I planned the whole thing."

The shrill chiming of my alarm clock interrupted our conversation, and I glanced at the open window. Muted light was now spilling in through it. Shit. Training.

"You are not going," I said firmly. "You are going to come and . . . exercise with me, and then we'll get pizza and read romance books in bed."

Aranare was waiting for us on the grassy clifftop beside the old graveyard. Today he'd worn a navy zip-up anorak and track pants, which reminded me of the Scottish coaches shouting at the football games that Granddad liked to watch on TV.

Aranare's arms were folded over his chest, and the wind ruffled his brown hair as the rising sun turned the cloud-strewn sky pink behind him. His eyes fell on Skye, who had covered her bruises as best she could and was wearing one of my hoodies and a pair of my jeans, hair put up in a messy ponytail. Somehow, she looked even more beautiful like this.

Aranare noticed, too. His mouth twitched in approval, but his amber eyes darkened as he took in the bruises. "What happened to you?"

"I don't want to talk about it." Skye avoided his gaze, looking out over the gray ocean.

"Alright, then." He cleared his throat, his cheeks coloring. "If you're here for training with me, don't think I'll go easy on you."

I bit my lip to hide a smile. In the two weeks I'd trained with him, I'd never seen his confidence waver, let alone his cheeks catch a blush.

"You ready?" Aranare asked me as he positioned his wooden sword before him.

The frosty morning wind tore across the clifftop, whipping my hair into a storm, but I positioned myself the same way, eyes slitted as I stared him down.

He shrugged and swung his weapon.

With a growl, I lunged at him, my driftwood staff slicing through the air in a frantic sweep.

Aranare met my blow with precision, his sword rising to block with a crack. "Again," he said, unmoved.

I gritted my teeth. Tears stung my eyes as I thought about what Parker had done to my friend and the guilt I felt for not checking up on her sooner. My shoulders burned, and my breath became ragged, but I spun and struck again—harder this time.

Anger gave me momentum. Every swing was a release. Every clash of our weapons, my fist slamming into Parker's head.

"You're not thinking," he warned, parrying my strike and stepping aside. "You're feeling."

"Good," I snapped, already pivoting into another attack.

And still, he let me come at him—again and again—until the morning mist thickened into low clouds and a fine drizzle kissed our faces.

My arms trembled, and the fire in me finally began to flicker into focus. Only then did Aranare lay down his sword.

I flung my stick onto the ground beside it, chest heaving.

"Your turn." He jerked his chin at Skye.

"I-I'm just going to watch," she mumbled.

"You may not want to tell me what happened to your face, lass, but I daresay you could use the means to protect yourself."

Her cheeks flushed, and I handed her my piece of driftwood.

Aranare retook his fighting stance.

Skye fumbled with the wood, her footing too wide as she rushed forward and slung her weapon at Aranare, who stepped calmly to one side.

The stick slipped from her fingers, clattering to the grass. "Graceful as a drunk seal," she moaned.

"There's only one drunk seal around here, and it's not you." Aranare winked at me, and I gave him the finger.

Skye tightened her ponytail. Her lips pulled into a pout.

"You're overthinking," Aranare said, retrieving the driftwood stick. "Combat is like the sea. You move with it, not against it." A smile softened the lines of his face as he strode over, handing the staff back to her.

As he stepped closer to correct Skye's grip, his hand brushed hers, lingering just a moment too long. She looked up, breath catching. Her cheeks flushed, and her emotions washed over me: desire.

"Again," Aranare murmured, moving back from her. A rouge colored his bronzed neck, and the hand that had been resting against hers trembled slightly.

I fought the grin tugging my lips upward and turned to the ocean, pretending not to notice the inklings of something starting behind me.

"That was awesome!" Skye's heartbreak had transformed into elation as we trailed back across the cliff toward the bay. I was glad the training had taken her mind off the hurt Parker had caused. Over the past two weeks, our sessions had also helped me process everything I'd been through.

As we passed through the industrial district, my gaze fell on where the Ferris wheel had once stood—now just a heap of rubble—and a shudder ran through me.

"Can I come with you every day?" Skye crossed her arms over her chest as if suddenly remembering the bruises on her face.

"Sure." I grinned. "I've got mindfulness training with Louisa next. Do you want to join?"

"Why are you doing all this training? You've been very strange since you left your job and went away—to where? America? I'm kind of worried about you."

"You're worried about me?" I choked on a laugh.

"Yes," she squeaked. "I am worried you might be having a quarter-life crisis or something because you haven't . . . you know."

I stopped and turned to her. "I haven't what?"

"You know, been with a man." She whispered the last part, her brown eyes wide.

"For your information, I have." I couldn't help but smirk, but at the same time, something deep within me trembled as I thought of Finn and his hands on me.

"Aranare?" Skye swallowed, and her cheeks flushed.

"Finn," I said casually, but the word was acid in my mouth.

Skye's hardened expression lit up at the mention of juicy gossip, and her squeal echoed across the bay. Some seagulls pecking at something on the cold cement took off into flight. She gripped my gloved hands with her dainty, manicured ones. "Tell me everything."

"It just happened." I shrugged. "But it won't happen again. Ever."

"Was it good?"

"Yes." I exhaled the word, and despite myself, a throbbing heat blossomed between my thighs as images flashed through my mind. Finn's unbuckled jeans, the length of him, the noise of pleasure he'd made as he slid inside me for the first time, and the need I felt rippling from him.

"That good, huh?" Skye nudged me.

We paused at the bay, where moored boats bobbed on the tide.

"I'll go home and get some clean clothes." Skye gestured to my hoodie, now dirty with wet grass stains from all the times she had fallen over in training.

"What about Parker?" My voice cracked.

"He won't be there. He had to go into Campbeltown for something."

"I'll come with you."

"No." She shook her head vehemently. "Go to your lesson."

"Skye, promise me you'll return to my place and won't go to his birthday party?

"I promise." She leaned forward and gripped my wrist, looking at me with sincerity.

A knot formed in my stomach as I watched her head in the opposite direction from me toward where Parker's house stood on the cliff.

6.

SKYE

What would I need? Sweatpants, makeup, hair curler (totally essential), and slippers. My hands shook as I shoved the items into the designer duffel Parker had bought for me on one of his business trips. Probably a guilt present.

I sank onto the leather ottoman at the center of the walk-in closet we shared. Tears pricked my eyes as I stared at his suits, arranged from pale gray to midnight blue to black, meticulously ordered by my own hands.

Did I really need to leave?

My gaze drifted to the half-packed bag. If I left, I'd lose all of this and have to return to the suburbs—to the house where my mother was drinking away her beauty, spinning tales of her youth with a cigarette in hand, and my father, worn from days spent breaking roads, came home to be met with her fury.

This was only the second time Parker had hit me. He was probably just stressed from work . . . But then, there were the other girls. That text message hadn't been the first red flag. There had been the lipstick smudged on one of his collars, the lacy underwear that mysteriously ended up in his briefcase ("Just a prank from the boys at work," he'd claimed). And, of course, the nights he spent "working late" at his place in Campbeltown.

I raised a hand to my bruised eye. It was swollen. The reminder strengthened my resolve, and I padded to the en suite bathroom to retrieve my makeup. My eyes fell upon the deluxe tub. Oh, how I loved reclining in it. What would be the harm in having one more bath before I headed to Morgana's? Parker wouldn't be back for a few more hours.

I let my dirty clothes fall from my body and clipped my dark hair into a messy bun. My muscles were aching from the day's training, and I thought of Aranare as I slipped into the steamy water.

Using a sponge, I squeezed hot water over my stiff arms. Aranare's trembling hand grazing mine flickered through my mind, and I started to ache somewhere else. Slowly, I moved the sponge lower, from my shoulder to my chest and over my navel.

I sank deeper into the water, resting my head against the cool porcelain edge of the tub. I thought of the flush in Aranare's cheeks when he looked at me, the way he sometimes mumbled or glanced away. A tenderness my broken heart craved.

As I moved the sponge lower, I pictured the protective look in his amber eyes when he'd seen my bruises. I ran the soaked loofah over the place I kept meticulously hairless for Parker, and then lower still, allowing it to offer a hint of pressure, wondering if I made Aranare nervous. I let out a slow breath as I pushed deeper.

A sharp bang jolted me from my fantasy, and I quickly put the sponge on the edge of the bath.

"There you are." Parker was standing in the doorway, watching me. My heart thundered so hard my chest felt like it might break under the force of its fists. He wasn't supposed to be back yet.

Instinctively, I crossed my arms over my bare breasts, the tops of them rising just above the water.

"Hey, don't do that." He rushed to my side, kneeling on the wet tiles as he clasped my chin in his hand and studied the damage he'd caused.

I took in his bright blue eyes, sandy hair, cleft chin, and the dimples that made their way into his cheeks when he looked at me like that. I still loved him for a moment. But no, it wasn't love; it was need. I was like a bird whose wings had been broken by this man and believed only he could fix them.

"I'm going to stay at Morgana's for a while." I pulled my face away.

"She doesn't know anything about us, baby. People will tell you not to be with me, but that's just because they're jealous of what we have." Parker jerked my face back to his. That look was there again, the same one he'd worn when he hit me. The same one he always had when he hurt me.

I flinched. Noticing, he sighed and stood up, leaning over me as I covered my breasts again. He bent down, kissing the side of my neck and tangling his fingers in the strands of hair coming loose from my claw clip.

"I said, don't do that." He removed my hands from my breasts and gently caressed one of my nipples. "You know I love you, don't you?"

I didn't reply, and he moved his hand lower so that it slipped under the water and across my hairless area.

"Don't you?" he asked again as his fingers brushed the space between my legs and he gently kissed my neck.

He rarely touched me like this. So tenderly. If he touched me at all, it was usually rough and quick, and then he would excuse himself for work or ask if I could make him dinner. This was different.

"Aye, I do love you," I whispered, and in that moment, I meant it.

He kissed my neck again, his fingers working the space between my legs. "Well then, if you loved me, you wouldn't leave. Especially not on my birthday, when I have bought you a new dress." He continued stroking me, and it felt so good. It was everything I had always wanted from him.

I leaned my head back into him, and he reached around me, holding my breast with one hand while the other moved between my legs.

"I am sorry I hurt you. It will never happen again," he breathed into my hair as he stroked faster.

"You p-promise?" I whimpered as my eyes rolled back, and a gasp escaped me.

"I promise." He removed his fingers from inside me, wiping them on the hand towel, his dimples in full effect as a grin split his face. "I've left your dress on the bed. The lads and I are going to have a few drinks at the Port House. I will meet you on the docks at 3 p.m."

He winked at me as he closed the bathroom door.

I climbed out of the water and pulled the towel around me. My cheeks were rosy with pleasure, but a sickening guilt shrouded my joy.

I pushed it aside. *He loves me. This will never happen again. He promised.*

My guilt disintegrated when I unzipped the garment bag on the bed and saw the black strapless designer dress Parker had left for me. I pulled it on and surveyed myself in the walk-in closet mirror. It fit like a glove, accentuating my curves, and my full breasts heaved with every breath due to the tightness of the bustier.

I powdered over the bruises, swallowing the knots coiling in my stomach at the sight of them. After painting my lips red, I pinned my hair into an elegant bun. Then, I begrudgingly pulled on stockings and a long black leather coat, because it would be freezing on the yacht.

I was about to shut the bedroom door and walk away when my gaze fell on the duffel on the floor. Guilt twisted as I remembered my promise to Morgana. Parker had lied—he'd hurt me. I paused. But he'd said he was sorry, said he'd never do it again, and deep down, some part of me still wanted to believe that.

And what about Aranare? He cared, which was comforting, but he didn't know me. Parker and I had a history. I owed him one more chance. It was his birthday, after all.

I released a shaky breath, and I shut the door on my half-packed bags.

Parker and his colleagues were clustered on the dock as I approached, a wave of awkwardness tightening in my chest.

Although Parker usually invited me to these things, I always felt like I wasn't entirely welcome. Plus, now there were bruises on my cheeks and lips. I had tried to hide them, but they were still visible beneath the makeup. At least these short winter days meant the sun would set soon.

I got up at night to grab a glass of water and walked into a door. I'm so clumsy.

That's what I would giggle and tell anyone who asked.

Parker grinned when he saw me, and despite myself, my heart fluttered. His designer sunglasses caught the last afternoon light as he strode down the dock. He was flanked by two workmates in navy suits, their loafers far too polished for the salt-stained planks beneath them and ridiculous for sailing the isles at this time of year.

I had tried to convince Parker to wait until the summer to hold his party, but he'd insisted on having it now—typical reckless Sagittarius. Luckily, the weather was mild, but darkness would soon fall.

Parker and his colleagues were laughing too loudly, the kind of conversation that left no room for anyone else. His blazer was slung carelessly over his shoulder, revealing a crisp white shirt, unbuttoned just enough to show off his golden tan and a glimpse of his gym-honed chest.

He turned to a girl—she must be someone from work, I assured my-self—who was trailing behind the men. She had long legs, glossy blonde hair, and a halter top that defied the winter sea breeze. She giggled at something Parker said, her hand brushing his arm in a way that made my stomach twist. I slipped my leather trench coat off my shoulders to reveal my own bustier, shivering immediately in the cold.

It was going to be a long night.

Parker's Wet Lass bobbed lightly in the bay, sleek and ostentatious with chrome railings and a bottle of champagne already chilling in a bucket of ice by the entrance at its rear. I quickened my pace as Parker helped the girl aboard with his practiced charm.

"Happy birthday, babe." I slung my arms around him, and his scent washed over me—Tom Ford Tobacco Vanille, which he always overdid.

The leggy blonde was watching me, a slight pout shadowing her features. My thoughts returned to the message I had seen on Parker's phone: *I miss you, baby.*

Parker peeled himself from me, offering a tight-lipped smile, the opposite of how he'd been in the bath. I could tell by the scent of his breath and the red in his eyes that he was already drunk.

He and his friends made their way into the sheltered area, but I lingered in the open stern, watching the sunset over the bay. It wasn't a huge yacht, about sixty-four feet long, yet it had probably cost him a few million. Well, his father, Douglas Stewart, anyway.

Parker had a good job as a partner at a law firm, but he was also a nepo baby. The Stewarts were well-known for their ties to the whisky industry and had spearheaded the development of Bayside.

If Aranare's family owned the older half of town, Parker's family owned the other. Although the Bayside development had failed, they had numerous successful developments across Scotland. Most of them lived in Glasgow, but they'd built a clifftop holiday home during the Bayside expansion. That was how we'd met.

I settled myself in the outdoor seating area in the stern, where oysters, caviar, and other delicacies had been laid out beside the ice buckets of Dom Pérignon. I glanced at Parker and his friends, who were now inside, slapping each other on the back and speaking animatedly. They were drinking whisky, so the champagne was just for show.

Thankfully, Parker wasn't driving the yacht tonight. He knew how, of course, but with all the gales we'd been having, I had begged him to hire someone for the occasion, and he had listened.

I helped myself to a glass and leaned back in my seat, sipping my champagne slowly. The evening darkened around us, and the wind picked up as the boat chugged away from the bay. Guilt curled in my chest for not returning to Morgana's as I watched Parker, his workmates, and the leggy blonde laugh together inside. What else had I expected? This was how it always went.

I pulled my iPhone out of my pocket and toyed with it. I should have let Morgana know that I was no longer coming; she must be worried. She still had no cell phone since she'd lost it somewhere, but perhaps I could find her grandfather's home number. I pulled up the browser. Damn it, I had no reception. The twinkling lights of Ruadán's Port glimmered alluringly in the distance but then faded altogether, replaced by the dark rushing of the sea.

7.

MORGANA

I couldn't focus on meditating. The cushion pressed uncomfortably beneath me, my eyes scrunched shut, fists clenched, even as the beautiful music curled around me.

My mind fixated on one thing: Parker. Foreboding filled me, the same sinking sense that had gripped me when we got the call about my grandmother.

"I think that's enough for today," Louisa said, appearing with a stack of dusty books and studying me closely. "Shall we sit?"

I stood, knees stiff from my time on the pillow, then crossed my arms and dropped into the seat opposite Louisa. "Why didn't you tell me about Aranare and your husband? What other secrets are you keeping?" I ground out. My worry over Skye had curdled into something sharp and confrontational.

Louisa sighed. "You were processing a lot already. I find that with these magical revelations, it's best to peel them back layer by layer, like an onion."

I scoffed, keeping my arms folded.

"I went through the same thing as you when I discovered this world existed . . . Then I met my husband and your grandmother."

My mouth was dry as I asked the question that had been troubling me. "You don't think I'm ready, do you?"

"Oh my dear, no one is ever truly ready to face destiny. That's what makes it so mysterious. All we can do is our best."

"And you think if we find the rest of this prophecy and I . . . fulfill it . . . we can stop the war somehow and save the ocean from the Shadow?"

Louisa nodded. "We can only *hope*."

I chewed on the inside of my cheek. Hope—the forge of greatness or the fool's sweet poison.

❦

It was freezing when I left the bookstore, and I ducked into the corner shop at the end of Saltmarsh Row to grab a stash of candy for Skye and me.

I'd hoped to find her waiting inside when I returned to Granddad's little house, but she wasn't there.

Granddad was stoking a crackling fire in the living room, and I strode into the kitchen to begin making us dinner: fresh fish with vegetables. It was his staple diet, and it was good for him that I'd acquired a taste for the white, fleshy meat while under the sea.

As we ate our dinner, my foot tapped a restless rhythm under the table, matching the swirling in my stomach.

"You okay?" Granddad surveyed me with dark eyes.

"It's my friend—she was supposed to come over." I looked at the old wooden clock. It was 6 p.m. "I might give her a call."

Leaving my barely touched meal, I raced upstairs and grabbed her cell number from where I'd written it down. I returned to the home phone and dialed, but got a busy signal. I tried again and again—the same signal. She must not have reception.

Dread pooled in my stomach. She had gone on the yacht.

I put my half-eaten dinner in the fridge, then did the dishes before climbing the narrow, winding steps to my tower and crawling into bed.

There was nothing I could do but lie there, my stomach churning. Skye had gone on the yacht . . . Helplessness consumed me as I stared at the ceiling for hours, unable to sleep.

The books on my dresser caught my attention: *Mythical Creatures of the Ocean* and *Myths and Legends of Ruadán's Port*. A fine layer of dust coated their covers. It seemed so long ago that I'd bought them from Aranare's bookstore.

I threw off my patchwork duvet and grabbed the one on Ruadán's Port, dragging it back into bed with me. If sleep wouldn't come, reading might help.

I flipped the cover open, skimming the pages. Aranare must have given me this book for a reason. He'd wanted to tell me who he was, and I had failed to uncover his secret.

My breath caught as my eyes landed on the name I'd been searching for: *The Lugh Sirens.*

Originally born of the sea, these Sirens interbred with Minoan settlers, who'd come to Orkney to mine copper, and then spread across Ireland, Scotland, Wales, and the Hebrides, blending ancient aquatic magic with human bloodlines and craftsmanship.

I expelled a shaky breath. Aranare's bloodline went back thousands of years and was connected to the Minoans, whom I had been studying with Louisa—Manannán's people.

I closed the text, thoughts drifting back to Skye as my stomach clenched.

I padded downstairs to try her phone once more. Again, I was met with the busy signal. She was still out of range. So I returned to bed, staring into the darkness until my eyes burned.

Sleep finally claimed me at some point, fitful and fraught with crashing dark swells and muffled cries for help.

8.

SKYE

Night had fallen, and it was biting cold on the yacht's stern. I'd slipped inside once or twice, but Parker and his friends barely acknowledged me. The blonde had made sure he didn't.

This was a mistake. I should have packed that bag and gone to Morgana's. We would've been curled up in her bed eating pizza by now. And tomorrow? Tomorrow, I'd have tagged along to her quarter-life crisis training—or whatever it was—with Aranare.

Maybe he'd have touched my hand again to guide my movements. Perhaps he'd have shown me how to beat the shit out of Parker if he ever laid a hand on me again. The thought made me smile.

"How's the champagne?" A man was standing above me. One of Parker's friends. Caramel skin, curly black hair, and straight white teeth that came together to make a handsome face.

"It's okay." I smiled, tilting my chin toward him as I twirled the slender champagne flute between my fingers. It was more than okay. It was Dom Pérignon, but I was in a sulky mood.

The man slid into the seat beside me. "I've been watching you out here. I hope it's not inappropriate, but I wanted to check on you because you look so . . . sad."

I couldn't find the words to respond as a lump formed in my throat. Instead, I grinned and brushed off his question with a dismissive hand.

"Beautiful and sad," the man said, surveying my face with his dark eyes before he shifted closer to me.

"Thank you." I tossed back the last of my champagne. His compliments made me want to cry. They struck some fractured part of me that longed to hear I was pretty.

"You're Parker's girl, right?" He grabbed the bottle of Dom from the ice bucket and refilled my glass.

"I'm Skye." I began to extend my hand but froze when I spotted Parker watching through the window, eyes narrowed. I drew it back. "Sorry, I have to go to the bathroom."

I moved away from the man toward a small deck area on the ship's side, where two stools sat on a strip of railless platform. Beneath me, the ocean churned, stars twinkling in a cloudless sky above. At least there hadn't been any of those unearthly storms for a while.

Hitching up my tight dress and wriggling onto one of the seats, I shivered and cursed my pride, wishing I hadn't discarded my coat. I glanced back toward the stern, where the handsome man still sat. I'd wait here until he went inside—no need to risk one of Parker's jealous outbursts.

"Why were you talking to him?"

Too late. I winced as Parker descended the stairs from the inside area and down to this narrow side of the ship.

"He just introduced himself, that's all." I shrugged. "At least *someone's* talking to me."

"I bet you were batting those big eyes at him and pouting those blow job lips."

Before I could answer, he lunged at me, one of his hands closing around my throat. Fear shot through my body, and all I could do was stutter "N-no" as his grip tightened. His breath reeked of alcohol, his bloodshot eyes darted back and forth, and his hair stuck out in wild tufts.

"You're just a whore, aren't you?" Parker shoved me from the seat, his hand still clasping my throat.

"Babe, p-please." My eyes darted wildly about the boat. The handsome man had disappeared inside. I wasn't sure whether anyone could see us through the darkened windows—and even if they could, would they care? They were sycophants to the Stewarts.

"What were you going to do? Suck his cock at the back of the boat?" Parker shoved me closer to the ship's edge, and ocean spray decorated the backs of my legs. The wind was in my hair as he moved his other hand to my neck and squeezed.

"Y-you're pathetic," I coughed.

"Pathetic, am I?" His eyes were no longer blue; they were white with rage. It was like the whites of his eyes had consumed his irises.

"Just a weak boy who has to beat his girlfriend to make himself feel like a man." I choked on the words as Parker released my throat and his fist collided with my face.

There was searing pain and a flash of blinding light, and then I was falling . . . falling toward the water. As its icy arms closed around my waist and its swirling blue swallowed my face, my mind drifted to laughing with Morgana and Aranare on the clifftop, driftwood sticks in hand, the sea wind in our hair. I smiled, because it had been a perfect day.

9.

MORGANA

"What's going on with you today?" Aranare asked after my magic had torn out of me and turned the sand around my sneakers into dust for the third time.

I'd woken with my stomach in knots, and the tension hadn't eased as I stalked down the slick road to the beach, where he'd been waiting.

"It's Skye." I collapsed on the sand as sobs burst out of me.

"What about her?" Aranare asked sharply.

"She was supposed to come to my house last night, but never showed up."

"Do you think she's gone to work?" He crouched beside me, worry shining in his amber eyes.

"Maybe. I just have a horrible feeling."

Aranare stood, raking a hand through his hair as he paced back and forth along the beach. "Come on then," he said at last, extending a hand to pull me to my feet. "Let's see if we can find her. I've got my truck here."

I wiped my tear-stained eyes and followed him to where his truck was parked on the boardwalk, a beat-up green Range Rover classic that looked like it might have been from the 1990s. The door creaked as he held it open for me, and I climbed in.

Aranare's brow was furrowed, his expression dark as we drove to Bayside and pulled into the parking lot. Surely, she was just at Tartan Treasures and hadn't called because she thought I'd be angry about her returning to Parker. That had to be it. I exhaled.

It felt strange passing through Bayside, the place that had started it all. I'd been so consumed by my training that I hadn't spent much time here since returning.

I couldn't help but glance into Ruadán's Port Pawn. The windows were dark, and a pile of letters and papers lay scattered by the door. It looked like neither Finn nor Mr. Inegar had returned in some time.

As we rounded the corner, Celtic Keepsakes came into view. Barry's son, Jamie, was manning the counter, looking thoroughly bored, but he waved when he spotted us.

I quickened my pace. The lights in Tartan Treasures were off, and a spike of panic pushed me into a jog. The store was dark. I scanned the windows and yanked the door handle. It was locked.

"Skye," I called, banging on the glass. "Skye!"

"She's not here." Aranare's voice was gentle, but his fear washed over me.

"I'm going to kill Parker." My fists curled into balls so tight I thought I might break a knuckle bone.

"Parker Stewart? That's her boyfriend who gave her the bruises?" His golden eyes pulled wide, brows sinking.

"You know him?"

"Aye, I know him. The Stewarts are a powerful family. They think they're untouchable. This is bad."

"Let's go to his house. Skye said it was on the clifftop near Finn's."

"Aye," Aranare said again, "I know where it is."

"How do you know the Stewarts?" I panted as we raced back through the center to his truck.

He waved a hand over Bayside. "They built this place."

"Are you serious?" I raised my brows as I yanked open the car door.

He nodded. "Our family business—Williamson Industries—once owned this land, including the cliffs on which the Stewarts later built those three fancy homes."

I'd walked to the houses from the docks before, but now I discovered you could drive there from the Bayside parking lot. We rumbled along the unsealed path, crumbling stone fences flanking either side. Aranare's hands were trembling as they turned the steering wheel.

"So what happened?" I clutched the door handle as the car jolted over the uneven road.

"The Stewarts offered to buy the land, but when we refused, things turned ugly. With their influence, the council declared it 'under-utilized' and approved it for development. The joke was on them—Bayside flopped after the Ferris wheel packed in."

"What about the pawnshop?" I asked as the narrow stone road widened into a driveway that sloped toward the cliff's edge.

"Finn's family owned that long before the Bayside development. It was part of the original stone cottages that were here."

Parker's house sat just before Finn's, closer to Bayside, but the landscape was designed to provide each residence with privacy. I wrapped my arms around myself, relieved we wouldn't have to pass Finn's towering glass windows.

Like Finn's, Parker's clifftop mansion had a turf roof and stone-clad façade that echoed the earth's natural contours, allowing the structure to blend harmoniously with the wild landscape.

"The Neptūnus Mer bought the house on the hill from the Stewarts, just to spite us, no doubt." Aranare laughed sharply as he parked the truck in the circular gravel drive.

I flung my door open, eyes scanning the property. The driveway was empty, and the house sat in silence.

I raced to the front door and banged on it. "Skye!"

No answer.

My pulse was pounding as I darted around to the front of the house, where floor-to-ceiling windows framed panoramic views of the churning Atlantic beyond the cliffs. I cupped my hands to the glass, squinting inside, but the open-plan living area and kitchen were empty. That was all I could see.

"Skye!" I pounded on the glass, tears blurring my vision.

"She's not here." Aranare put his hand on my shoulder and pulled me from the window.

"They were going on Parker's yacht. Perhaps they're still at sea."

"Let's go down to the bay, then."

Aranare's entire body was tense as we jumped back into his truck, and I could sense his unshielded emotions: a mixture of concern and boiling fury.

The Range Rover's engine rumbled to life, its splutter matching my anxious heartbeat, and we drove in silence across the grassy clifftop and down through Bayside to the docks. My eyes swept the moored boats as Aranare eased the truck into park.

The afternoon had darkened, and gray clouds gathered overhead as we jumped from the car and raced to the concrete boardwalk, where the moored boats bobbed. My stomach turned. *Parker's Wet Lass* was docked, its chrome railings drifted with the rising swell.

"Come on," I said, racing down the stone steps to the granite sand, Aranare on my heels.

He'd been silent since we left Parker's, his face drawn and a muscle ticking in his jaw.

We combed the beach, calling Skye's name until my throat was raw, my fingers numb with cold. The sun had sunk low on the horizon. How long had we been down here? I didn't even know.

Emotion welled up behind my ribs as I turned to Aranare. "I think . . . I think we should get my coat, and I'll check SS *Jones's Lady.*" The suggestion sank into my stomach like I'd swallowed a stone.

"She's not down there. Don't even say such a thing." Aranare clenched his fists, and his anger radiated.

"Can you just take me to my place?" I turned away, unable to hold back the tears.

He exhaled and then nodded.

"Wait here," I told him as he pulled the truck up outside Granddad's house a few minutes later.

I burst through the front door and flew up the narrow attic stairs, two at a time, racing to my bedroom to snatch my grandmother's fur coat.

Granddad was watching the news by the fire when I darted back past the living room. "There's fresh fish on the table," he called.

"Tha—" I paused when I caught the newsreader's voice. "Ms. Davies reportedly fell from her boyfriend, Mr. Stewart's, yacht last night. Authorities say he is cooperating fully with the investigation."

"Turn it up!" I gasped breathlessly as I rushed to Granddad's side and grabbed the remote from the coffee table.

Parker appeared on the screen. I remembered his blue eyes and cleft chin from the Samhain festival. His face was pulled into an expression of sadness. "We think she fell . . . or maybe she jumped. She was sitting in the stern, and when we docked, she was gone. I just hope that, somehow, she finds her way home." He stifled an exaggerated sob. "I'm sorry, I can't." He pushed the news anchor's microphone to the side and turned away from the camera.

My nails dug into my palms as I sprinted back to Aranare. His truck was idling at the curb, headlights casting twin pools of yellow across the narrow street.

"Let's go now!" I drummed my palm on the dashboard and clutched the coat to my chest, casting my eyes to the sky. The sun had almost set. We needed to hurry.

We were soon at the beach, and Aranare was behind me as I tore down to the soft sand, shrugging on my Selkie jacket as we ran.

"I'm coming with you this time," he growled.

I nodded, exhaling as my gaze swept the bay one last time. Waves lapped against the jetty to my right, and to my left stood Merrow Rocks and the old stone lighthouse Finn and I had once climbed. Its light was on, casting a golden glow through the windows. My breath hitched as a silhouette moved within its glass crown—a woman.

"Skye!" I gasped.

I ran across the damp sand, slipping slightly as I scrambled over the slick rocks, making my way toward the lighthouse.

"Morgana?" Aranare was at my heels.

"I saw a woman. Come on!" I grabbed his wrist, yanking him after me.

We were both breathless when we reached the grassy ledge above the rocks just below the lighthouse. I grasped the handle and tried the door. It was locked. I threw my shoulder into it like I'd seen Finn do, but it didn't budge.

"Here." Aranare coughed, gently moving me aside with an exasperated sigh. He hovered his palm over the door, and it clicked open. "We're magic, remember? If we can affect the brain—the most complex structure in the universe—I think we can handle a lock." He chuckled, stepping inside.

I took two steps at a time. "Skye," I called, but my chest was tight from a stitch.

"Morgana?" her familiar voice answered, and my shoulders sagged in relief. "Morgana, don't come up here."

At the top of the stairs, I found her curled in the corner on the dusty floor. Her dark hair had slipped from its bun, strands clinging to tear-streaked cheeks. She was clasping an old sheet, tattered and torn, around her, but she was alive.

Relief flooded me as I took her in. She hadn't drowned and ended up on SS *Jones's Lady*.

"Get away from me." She held up her palm to shield herself from my gaze as Aranare burst up the stairs behind me.

I rushed over, kneeling on the dusty concrete beside her. "What happened?"

"Don't come near me," she cried, pushing herself further into the brick wall.

"Skye, it's me." I searched her eyes but found only fear staring back at me.

"Just tell us what happened." Aranare knelt on her other side, and she shrank against the wall, pressing herself as far from us as possible.

"I'm sorry I went on the yacht." Her eyes filled with tears.

"It's okay." I took her hand. It was cold, and some acrylic nails had fallen off.

"Parker, he—" She gestured to her neck, and I noticed the bruises on it and more around her eye. My teeth gritted, and Aranare blew out an angry breath.

"I fell overboard into the ocean." Skye burst into shaky sobs.

"We'll take you to the hospital, and after that, you can stay with me. You never have to see him again."

She shook her head frantically, continuing to press herself against the wall.

"You're safe now," I said as I squeezed her fingers. "Let's get you home and warm."

"Get away from me," she screamed, yanking her hand from mine.

"You'll get hyperthermia." I reached for her again.

"I said, don't touch me!" Skye's brown eyes blazed gold, and with a sweep of her hand, a surge of wind slammed Aranare and me against the opposite wall.

"What the hell?" I spluttered as I picked myself up.

Skye's eyes widened in horror, and she stared at her hands. Then she scrambled to her feet and rushed to our side. "I'm so sorry. I told you to stay away—it's not safe. I . . . I'm a monster." Her voice broke as she collapsed into trembling sobs.

"You're not a monster." I turned to Aranare, who was watching the scene unfold with a look of calm contemplation in his eyes.

"I am!" Skye wailed. "I'll show you." She stopped sobbing and stood in the center of the lighthouse, her eyes scanning the space until they landed on a plastic bucket that must have been used to gather water from a leak in the roof. She raced over to it, plucked it from the floor, and emptied it over her head.

"Skye—" I reached for her but then froze, my breath hitching, as scales blossomed across every inch of her body, ripping the old sheet further as they slithered across her full breasts and over her torso. They were beautiful, the scales. Baby blue fused with pink and aquas, like the inside of an abalone shell.

I knew I needed to say something—after what I'd seen, this was nothing—but I couldn't find the words.

A single tear rolled from Skye's eye, and my mouth fell open as wings sprouted from her back. She cried out, her face contorted in pain as the thick, beautiful wings grew, feathered like something pulled from an angelic painting, but like the scales, they shone in greens and blues and were spanned with what looked like webs.

"See?" Her hazel eyes dimmed. "I'm a monster."

"You are the most beautiful thing I've ever seen," Aranare said, his voice hoarse. The words snapped me out of my shock.

He was right; she was.

"So, what happened after you hit the waves?" I chewed on my lip as I took her in. The water she had doused herself with had started to dry, and her scales were disappearing.

"Well, I blacked out from the punch, and when I came to, I was sinking. The water was in my lungs, pushing me down and suffocating me. I couldn't breathe. That was it—I knew it. My heart slowed, and peace overcame me. I was dead." Skye's wings vanished, and she startled, then sank back onto the sandy stone floor, wrapping the torn sheet around herself as the rest of her scales faded. "Then a woman appeared to me. She told me her name was . . . it was something strange, like 'a cup—'"

"Agápē?" Aranare interrupted her.

My mouth fell open. *The Siren Goddess of Love.*

"Yes, that was it." Skye's eyes lit up. "She told me that I was a descendant of hers and that I had a choice. I could die, or I could be given a second chance to live out my destiny. Naturally, I chose the second chance. I didn't realize it would come with wings and scales." She fell into tears again.

Aranare and I exchanged a glance and gave each other a silent nod of agreement.

I sat down beside her and rubbed her heaving back. "You are not a monster, and you are not alone. We have a lot to talk about, so Aranare and I will take you back to my house for a hot chocolate."

Skye nodded, hiccuping back tears.

"But first, I think Aranare wants to show you something."

Aranare pushed himself up, his hand dug into his curls as he turned to meet Skye's gaze. A ripple of energy scintillated through the air as he stepped forward, his chest rising with a slow exhale. He yanked his sweater over his head, tossing it aside with his T-shirt, revealing a bronzed torso and sculpted abs that rippled with every breath.

The wind howled through the cracks in the lighthouse momentarily, and then everything fell silent. Scales, iridescent and dark as the midnight sea, unfurled across his chest and shoulders in a smattering of glistening greens and blacks. They glittered along the sculpted planes of his arms, torso, and throat. His amber eyes burned brighter, like Skye's had.

From his back, wings erupted—not feathered like Skye's, but sleek and translucent like a fish's fin, leathery and dark in places, but edged with an oily pearlescent sheen. They stretched high and wide, glistening like hematite.

I inhaled sharply. Aranare was no longer just handsome. He was devastating. A creature born of ocean storms and wind-swept beaches, every inch of him radiated power. And yet, even in his transformation, something human flickered in his gaze as it settled on Skye, her mouth open in awe as she watched him.

10.

SKYE

Their voices morphed into nothing, a shrill ring on the periphery of my being. I thought I heard them say Finn was a merman and that the storms had been created by some dark lord whose name sounded like it rhymed with banana.

There was a prophecy, and they were going to find it. Had Morgana said something about the Drowned?

It was all too much. The edges of my vision blurred, and I raised a hand to my temple. "I need to get some rest . . . " I pushed my hot chocolate aside. "Is it okay if I sleep here?"

"You will stay with me from here on out." Morgana sprang up from the rickety kitchen table, her eyes soft with concern as they swept over me, so tender it made my stomach twist. Her sympathy was a mirror, reflecting everything I was trying to forget. "You can borrow some PJs and have a shower."

"No!" I recoiled at the mere thought of water.

"It won't always be like that," Aranare said quietly.

"Like what?" Morgana whipped her head to him.

"She's afraid of water touching her." He gestured to me, and I trembled at the thought, rubbing my hands across my arms.

"When you asked me where my people were from that day at the café, you knew." I glared at him.

Aranare's cheeks flushed under my gaze, and he looked away. "I didn't *know*, I just had a sense there was something more to you."

"That's why you could see Donahue. I should have realized it earlier." Morgana slapped a palm to her forehead.

"What?" My brows drew together in confusion as I turned to her.

"The man with the sunken face at the Ferris wheel that night. Only those of the ocean can see the Drowned, and you saw him too."

I stared at her in disbelief, but she shoved her chair back and rushed over, sweeping my hair aside and tugging down the collar of the sweater she'd loaned me.

I jerked away from her. "What are you doing?"

"Look, the Symbol of the Ocean." Morgana gestured to my shoulder, where a tattooed wave was now burned into my skin. Above it, a crescent moon had begun to rise.

"I'll show you mine if you show me yours." Aranare grinned and stood, lifting his shirt.

My mouth popped open, and I hastily clamped it shut. He had the same marking above his rippling abs, on his right pectoral.

Morgana giggled and pulled down the shoulder of her shirt to show me hers.

"Why were my wings made from feathers and yours were different?" I grimaced at the memory of the things that had sprouted from my back, and the feeling of my skin distorting to accommodate them.

"I'm related to the Lugh clan. You, on the other hand, are related to Agápē, the Siren God of Love, and the clan located in the Mediterranean."

"Oh." I nodded and tried to look nonchalant as I waved goodnight to Aranare and Morgana, but my heart was pounding as I climbed the narrow stairs to Morgana's bedroom.

Morgana lingered in the kitchen with Aranare, and I was glad. I needed some time alone.

I grabbed a pair of PJs from her dresser and collapsed onto the bed, eyes fixed on the ceiling railings. A single tear slipped from the corner of my eye. I wiped it away quickly, half-afraid it might trigger my Siren form, but it didn't. And before I knew it, sleep had taken me.

I awoke with a start, gasping as the horrors of the night before came flooding back.

Cool early morning light filtered through the window, and my breathing relaxed. I was in Morgana's bed, her chest rising and falling beside me. She looked so peaceful, but how could she be when she had gone through the same thing as I had only months ago?

I padded downstairs. Aranare was asleep on the couch in the living room, the final embers of last night's fire glowing feebly beside him. He was shirtless, and one of his bronzed forearms rested on his blanket.

I moved past him and toward the front door.

"Where are you going?" He was behind me suddenly, still shirtless, his hand encircling mine on the doorknob.

I turned my head and met his amber gaze, and he quickly pulled back his hand. Sleep had messed up his chestnut hair, and faint pillow lines etched his bronzed cheek.

"I need to speak to my mother."

He nodded in understanding. "We'll come with you. You shouldn't be alone after what you've been through."

I flushed, wondering what state my mother would be in. Surely she hadn't hit the drink yet, but you never knew with her.

"I'll make you a coffee," said Aranare gently.

When I didn't move, he wrapped his hand around mine again, coaxing my fingers from the door handle.

I let him lead me to the kitchen.

Dad's truck wasn't in the driveway when Aranare pulled up. Good, he must have already left for work.

I exhaled as I took in the whitewashed stone residence and its brown-shuttered windows. The space felt cramped and suffocating—nothing like Parker's clifftop home. Just thinking his name tightened something in my chest. I couldn't forgive what he'd done, but I felt lost at the thought of building a new life without him. He had been my world.

We found Mom on the couch in the living room, engrossed in her favorite daytime television, a cigarette in one hand and a glass of cheap white wine in the other.

"Honey, you're home." She leapt up at the sight of me, flinging her slender arms around my neck. The sharp scent of smoke clung to her, and the chardonnay in her glass sloshed perilously near the rim. "And you brought friends. I'm Yvonne." She turned to embrace Aranare and Morgana, lingering a wee bit longer and tighter on him.

"Sorry," I mouthed over her head, and he grinned.

"I need to talk to you." My eyes pinched, and I folded my arms across my chest as my mother plopped back down on the couch. This time her wine managed to spill over the side of her glass.

"Are you going to sit down?" She gestured to the other lounge chairs—cheap, worn things upholstered in prickly carpet-like fabric that she had tried to disguise with frilly cushions and faux-fur throws.

Morgana took the lone chair. Dad's chair. The thought of him sharpened my expression into a glare.

My mother, cigarette in hand, patted the couch beside her with her long, lacquered nails, scattering ash onto the cushion as she looked at Aranare. He sat, and she turned to me, expectant.

"I'm fine standing."

She shrugged and took a long draw on her cigarette. I batted the fumes away in an exaggerated gesture.

She was beautiful, my mother, or she used to be. She wasn't now, but somewhere beneath the puffiness, smeared mascara, and garish pink tracksuit, traces of it still clung to her. Yesterday's makeup lingered like a shadow beneath her eyes, and she'd coated her full lips in a hideous dark lipstick that didn't match the tracksuit.

"What is it, hen? You haven't visited us since you moved in with Parker. Not that I blame you. He's a right catch, that one." She squinted at me, eyes bleary with drink. "And what happened to your face?"

"I don't want to talk about that, I want to talk about my father."

"Your father's at work. Useless wee shite, so he is."

A muscle in my jaw clenched. My dad was the nicest man you'd ever meet, but he was sad and tired after years of never being good enough for my mother.

"You did well to snare that lad. The Stewarts are a good family. You'll have a better life with him." My mother nodded knowingly, looking at Morgana and Aranare for support.

Morgana offered her a polite, tight-lipped smile, but Aranare's fists were balled up beside him on the vulgar couch.

"I was a great beauty once, you know . . ." Mom sighed, and I rolled my eyes.

Here we go.

Her rosy cheeks caved as she drew on her cigarette. She exhaled a plume of smoke into Aranare's face while peering at him earnestly. "Folk always thought I would leave this town and make it big somewhere like Hollywood." She stubbed her smoke into an ashtray on the small table beside the couch.

"I know you cheated on Dad," I interrupted. Tears bit at the corners of my eyes as I glared at her.

"I gave up my whole life for that man," she slurred, taking a long gulp of her cheap chardonnay, probably from a box.

"But there was someone else, wasn't there?" My voice was sharp, though it trembled beneath the surface.

"Skye," Aranare said gently. "It may not have been entirely her fault. Our kind can be . . . hard to resist when we want to be."

"It would have been her fault. You don't know her."

Mom took another gulp of wine, her eyes glassy.

Aranare stood and moved to me, placing his hand on the small of my back. "The Agápē Sirens are skilled in mind magic. Why don't you try using it on her?" He jerked his head at my mother. "They draw everything from the power of love."

He traced a finger across the fabric of my sweater, just above my heart, and warmth bloomed beneath his touch as his hand hovered close to the swell of my breasts.

"Just like your mama." Mom's hiccup of a chuckle as she looked between Aranare and me reignited my anger.

I turned to Aranare. "Tell me what to do."

"Just as Morgana can channel peace, you should be able to flood the room with euphoria, drawn from love. Like a wave of ecstasy. When she feels that, she'll tell you everything you need to know."

I blew out a breath.

"That's it. Relax." Aranare stepped behind me, folding his arms across his chest.

I peered over my shoulder at him. "What do I do now?"

"Think about the feeling of love. *New love.*" He moved closer, his body now only inches from mine. "You know the feeling?"

I swallowed and nodded.

"Good." He grazed my elbow with his thumb. "Let that feeling fill you until you can feel it throughout your body."

I focused on the subtle heat of his hand against my skin, how something so small could set me alight. I could feel his nearness like a pulse, knowing that if I stepped back just once, I'd be pressed against him. I let the euphoria flood through me and closed my eyes.

"Now ask your questions." Aranare's voice startled me. I had surrendered to the rush, the electric thrill of new love coursing through me like a spell I didn't want to break.

"This wine tastes like the gods' own honey!" my mother cried, smacking her lips and throwing the glass back. "I am in love with life today." Her eyes were glistening and wide with a happiness I had never seen on her before, and that made my heart clench, but only momentarily.

"I did it." I swung back to Aranare.

He nodded.

Morgana giggled. "Yvonne . . . Yvonne. Do you have any of that wine for me?"

"In the fridge, love. Boy, are you bonnie. Just look at those green eyes. I bet the boys go daft for you." Mom cackled, and Morgana laughed with her.

"What the fuck?" I mouthed at Aranare.

"It must have worked on Morgana as well. She's terrible at shields," Aranare choked out. "Oh, this is going to be good."

Morgana came swooping back into the room carrying a glass of the yellow wine in one hand and the box in the other. "I feel like dancing, don't you feel like dancing, Yvonne?" She pulled my mother off the couch, and they started twirling around the living room.

"You've got this," Aranare whispered. "Control the situation."

"Mom, Morgana . . . I think it would be *really* fun if you both sat down."

"Yes." Morgana grinned at me, eyes wide. "I love this couch." She threw herself down where Aranare had been sitting, and Mom slipped back into her seat, plucking a fresh smoke from the pack on the table.

"Mom, tell me about my dad, my *real* dad." I turned to her.

"Oh yes, I *love* a love story," Morgana crooned, caressing one of the threadbare cushions as she surveyed my mother.

"Oh, you lassies." Mom placed the cigarette between her clumsily painted lips.

"Here, let me." Morgana lit it for her.

"He was a bonnie lad, just like that one." She nodded at Aranare. "I was at the Port House one Friday night with Suze when he walked in. The way that man commanded a room, if you know what I mean . . ." Mom winked, and Morgana let out a high-pitched giggle, nodding along with the story while slinging back chardonnay.

"I could tell he wasn't from around here," my mother continued. "He was taller than any of our men; he had ebony curls, dark stubble on his shapely chin, and green eyes. Every woman in the bar stopped to watch him, from the oldest fish wives to the teenagers playing pool. But . . ." She paused for dramatic effect. "He took his drink, and he came over to *me*. 'Omorfi,' he said as he took me in. 'My name is Vasileios.' His accent was thick and foreign. He held out his hand to me, and I didn't think once of your pa as I took it. I could only see him."

"See, not her fault," Aranare whispered.

My teeth remained gritted.

"Then what happened?" Morgana hiccuped.

"He led me into the night, and we made love under the stars."

"Made love? Please." I scoffed.

"It's true." My mother nodded, taking a long draw on her cigarette and exhaling the smoke. "He knew his way around a woman's body in a way your father didn't."

"Ugh, too much information!"

Morgana giggled. "I hear you, girl."

I threw her an exasperated stare, and Aranare snorted a laugh at my side.

"He ruined me after that. No lad could ever love me the same." My mother shook her head and held her hands apart, indicating size, while Morgana clapped her hands over her mouth in shock.

"I think I've heard enough." I turned sharply to Aranare, closing the distance between us. He stepped back, catching my forearms gently in his palms.

He nodded at the scene unravelling before me. "Just clap your hands."

"Skye! I love your mom." Morgana took my mother's hands and held both of them at her chest, as if they had been friends for years.

I clapped my hands.

11.

MORGANA

In the week following Skye's transition, Aranare trained us both daily, first in combat and then in some form of magic-wielding.

We toiled for hours beside the old graveyard, our wooden sticks clashing. Even as mist curled around our ankles and sleety winds lashed at us, we trained.

When it came to magic-wielding, we often worked on allure, Aranare trying to break through our shields, then switching as we attempted to breach his. My ability to resist his influence and summon my own steadily improved, but the rest of my magic remained unpredictable.

On the other hand, magic came naturally to Skye. She didn't seem burdened by the battle to control her mind like I was. And without powers that could reduce people to dust, she was less hesitant to practice with them. But she loathed combat. She spent most of our sessions sitting in the grass, watching, while I'd managed to disarm Aranare over ten times.

Today, we'd been practicing my perilous dust magic down at the beach, and my muscles ached with every step, exhaustion settling deep in my bones as we trudged back to the boardwalk after four relentless hours of training. It hadn't been too bad. Most times nothing had happened, and twice the power had torn from me violently, turning the sand around us black and causing Skye to shriek. But I had also managed—on three separate occasions—to turn a single shell to dust.

"Full moon tomorrow." Aranare jerked his chin toward the darkening horizon, leaning against the open door of his green Range Rover.

The ocean breeze caressed us, and the waves sighed as my stomach hollowed out. I was severely underprepared for our trip beneath the waves.

"You're coming with us, right?" He turned to Skye, aiming for a casual tone, but the flush in his cheeks and the bob of his throat betrayed him—her answer meant everything.

Sometimes, I caught a lingering glance between them or noticed Aranare's careful attention during training, but Skye was clearly still torn up over Parker.

"I still don't know," she mumbled, suddenly absorbed by a fraying hole on the sleeve of her sweatshirt.

My chest tightened. I hoped she would choose to stay with me, because if she didn't, I was worried she would return to Parker.

"Skye," I said gently. "You can't stay here."

"I know." Her throat constricted, and her eyes filled with tears. "But those scales . . . the wings."

"Releasing your wings is a choice." Aranare's eyes flickered with understanding. "Magic mastery has come easily to you. If you don't want to unfurl them, then don't."

"But you want us to go down there?" Skye lifted a trembling hand toward the waves, swollen and dark beneath the evening wind that whipped across the bay.

I stepped closer, wrapping an arm around her back. Her face blanched, and her shoulders shook. I knew she was remembering what it felt like to sink beneath the surface.

"This time, it will be different," I said quietly.

She nodded, but her bottom lip was trembling.

Aranare's eyes shone with agony as he watched her, and then he shot me a look that said, *Talk to her.*

That night, Skye and I lay curled together, the moon glowed through drifting clouds beyond the window, luminous and nearly full.

"My whole body feels like it's in pain," Skye groaned, pulling the patchwork quilt up to her chin.

My bed was only a single, so we slept head to toe, but I didn't mind. It kept the shadows and aching loneliness that had haunted me since I'd returned to land at bay.

"Tell me about it." I massaged my shoulders.

"How did you come to terms with . . . you know, becoming half a seal?" Skye toyed with the sleeve of her sweater.

I rasped out a chuckle. "You never fully come to terms with it, but once I discovered that part of myself, I had to explore it. It was scary, but I'd have carried more regret if I hadn't."

She met my gaze, nodding slowly, but there was a heaviness behind her reflective eyes.

"I'll understand if you don't want to come, but I really hope you do." I leaned forward, threading my fingers through hers and gently squeezing them.

"Thank you," she whispered.

Sleep found us eventually. I don't know how long I'd been out when the soft creak from my bedroom door stirred me. Skye was gone.

I crept down the dark stairs, keeping to the shadows, following the sound of muffled sobs. Peering into the kitchen, I saw her clutching the home phone. She dialed, then stood silent as the answering machine clicked on: "Hi, it's Parker. You know what to do . . ."

My stomach dropped as she dialed again and again, tears tracking down her cheeks as his voice echoed from the answering machine.

I slunk back upstairs and got into bed, but couldn't get back to sleep. I lay staring at the ceiling, the nearly full moon casting pale light across the room and tying my insides into knots. I couldn't leave Skye behind tomorrow, but I couldn't stay either. She had to come with us. And if she didn't, I'd have to ask Aranare to stay. Her safety was more important than my training.

When the door creaked open again, I shut my eyes and pretended to sleep. Skye slipped in beside me, and I reached out, resting a hand gently on her leg to let her know she wasn't alone.

12.

MORGANA

And just like that, the full moon was upon us, and we were to spend our last day on land training with Louisa and then Aranare.

From under my lashes, I glanced sideways at Skye, who was sitting cross-legged beside me on the bookshop floor, perfectly poised.

"Okay, girls. That's thirty minutes." Louisa swept into the bookstore's dim back room and silenced the meditation music with a flick. "Morgana, you're still overthinking things. You need to focus on your breathing and quiet that mind. Magic is a balance of trusting your heart and mastering your mind."

I rolled my eyes. I had trusted my heart when it came to Finn, and where had that gotten me?

Finn. Just the thought of seeing him made my fist tighten around the edge of the meditation pillow. If I wanted answers, I couldn't reveal what I knew about his father—or what I suspected about him. But I was terrified that everything I felt would spill out when our eyes met.

We were headed to the Kingdom of Thálassa, and though Finn had promised I'd be safe under the Mer emissary's protection, fear coiled within me—the fear of ending up in yet another dungeon.

But I had to go. Not just to uncover the prophecy, but to see Thálassa with my own eyes—the kingdom where my grandmother once lived, side by side with Finn's mother, Abalone.

I remembered her words from the diary entry. *After the last of my family succumbed to the Shadow, they embraced me as one of their own.*

"Skye, will you accompany Morgana to Thálassa?" Louisa's question brought me back from my tumultuous thoughts.

"I've said I don't know. Would you stop asking me?" Skye nibbled on her bottom lip, her cheeks flushing.

Louisa surveyed her. "There's a reason Agápē chose to save your life and offer you a chance to claim your heritage. As Manannán's presence grows, the old gods will find a way to return."

Skye avoided Louisa's stare and picked at her nails.

"So Aranare tells me that you've mastered your ecstatic magic," Louisa said, still looking at Skye.

"Yep. I can make people happy or allure them to me? A fat lot of use that will be on a battlefield." Skye pouted.

The conversation about the Sirens from the throne room swam back into my head, mostly weaving light magic and mind illusions.

"Do not discount your magic. As a descendant of Agápē, you should be able to give people dreams and walk into the memories of others as a dream. But dream weaving is highly complex—"

"Are we going to weave a dream today?" Skye's eyes widened.

"No." Louisa exhaled. "We are not trained to teach you. It's a skill unique to Agápē's people. That's why I think you should go to Thálassa. It's where Agápē herself came from."

Skye nodded, still chewing on her lip.

"Will Skye's magic work on the dead?" I asked, remembering how I couldn't sense the Drowned's emotions.

Louisa's brow furrowed. "I'm not sure, but throughout mythology, Sirens have often been associated with death and are known as harbingers of the underworld. So, I think it's likely."

"Could you tell us what magic you expect us both to have? It might help with the journey." I crossed my arms and lifted my chin, meeting Louisa's gaze with a defiant stare.

She let out an exasperated sigh. "It's not that simple. Ocean magic is as wild as the tides. Some of it comes from ancient pacts with the gods, some is drawn straight from the sea, like the Mer's, and then you've got evolution and crossbreeding layered on top . . ." She turned to Skye, her voice softening. "You have to trust that Agápē brought you back for a reason. Let her guide you." Then, she looked at me. "And you need to stay in the realm of peace and light. Don't let the darker side of your power take hold."

A knock sounded at the door, and Aranare appeared, leaning casually against the frame, his amber eyes sweeping over us. "Good morning, Mom. Are you lassies ready to train with me?"

I stood, legs stiff from sitting on the cushion, keen to work up a sweat in combat.

As we followed Aranare out of the bookshop, Louisa caught my wrist. "Good luck . . . with everything," she whispered.

I nodded, and a sob curled in my throat. "You'll check in on Granddad?"

"I promise," she said, giving my wrist a quick squeeze. I smiled, and in that moment, Louisa and I understood each other. I was doing this for my grandmother, Iona, finishing what she and Louisa had begun.

Then, I followed Aranare and Skye into the gray morning.

"Can we do magic-wielding now?" Skye whined from the grass where she had sat for the whole combat lesson.

Aranare let out a low chuckle. "Alright then, let's start with shields."

She scrambled to her feet, and we took our positions facing Aranare. He folded his arms as he did every morning, his brown hair stirring in the early breeze, his expression smug with a hint of a smile.

This time, I noticed his allure as it rolled out from him, winding through the air and brushing against my mind—the scent of wood and something like honey.

My pulse faltered as I felt the tug, like an invisible hand drawing me closer, whispering promises against my skin. Skye swayed slightly beside me, eyes half closing, as if caught in a perfect dream.

A flash of defiance sparked in my chest, slicing through the haze. I gritted my teeth, reaching for my power and anchoring my mind's shield. Beside me, Skye shook her head, blinking the fog from her eyes.

I met Aranare's gaze, my chin lifting. "You'll have to try harder than that."

His smile only widened, a glint of challenge in his eyes. "Your turn," he said, voice a velvet purr.

Skye glanced at me, and Aranare lifted a brow in invitation.

I shot her a conspiratorial grin. "We've got this."

With a slow inhale, she closed her eyes, centering herself before releasing her breath. I followed suit, reaching again for the orb of power inside me.

Out of the corner of my eye, I saw a ripple of warmth bloom from Skye, soft and golden, like Aranare's had been, twisting through the air like the first winds of spring.

Aranare's body tensed. His smile faltered for half a second, eyes darkening as Skye's allure brushed against him. He gave a low growl of approval, his gaze locked on her now, more focused, more fierce.

Distracted, I inhaled and tried to summon my power again. I felt it stir, a silver spark inside my chest, and I pushed it outward, but it flickered, like a wave that never reached the shore.

"Well done, Skye. Almost, Morgana." Aranare threw me a sympathetic shrug.

I clenched my fists at my sides, frustration burning hotter than my embarrassment. This was our final lesson before heading underwater.

"I need to help my uncle over at Bayside before we leave, but let's finish with another try at your stunning magic. It would be good to master that before we go to Thálassa."

I crossed my arms. "I don't understand how this magic will be useful."

"As it strengthens, you'll eventually be able to shape it into weapons, but we're not even close to there yet."

I focused hard on Aranare, letting my magic rise, willing my frustration not to bleed into it, but unease twisted within me. "I'm sorry, I don't think I can." I was terrified I'd turn him to dust instead of sending him to sleep, and that fear might be shaping my magic.

"You'll never get there if you don't try. I trust you." Aranare nodded in encouragement, and he and Skye stepped back, waiting.

I scrunched up my eyes. *Stun, not end. Stun, not end.*

I opened my heart, and the silver orb flickered. Taking deep, steady breaths, I let my heart pump the power through every inch of me. I forced the fear down, because that's what tended to make things go haywire.

"King Neptūnus. Parker. Teachie. Rackham."

They're the only ones I want to end. Not anyone else. Not Aranare. Not Skye.

"King Neptūnus. Parker. Teachie. Rackham." I kept my eyes screwed shut and repeated the names from my turn-to-dust list like a mantra.

Shit. Please don't let me turn Aranare and Skye to dust.

My body vibrated with the power thrumming through my veins, desperate for liberation. I visualized calm, and with one final exhale, I released.

The world stilled, and I became weightless, suspended in the air with my eyes closed. I couldn't move, but I didn't want to. The stillness was so serene, so lovely, I could have stayed there forever.

A vision formed behind my closed eyes, and I knew immediately who it was: Manannán, the bronzed Minoan sailor. This time, he was on his boat, moving across the creaking deck, his sun-darkened skin glistening with sweat and salt. Copper bracelets clinked at his wrists as he hauled a rope through his hands, securing the sail with a knot. His loincloth, simple and girdled at the waist, flapped in the sea breeze, revealing muscular thighs. His son was with him, and he watched his father in awe.

Manannán shaded his eyes with his forearm, noticing dark clouds on the horizon. He turned to the boy. "A storm's coming. I shouldn't have brought you—it's too dangerous."

"But you're the best sailor in our kingdoms, Daddy. I will be fine with you."

Manannán chuckled and ruffled his son's hair.

The vision faded as I hit the wet ground with a thud, Skye and Aranare swimming back into view, looming over me.

"What happened?" I asked, looking around blearily.

Aranare was laughing so hard he could barely speak. "You—you—" He choked, wiping tears from his eyes. "Well, it's safe to say you mastered it, but you used it on yourself."

"Shut up." I stood, flipped him off, and burst into laughter too.

Skye wasn't laughing. Her eyes were narrowed on me, her cheeks flushed with anger. "Why were you muttering Parker's name?"

Shit. My throat bobbed.

"It was my turn-to-dust list," I mumbled.

"Why is *he* on your turn-to-dust list?"

"He tried to kill you, Skye."

"I-I can't. I need to clear my head," she snapped, turning on her heel and striding back down the cliff.

"Skye." I jogged after her, grabbing her arm. "I'm sorry."

"I just need some space." She shook me away, avoiding my gaze. "I'll meet you at the jetty."

"We leave at sunset," I called, my shoulders slumping as tears of worry formed in my eyes.

She ignored me, waving a hand over her shoulder, and a shadow of fear crept over me as I stomped back to Aranare.

"Do you think she'll go back to him?" he asked, arms crossed, eyes narrowed, a muscle ticking in his jaw as he watched her disappear down the path.

"I don't know . . ." My throat tightened.

"I'll deal with this." A ripple of anger rolled off his frame. "You should check in on your grandpa before we leave."

13.

SKYE

I had been walking for what felt like hours, and somehow, I found myself on the clifftop, pacing back and forth near Parker's drive. The cold wind was toying with my hair and plucking at my sweater. Well, it was Morgana's sweater. All my clothes were still at Parker's.

The thought dragged my gaze to his architecturally designed pad, nestled into the cliff's plateau.

I missed my clothes. My makeup. My heels. I wrinkled my nose in dismay at the jeans and sneakers I was wearing, but they would vanish if I returned to my Siren form.

As the reality sank in—that Morgana and I would soon be diving deep beneath the waves and swimming to the Mediterranean—a restless urge to see Parker had begun to gnaw at me.

I returned my gaze to the house in the distance.

Maybe I didn't have to leave with Morgana; perhaps I could slip inside, use my powers on Parker, and curl up against his muscled chest like I used to.

We could be happy.

If I stayed with him, I would never have to take that weird, scaly, birdlike form again. I couldn't deny how much I enjoyed magic-wielding lessons, and the attentions Aranare gave me, but the thought of claiming my beastly form filled me with dread. Like, once I embraced it again, everything would become permanent.

If I used my new powers of allure or ecstasy inducement on Parker, he would love me and only me, and he would never hurt me again.

We could be happy. I repeated the notion to myself.

The wind picked up as I gazed out over the ocean. The sun hung low on the horizon. Sunset was near. That was when I was meant to meet Morgana and Aranare, when we were supposed to go beneath the waves.

I swallowed but couldn't bring myself to move. This was all I'd ever wanted—this life with Parker.

I returned my focus to his stone-clad home. It was smaller than Finn's further up the cliff, but equally luxurious. My walk-in closet, my patent leather Christian Louboutin boots—the things Parker bought for me were things I could never afford on my own, and I didn't want to give them up.

I brushed the space beneath my eye where he had punched me. The bruise had faded, but the gesture brought an unwanted thought curling into my mind. *He tried to kill you.*

Perhaps he hadn't meant to. It had all happened so quickly on the boat. And if I used my powers, it would never happen again. He would love me the way he had when we first met.

I had clung to that feeling. It was what kept me waiting through all his nights away, what pulled me back even after he bruised me. How he had treated me when we first met—like I was the only girl in the world, like he needed me more than air. The feeling had quickly faded, yet I had always hoped we could find our way back to it.

And now, we could, if I used my powers.

I made my way down the drive, which wound through the rich grass on the clifftop to the front entrance. Parker's electric Porsche Taycan was in the driveway, and my chest hollowed out at the sight of it. He was home.

The dark wooden door I'd come to know so well was ajar. *Strange.*

Stepping inside, my shoulders hunched as a crash rang out. The noise was coming from the dining room. I rushed down the familiar stone walkway, the floor-to-ceiling windows wrapping me in ocean views and afternoon light as I reached the expansive living and dining area.

A cold sweat prickled at the back of my neck, and I froze in the doorway. Aranare.

He was shirtless, back muscles flexing as he prowled back and forth, circling Parker, who was sprawled on the shattered dining table.

"What are you doing?" I cried, lifting my hands to my mouth in horror.

Aranare didn't notice me. His Siren form was barely contained beneath his bronzed skin; scales were beginning to spread across his forearms and gleam under the kitchen's downlights.

My lips parted, but no more words came out as he continued pacing.

Parker pulled himself from the wreckage, fists clenched, his sleek hair disheveled and blue eyes wide with fear. "Get out of my house, you fucking freak," he spat, but his voice was trembling.

Aranare lunged forward, ramming into him. Back and forth they went, a tangle of grunts and limbs, until they both crashed into the marble kitchen island. A bar stool clattered to the ground.

I clamped my hands over my mouth again, unable to move, the scene unfolding before me as if at lightning speed. Parker shoved Aranare from him and scrambled to his feet, swinging wildly. His knuckles connected with Aranare's cheek, but the Siren barely flinched. He bent Parker's arm behind his back, pinning him against the counter.

Terror clawed its way into my core as a wine glass exploded beside my feet.

No! They are going to kill each other.

Muscles taut, scales rippling, Aranare bared his teeth—sharp now, not quite human—as the leathery wings ripped from his back. This wasn't the man who'd trained with me on the cliffs, laughing in the wind. This was something else. Something beautiful but deadly.

Parker writhed, shouting, but Aranare pressed harder.

"Aranare!" I shrieked, my voice breaking. "Stop!"

He turned, eyes connecting with mine. They remained wild, but softened as he gazed at me. His grip loosened, and Parker crumpled to the floor, gasping.

I rushed to Parker, kneeling beside him. His blue eyes widened as he noticed me, his face paling as if he'd seen a ghost.

"Wh-what the fuck is this?" he choked out, his eyes darting between us.

"It's okay." I reached for him on instinct, drawing his head into my lap.

Aranare let out a low growl; his entire frame vibrated as he paced to and fro.

"What are you even doing here?" I glared at Aranare, whose chest was heaving, his scales still rippling.

He didn't answer. He just shook his head, a flicker of sadness in his eyes as he observed Parker cradled against my chest.

"I-I . . ." Parker rasped, a cruel smile curling on his lips as he looked between Aranare and me. "I knew you were a slut."

I barely saw Aranare move, but something rushed past me, like a gust of wind. The next thing I knew, he was kneeling beside me, a knife from the kitchen gleaming silver as he held it against Parker's throat.

"Stop," I cried through a veil of tears, and Aranare froze, holding the blade in place.

"You can have her—she was a rubbish fuck anyway," Parker spat.

Rage consumed me, and my Siren magic vibrated beneath my skin, a hot brilliance slithering through my veins and igniting my insides. Aquamarine scales blossomed along my arms, and an animalistic snarl escaped my lips as talons shot from my fingertips. My back arched as the skin behind my shoulders bubbled, then shredded, wings tearing free. They draped onto the floor behind me, feathers brushing against my back as they cloaked my kneeling form.

A sneer of disgust shadowed Parker's face as he looked at me, eyes traveling from my claws to my wings. Warm power burned in response, and I snatched the knife into my own hands, slicing into the soft skin at his throat. Crimson blood spilled from the wound as I dragged the blade across. I pulled back, looking in shock at my bloodstained hands.

Bile rose in my throat as the weight of what I'd done sank into my stomach. "No," I sobbed, pressing my fingers to the cut. My anger ebbed and my scales faded, but the blood was everywhere.

"I'm sorry, baby." Parker choked, his head falling limp as blood trickled from his parted lips.

I stared at my crimson-splattered hands.

Parker was dead.

I had killed him.

Everything around me blurred, slipping in and out of clarity as my breath came in ragged gasps. Aranare . . . If he hadn't come here, then this would never have happened.

"Wh-what did you make me do?" I rasped out, glaring at him through a blur of angry tears. I pulled Parker's head tighter against my chest, refusing to look at the warm, sticky blood spreading over my thighs.

Aranare didn't reply. He turned from the scene, raking both hands through his hair.

A hot slice of anger flared through me, and a guttural snarl tore from my throat as I shoved Parker's lifeless body aside. Aranare barely had time to raise an arm before I barreled at him. Wings splayed, I clawed at his chest, scratching and crying like a beast. And I was a beast—a monster.

I dashed back to Parker's body, grabbed the sticky knife, and threw myself at Aranare again. My strikes were wild, one landing, carving a gaping wound down his right shoulder.

He caught my wrists, holding me still. I glared at him, chest heaving and breath sharp. A flicker of pain crossed his face, and his eyes glistened as if he were fighting back tears.

"What were you even doing here?" I asked again, my lip trembling as more scales glittered along my arms. I wrestled with my magic, shoving my Siren form back. Heat flamed behind my shoulder blades as the wings retreated, skin fusing over. I would never let those repulsive feathers come out again. They made me do terrible things. They made me a monster.

"He hurt you." Aranare's gaze burned into mine, his eyes still gleaming gold.

"I don't need your protection. If you hadn't come here . . . hadn't given me a knife . . ."

"What then? Would you have gone back to him? Played happy family after everything he'd done?" His jaw was stiff as he stared back at me. Blood was leaking from the wound I'd left on his shoulder.

I held his gaze, refusing to back down. Several beats of silence passed between us, and still he said nothing. I could feel the tacky smear of blood on my hands and beneath my nails. Parker's blood. I hated Aranare for being here, but most of all, I hated myself—hated the monster I'd become.

"I will *never* forgive you for this," I finally hissed, letting cold hatred work its way into my features.

"I understand, and I'm sorry." Aranare's shoulders sagged, his chest heaving as his scales disappeared and his wings melted into the flesh on his back. "But I would never forgive myself if I'd done nothing and he hurt you again."

"Get out!" I sobbed, returning to Parker and drawing his limp torso up to my chest.

Aranare surveyed the scene with sad eyes before striding out of the room.

14.

MORGANA

Skye and Aranare were not at the jetty, where we had planned to meet. It was biting cold, and I nestled my fingers into the pockets of my grandmother's fur coat, my dagger strapped around my waist.

The sun had almost set, and my gaze kept returning to the horizon. If they didn't arrive soon, I would have to go alone.

I made my way to the water's edge, the last blush of sun fading behind the sea. Golden light stretched across the dark waves as I craned my neck, eyes flicking toward the path from the town.

Skye had said she needed to clear her head and would meet me here, but I had a sickening feeling she'd gone to see Parker instead.

My heart beat faster with each passing minute—both of them were late. Too late.

If I had to go alone, at least Aranare would be here to watch over Skye. Still, I'd give them one more minute. I tapped my foot in the sand, nerves prickling beneath my skin.

Wind tugged at the loose strands of my hair, and the cold crept up my legs as I stepped into the tide, dread twisting in my chest like seaweed, wrapping tight. Where were they?

Sneakers slapped on slick concrete, the rhythm was stumbling and frantic. Skye emerged on the boardwalk, breathless and streaked with . . . blood?

It stained her sweater, smeared her hands, and painted the side of her neck. Her eyes met mine, and the knot in my chest tightened.

"Whose blood is that?"

"Parker's." Her lip trembled.

I gripped her wrist, pulling her to a halt. "Where's Aranare?"

"He won't be joining us anymore." She wiped a tear from beneath her eyes, but her lips thinned as she turned back to me. "Come on, let's go."

My stomach hollowed out. No Aranare meant no more training, but something in Skye's expression told me now wasn't the time to press her about what had happened. And we had a sunset to catch.

I took her hand in mine, and we stepped into the waves. The chilly water kissed our skin, and magic hummed beneath my ribs.

"I-I don't know if I can." Skye's hand trembled. The sun had almost dipped below the horizon.

"You are much better at magic-wielding than I am. If I can do it, so can you."

"It's not that. I'm just not sure I *want* to." She stopped, waist-deep in the waves.

I gestured to the sliver of sun left on the skyline. "You can stay here, but I have to go."

"I can't stay here, not anymore. Parker . . . the police . . ." Skye sobbed, and she pushed past me, striding out into the surf.

I followed, clearing my mind, blocking SS *Jones's Lady* from my thoughts and imagining myself free-falling into the sea. The salty waves welcomed me like an old friend.

With one last look at the fading sky, we dove.

The ocean embraced us as we vanished beneath the surface to become wild creatures of the sea.

15.

SKYE

The water engulfed me as I dove beneath the waves. The icy bite of the Atlantic nipped at every inch of my skin like frostbite, its midnight blue waters swirling around me in a mist of bubbles.

Magic coursed through my body, its warmth seeping into my frozen human limbs. A part of me wanted to resist, surrendering to my human frailty, letting my teeth chatter and my lips turn blue. A part of me wanted to die a human death in these waters—the death I should have had if Agápē hadn't given me a second chance.

But Morgana's hand remained clasped in mine, and for her, I exhaled, leaning into the magic, allowing it to work through my body as the transition unfolded.

My heart clamored as I recalled the last time I'd felt my body shift in this way, in these same cold, dark waters. But the last time I'd been a victim. This time, I was the perpetrator. Last time I'd been a human. This time . . . this time I was a monster.

As the magic enveloped me, aquamarine scales unfurled across my skin, glistening over every inch of my body. Though my form remained human—my breasts still soft against my chest, the warmth of my woman parts lingering between my thighs—my curves were now sheathed in a sleek, glittering bodysuit. They formed a natural corset across my torso, leaving my neck and shoulders bare.

Morgana released my hand and swam forward, her thick coat billowing in the swell. I gasped as I watched a similar transformation take hold of her body, but where scales clung to my skin, she was cloaked in glistening fur.

I jolted, a hiss escaping my lips as my fingers and toes lengthened, slick webs flaring between them, and then with another pulse of magic, the claws came.

They weren't the claws of a beast—they were delicate, as if some artful manicurist had shaped my nails in the style of arched vampire acrylics. But they were still claws, real, sharp claws, not pieces of plastic glued in place.

I brought my hands to my face, and my dark hair curled around me in the water. I could see everything so clearly, see the blood that remained on my webbed, clawed hands. It was dark crimson against the deep blue, but slowly, the water was cleansing them. The blood, which had congealed, softened under the ocean's caress, drifting like unraveling red ribbons from my hands, cheeks, and chest.

My stomach knotted, and I sucked in a breath, crying out in a bubbly gasp as something broke from the skin of my neck.

Gills! I ran my hands across the newly formed grooves.

Pain seared behind my shoulder blades as wings strained against my skin, desperate to break free. I hissed, pushing the sensation away. I would not let those grotesque feathered things emerge. Obeying my will, they retreated, and a part of me was glad. I couldn't control the creature I'd become, but at least I could control this.

"Are you okay?" Morgana turned to me, catching the pain that must have been twisting my features as I fought to keep my wings at bay. Her red hair drifted around her face in the dark waters. I noticed the fingers she used to sweep it aside were now webbed. Only bubbles had left her lips, but I heard her familiar voice in my mind.

"No." I shook my head, tears trying to fall from my eyes, but the water claimed them just like it had claimed the blood.

"Skye." Morgana's eyes searched mine, their color like frosted Uranus in the murky light. "Parker deserved whatever you did to him."

"I-I took someone's life. I'm a monster. And Aranare . . . If he hadn't been there . . ." My bottom lip quivered, and I held up my hands again, but all the blood had now been swept away by the water.

Morgana clasped my webbed hand with hers. "We're in this together," she murmured, giving it a little squeeze.

I let her pull me into the blue-lit expanse. Moonshine filtered down from somewhere above, casting ripples of shimmering light that danced before us, breaking with every stroke only to reform again.

We swam on and on, and as we moved, I let my world collapse in on itself. I let the weight of everything that had happened flood me, as if the entire Atlantic had poured into my being. I drowned in the feeling until nothing remained but swirling darkness. A darkness that I shoved down deep, letting the ocean close over the hollow in my heart.

16.

ARANARE

I'd loved her since first seeing her at my uncle's cafe, but I'd managed to keep it at bay until now. Because when Sirens love, it can become something primal.

We have a deep connection with love. We can sense it in others and harness its power to wield our magic, but when *we* love, it makes us go daft. It hits us with an all-consuming intensity.

It's like new love's fluttering butterflies, the breathless thrill of a first kiss, the electric spark of skin brushing skin. It's aching. It's euphoric. And that feeling never goes away.

I waited in the Bayside parking lot, hands tapping against my beat-up truck's worn steering wheel until the port was shrouded in darkness. Skye and Morgana would have disappeared beneath the waves at sunset.

I hissed as I shifted the car out of park, blood soaking through the makeshift bandage on my shoulder. The gash was deep, likely to scar. I turned the key, and the engine coughed before rumbling to life.

It was time to return to Parker's house and clean up the mess she'd made. *We'd* made. The Stewarts were a powerful family, and I didn't want them coming after her.

The truck jolted down the uneven road, every bump echoing the tension in my chest. I glanced over my shoulder into the back, where I'd loaded an old black tarp, bleach, and rope.

I'd done this before, but not many times. We Lugh Sirens tried to keep our lives among humans as uncomplicated as possible, but sometimes things arose, such as family, land, and politics, and you had to do what needed to be done. If anyone threatened my family, I had no problem making them disappear. Family came first, before all other things.

Making people "disappear" was easy in a town plagued by drownings, and in a bit of poetic justice, I was going to make Parker's death look like a drowning-suicide over his broken heart.

When I pulled in, I saw Skye had left the door ajar, and my chest tightened as I imagined her fleeing the place, tears streaming from her bonnie eyes, pain shadowing all her features.

"I will *never* forgive you for this." Her words crept into my mind, sharpening the ache in my heart.

Why had I even come here? She'd asked me that more than once. What had I been planning to do? I wasn't sure exactly. All I knew was that I wanted to make sure he never hurt her again.

When Sirens give their heart to someone, it's as if a tiny part of it has been branded with that person's name. We call it a Tidescar because the tug on the heart is akin to the pull of the tides.

I'd fought my feelings for Skye, but as everything unfolded here with Parker—seeing her pain, her strength—I had let my guard down and allowed my heart to swell with love. A violent pang tore through my chest as I walked out the door, and that's when I knew I'd let her in.

A Tidescar can be torturous—it can form even when love is unrequited.

The bond clicks into place once we open our hearts and never loosens its grip. Not if the person lies. Not if they cheat or hurt us. When we've given away a piece of our Siren soul, no matter what happens, we can never take it back. The good news? We can form more than one Tidescar in a lifetime. And with time, we learn to guard our hearts—to wait until we're sure the love is returned before letting the bond take hold.

I'd slipped up when it came to Skye.

I rolled Parker's body into the tarp and tightened the rope around it. Then I put on a pair of plastic gloves and shook out a garbage bag, picking up anything that suggested a struggle had occurred here.

I'd only borne one other Tidescar on my heart. It had formed ten years earlier, and though she was long gone, the scar remained—a subtle ache when I thought of her, like the tide pulling me from a distant shore where she still stood, to where I was powerless to return.

After that, I'd sworn off love. I was careful not to scar again. And it had worked until Skye had turned to me with tears streaming down her face, and the attraction I'd been fighting for her had exploded into something primal.

I threw the garbage bag in the back of my truck and returned with a bucket, kneeling on the floor to deal with the blood. It was everywhere and had congealed across the polished stone like spilled sauce.

I sponged away the blood, wrung the cloth out into the bucket, and then soaked up some more. I wiped my sweaty forehead with a gloved hand.

My legs were stiff when I finally rose and surveyed the stone floor for any traces of red. When I found none, I coated the space with bleach. Exhaling, I pulled off my gloves and loaded my stuff into the back of my truck. It was time for the setup.

I unlocked Parker's phone and flicked open a music streaming platform.

What would a douche like Parker listen to before committing suicide over a lass? I put the whiniest track I could find on repeat, blasting it from the stereo.

The music wound around me as I pulled Parker's finest scotch from the liquor cabinet and emptied it down the sink, leaving the bottle and a glass on the elegant living room table.

I left the door leading to the cliff face ajar, padding into the expansive bedroom and walk-in closet where Skye's things still hung, fighting against the feelings seeing her clothes and the bed they'd slept in together evoked.

I tossed Parker's jeans and shirt near the doorway, making it look like he'd stripped them off in a rush before running toward the cliff. Then I sank into the couch and picked up his phone again. I opened the message thread with Skye—there was a heart beside her name, and her display picture was a photo of her blowing him a kiss. I had a feeling she'd set it herself, but the sight of it still twisted something in my gut. Had she unwittingly created a Tidescar for Parker?

The urge to scroll through their messages gnawed at me, but I resisted. Instead, I began typing the words of a desperate man—messages he might have sent her.

I love you, baby.

Come home, I can't live without you . . .

It has been torture with you gone, a torture I can no longer endure . . .

I am sorry. I had to do this. I love you.

I wiped the phone clean of fingerprints before placing it beside the empty scotch glass on the coffee table. Writing the messages had come easily, like I was speaking to her, saying the things my heart yearned for.

I leaned back into the couch, allowing a bit of my allure to radiate through the house so that when the authorities arrived, they wouldn't smell bleach or blood, just the faint scent of honey and heather. Then I gathered

Parker's tarp-wrapped body into my arms and hoisted it through the glass doors and onto the cliffside. The wind howled around me, my muscles straining under the weight. I took one breath, then dove.

My Siren form rippled to life, obsidian scales glinting across my chest and forearms, wings splaying before I hit the water. Gills flared along my neck as I dove deeper, my legs merging to become an onyx tail, which beat against the current.

I unraveled the tarp as I sank, laying Parker's body on the ocean floor, my tail keeping me afloat. I tucked him between some worn rocks and tangled seaweed at the cliff's base. I weighed down his drifting clothes with stones, anchoring him so he wouldn't float to the surface.

Blood bloomed into the dark water, and a slow grin curled my lips. Soon, the sea's wild beasts would come. And if anyone did find him, there wouldn't be enough of him left to guess how he'd died.

What a night . . .

I raked a hand through my wet hair, keeping the other on the leather-clad steering wheel of my Range Rover. I exhaled as the lights of Ruadán's Port faded, the truck rumbling past the old graveyard and onto the rugged deserted road that clung to the cliff's edge.

Fresh blood was seeping from the gash Skye had left on my right arm. I'd lost the bandage during my dive and would need to patch it up again.

The elongated yellow shadows of my headlights danced across the worn road, illuminating the crumbling brick fence on either side as they passed. The beams wavered like a drunk staggering home, still trying to dance to the tunes from the bar.

After fifteen minutes of driving along the clifftop, the headlights trembled across my stone cottage as I pulled into the yard. I got out and slammed the front door of my wee house shut behind me, blowing out a breath as I took in the space. My space.

I'd refurbished the one-bedroom cottage by hand. Its packed stone walls met a stone floor, and there was a modest kitchen, a hearth set into the wall, and a wooden table with chairs I'd carved by hand.

My breath misted in the cold air as I lit a fire, poured myself a whisky, and sank onto the couch, muscles tense as I rebandaged my arm.

I liked the solace of this place. I spent most days helping my uncle fish or my mom in the bookstore. Not that I didn't love my family; we were close, the Lugh Sirens.

We knew the blue-blooded oceanic families—like the Neptūnus Mer—looked down on us for being half-breeds, for choosing the land over the deep. But that only drew us closer. Family was everything to us, but having this place to call my own was nice—an escape.

I pulled a peeling novel from the small pile on the dusty floor beside the hearth and sipped my whisky. I didn't have a TV, just a collection of my favorite clothbound classic novels I'd taken from the bookstore: *Wuthering Heights, Anna Karenina, The Count of Monte Cristo, Far from the Madding Crowd . . .*

I exhaled, taking another sip of scotch before flicking to my marked page in *The Great Gatsby.*

PART TWO

The Kingdom of Thálassa

17.

MORGANA

A sense of pride swept through me as we swam over the plumes from the Therme Skótos heat vents, SS *Jones's Lady* looming out of the gloom ahead. I'd controlled my transformation and no longer needed to wake up in my grimy Drowned cabin. Still, a part of me ached because I knew I'd been granted that special room on SS *Jones's Lady* because of my father.

Skye and I alighted on the sand before the doorway of the corroded ship, and her nose scrunched up as she took it in. "*This* is where you've been living down here?"

Light from the coral pillars and glowing portholes shone across the scales now covering her body. They glimmered pink when she moved through the water. She didn't have a tail, she had legs like me, and scales curved over her breasts in the shape of a corset. It seemed her wings only protracted when commanded, and I hadn't seen them since she'd first revealed herself to us in the lighthouse.

She should have been screaming and crying in her new body, in this strange new world, but it was as if she'd bitten back her tears and shut down, letting something inside her harden as we swam. By the time we reached SS *Jones's Lady,* she was smiling again, her trauma buried somewhere. Yet beneath that smile, I could sense a sadness so deep it was almost a darkness.

I stepped toward the swinging doors of the tavern, light spilling through them and pooling around me on the sand. My hand hesitated at the entrance. "The Drowned are . . . well, you'll see." I sighed and pushed the doors open.

The bar fell silent as we strode inside. I was used to it, but their eyes weren't on me this time. Every gaze was fixed on Skye. Some of the men's mouths hung open.

I cast a sideways glance at her full breasts and shapely figure. Instinctively, I stepped closer, eyes darting across the room for any sign of Teachie or Rackham, but neither was in the bar.

Skye emitted a sharp noise of shock as she took in the rest of the unruly Drowned and the anglerfish lights shoved into glass jars on the tables.

"Morgana, welcome back." The Captain stepped out from behind the bar, his wooden leg thudding through the room as he hobbled over to hand us a bottle of rum.

I sipped the spicy liquid but remained in the doorway, scanning the space for Rory Balfour, my father, as I did every time. As usual, no one had the kind face I had seen in the paper or my grandmother's photo album.

I spotted Edward playing chess with his friend Daniel at our usual table in the far corner. His eyes lit up when he saw us, and he waved us over. Gripping Skye's hand, I led her through the eclectic mix of tables toward them.

"Good game, Ed." Daniel grinned, snatching his mustard-colored military cap from the table and allowing Skye to take his vacated seat. I slipped into the chair on Edward's other side.

"I say, I've never seen a Siren in such close quarters before." Edward leaned forward, eyes wide with wonder as he took in Skye's gleaming scales.

"This is my friend Skye," I said gently. "She's recently *transitioned.*"

"Is she . . . ? Surely not." Edward's brows drew apart, and his eyes widened.

I rolled my eyes. "Yes, she is descended from Agápē."

"Smashing," Edward breathed.

"I can't believe all this." Skye's throat bobbed as she scanned the bar.

Edward folded his arms and gave me a pointed look. "So, what's the plan?"

"We meet Finn under the archway of Archōn Agorá tonight."

Edward's mouth thinned at the mention of Finn, but he nodded.

"I know you wanted to come with me when we last spoke." I gripped Edward's freckled wrist and looked at him with sincerity. "But if you've changed your mind, that's okay."

"Changed my mind?" His nostrils flared. "I'll have you know I've even prepared supplies for the journey." He plucked a netted bag from under the table and rattled it, rum bottles clinking merrily inside.

"You couldn't pack something a bit more useful?" I snorted.

Edward raised his tumbler in cheers. "I'm quite content with rum."

I met his glass with mine and leaned back in my chair. Some of the Drowned continued to stare, their gazes either lecherous, curious, or malicious.

The Captain, noting their looks, caught my eye and hobbled over to a woman in a ripped beaded dress seated near the piano. He squeezed her shoulder and chuckled. "Evelyn, play a tune, would you? These Drowned need a distraction."

Evelyn—I remembered her as the woman who had helped the pirate José after the prince, *Finn,* had tortured him. That felt like so long ago now.

The Drowned returned to their drinking as Evelyn settled at the piano, though a few still cast glowering looks our way. Skye had fallen into a somber silence, her eyes tracing the anglerfish lights strung across the mottled ceiling, glowing like a sky full of stars.

I nudged her. "Why don't you see if you can use your gifts on the Drowned before we leave?"

She adjusted her stance, masking her downcast expression with a quick grin, as if not wanting me to glimpse her sadness. "I don't know." She toyed with her rum, her eyes darting across the rowdy patrons.

"Look at them." A rush of sympathy coursed through me as I observed the sad, drunken, tattered souls. "They deserve to feel the ecstasy of new love."

"You think you can shield yourself this time? I wouldn't want you to end up in that guy's lap." A genuine grin split Skye's face as she jerked her thumb at a toothless pirate sitting across from us.

"I managed to shield myself from Aranare." I regretted the words as soon as they tumbled from my mouth.

Skye's expression darkened at the mention of his name, but she pushed it aside, settling into her chair. Her long raven locks spilled over the back as she closed her eyes and exhaled.

This time, with my shields in place, I remained unaffected. This time, I could see the magic of love at work.

It started with the music. Evelyn was at the piano, throwing back her head and caressing the keys with a newfound passion. The tune became sultry and mournful, like something from a 1920s cabaret bar. Her bejeweled dress sparkled in the anglerfish lights, and she closed her eyes and began to sing. It was a haunting melody—a song of two drowned lovers.

One died at sea and the other from grief. Eventually, their bodies washed ashore on the same beach.

I glanced at Edward, his eyes now fuller and his face slack as Evelyn's music spread through the venue, woven with the threads of Skye's magic.

"It's working!" I turned to Skye, who nodded gleefully, dark curls bouncing.

My eyes widened as the Drowned began scraping back their chairs and pulling partners onto the dance floor. The Captain hobbled out and helped a few Drowned shove the tables aside, clearing space. As he passed, he shot us a wink. Clearly the magic had not affected him.

"By golly, this song." Edward's voice drew my attention. I turned to find him resting his chin on his elbow, gazing dreamily at Evelyn. Beside her, the Captain now played, their voices intertwining in a heartfelt duet.

"May I have this dance?" Daniel stood beside us, his hat tucked under one arm, the other extended toward Edward.

Edward flushed and nodded. The two of them moved onto the dance floor, swaying slowly, cheek to cheek.

A timid Drowned boy approached our table. He must have been young, perhaps eighteen, as he still had acne. He was wearing the tattered uniform of a soldier. "Could I ?" He glanced at Skye, then quickly looked down, a flush rising to his cheeks.

She turned to me, stifling a giggle, before sweeping the wide-eyed youth into her arms and leading him across the room. He rested a hand on her scaled hip, holding her carefully, as if drowning had been worth it for this moment alone.

"Fuck it." I laughed and joined everyone on the dance floor, linking arms with some of the merry Drowned. Who knew what awaited us in the Kingdom of Thálassa? We might as well have some fun.

The Captain pulled Evelyn from her seat at the piano, her long beaded dress glinting as he spun her around the room. A man in modern clothes—a leather jacket and dark jeans—took their seats, and he began to play a tune I recognized.

"Wicked Game" by Chris Isaak. The song caused goosebumps to form on my arms, and for a moment, it felt like the world had gone into slow motion as my mind was consumed with thoughts of Finn.

All around me, the Drowned were dancing, drinking, and smiling. Their eyes lit up like they had at the Mourning, filled with love. I realized love was both life's elixir and the most dangerous poison of all.

Evelyn gazed into the Captain's eyes, and he spun her away only to pull her back against his chest. Nearby, Daniel and Edward waltzed, holding each other close, as if this had been what they'd always wanted, even if neither had found the words to say it.

The youth dancing with Skye grinned, his face shining with boyish delight as his hands wandered lower. She slapped them away with a sharp look, then rolled her eyes. "Okay, for one song." The young soldier's face lit up with glee as he eagerly slid them back down.

I spun around, linking arms with a Drowned in a full-skirted dress, then somehow found myself back at our table, tucking my hair behind my ears as the song swelled, tugging at my aching heart.

The bar's swing doors burst open, the pianist froze midnote, and silence swept through the venue. I stiffened, heart pounding.

Teachie and Rackham were standing in the doorway.

18.

MORGANA

All eyes flicked to Teachie and Rackham as they sauntered into the Avenue. They stopped at the bar, arms folded, surveying the Drowned, still frozen on the dance floor, with matching wicked grins.

They were no longer the pirates I remembered. Rackham's beaded braids hung limp, patches of his scalp exposed. The skin beneath Teachie's right eye had peeled back above his old scar, revealing muscle and bone. Silver glimmered in the whites of their eyes and wreathed their skin. *Mer blood.* My stomach tightened as the memory of their rough hands on my body surged back.

"What the fuck?" Skye cried, letting go of the youth she'd been dancing with and clapping her hands. Her ecstatic magic evaporated.

Around us, awkward shuffling and low grunts filled the air as Skye's influence loosened its grip on the Drowned, sending them retreating from the dance floor. Daniel and Edward released each other, and Edward hurried to sit beside me, his face flushed bright red.

Skye quickly scurried over, settling in next to us also. "Are they glowing silver?" she whispered.

"Mer blood. I'll explain later," I whispered out of the corner of my mouth.

The heavy clomp of a wooden leg echoed through the room as the Captain left Evelyn's side and limped forward to face the pirates. "Teachie, Rackham, how nice of you to rejoin us," he said, offering them a bottle of rum from the bar.

Teachie grunted, swatting the bottle from the Captain's hand. It shattered against the floor, the sharp crack slicing through the silence. More silver-stained Drowned emerged in the doorway, as if the noise had been a signal.

The Captain glanced toward the table where Edward, Skye, and I sat grouped. His one good eye gleamed gold as it met mine, and something in his look twisted my insides.

I sucked in a breath as the Captain raised his right hand, fingers splayed. A hum filled the air as a golden orb materialized from nothing, hovering before the pirates. While their eyes were fixed on the light—distracted—he shot his left hand behind his back, and a wave of pale blue luminescence cascaded outward, like mist woven with moonlight. It rippled through the tavern, curving around me, Edward, and Skye until it formed a glittering dome that shimmered like a heat haze.

"Hey," I cried, shoving back my chair and rushing forward, only to rebound. "Hey!" I pounded against the glistening veil of magic now enclosing the three of us, but no one looked our way. The Captain was shielding us.

Edward's words rippled through my consciousness: *No one knows much about the Protectors. It is rumored they have ancient powers, but they are dormant unless activated by the need to defend.*

"Your magic won't work on us anymore, old man," Rackham growled, slashing his knife through the Captain's glowing orb, unaware it was only a distraction. His toothless grin split wide as the light disintegrated.

"We are not here to fight with you," Teachie proclaimed, addressing the bar. "We are here to offer you a kingdom. Join Manannán in fighting the Mer and live to tell the tale. Or stay with him"—he jerked his chin at the Captain—"and die."

"You want us to fight against the Mer?" an old fisherman asked, looking around nervously.

"With the Lord of the Drowned on our side, we'll claim their kingdoms," Teachie cried. "I've seen the inside of the Neptūnus palace—Mer Prince Aigéan tortured me for days in his stone chambers. But he got distracted, and I escaped."

Wait, what? Finn had tortured Teachie. Could it have been because of me? No, I never told him who gave me the bruises; it must have been a coincidence.

"You saw the castle?" a woman asked. "What was it like?"

Teachie snarled. "While we wallow in ships like this one, they live in opulence."

"This is madness. These men are almost rabid with Mer blood," the Captain interjected.

"Enough time has been wasted," Rackham grunted. "Join us and live, or stay with him and die."

Chairs scraped back as the Drowned rose, shuffling to gather behind Teachie and Rackham. Only Evelyn and Daniel remained seated.

"So you chose death." Teachie's voice was laced with violence as his eyes swept the two of them.

"Daniel, no," Edward cried, pounding on the dome that held us, trying to get Daniel's attention, but no one looked our way. The shield made us invisible.

Evelyn threw back her shoulders, her spangled dress catching the light as she walked to stand beside the Captain, and Daniel followed. Teachie's large, ringed fingers twitched over the knife in his belt, eyes flashing as he surveyed the three of them.

"No!" I joined Edward, hammering on the magic shield. "No, you can't do this."

Neither Evelyn, Daniel, nor the Captain looked our way, but the Captain said to no one in particular, "The rest of the prophecy must be found. Find it, and end this."

"There is no second half to the prophecy—we make our own fate." Teachie bared his teeth. With that, he pulled the blade from his belt and slit Daniel's throat.

"No," Edward breathed, softer this time. His hand pressed against the magic shield as he slid to the floor, shoulders shaking.

I rushed to his side as Skye let out a choked sob.

Daniel's body crumpled, and then, like Donahue's had done, dissolved into its surroundings. Edward let out a strangled sob, and I gripped his arm in reassurance.

Teachie turned to Evelyn next. Her shoulders were trembling, and her breasts heaved beneath her embellished bodice, but she kept her neck straight, holding Teachie's gaze as he approached and placed his knife to her neck.

The Captain's gray hair was disheveled, his chest heaving as he looked at Evelyn. Fear flickered in his amber eye.

He's exhausted from holding our shield.

"I'll find you in another life," Evelyn whispered, and she linked her fingers with his as Teachie's blade slid across the flesh of her throat.

She crumpled and fell, choking and coughing as her skin split and then knitted itself back together. She didn't die.

"Well, well, well . . ." Teachie threw back his head and laughed, glancing between Evelyn and the Captain. "We'll have some fun with this one instead." He grabbed Evelyn by the arm and threw her into Rackham, who held her against him, slicking his silver-stained tongue up her bare shoulder in a way that made me want to be sick.

"Do not touch her," the Captain growled, and light exploded from him.

Furniture shattered in every direction, but though our shield trembled, it held.

All around Teachie and Rackham, Drowned men writhed and shrieked as their bodies were flung into the air, twisting into glittering, tortured orbs that floated through the tavern door, bound for the Garden. Only Teachie, Rackham, some of their cohort, and a scattering of Drowned remained standing when the carnage cleared.

"She will pay for that." Rackham tore at Evelyn's bodice, exposing her breast just as she snatched the knife from his belt and drove it into her own throat.

This time, she dissolved into her surroundings like Daniel, tiny bubbles swirling upward, dancing around the Captain as they sang their song of release. The blade clattered to the floor.

Teachie reached for the Captain, the whites of his eyes now pure silver, but he paused as a looming presence filled the doorway and a new Drowned entered the room.

My blood chilled, and Skye gave a little gasp at my side as the man stepped from the shadows into the light. Like the other Drowned who had been using the Mer blood, he had deteriorated. All his hair had come away, and silver stained his skin, but whereas the others remained distinctly human, this man was part beast. Scales crept up the back of his neck, spreading across his face, and crowning his bald head. Worst of all, one of his arms was a writhing tentacle.

"The Fisherman," Edward hissed.

"What?" A shudder worked its way down my spine as I watched the man's face twist into a wicked smile.

"I've heard tales of the Drowned man with a beast's body who overthrew Port Royal's Protector and claimed the title for himself. He despises the Mer. They call him the Fisherman for the sheer number he's slaughtered. No surprise he's working for Manannán now."

The Fisherman's gaze swept the bar, and for a moment, I thought he might see us, but the Captain grunted, emitting more magic, and our shield strengthened. The newcomer stepped forward, and my stomach hollowed as he wound his tentacled, squid-like arm around the Captain's neck.

I pummeled the shimmering veil before us, tears blurring my vision. My pulse stuttered as I remembered I had magic—magic that could rival the Captain's. I reached clumsily for the silver orb of power within me, thrusting it into my palms and channeling it into the walls that held us. Electricity crackled as it collided with the shield, which wavered but held.

The Captain grunted in the Fisherman's grip, and my stomach sank. Holding the protective bubble was already draining him, and my power pressing against it only made it worse. I pulled back my palms, and my magic extinguished.

The Captain struggled, clawing at the slimy tentacle around his neck, but he was spent, drained from protecting us.

Skye shrieked, and Edward let out a garbled sob. We pounded against the dome again, but still it held firm.

The Fisherman hoisted the Captain higher, until they were eye to eye.

"*You*," the Captain rasped as he took in the man's face.

The Fisherman's smile was a cruel slash, his silver eyes gleaming as the scales along his cheek caught the light. He tightened his tentacle, and the Captain slumped against it.

"The Protector has fallen," the Fisherman growled to the remaining Drowned, his voice dark as a bottomless ocean cavern. "SS *Jones's Lady* now belongs to us. Let's move on."

He let the Captain's body fall to the floor, where he collapsed in a crumpled heap of white and navy fabric, his cap landing beside him. His breaths were ragged, worn from the effort of protecting us with his magic.

As the beast strode toward the door, his tentacled arm slithered back, curling over the Captain's cheek. Bile rose in my throat as it retracted. Where it had lingered, faint suction patterns radiated outward like bruised halos, the Captain's skin turning a sickly greenish hue as if tainted by salt and rot. The Fisherman had left a circular brand.

The swinging doors closed behind him. Teachie and Rackham were on his heels, the remaining Drowned shuffling after them. One or two cast a guilty glance toward the Captain, whose chest was still rising and falling, though barely.

The magical shield still held. I continued to hammer my fists against it, sobs rasping from my throat as the Captain's chest shuddered. With one last shaky breath, he disintegrated, joining his two loyal friends, Daniel and Evelyn, and my heart broke as the bubble collapsed.

The Captain was dead.

Tears brimmed in my eyes, and I dropped to my knees where he'd lain moments before. My mouth thinned, fists clenched, and I let those tears harden, frosting over into seething anger.

I now had four people on my turn-to-dust list: Teachie, Rackham, King Neptūnus, and the Fisherman.

19.

MORGANA

We walked in silence, following the gnarled pillars of Therme Skótos upward, traveling at Edward's slower pace. The mood was somber, as if a dark cloud hung over each of us. Anguish shrouded Edward's face, and Skye's expression remained impassive as she scanned the underwater surroundings, but I could sense her lingering pain.

The world seemed to fade in and out of focus as I repeated the same story to myself over and over.

The Captain was dead. There would be no more of his kind smiles or all-knowing nods; his little sea snake was gone, too. There was one less Protector in the Kingdom of the Deep. Edward had said there were seven—the spirits installed by the gods to keep the Drowned in check. With Port Royal and SS *Jones's Lady* fallen, only five remained.

The world felt like an ever-darkening abyss. I wanted to curl up in a ball and sleep for days, but I couldn't. The Captain, Daniel, and Evelyn had given up their lives so we could continue on the quest to find the prophecy.

It had been the Captain's dying wish. *The rest of the prophecy must be found. Find it, and end this.*

Every twisting strand of seaweed resembled a tentacled arm, every glittering fish a flash of the mottled scales on the Fisherman's cheek.

"Teachie, Rackham, King Neptūnus, the Fisherman," I muttered, repeating my turn-to-dust list as I clenched my webbed fists. And Finn— should he be on that list? I didn't know. But I couldn't say he shouldn't be, either.

My chest tightened at the thought of seeing him again. I kept scanning the dusky gloom ahead, half expecting his Mer form to emerge from the shadows.

"Do you really need to drink that now?" Skye's reprimand snapped me from my churning thoughts. Her brow furrowed as she watched Edward pull a bottle of rum from his jangling sack.

"Don't mind if I do," he said, popping the cork, but there was a pained look in his eyes, as if he were trying to hold back tears. "To the Captain— and Daniel." He took a generous swig.

"To the Captain." I grabbed a bottle from Edward, grateful for the brief reprieve from my mind, and tossed back the spicy liquid.

Skye shrugged and accepted one as well. Her long curls swayed as she angled her chin to drink.

We followed the stalagmites of Therme Skótos until the gloom thinned and the Atlantic's rainforest unfolded before us. Skye gasped as a flourish of colorful fish burst from between coral-clad pillars. Wispy branches swayed in the current, wavering masses of pearl, crimson, and dark green in the midnight waters. Now and then, their delicate tips brushed against our ankles as we passed.

"Best not put your hand in there," Edward cried.

Skye was peering into a giant clam, her dainty, clawed fingers clutching its lip. She jumped back like a guilty child. "Why? It's amazing," she gasped, emitting a sea of bubbles.

"Why? Because they'll snap shut and hold you fast! Everyone knows that." Edward let out an exasperated sigh. He broke off a branch of coral and rolled it between his freckled fingers before letting it tumble to the seabed.

After a few hours of walking, Edward's rum sack was considerably lighter, and the coral had begun thinning, replaced by plain stones.

I ran my hand across the nearest monolith. *Runes.* We had reached the outskirts of Archōn Agorá. Flecks of debris danced between the tumbled poles, glinting white against the blue surroundings.

We continued through the ancient pillars, past the statue of Agápē's vacant eyes. I looked into their stony depths and recognized Skye's likeness this time.

"That's her," Skye whispered, pausing beside me to study the eroded statue of the beautiful Siren goddess, half-submerged in sand.

I nodded, glancing at Skye. Pain flickered in her eyes as she gazed at the figure's marble hand reaching toward the surface.

I drew her away, and we continued through the scattered stones, some etched with the Runes of the Ocean. I wondered what this place would have looked like in the Days of Gods.

"Ouch!" I flinched as Skye's claws dug into my arm, and she drew a sharp breath beside me. I followed her gaze, and my stomach tightened.

In the shadow of an eroded archway, Finn was waiting. His face was partially shaded, but his tail glimmered jade in the cool light. Its tips shone red, as if dipped in blood. He was wearing a breastplate of tarnished silver, like that of his guards, and the packed muscles of his torso rippled beneath it. Around each of his wrists were silver filigreed bracers. His dolphin Pháos hovered beside him, angling its head and chirping as it surveyed us.

I exhaled in a mist of bubbles. My throat felt dry as my eyes darted across his abs, and in that moment of weakness, his words crept into my mind. *You are my moon . . .*

He had said he loved me, yet I was sure he was keeping information from me. The book on mythical creatures had described the merfolk as treacherous. Maybe I'd been a fool for ever letting him in, for believing that this world and its inhabitants could be anything other than dark and dangerous.

Finn drifted from the curling shadows of the archway, a smile flirting with his lips. "You sure know how to keep a merman waiting."

A pang sharpened in my chest, and for a moment, breathing became difficult. Where this man was concerned, my heart was a battlefield in which love, hate, desire, and distrust clashed like opposing tides. My feelings for him weren't simple—they were a raging storm, which wouldn't help me now when I needed to have my wits together.

I squared my shoulders and assumed a commanding stance.

The plan was simple: pretend nothing had changed, find out what he knew, and find the prophecy. Finish what my grandmother had started and honor the Captain's dying wish. My new family was on either side of me, and a deadly power roiled within me. A power that could turn the world around me to dust.

"My apologies, Your Highness." I did a little mock curtsy, and my red hair swirled.

Skye was frozen beside me, and her eyes moved slowly from the tip of Finn's tail to his dark hair tossing in the swell. "Oh yeah . . ." she whispered, still clutching my arm. "I get it now."

Pháos moved in a spiraling arc, returning to hover beside Finn and cocking his gray beak. The corners of Finn's mouth twitched as he patted the dolphin.

Edward stood motionless on my other side, his expression a mix of awe and arousal. I gave him a shove, and he snapped out of it with theatrical flair, narrowing his eyes in what I assumed was his premeditated *I don't trust you* glare, aimed squarely at Finn.

"I hope you don't mind I brought these two along," I muttered, lifting my chin high.

"The more the merrier." Finn's gaze swept us lazily. "But wait, is that Skye?"

"Her boyfriend pushed her off a yacht."

"Men." Finn's black eyes twinkled as he moved forward to embrace Skye, who was still speechless. "Shall we?" He gestured with his tattooed arm, his silver cuff glinting in the emerald light.

"We shan't go anywhere until you tell us why we're bound for the Kingdom of Thálassa. I don't fancy finding myself in another dungeon." Edward had found his tongue.

"Edward, so pleasant to see you again, too." Finn's dark eyes were on him, and Edward flushed.

"We are going to see my mother's brother, King Proteus, and his queen, Peisinoe, who is a Siren skilled in dream magic. I am hoping she will offer us a dream that will help us find the prophecy."

"Dream magic . . . Like Agápē's dream weaving?" Skye exhaled, and bubbles danced around her.

"Yes." Finn raked a hand through his dark hair. "Then, after that, we will travel to the Kingdom of Okeanós for the summit. Pisceon and Glacies are rallying all the houses to attend as we speak."

"And what takes place at this summit?" Edward asked, folding his arms across his chest, the burlap sack full of bottles clinking.

"All the Mer and Siren houses will meet and decide if we will go to war." Finn waved a webbed hand. "Satisfied?"

Edward narrowed his eyes and angled his chin in a haughty gesture.

Finn swept toward me, his hand brushing my lower back as he looked down at me. I stiffened. Something flickered in his gaze.

Shit. He noticed.

Pulling myself together, I flashed him a charming smile. "After you, Your Highness."

I was glad Edward and Skye were with me—if they hadn't been, Finn might have pulled me close and started spouting the sentiments he'd shared the last time I saw him. And then what? I wasn't sure. Maybe I'd kiss him and mean it . . . or maybe I'd kill him and mean that too. I needed to get a grip, or I would ruin all my plans.

Finn withdrew his hand from my back, still watching me with a strange look.

I straightened, willing the ruddiness from my cheeks. "Let's stop wasting time. Which way?"

"Before we go, we need to settle something." His thin mouth morphed into a devious grin as he looked between us. "Which one of us is going to carry the Drowned boy?" He jerked his head at Edward.

"There will be no carrying me." Edward rattled his bag of rum at Finn.

"Suit yourself. We can carry you and get to Thálassa in a day, or walk and arrive in three months."

"He has a point." I rubbed my chin.

"Great," said Finn, clapping his hands together before surging forward and throwing Edward under one arm, his tail beating against the water.

"Unhand me at once," Edward yelled, his cheeks stained crimson.

I rasped out a chuckle as Finn brushed his dark hair back from his forehead and winked at me.

"This is disgraceful, do you hear me?" Edward wriggled against Finn's muscular embrace, his maroon uniform billowing in the swell as the merman began to swim.

We kicked off into the ocean, Pháos slipping through the blue like liquid silver, Finn at his side, his tail slicing through the water ahead of me.

As I watched his sculpted back muscles ripple, the sting of his betrayal burned bright. The Neptūnus family had killed my grandmother, and I suspected Finn was the one who'd done the deed. This man was now my sworn enemy. I hovered there momentarily, letting that reminder envelop all other memories, allowing my heart to barricade itself in an icy fortress of cold hatred that smothered all other emotions.

An eerie calm swept over me. I would use that anger—the hate and mistrust—to get through this. Then, after it was all said and done, when we'd found the prophecy and I had kept my vow to the Captain and my grandmother, I would confront him, but until then . . . until then, I needed to be an impregnable fortress.

The rest of the prophecy must be found. Find it, and end this.

20.

MORGANA

The sea grew darker as we descended into the deep along the coast of Ireland. We would travel this way for hours before curving into the Strait of Gibraltar, which separates Spain from Morocco, and then into the Mediterranean Sea. According to Finn, the palace of Thálassa was somewhere between Italy and Greece.

Sometimes we swam through warmer, shallower waters, giving me a chance to surface and replenish my oxygen. But soon, we'd return to the depths, where we were less likely to encounter humans. Finn and Edward were invisible to them, but I wasn't, and we still weren't sure about Skye. She was half-human, too.

Silence settled over us as we swam. Each of us was weighed down by our own shadows and fears. Thankfully, Finn carrying Edward meant he was keeping his sweet sonnets and wandering hands to himself.

Finn set a fast pace—faster than I'd ever swum—our powerful bodies cutting through the water in a blur, propelled by our inhuman speed.

Skye glided gracefully behind him, the aqua-tinged scales on her legs shimmering as she kicked. Her face was calm, often smiling, but I could feel the ache of her sadness as I drifted beside her.

Finn kept one strong arm wrapped around Edward, who didn't look like he minded being pressed against the merman's muscular torso as much as he claimed. Sometimes, Pháos would swim with us. Other times, he would disappear for hours. I remembered Finn's words. *He's a wild animal of the sea. He chose me.*

We'd been traveling for hours, and a dull ache had formed in every one of my muscles, when Finn finally held his palm up, signaling us to slow.

"How much longer?" Edward's groan broke the silence. With dramatic exaggeration, he raised a hand to his forehead, still caught in Finn's muscular embrace.

"We are almost at the Pillars of Hercules, marking the Strait." Finn nodded. "Once we get to them, it will only be a few hours to Thálassa."

Skye careened backward, turquoise scales glittering as her arm shot up. "Stop!"

Drowned.

Three of them emerged from the shadowed ridges of a seafloor trench, their frayed clothes rippling in the swell.

Finn stiffened.

My fingers curled into fists as the Captain's crumpled body swam into my mind.

One of the Drowned men looked up, his gaze locking with mine. I exhaled in relief—their eyes were clear, not silver-stained. But the moment they spotted us, they leered upward hungrily.

"They've seen us!" Skye hissed, her voice a high-pitched ribbon through the water.

"Without Mer blood to propel them, they can't catch us. Just ignore them and swim over." Finn rose above the trench with Edward, and we followed. "We Mer are used to dodging brainless, blood-hungry Drowned."

Edward let out a disgruntled huff.

Soon, the ragged Drowned disappeared into the gloom and the water lightened. Color blossomed beneath us, and more fish appeared.

I turned to Finn in a tangle of hair. "Teachie said you tortured him and he escaped . . ."

Finn's eyes flashed onyx, and his jaw tightened. "He hurt you."

My stomach flipped, my throat constricting. So Finn had found out who'd left the bruises and made it his business to take vengeance. I slowed, my breath growing ragged.

Noticing, Finn dropped back, eyes searching mine. "You okay?"

I nodded, and he linked the fingers of his free hand through mine.

"Do you two mind?" A harsh breath escaped Edward's nose.

Finn pulled his hand back, but my fingers twitched where he'd brushed them. For once, I was grateful for Edward's unceremonious interruption.

A trill echoed through the water. Pháos had rejoined us. The dolphin was chirping and jerking his head.

I gasped as I took in the colossal stone statue materializing out of the gloom. The remains of a Grecian-looking marble pillar jutted from the seabed, wrapped around it was a carved sea snake, its inscriptions faded beneath layers of barnacles and coral. It was split down the middle, its marbled halves leaning away from each other like lovers torn apart midembrace.

"One of the Pillars of Hercules," Finn said, studying the ruins. "You humans think of them as two rock formations above land, but to the creatures of the sea, these are the true pillars. It is said that Hercules created this narrow passage to protect the Mediterranean from the monstrous creatures of the Atlantic."

Algae clung to every crack, and sea fans waved like bedraggled banners from the fallen architrave. Schools of silver fish darted between the ruins, weaving through crumbled capitals and broken blocks that once towered long ago.

"Where exactly is the palace of Thálassa?" I asked as I ran my hand along the grooves of one of the ancient stones.

"Between Syracuse and Kalamata," Finn said, gesturing in that direction. "But first, we have to pass through the Sunken Bazaar. It runs along the Moroccan coastline into the Mediterranean. The market's full of shady characters, but it's the safest path, warded from humans. The merchants will call out to you as we pass. Whatever they say, whatever they offer—don't go in."

We weaved between the crumbled Pillars of Hercules and the surrounding ruins, then onto the Strait of Gibraltar, veering toward the Moroccan coastline. The water was warmer now, and I knew that we were reaching the Mediterranean as various fish swarmed around us and corals in all colors sprouted on the seafloor below.

We had only gone a few miles past the pillars when the first stalls of the Sunken Bazaar began to appear. It was impossible to miss, like a serpentine labyrinth of bright colors beneath the waves.

Ancient stone arches, half-eaten by sea life and time, marked the entrance, draped in swaying curtains of slimy kelp veils. We slipped inside, and my gaze flicked upward. Glass lanterns of different shapes and colors bobbed overhead, casting flickers of light that danced in mosaics across the sand. As we moved deeper into the bazaar, colorful shops appeared on either side of us, but we followed the path between them, swimming just above the seabed.

"What kind of things can you buy here?" Skye asked as a Drowned man in a long tunic stepped out from his stall and brandished a glowing orb in our direction.

"Anything from cursed jewels to vials of Mer blood," Finn spat, waving away the merchant with his free hand.

Stalls fashioned from shipwreck timber and bleached whale bone lined the winding pathway. Tattered nets were strung above them, decorated with seashells, seaweed, and flickering anglerfish trapped in glass globes.

"Pretty girl, pretty girl," a merman called from his store, waving at Skye. He had dark hair, dark skin, and equally dark eyes. "I have a special love potion just for you. Come here and look." He held up a glowing bottle, and Pháos trilled in disapproval.

We kept swimming, but I peered into the sprawling stalls on either side of us, where merchants of every underwater persuasion haggled with passing buyers. Mer with twitching gills, Drowned with hollow eyes, and some other aquatic creatures whose species I didn't know. Perhaps some of them had been mentioned in the mythical creatures book.

"Drowned boy," a woman with long, flowing dark hair and a colorful skirt called up at Edward. Her stall was a gypsy caravan. Barnacles clung to its wood, and the structure was half-sunken in the sand. "Don't you wish to walk upon the land once more? I can offer you that."

Edward's eyes widened. "You can?"

"Yes, Drowned boy. For a price, of course." The woman grinned, and one of her teeth glinted gold.

"Unhand me." Edward squirmed against Finn's arms.

"Ignore her. There is no cure for death," Finn said, but his words were gentle.

We continued past the stores, which stretched for miles, and soon we had been offered an array of things: vials of silver Mer blood, charms carved from the bones of ancient "gods," pearls that would grant the wearer all of their dreams, and treasure maps inked on stingray hides.

"Surely some of this has to be real, or they wouldn't have any trade at all." I turned to Finn as a toothless man in a turban waved another love potion in my face.

"Yes." Finn blew a bubbly breath, and his gills flared. "But the question is what you have to give in return."

"Where is Skye?" Edward asked from Finn's chest.

I whipped my head around. "She was with us a moment ago."

Finn shook his head as we scanned the surrounding stalls. "I just *knew* this would happen."

Pháos clicked, flicking his gray tail and snapping his beak.

"There!" I cried as Skye's turquoise-scaled body slipped into a colorful pavilion and a henna-covered hand closed the door. We pushed past an array of dyed threads hanging from strands of seaweed strung between the stores, and lanterns tinkled in our wake as we followed her into the vibrant gypsy tent.

"Would you look at these?" Skye turned to us as we burst through the entrance. She held a beautiful necklace in her hands, its gemstones sparkling even in the gloomy light.

"Don't touch it," Finn snarled, dropping Edward in the doorway as he lunged forward, snatching it from Skye's hand and slamming it onto the counter.

"Jewels blessed by the Kingdom of Thálassa." The mermaid shopkeeper glided out from the back room clutching an array of brilliant pieces, but they fell from her henna-marked fingers when she saw Finn.

"Your Highness." She bowed her head.

"Mer from the Kingdom of Thálassa can store fragments of magic in objects, but there is no way to tell if that magic is good or bad," Finn ground out.

I remembered the jewels belonging to his mother, Abalone, which had sparkled with otherworldly beauty on my neck.

The mermaid peddler woman grinned, her amber eyes glowing. "Oh, these are good magic, sire, only good."

"Well, we are not going to take that risk." A muscle ticked in Finn's jaw. "Come on, Skye."

"But they're so beautiful." She cocked her head to one side.

"Yes, aren't they? And this one would look stunning on you," the old mermaid gypsy said, holding up a ruby-red choker with sparkling crystals.

Finn spun toward the woman, his silver breastplate clinking as the shadow of his beastly form flickered across his face. "The Mer of Thálassa very rarely use their artifacts' magic, so why don't you put your wares away before I am forced to investigate where you got these?"

Skye let out a small gasp.

"You'll get used to it. So temperamental, these Mer," Edward muttered from the doorway.

21.

MORGANA

I knew we were nearing the outskirts of Thálassa when the seafloor grew more purposeful. Small Mer mounds adorned sandy dunes, and around these was carefully arranged seaweed. Coral and kelp lined the sandy paths we followed, and here and there, algae-covered sculptures of Mer appeared like beacons to guide us toward the palace.

A shrill clicking rang through the waters, and Pháos reappeared, angling his head in a way that suggested he was distressed.

Finn reached out, running a calming hand along the dolphin's snout until the clicking eased. "Show me," he growled.

Pháos jerked his head, asking us to follow, then dove in a wide arc before flickering off across the seabed. Finn swam after him, still holding Edward.

Skye gripped my arm with her dainty clawed hand. "Don't tell me he can talk to the dolphin."

"It seems that way." I shrugged as we followed after them.

We reached a patch of rippling seaweed, where cries of distress echoed from within. Pháos trilled urgently, snapping his snout toward the tangled strands. With a flick of his emerald tail, Finn set Edward down and rushed forward, parting the green tendrils with his hands.

My breath hitched at the sight of the injured dolphin. The skin on its back and fins was a lighter gray than Pháos's, fading to a pale belly, its short beak opening and closing with desperate pleas. A black fishing net bound its body, tightening with each panicked thrash. Deep gashes scored its flank where the fibers had sliced through flesh.

Skye gasped beside me, and Pháos trilled louder, darting in frantic circles.

"Hey, it's okay," Finn said softly, touching the injured dolphin's forehead. "I'm going to get you out, but you need to stay still."

The creature quieted. Its dark eyes, set just behind the curve of its mouth, locked on Finn, who reached for one of the blades strapped to his back and began slicing through the coarse net.

"Let me help," I breathed, drawing my dagger. Parting the seaweed, I knelt on the dolphin's other side.

I carefully sliced through the netting, my stomach sinking as more of the dolphin's body was revealed. Deep gashes marred its smooth skin. I glanced up at Finn; his jaw was clenched, his expression shadowed as his eyes lingered on mine for a moment. The dolphin remained still as instructed, letting out the occasional soft click, as if in thanks.

It took us the better part of half an hour, working slowly to avoid worsening the wounds, but at last, the creature was free. It spiraled upward when we cut the final bond, the shredded net slipping from its body as it clicked joyfully, but then it faltered. Blood from the gashes seeped into the water, and the animal swayed, listing to one side. Pháos began circling, chirping a frantic call of distress.

"No." Skye sobbed, bringing her hands to her mouth.

I glanced at Finn, whose features were pained.

"Shhh. Let me try something," he told the dolphin as he drifted toward it, his emerald tail swishing to stay level, brows lowered with focus. He reached out with webbed fingers, murmuring in the ancient tongue of the sea. "Sōzō hos ti fractos."

As his palms hovered over the creature's wounds, light bloomed from them, and the gashes began to close, torn flesh sealing with a gleam before fading back to its natural silver gray.

Skye sucked in a breath and gripped my arm again with her clawed fingers. At this rate, her clutching was bound to leave a mark.

Finn exhaled, his face etched with tenderness as he brushed the dolphin's dorsal fin. "There you go, little one," he whispered.

The animal chirped, nuzzling into his touch, then Pháos and his newly healed friend circled one another before they swooped off to celebrate. Their happy clicks echoed through the waters as they disappeared into the blue.

I turned to Finn. "What was that?"

"My healing magic." He stared at his hands. "I thought I'd lost it years ago, but I felt its tug just now . . . I-I think it's back."

When his eyes met mine, awe and joy lit his features, and my stomach tightened. Did he think his feelings for me had brought it back?

No—it couldn't be. I shook the thought away, but when I glanced at Finn again, he was still watching me like I was the miracle.

I rolled my shoulders, shaking away his gaze.

If the Neptūnus castle had been dark and magnificent in a twisted, eerie way, the Kingdom of Thálassa was its radiant opposite. The water here sparkled a light aqua, sunlight streaming through its depths. It bathed the Corinthian pillars lining the path to the palace, which stretched through beds of coral, in a glow, offering the impression of having been blessed by some high god.

Beyond the pillars, a towering stone structure rose from the seabed. Its square perimeter was lined with arched openings, each corner crowned with a flat rooftop, where lilac-tailed Mer guards stood watch.

As we drew closer to the castle, a set of vast stone steps appeared, at their top more marble columns supported the entrance—tall, crimson ones topped with cerulean-blue capitals. Behind them, a mural of bright dolphins danced above the square doorway.

They stirred something in my memory. At first, I couldn't place it, until I recalled the vision I'd had in the bookstore with Louisa. This ancient architecture was similar to the designs I'd seen adorning Thera's shores, where the human sailor version of Manannán had lived long ago. These columns must have stood since the Days of the Gods. The thought sent a shiver rippling through the fine fur on my arms.

Beside me, Edward and Skye were taking in the structure with the same wonder.

"Prince Aigéan." A lilac-tailed merman—presumably the Thálassian herald—drifted out to greet us. "King Proteus awaits you in the throne room."

"Thank you, Elias." Finn nodded at the herald.

Elias led the way inside, and I looked around in wonder as we passed into another room decorated with paintings of the ocean's creatures. Above the throne room doorway, the Insignia of the Ocean was rendered, which revealed details the earlier carvings I'd seen lacked: a purple-haired mermaid, a Drowned man etched in shadows, and a sea beast with writhing tentacles that brought the Fisherman's arm to mind. There was also a seal, and a Siren—though in this depiction, she had a sweeping tail, not scaly legs like Skye's.

The colors faded as we stepped into the throne room, a plain off-white marble chamber lit by a decadent chandelier that swayed with the current. Six thrones lined the space, with the grandest at the center, where the lavender-haired Mer king lounged beside his Siren queen.

Purple hair—of course. Just like Abalone. My throat ached with a wave of sympathy for Finn. This was his dead mother's kingdom. I shook off the emotion and stood taller, reminding myself that he couldn't be trusted. Instead, I focused on the royals before me.

"Uncle." Finn bowed his head, and I rushed to follow suit, pulling Skye with me.

"Come now, there will be none of that around here. This isn't the Neptūnus Kingdom." King Proteus chuckled, as did the six royals by his side.

He glided down from his throne, purple tresses cascading to his shoulders. His eyes were deep umber, and his skin golden brown in the chamber's light. Age had carved furrows into his brow, but his face still carried traces of handsomeness.

"This is my wife, Queen Peisinoe." He gestured to the woman seated to his right.

She smiled at us. Her hair and eyes were dark, like Skye's, and the scales covering her body were the same translucent aqua. She must be from the Agápē line.

"If you have legs, why does the Siren on the insignia above the door have a tail?" I blurted out, my gaze drifting over her.

"The Siren is a creature whose image has changed over time, shaped by artists, cultures, and eras. People assume we were adapted to fit their propaganda, but the truth is, we evolved. Agápē believed in love above all else. Her people were once winged, claw-footed, and scaled, but they interbred with Mer and humans. Now, some of us have legs, wings, or Mer-like tails, though claws have become rare." Queen Peisinoe's gaze moved to Skye with a welcoming smile.

"And this is my daughter, Porphura," King Proteus boomed, waving to a purple-haired mermaid on his left. She had porcelain skin, like her mother's, and deep-brown eyes, like her father's. Her tail was a rich indigo, and matching scales adorned her torso and chest.

Porphura grinned at Finn. "Nice to see you, cousin. This is my wife, Layla Okeanós." The mermaid beside her had dark skin and a golden tail. Bronze earrings hung from her ears, and a crystalline headband shone in her ebony hair, which was arranged into hundreds of tiny plaits.

King Proteus motioned to his far right. "And these are my sons, Damon and Alexandros."

I turned to the two males, and my breath hitched as I drank them in. They were twins. Both had strong stubble-shadowed jawlines, thick dark brows, and wavy hair that drifted in the ocean's current.

Although their faces and chests—which my eyes kept darting to— were identical, they weren't entirely indistinguishable. Like his father, Alexandros had lilac hair and a matching tail, its scales glittering like amethyst in the aquamarine light. Damon had black hair, and his torso blended into a dark tail, but its scales glinted a deep plum.

"And who are our lovely guests?" Damon asked.

I flushed as his eyes lingered on me.

Skye stepped forward. "I'm Skye, and this is Morgana and Edward."

"It is our pleasure to welcome you," Alexandros said, his gaze moving from head to toe over Skye's curvaceous body.

Finn coughed, drawing the attention back to himself as he turned to Queen Peisinoe. "My father says you have agreed to grant us a dream."

The queen rose, and her aqua scales glittered over pale skin. Her long, dark hair flowed behind her as she approached us. "For thousands of years, the Sirens have remained neutral in the feud, but now . . . " She stopped, her eyes welling with tears as she turned to her husband. "Now Proteus has fallen ill with the Shadow. I need to find a way to save him."

Finn's brows drew together. "Uncle, is this true?"

King Proteus scooped back his hair to reveal a trail of spidery black veins creeping across the side of his throat.

A cold shiver crawled down my spine. Beside me, Finn's throat worked, and he toyed with the silver armlet on his right wrist.

"Our healers have managed to slow the disease, but I am willing to defy the gods and offer you a dream of what you most desire, hoping it leads you to the prophecy and a cure." Queen Peisinoe stifled another sob.

Finn nodded. "Thank you, my queen."

He was being granted the dream? That meant I'd have to follow him wherever it led—and my throat tightened at the thought.

"I think you should offer us both a dream." I stepped forward. "Y-Your Majesty," I added quickly as the Siren queen turned her dark eyes to me.

Finn spun toward me, his brows furrowed and face suddenly pale. "Morgana!"

His reaction only steeled my resolve. I lifted my chin and locked eyes with the queen. "I am related to Iona Selich. She was Abalone's closest friend and spent time in this kingdom long ago, and I think it's more likely that *I'll* see where the rest of the prophecy lies."

Queen Peisinoe observed me with curiosity in her dark eyes.

"Using too much dream magic will exhaust her." Finn's tone was sharp. "*I* will lead us there."

The queen held up a hand. "I will offer you both a dream," she said, looking between us. "My husband's health is worth my exhaustion." She turned to King Proteus, her eyes filled with sorrow.

Noticing her gaze, the king shook the fear from his eyes and rolled his shoulders. "Yes, well, let us be merry and forget about this for tonight." He forced a wide grin. "It is not every day my nephew comes to visit."

Finn took a second, composing himself enough to smile at the king, but his eyes remained dark.

"Elias will show you to your rooms. We Thálassians are the keepers of pleasure, and tonight, you'll experience one of our kingdom's famed indulgences—a pleasure party at the sunken palace of Baiae." King Proteus clasped his hands over his muscular chest.

"Wicked." Edward's eyes sprang wide.

A muscle in Finn's jaw clenched. "Uncle, you know that my father's half-brother, Taranis, has been possessed by Manannán. A war is coming."

"Yes, yes." Proteus waved a hand. "Pisceon and your lovely wife-to-be have been to see us. The castle is warded. All the more reason to party."

The herald, Elias, drifted away from the king to lead us to our rooms, and I started to follow.

Finn caught my arm in a firm grip. "What do you think you're doing getting a dream?" he snapped, his black eyes flashing.

"The same thing you are," I shot back, yanking myself free and following Elias up the stone steps that led to our chambers.

This was perfect. If I was granted a dream of the prophecy, I could set out alone. I wouldn't need Finn at all. That was probably what he feared. I cast one last glance over my shoulder. He was still watching me, arms folded, dark eyes narrowed, the muscle still ticking in his jaw.

I bit my lip to stop my grin. Perhaps I would only have to pretend I trusted him for one more night.

22.

SKYE

As soon as I was alone in my chambers, the darkness crept in. When I'd been around the others, it had been easier not to think about everything that had happened. About what I'd become.

I glanced around the room I'd been shown into, chewing on my lip as I took it in, my breathing becoming shorter and sharper. The gills on my neck flared. I clamped my hands over them, then tore them away as suffocation gripped me and my vision swayed. Stepping farther into my new bedroom, I willed the anxiety clutching my chest to release its hold.

More pillars adorned the area, meeting a polished marble floor, and the roof was decorated with finely painted squares of red, white, and blue. In one corner stood a limestone basin and an expansive mirror, and the stone bed was topped with a sea sponge mattress. A marble balcony looked out over the turquoise waters, coral gardens, and colossal structures beyond.

My breath hitched, fear dissolving in a sharp burst of pleasure as my eyes fell on the jewels laid out before me, shining from the carved shelf below the mirror. I presumed they were to wear to the party.

Rushing over, I clutched them to me: gleaming bracelets inlaid with colorful stones, matching earrings and necklaces, and a finely carved golden crown featuring strands of seaweed woven together.

I lifted one of the earrings to my cheek, and my stomach tightened as I faced my reflection. My long hair tumbled over my pale shoulders, the translucent aqua scales forming a corset across my rising chest. My breath turned ragged again as the mirror reflected the gills, now carved into either side of my once porcelain neck.

I gripped the edges of the basin, a wave of nausea rolling through me, as everything I had been pushing down, pushing away, came flooding back. Parker's head lolling, his sticky blood staining my thighs . . . under my fingernails . . . And Aranare had been there. *I would never forgive myself if I'd done nothing and he hurt you again,* he had said.

Sickness expanded in my gut as more memories surged through the floodgates of my mind. The Drowned . . . I'd screwed my eyes shut when Evelyn and Daniel's throats had been slit, and then there had been that monster with a tentacle for an arm who'd had killed a man right before our eyes. The world warped as panic and devastation churned within me. I exhaled, releasing a stream of bubbles into the water.

This doesn't have to be my life. I can change back anytime.

But for what? Aranare was dead to me. Parker was gone. And the police . . . they were probably out there, searching for me. I'd killed a Stewart—a member of one of the most powerful families in Scotland.

This. This was my life now. I'd made a deal with Agápē.

My breathing quickened again, and hot tears welled at the corners of my eyes. I wiped at them angrily, scooping up the scattered jewels, then turned away from the reflection I no longer recognized.

Moments later, I knocked on the door to Morgana's room, which was next to mine. I steadied my breathing, forcing a practiced smile and bracing myself as she opened it.

"I can see why you like this place." I kept my grin wide as I swanned into her room. "Shall we get ready for this pleasure party together?"

"Erm, sure." Morgana sat down awkwardly on her sponge-covered bed.

"Let's see." I drifted over to the mirror, where jewels had also been laid out for her, releasing a shuddering breath.

"What do you think they mean by a pleasure party?" Morgana chewed on her lip as I pinned half her red hair up, letting the rest cascade over her shoulders.

I winked at her and draped a delicate golden chain across her tresses. "Oh, honey, I think it's self-explanatory."

Morgana flushed.

I handed her an elegant bangle for her upper arm and painted flourishes of glitter across her eyes. "Do you think you and Finn will—"

"No," she said quickly.

"What happened between you guys?" I rifled through the rest of her jewels, choosing pieces for myself.

"He—It's a long story." She waved a hand, her mouth falling into a thin line, and I got the message.

I shoved a golden crown onto my head and spun around, wanting to offer a distraction from whatever thoughts were darkening her. "Do I look like Helen of Troy, beautiful enough to start a war?"

"You've seen *Troy*?" Morgana raised her eyebrows incredulously.

"Girl, if it's got Brad Pitt in a skirt, I'm there for it."

Morgana giggled, standing to survey herself beside me in the mirror. "Did you know this whole war beneath the waves started with a woman? My ancestor, Siana Selich. Manannán, the God of the Drowned, and Mer

Prince Kyano Ătlanticus went to war over her." She sighed, toying with one of her cherry strands.

"Now *that* is a history lesson I'd pay attention to." I hooked two stunning gold earrings into my own ears. "How about those twins, though? I wouldn't mind if they wanted to go to war for me . . . or on me."

Morgana stifled a chuckle, and my mouth twitched upward. I'd caught the worried glances she'd been casting my way throughout the journey, and I wanted to show her I was okay, even though that was far from the truth. But this was how my life had always been—wearing a smile so no one would see the sadness that lived inside me all those years with Parker.

When I'd finished adorning myself, I glided over to the mirror. Taking a shaky breath and letting it release, I lifted my eyes to survey my reflection. The twinkling crown nestled in my hair, which I had artfully pinned half up and half down, brought out the deep hazel of my eyes. The bracelets and earrings glittered in perfect contrast with the scales on my forearms and the bustier that now encompassed my breasts. My beastly form looked almost . . . beautiful.

No. I pursed my lips, pushing down the thought.

There was a soft knock at the door.

"Come in," Morgana called, moving to sit on the sponge bed, and I wafted over to join her.

The gorgeous twins, Alexandros and Damon, glided into the room. I elbowed Morgana, whose cheeks turned ruddy.

Alexandros's purple tail beat against the water, and he was wearing a golden necklace and rings. Damon had a bronze coronet in his ebony hair, his dark scales glinting in the aquamarine light.

"Can we escort you downstairs?" Alexandros held out his arm to me, and my stomach fluttered as the muscles in his chest rippled with the movement. He had an Italian accent—or maybe it was Greek. Whatever it was, it was hot as hell. I could hear it in my mind even though only bubbles were coming out of his mouth.

I flashed him a smile before resting my scaled arm on his. Beside him, Damon offered an elbow to Morgana, who hesitated.

"Come on." I grinned at her. "Let's see what this pleasure party is all about."

She sighed and allowed Damon to take her hand.

Our chambers opened onto an expansive marble corridor beside a balcony overlooking a square central courtyard, where stone lounges lay artfully strewn among coral and seaweed gardens. The hallway led to a staircase that descended to the throne room, where the others awaited us.

A flicker of delight ignited within me when we arrived and I saw them all equally decked out in gold finery. Even Edward had been given a gleaming necklace, which hung beneath his porter's collar, and like me, he was wearing a crown. Finn had gone for the understated look, removing his silver breastplate, swapping his silver cuffs for bronzed ones, and adorning his fingers with thick golden rings.

Like me, the rest of the Thálassian royals had draped themselves in as many bright jewels as possible. Perhaps I would fit in here after all. The passing thought tightened something in my chest.

Queen Peisinoe glided forward. "Walk with me, daughter of Agápē. This transition must be hard for you, but you are with family now." She gestured toward the marble pillars that marked the room's entrance.

Alexandros continued to hold my arm as we drifted beside the queen. *Family*, she'd said. The word struck a chord in me, reverberating with both hope and loathing.

23.

MORGANA

The sunken pleasure palace of Baiae was off the coast of Naples, and we traveled to the party in a royal procession. The Thálassian court and Skye drifted at the front of the group, a blur of dark hair and purple scales glittering through the turquoise waters. Edward, Finn, and I brought up the rear.

The waters here were shallower than in the deep, dark Atlantic, and we could see night falling in soft shadows across the waves. Once again, I was glad Finn was carrying Edward—it meant I could keep avoiding his wandering hands and sweet sentiments.

I just had to get through tonight. Tomorrow, I'd receive the dream at the ceremony and could set off to find the prophecy, without him.

As we swam, Edward, who seemed to have forgotten his mistrust of Finn while caught in his muscular embrace, rattled off a history lesson. "They called Baiae the 'city of sin,' you know."

Finn chuckled. "Did they now?" His gaze found me, and dark butterflies took flight in my stomach.

"Before it was swallowed by the sea, it was a place where the wealthy and powerful of the Roman Empire came to conduct their illicit affairs . . ." Edward waved his arms animatedly, almost smacking Finn in the jaw once or twice.

We swam quickly, and soon we had left the curated coral gardens of the Thálassian palace behind, drifting over basins, ridges, and an array of sea life as we slipped through the Strait of Messina and up the front of Italy's boot. As we neared the outskirts of the sunken city of Baiae, crumpled ruins littered the waters.

"Don't we need to worry about humans?" I swallowed, remembering they could see me.

Finn rubbed a hand over his jaw. "The city will be warded, like our castles."

"Spiffing!" Edward's eyes were alight with excitement.

Eroded brick walls covered in algae led the way into the space. Lights had been strung from broken-down arches, and floating glass orbs littered the waters above. The sand had been cleared from intricately tiled floors, their hexagon patterns shining under the illuminated spheres.

I reached the rest of the Thálassian royal party and Skye, who had paused at the outskirts of the dance floor. Finn glided up beside us, placing Edward down. My chest swelled with wonder as I took in the space.

"This is *our* pleasure palace, which we built in the ruins of sunken Baiae. The humans can't see it, of course. To them, it looks as decayed as ever," Princess Porphura explained, her violet hair billowing around her face as she turned to me.

Layla giggled, her many gold bangles gleaming in the turquoise light as she grabbed her wife's hand and led her into the party. "Come on, let's get a wine."

Alexandros, Damon, and the king and queen drifted after them, and we followed cautiously behind. The remains of Roman statues depicting voluptuous women and men rose from the blue, decorated with algae and shaped by erosion, as schools of fish wove between them.

"Nymphs," Edward said, gesturing to the statues. "This was once the emperor's dining hall."

Music rippled through the water in seductive notes, and Mer dancers, bare-chested and adorned with pearls, spun in hypnotic circles around the space, using kelp as ribbons. They would lean over one dining guest and then move on to the next, teasing and sultry.

My mouth fell open, and I hastily clamped it shut.

The nymph statues that surrounded the space were hung with lights, providing a magical ambiance, but beyond them, night had fallen, cloaking the sea in darkness.

Tables curved around the edges of the dance floor, laden with what I now recognized as Mer delicacies: seafood towers, kelp sushi rolls, rose-gold clams bursting with caviar, and cups of what looked like red wine. We were in the Mediterranean after all. I eyed the food gratefully; I was getting sick of wild fish.

Sweet perfumes floated like mist through the currents, stirred by flirtatious glances and brushings of dancing tails.

"What the actual fuck?" Skye whispered from beside me.

"The philosopher Seneca once said of this place, 'Baiae is a place to be avoided. People wandering drunk along the beach. The riotous revelry of sailing parties . . .'" Edward gestured to the sultry Mer dancers.

Finn smirked. "This Seneca sounds like a bore."

Mer of all colors, shapes, and sizes, and even some Sirens, were taking partners to the dance floor or sitting draped over coral lounges set around the polished tile floors, their scales glinting as they sipped from conch goblets. Some of the females were bare-chested like the dancers, others wore shell bras, or body glitter matched to the hue of their scales.

"Your Highness." Elias rushed forward from the merriment to bow to King Proteus. "Your table awaits."

The herald led us to a long table at the head of the dance floor. Above us, on raised ruins, musicians strummed on harps, creating a beautiful, enticing song. Along the length of the table, sponge couches allowed the Mer to recline with ease, while at the head, carved stone seats accommodated sweeping tails.

"Did I mention I get it now?" Skye arched a brow, her gaze drifting over the many rippling torsos filling the space as I sat, and she slid into a sponge seat beside me.

Alexandros lounged on Skye's other side, while Damon claimed the stone throne at the head of the table, beside me. At the opposite end sat King Proteus and Queen Peisinoe, with Finn beside them, Porphura and Layla flanking him. Edward had taken the seat next to Alexandros.

Damon reached across the lavish spread, plucking up a plate of prawns and offering them to me, his purple-flecked eyes lingering on mine as I accepted one. I glanced across the table at Finn. His expression was dark, eyes fixed on me, clearly noticing his cousin's attentions. I quickly turned away, offering Damon my most charming smile.

I could still feel Finn assessing us, and the realization tightened something in me. I leaned into the attractive Siren man beside me and laughed as if he'd just said something amusing. Damon's gaze flicked to Finn, then back to me, a knowing smirk playing at the edges of his mouth. *Shit.*

He reached for a strand of my hair and toyed with it. "You look beautiful."

I exhaled in relief. He was willing to play along. I offered him a smile from beneath lowered lashes.

Double shit. What was I doing? Was I really about to play the jealousy game? Some dark part of me purred at making Finn hurt. The Neptūnus family had killed my grandmother—if I had to spend the next few days pretending to love the man who'd torn out my heart, the least I could do was this.

Heat crept up my neck as I turned from Damon only to meet Finn's gaze. His jaw was rigid, his eyes dark as onyx. I needed some Mer wine.

"May I?" Damon asked, as if he'd read my mind.

I glanced again at Finn, whose knuckles were white around the fork he was shoving into glistening caviar.

"Is it Moon Wine?" I didn't particularly want to find myself comatose at this pleasure party.

Damon chuckled. "Moon Wine is for ceremonial celebrations only. This is regular wine."

I held out my conch shell. The muscles in the Siren's bronzed torso—half-adorned in gleaming black scales—tensed as he poured the enchanted wine and passed it to me.

"Salute." He kept his dark eyes on my face as he raised his drink.

"Is it weird for you to eat fish when many of you *are* fish?" I blurted out as I helped myself to some kelp sushi rolls.

"In the world of the deep, it is common for bigger fish to prey on smaller ones, and we are the biggest fish of them all." A faint gleam lit Damon's eyes at that, his tail fin fanning where it curled behind his chair. "But we only take what we need, never more."

I nodded, gulping back more wine.

"So, cousin," Alexandros, the lavender-haired twin, addressed Finn. "Tell us more about this impending threat."

Finn sat up straighter, adopting his princely tone. "We believe that Manannán has returned and is using Taranis's body as a . . . vessel."

King Proteus looked between them. "Would you save talk of such dark things for another time? This is a party."

I noticed Princess Porphura observing me as I helped myself to some seaweed salad. "And you're related to the lost Selkies . . . to Iona?" she asked softly.

"Yes," I managed through a mouthful of kelp.

"It must have been hard . . ." She eyed me thoughtfully. "To have been thrust into this new world with our ancient feud hanging over your head."

I let the wine settle on my tongue before swallowing and meeting her gaze. The purple-haired princess's eyes showed no malice, so I offered her a smile.

"My sister did enjoy Iona's company. They were thick as thieves." King Proteus grinned at me as he reached for a vat of wine, and a pang shot through my chest as I recalled the stories my grandmother had penned in her diary about her and Abalone's adventures.

My eyes drifted to Skye and Edward as I chased the silence with a mouthful of red. Skye was now giggling with Alexandros, and Edward was leaning in to talk with the king and queen. They were my friends, just like Abalone had been my grandmother's. Perhaps after we found the prophecy, there was a future where we could all be happy in this new world.

Finn's mood darkened as the night wore on. When I'd glanced his way earlier in the evening, he'd been speaking with the princesses, Porphura and Layla, but now his brows were drawn, his mouth set grimly, and he was twirling a knife across the table. Unlike the rest of us, he hadn't touched his wine.

Skye was deep in conversation with Alexandros, and Edward, cheeks flushed, was still happily chatting with the king and queen. The Thálassian Mer seemed far more tolerant than the Neptūnus court, and to Edward, sitting in the restored heart of history as an honored guest of the Mer, it must have felt like a dream come true.

Damon's thumb brushed over mine on the table. "Would you like to dance?"

My gaze moved to Finn, still twirling his knife, then I let Damon take my hand and guide me from my seat. His black tail swished, glistening with hints of purple, as he led me onto the dance floor.

He held me close, his body flush against mine, glittering scales grazing my fur, the taut pull of his abs shifting with every movement. When our eyes met, I saw his were a rich brown. His shoulder-length ebony curls drifted in the current. He spun me away, and when I turned back, his gaze stripped me bare.

"You are utterly unique," he purred as he curled me into his chest. "I have been on this earth for over three hundred years and never seen anything as rare and beautiful."

Heat bloomed low in my belly, and I flushed. He was undeniably handsome, but something about this attraction felt wrong.

I forced the sensation aside, shifting my focus to the Mer behind Damon's shoulder. All around us, couples were slipping away into the shadows beyond the hall.

"Would you care to join me in the gardens?" Damon gestured to the darkness, where the naked statues of old were scattered among coral-covered ruins and no lights hung.

My throat bobbed as I noticed Skye and Alexandros slipping into those shadows. "Not tonight." I put my hand against his sculpted chest. "I have to get some rest for the dream ceremony tomorrow."

Damon nodded, understanding flickering in his eyes.

I scanned the table, and Finn was gone. Porphura and Layla had taken to the dance floor, while Edward remained with the king and queen, gesturing wildly as he spoke. His maroon uniform puffed in the swell, the gold chain across his chest catching the light. I almost laughed—he looked like a wannabe drug lord.

As Damon drifted off, sweeping another mermaid into a dance, I searched for Skye, but she still hadn't returned from the gardens.

An aching loneliness swept over me as I journeyed back to the palace through the dark Mediterranean by myself. I'd tried to fill the emptiness with Damon, but in the end, Finn was the only one who I wanted to hold me close. And he had betrayed me.

I hadn't lied to Damon—I was tired. We'd been traveling all day, and tomorrow, if my dream was granted, I would be off searching for the prophecy.

When I reached the palace of Thálassa, it was dark. No doubt the whole court was at the pleasure party. The guards remained sentinels on the rooftop, but the castle was shrouded in shadows.

I swam toward the floor where my room lay, up the stone steps to the long corridor. It was cloaked in the ocean's gloom, but my senses guided me through the dark. I was about to open the door to my chambers when a fist closed around my arm. I turned to find myself pressed against a heaving chest as Finn pulled me in. Muscles tensed beneath me, his glittering tail flickering below. Drawn brows and a sharp jaw. He stared down at me, holding me tight against his body.

"Is everything okay?" His mouth was thin. "You're acting differently."

"Am I?" I replied coolly, pulling away.

"When I saw you last, you said we had hope. Now I'm starting to feel like that has changed." His dark eyes locked with mine, and I held his gaze. There was no trace of scheming—only a broken man, silently pleading.

"I—I . . ." I looked away, forcing my thoughts into order. This was King Neptūnus's most trusted enforcer. This had to be an act.

I couldn't let him know I knew what his family had done—what I suspected he'd done. If he caught on, he might never reveal his plans . . . or the king's. Slowly, I turned back to him, lifting my chin. "You're engaged, Your Highness."

"But you know that we have an understanding," he breathed, reaching out to trace my bottom lip with his calloused thumb. "Morgana, I cannot get these lips from my mind."

His tail stiffened against me, and that traitorous space between my legs warmed as a flare of the girl who'd once loved him rose to the surface. If I wanted to pretend nothing had changed, I had to cling to that feeling and use it to keep up the act.

My throat tightened as I let the sensation wash over me, and my gaze drifted to the sculpted abdominal muscles that tapered and dipped, tracing the path to his gleaming tail. Trembling, I slid my free hand to the small of Finn's back, where firm muscles framed his spine. My fingers grazed the dimples etched just above his tail.

I can do this . . . pretend.

Grunting and biting his lip, Finn pulled me further into him, and something undulated between my thighs. The water pressure was moving between them again, stroking me.

It felt good, so good. *Damn it.*

I bit back the whimper that wanted to escape me as I moved my hand from Finn's back, fingers tangling in his hair. He held me close with one hand, the other guiding my face to his. His lips brushed mine, but he didn't kiss me. Instead, he pressed our foreheads together, savoring this moment of closeness. His breathing was ragged, matching mine, and I could tell how much he wanted this—wanted me.

The water pressure between my thighs made me throw my head back as pleasure swept through me in arching pulses. For a heartbeat, I almost surrendered to it—to him. The sensations tore me from the darkness gnawing at my soul whenever I let my guard down, a blackness that was filled with silver-stained Drowned and the Captain's crumpled body.

But reality came crashing in, shattering the arousal in an instant. The Neptūnus family killed my grandmother—this man was my enemy. A wave of guilt churned in my gut and clawed up my throat, choking me with shame. I couldn't do this . . . I couldn't even pretend.

"No," I cried, pounding against his chest as tears filled my eyes—tears of confusion, tears of anger. Anger at him. Anger at myself. And most of all, disgust.

All composure left my being as I whipped my dagger from its sheath at my hip and pressed it against the soft skin of Finn's throat. His eyes flared, and he threw up his hands.

I pressed the knife deeper. "I fucking hate you!"

"You hate me?" He pulled back from the gleaming blade, his eyes searching mine, but I moved with him, keeping the metal pressed against him.

"Yes, I hate you." I let out a cold laugh—a hollow, wretched sound. The knife had drawn blood, and a glistening crimson trickle ran down Finn's neck before the water licked it clean.

"I deserve it," he gasped, and his sharp teeth and globe-like eyes flickered.

I pressed the blade deeper, and Finn closed his eyes, his monstrous form fading, chest rising and falling beneath me.

"Don't. Put. Your. Hands. On. Me. Again," I said. Each word sliced like the razor that was kissing his flesh.

Finn lifted his chin, pressing into the dagger, and another drop of blood slid down his neck. "Do it. End this torment. Since the moment I first saw you, some part of me has always known you would be my undoing."

My hands were trembling, and with a stifled sob, I withdrew the knife. "Let's just find the prophecy and be done with this."

Finn brought his webbed hand to his throat, where a small cut remained. "Why do you hate me now? What's changed?" His tone was sharp. Too sharp.

A few glasses of Mer wine, and I was throwing my plans out the window and giving myself away. I was better than this. I exhaled slowly. Once I had the dream of the prophecy, I could set out to find it alone, and I'd never have to see Finn or pretend again.

I remembered all the times he had met my heart with a façade of impenetrable ice. Pain lanced through my chest, but I stood motionless, forcing it down until the darkness I'd been fighting swallowed my soul.

"While I was on land, I had some time to think." I steadied my breathing. "You're right. I do deserve better than this, and you. I'm sorry if I seem cold, but let me clarify. There is no longer hope for us."

"This is truly what you want?"

"Yes." Tears tried to spill from my eyes, and I was grateful for the watery atmosphere as I kept my expression impassive.

He pulled back, eyes darting across my face. An excruciating silence followed. It took everything I had to keep my features cold, holding his gaze as he continued to survey me.

"I understand." Finn finally spoke. He dipped his chin in the barest of nods, his pained expression pulling into one of indifference, before he moved away into the shadows of the corridor beyond.

24.

SKYE

I'd slept with five men before I met Parker, and I thought about them now as I followed Alexandros into the gloomy gardens beyond the party's lights.

This was a pleasure party. I knew the rules. It was the Mer equivalent of "Netflix and chill." I'd known what this merman wanted when I agreed to leave with him, and I desired it too. I wanted to lose myself in the sweet wine swirling through me, and in Alexandros's sculpted body. I wanted to *forget*.

As the gorgeous lavender-haired merman led me between the crumbled nymph statues, Parker's dead eyes slunk into my mind, and I could almost feel his fury at the thought of me being here, with someone as handsome as this. But maybe that was the point. Maybe that was why I needed this.

The air between us thickened, and I breathed it in. Moans and gasps rose from the shadows where other Mer lay together in the gardens. How would this even work with a tail? Alexandros's amethyst-tinted tail flickered before me as he led the way further and further from the light. I figured I would find out soon enough.

We reached a glade, where the lifeless eyes of eroded Roman statues looked down upon the sand and sea life before them, and the merman stopped, turning to face me. I dragged my gaze from his dark eyes to his muscular chest, covered with the same stubble that adorned his jawline.

I moved forward, taking hesitant steps, until I was standing before him. Hovering on his magnificent tail, he loomed above me, and I tilted my head back, taking in his sharp features and the subtle flex of his chiseled torso. Bubbles emerged from the rocky masses on the edges of the glade, and I gasped as heated water caressed my ankle.

"They call this place Campi Flegrei. The whole of Naples sits inside a giant volcanic crater." Alexandros stared at me thoughtfully.

"Oh." My throat bobbed.

The merman flicked his fin lazily. My gaze rested on his chest, then drifted lower to the shaped lines carved into his abdomen and the trail of dark hair that disappeared into the seam of his deep purple tail.

"Pleasure is not something we should feel ashamed of." Alexandros thumbed my chin, guiding my gaze to his, as if he'd read my thoughts and seen the storm of feelings warring inside me. "I have had many lovers—men, women—and it is always something sacred."

I nodded, pushing down the nerves rising inside me.

His eyes searched mine, and his face was gentle. "Bella, you're so sad, and I want to make you happy."

A sudden wave of emotion surged up, blurring my vision with unshed tears and causing my shoulders to tremble. I hadn't had time to process Parker's death, my fight with Aranare, or the disorienting grief of leaving everything I'd known behind. But Alexandros's understanding eyes unlocked it all, and I began to sob.

Without a word, the merman pulled me into his arms, and I surrendered to the flood of feelings. My body heaved against his, and I cried and cried, burrowing my face into his neck and tangling my fingers in his fuchsia hair. All the while, he held me close, strong and silent.

I wept until I couldn't weep anymore, and as the tears subsided, the pain gave way to the sensation of my lips brushing the merman's neck, my hands in his hair, his chiseled body against mine.

I pressed my mouth into his clavicle, and he responded to my kisses with a soft moan, moving his hands from my lower back to rest upon the curves of my scaled ass. Our mouths found each other, and our tongues clashed in a fiery embrace as I transferred all the hurt and confusion I had been feeling into the kiss.

I pulled back and met Alexandros's hungry gaze. His lips were swollen from the urgency of mine, his indigo tresses drifting around his face.

"Wait." I pressed my palm into his chest with force as my stomach twisted. "Are we . . . related?"

He chuckled and toyed with a strand of my hair, sending a tingle through my spine. "The Agápē line is ancient and broad, more like a tribal identity than a literal bloodline. So no, we are not related."

I released a relieved breath, my thoughts returning to Alexandros's sensuous mouth and his twelve-pack flexing each time he flicked his fins.

"How do we . . . ?" I swallowed as I dragged my gaze across his abs to his tail.

He placed a webbed finger against my lips as if to say, *Relax, don't speak. I will show you,* as he glided his other hand down to meet mine, guiding it to his scaled tail just below his defined stomach, where his manhood would have been had he been human. Pressing my hand into the space, he emitted a gravelly moan, and I understood.

I pushed harder and faster, stroking the place like I would have handled the length of him if he were a man, and his tail stiffened beneath my touch. At the same time, he reached between my legs, where my womanhood remained. His fingers caressed me there, and I arched with the pleasure of it all.

Our bodies came together, and his hand slid through my hair, angling my head up so he could kiss me again. I gasped as his lips moved over my neck, dragging his open mouth down to wrap his tongue around my nipples, peaking beneath the scales.

Head tipped back, I groaned as he nipped, cupped, and sucked my heavy and aching breasts. At the same time, his thumb circled my sensitive area, while his other fingers dipped inside. All the while, I continued stroking him the way he had shown me.

No one had ever touched me like this, with such adoration and attention to my needs. I gave in to the feeling, my pleasure growing as the merman's breathing grew increasingly ragged.

Pulling back from me, he whispered "Bella" as his eyes roamed over my face.

He kept his fingers inside me, and the noises I was making alerted him that I was close. He threw his head back, his chest muscles tightening, and a low groan escaped him as if seeing the look of ecstasy on my face was breaking him. I stroked his tail harder and faster.

He grunted beneath my touch, and I moaned with him as the pleasure encompassed my entire body, shooting from between my thighs to my arms and neck to engulf me in the heightened sensation.

The ocean around us felt so still afterward, like an explosion had stopped the world for a moment.

I exhaled, shaking my head. "That was—"

A devilish grin split Alexandros's face, and he caressed my cheek. "It is a cure for the sadness, is it not, bella?"

25.

The dream ceremony was to be held in the sacred temple of Thálassa's Kingdom. The space was ancient and magical, steeped in an energy that vibrated against my bones.

At the temple's center lay a circular platform of white marble, and the area was hemmed in by stone columns that rose like pale tree trunks toward the structure's roof, each wrapped in bioluminescent sea vines.

Finn and I were guided in separately by finely cloaked Mer priestesses with silver-painted lips, and I was glad of this. I'd held a dagger at the throat of the most dangerous and erratic Mer prince in the Seven Kingdoms. So, no, I didn't exactly feel like being alone with him.

Finn hadn't wanted me to receive the dream, whether for fear of losing me or fear I'd uncover the prophecy before him and his family—maybe both. But none of that mattered now. Once I had my dream, I'd never have to see him again.

Statues of the old gods lined the sandy floor around the platform, and I turned in place, letting my gaze roam over them. Behind me, Poseidon emerged from the crest of a marble wave, power etched into every line of his stance. Agápē swooned beside him, her Siren form immortalized, with vacant eyes and wings splayed. Síocháin, carved from the same pale stone, swam alongside her in the shape of a seal.

On the opposite side loomed Cetus, the sea monster's tentacles stretching across the floor, their stone weatherworn and dusted with sand. And there, beside him, stood Manannán, the Drowned God. I recognized him immediately—it was the likeness of the Minoan sailor from my visions.

The Mer priestess behind me silently instructed me to kneel before one of the four low stone basins filled with mirrorlike water at the center of the marble circle. Across from me, Finn leaned over his own bowl, propped on his elbows, tattooed muscles flexing as his tail swished behind him.

We were positioned directly across from one another, but my gaze kept returning to the statue of the Drowned God behind Finn. It felt almost like I'd begun to know Manannán.

Queen Peisinoe appeared before us, crowned with a headdress of coral and green glass beads. A translucent cloak—identical to those worn by her priestesses—floated around her shoulders. Her silver lips gleamed in the light flowing into the temple from strategically placed openings. Unlike the priestesses, who kept theirs on, Peisinoe had thrown her hood back to conduct the ceremony.

The rest of the royal court and our companions were not permitted inside, as this ritual was sacred.

The chants began, melodic and haunting, as more priestesses entered the space, and the water in the bowls before us turned crystalline with magic.

"Dream weaving is an art sacred to the Sirens and not to be taken lightly." Peisinoe raised her palms as she stepped between Finn and me on the stairs leading to the pools. The priestesses continued to chant in the background. "The Shadow haunts our people, and we ask Agápē, the Goddess of Love, to bless us with dreams of what we desire most." She turned to the statue of the Siren goddess and bowed her head. Her priestesses also bowed.

Tendrils of mist rose from the basins and twisted around Finn and me as whispers echoed through the space—memories not yet lived, emotions not yet felt, the dreams and desires of those who had come before us.

The chanting swelled as the two Mer priestesses drifted up behind us again. I lifted my chin to meet Finn's dark eyes. His hands gripped the edges of the basin, knuckles white with tension. He wore no breastplate, just the silver bracers on his wrists, and in the emerald glow, the inky markings on his right arm and the Symbol of the Ocean on his pectoral shone. The new heart-shaped tattoo in the center of his chest burned with a silver light.

A chill prickled my skin as I replayed everything that had passed between us. I gritted my teeth, forcing myself to focus. Soon, I'd have my dream—and never have to see him again.

I dragged my gaze to the swirling, crystalline water in the stone basin before me, and magical whisps continued to rise from it as my hair spilled over my face, its ends dancing on the surface of the pool.

"Let your desires fill you," Peisinoe commanded as she stood before us on the dais. "Feel them in every inch of your bones."

I want to find the prophecy and save the ocean—for my grandmother and the Captain.

I repeated the mantra, eyes squeezed shut, clearing my mind until only that single desire remained.

"When you can feel your desires radiating through every inch of you, dip your face into the pool to sleep and see your dreams."

I drew my eyes from the basin to glance at Finn. His gaze was already on me, burning with a dark intensity. I bit the inside of my cheek, looking back at the crystal water. Exhaling, I immersed my face.

I was met with a breathtaking prism of fractured lights and colors. It was so intense and beautiful that my tears streamed like rivers into the pool. The lovely lights dissolved around me, and I floated above a ship on a stormy sea. I held my hands before my face, but they were invisible. I tried to move, but I remained anchored, gazing down at the ship below as the ocean tossed it to and fro. This was where my dream had led me.

The ship was long and wooden, with oars lining each side. I recognized it from my previous vision. Manannán.

I forced down the lump in my throat. Lightning forked through the sky, and the dark waves tossed the boat as they crashed across its deck.

"The Atlantic is angry," a sailor yelled, pulling at one of the oars.

"This is the work of Poseidon!" cried Manannán, the Minoan man, who was also rowing furiously. Rain plastered dark hair across his bronzed face, and his olive eyes were pinched with fear.

"Father." The young boy, whom I recognized as his son from the previous visions, clung to the mast as the boiling waves tossed the boat.

"Hold on, and don't let go!" The color drained from Manannán's face as an inky wave swelled until it loomed above the ship.

An ominous weight settled over me. More waves rose behind the first, towering and merciless, the work of the gods, just as Manannán had warned. They crashed against the vessel, shattering it as Manannán rushed to the mast, scooping his terrified son into his arms. Wave after wave pounded the ship until it vanished beneath the surface, leaving behind only splintered wood and the screams of drowning men.

A sob escaped my lips, tears streaming down my cheeks as I hovered above the scene, helpless to do anything but watch.

"Papa," Manannán's son screamed as the waves tore him from his father's chest.

"It will be okay, son, I promise," Manannán cried, battling against the current pulling them farther apart. Tears streaked down his face as his son let out one final, terrified cry before being dragged beneath the heaving sea.

A heart-wrenching wail left the sailor's mouth, and I sobbed alongside him.

"Poseidon, you beast!" He hurled the words like a weapon, lifting his face to the heavens as the dark waves continued to roil around him. His crew, son, and all but a few splinters of wood had vanished beneath them.

A booming voice echoed across the ocean, carried on the tides. "You are a great sailor and lover of the seas, Manannán."

I knew it was the voice of Poseidon.

"I will never forgive you for this, or the seas." Manannán spat the words into the churning water, clutching a piece of wood to keep himself afloat.

"As the civilizations of man thrive, more humans drown. We sea gods are above ruling over such a powerless race. I want you to rule the Kingdom of the Drowned."

"Never." Fire filled Manannán's eyes as he hissed the word.

Poseidon's long, slow laugh reverberated across the waves, and thunder rolled behind it. "I am giving you a choice: rule over the Kingdom of the Drowned as a god and see your son provided a peaceful afterlife, or die here now and condemn both of you to a life of purgatory under the sea."

A shuddering sob escaped Manannán as he floated among the waves, still clutching the wood, and he gave a slow nod.

Poseidon's laughter cracked through the sky as lightning struck the sailor, jolting his body and sending magic skittering across every inch of his skin.

When the lightning faded, Manannán's body trembled with fury, the water lapping at his waist. "You may have thrust the Kingdom of the Drowned upon me, but I will always be a man. I wasn't fashioned out of sky and stars like you were . . . I will never forget my boy's fearful eyes as he was tugged from my arms. I will never let go of the pain, and I promise you, Poseidon, God of Seas and Skies, that will be your downfall."

Poseidon's booming laughter echoed as Manannán—the man—was dragged beneath the waves, where I knew he would soon become the God of the Drowned.

The sacred Doric temple swam back into view as the Mer priestess at my back gently pulled me from the glittering water. I spluttered, shaking with tears, as I rested my forehead against the basin.

"The dream magic is powerful. It is normal to feel disoriented," Peisinoe said gently as she wafted to my side.

Across from me, Finn was drawn from his stone pond by another Mer priestess. His dark fringe dripped across his forehead, as he brushed it back his eyes were intent on mine.

Peisinoe knelt beside me. "Did you have a dream of the prophecy?" She was no longer a powerful Siren queen—she was simply a lover, eyes pleading for a cure to her husband's sickness.

I flushed as my vision came flooding back. I hadn't dreamed of the prophecy's location. I had been distracted by the statue and dreamed of Manannán, the love of Siana's life. The thing that, perhaps at one time or another, she had desired most.

Heat crept to my cheeks and ears as Peisinoe surveyed me. I shook my head. "I didn't, I'm so sorry."

"It's okay." She touched my wrist gently, but her tone was filled with anguish, and she turned to Finn. "How about you?"

"Yes, I know where it is." Finn exhaled, the breath laced with relief as his gaze met mine again.

A cold knot formed in my stomach. Hot tears filled my eyes, and I pressed my lips together to stop them from trembling. Muttering apologies to the Mer priestesses and Peisinoe, I stormed from the temple, cursing myself for not mastering my mind.

26.

MORGANA

My stomach was a distorted mess of knots as I paced back and forth in my chambers. I'd planned to dream of the prophecy, then leave Finn and find it alone. But instead, Finn had seen the vision, and all I'd seen was Manannán.

I stalked the length of my magnificent stone-hewn room for the hundredth time, hair streaming behind me with each restless stride.

I'd meant to feign belief in Finn's words, to uncover everything he and his father knew. But I'd let my anger win and had ruined that, too. Now, he might set off without me to find the prophecy, which would mean I'd failed to honor the Captain's dying wish—the wish he'd given his life to protect, hoping I would see it through.

In short, I was failing at everything. I sank onto the spongy bed and put my face in my hands, my red strands curling around me to offer comfort I didn't deserve.

I hadn't left my chambers since the morning's dream ceremony, but I could tell night had fallen by the darkness which had crept over the waters around me. Had Finn left to find the prophecy while I was here, stewing?

After hours of mulling everything over in my mind, the only conclusion I could arrive at was that I'd have to convince Finn to take me, but now that I'd told him I wanted nothing to do with him, that might prove . . . difficult.

Swallowing my churning emotions, I flung open my door and strode down the stone corridor to the room I'd seen Finn slip into after our disagreement the previous night.

I wrapped my knuckles against the door. No answer.

I knocked again. When there was still no answer, I pushed it open.

Finn was floating in the room's center, using straps to buckle daggers to his chest, his dark hair caressing his face.

"Morgana!" He startled when he saw me, drifting away, one muscled arm pressed behind his back. "What do you want?" His expression darkened, as though my cold words still haunted his mind.

The anger I'd been grappling with since I'd first laid eyes on Finn at Archōn Agorá rekindled, searing through my veins and bubbling to the surface. "You did this on purpose, didn't you? That's why you didn't want me to have a dream . . . So you and your father could find the prophecy without me."

"No, that's not it at all," Finn breathed, dragging a hand over his face.

"I—I want to come with you." The plea tasted like acid in my mouth, but my promise to the Captain burned sharper.

Finn's face hardened. "I'd have thought the idea of being alone with me would repulse you, after what you said."

I folded my arms and stared him down. "I won't take it back, and I'm not going to beg you. But if you care for me like you claim, you will let me come."

Finn drifted back and forward, muscles tense, one arm still behind his back. What felt like minutes passed until he paused, leveling me with a glare.

The silence that came next was stretched. My pulse was pounding as I held his gaze.

A softness crept into his drawn expression—a flare in his eyes as he surveyed me, a genuine shred of something cutting through his impenetrable mask. Brows furrowed, he rubbed his chin as if thinking. "You're connected to the prophecy somehow, so . . . it could be beneficial to have you there."

"Great, so it's settled."

Finn nodded curtly. "However . . . *difficult* it might be to be around you after what you've said to me."

My throat indented as I swallowed, but I ignored his comment. "Where are we headed?"

"We are going to the island of Santorini," Finn grunted through gritted teeth. "After we find what we need there, we can return and travel with the others to the summit."

I blinked hard, trying to steady myself. Once known long ago as Thera, Santorini was the island where Manannán had resided, as I had seen in my visions.

"If you don't mind." Finn gestured to the door, one hand still behind his back. "Since you barged in, I'll need a minute to finish getting ready. Meet me in the throne room—we're leaving the second I'm done."

"Are you sure you don't want me to come?" Skye trailed behind me as I descended the expansive stone steps leading to the Thálassian throne room. I'd roused her and Edward to come and see me off.

I fingered my dagger, now re-strapped across my hips. "You need to stay here and learn Agápē's magic with Peisinoe. I have to do this alone."

Edward let out a huff of indignation from my side just as Finn emerged behind us from his chambers. He gave a curt nod before gliding past us and descending the stairwell.

Skye grabbed my arm. "What's going on there?"

"I clarified that I was no longer interested, but he's agreed to take me with him, and he's not happy about it."

"What? I thought you would have climbed that Mer body like a tree."

I grinned. "Someone had fun with Alexandros."

Skye flushed.

"Have you not told her yet?" Edward's eyes narrowed at the doorway leading to the throne room at the bottom of the stairs.

"Told me what?" Skye asked sharply.

So much had happened I still hadn't found a moment to speak with her about what Finn had done. Maybe I dreaded saying it aloud, as if speaking it would make it real, so I'd kept it all inside. Perhaps that was why my heart had betrayed me, ruining my plans by letting my anger spill over.

"We cannot trust him. I shall explain everything later," Edward muttered, then turned to me, silently asking if that had been okay.

I nodded.

Skye gasped, grabbing me by the hand. "If that's true, you can't go with him."

"The Captain used all his magic to raise that shield and protect us because he knew the prophecy named me. I have to try to find it."

"Then let me come with you," Skye pressed, stopping on the stairs.

I turned and grabbed both her hands in mine. "I think Louisa was right. Agápē brought you back for a reason. You need to stay here and find out why—it might give us an edge at some point."

Skye's lower lip quivered, but she nodded. Guilt washed over me for reminding her of what she'd become.

I kept her hands in mine. "If you learn to conduct a dream ceremony, this could prove very useful. I'll be back in a few days, and we'll all go to the summit together."

"And you have me to keep you company." Edward put a hand on Skye's scaled arm, and she bit back her tears, nodding.

As we reached the bottom of the stairs, laughter echoed from beyond the stone pillars lining the corridor. The voices were unfamiliar, and I exchanged a glance with the others before we quickened our pace down the marble hallway. The sound grew louder as we neared the threshold, and then we stepped into the throne room. It was lit by the shades of moonlight and the three-tiered crystal chandelier hanging from its decadent roof. Its glow fell upon Pisceon, Finn, Glacies, and King Proteus, floating in a group before the six towering thrones.

The laughter died away as we approached them, and my throat constricted. The last time I'd seen Finn's cousin Pisceon and his bride-to-be Glacies, I had put them into a bewitched slumber.

King Proteus swept a webbed hand against Pisceon's back. "These two have come to report their success: all seven Mer kingdoms and the four Siren houses have agreed to attend the summit. They'll remain here with us until we depart."

"If it isn't the little shifter." Pisceon turned to me and pulled himself from Proteus's embrace, his mouth tugging into a grin. "Should I be afraid of you knocking me out again?"

I folded my arms and rolled my eyes.

Finn's gaze flicked to me, but he quickly looked away. He was wearing the ornate wrist guards again, and the daggers he'd been fastening when I barged into his room remained on his back. He hovered beside his future wife, who was looking radiant as ever. Her obsidian tail glistened in the shifting light, and her long, pale hair twisted elegantly in the swell. A silver breastplate adorned her torso, much like Finn's, giving her the air of a Nordic warrior queen.

Pisceon's eyes traveled across Skye and Edward, his face falling into a scowl. "And you're all going on this quest to Santorini."

"The Siren girl and Drowned boy are staying with us. Oh, we will have some fun!" Proteus winked.

"Really, Proteus?" Pisceon swung to the king, muscles flexing as he raised a brow. "You're going to allow the Drowned boy to stay?"

"Come now, Pisceon. This is not the Neptūnus Kingdom."

"If you'd seen what we'd seen"—Glacies's eyes flashed—"you would not be so quick to harbor one."

"Mer dead and drained . . . Their bodies were scattered across the Atlantic. All the work of Manannán's henchmen." Pisceon's jaw clenched, and his eyes narrowed on Edward.

A cold shiver crawled down my spine as memories of the Fisherman's scaly face, silver eyes, and beast-like tentacle crept into my mind. I rubbed the goosebumps from my arms.

"This attitude is exactly *why* we have wars. We've gotten to know this young man and enjoy his company." Proteus waved a hand at Edward, whose face was burning with pride.

Pisceon looked to Finn. "Cousin, I trust you got the dream you needed."

"I did," Finn said stiffly, his gaze darting to the right.

Something twisted in my gut as I glanced between them, my fingers tightening unconsciously around my dagger. So Pisceon and Glacies knew we'd come here to get a dream about the prophecy.

Pisceon folded his muscled arms. "You need to move fast. Darkness spreads through the Atlantic as Manannán grows stronger. We tortured and interrogated several Drowned. They revealed that he has built an underground fortress near Port Royal. That's where the Drowned are gathering their forces."

I choked back a rising tide of emotion. If all the Drowned were gathering at Port Royal . . . could my father be there too? Would he have stood against Manannán's henchmen, or would he have joined their ranks? Maybe I could find him after we uncovered the prophecy—even if it meant walking straight into the lion's den.

I stepped to Finn's other side, lifting my chin, fingers still grazing the hilt of my blade.

Turning to Glacies, Finn kissed his wife-to-be's porcelain hand. "I hope you enjoy the hospitality of the Thálassians while we're gone." Then he winked at Pisceon. "And you too, cousin."

Pisceon offered him a tight-lipped smile. The ever-joking Mer was gone, replaced by someone worn, his eyes darker, his face drawn. Whatever he'd witnessed on that journey had changed him.

My stomach remained in knots. The last time I'd seen Glacies, it was clear her heart belonged not to Finn, but to Princess Aarna Okeanós. Yet she'd still questioned Finn being tasked by his father to follow me. Her composed demeanor suggested that she and Pisceon knew exactly why Finn and I had come here, which meant King Neptūnus knew too. The thought chilled me to the bone.

"We look forward to seeing you both return safely and attending the summit," Proteus boomed with approval, clasping his hands before waving us away with a sweeping gesture. But behind the bravado, I saw it in his eyes as he reached beneath his purple locks to stroke the spidery black veins on his neck: *fear*.

27.

MORGANA

Pháos joined us for the swim to the island, and the silence that weighed over Finn and me was broken only by the dolphin's odd click or chirp.

I glanced at Finn from the corner of my eye. His jaw remained tight, his gaze dark—he was no doubt replaying the cruel things I'd said. *Good.*

My mouth was dry as I kicked through the moonlit water, frustration burning inside me. If only I'd spent more time mastering my mind. But it was too late for regrets. I was bound for Santorini, alone with my sworn enemy, Prince Aigéan—King Neptūnus's most dangerous henchman. I needed to keep my wits about me.

Although I'd jeopardized my plan by telling Finn I no longer cared for him, he didn't know I knew the Neptūnus family had killed my grandmother. I planned to keep it that way.

My fingers brushed the hilt of the blade strapped to my thigh. I might not have mastered my mind or my magic, but with a dagger in hand, Aranare had made me dangerous.

The colorful coral beds surrounding the Thálassian palace stretched beneath us for what must have been miles, their brightness dulled to indigos, deep blues, and greens in the water. Soon, the coral dispersed, and our surroundings became unkempt. Sandy turrets wound below, rocks scattered here and there, and dark seaweed clumps swayed with the current.

We hadn't spoken since leaving Thálassa, and the tension between us was growing thicker. I kept my strokes smooth, calm, refusing to meet Finn's gaze, although I'd seen him observing me in my peripheral vision a few times.

Finally, I broke the silence—if I was going to do this, I needed to know more about his plans. "So your dream told you the prophecy is on Santorini?" I pinned him with an incredulous stare.

He gave a low grunt, folding his arms across his sculpted chest.

I shot him a glare. "Seriously?"

"What?" Finn stopped moving, his tail beating sharply against the water as a muscle feathered in his jaw.

"I don't want to be on this journey with you any more than you want to be here with me. But do you think you could set your bruised ego aside while we find the rest of the prophecy?"

"My bruised ego?" Finn's eyes flashed onyx, and he laughed without warmth. "You never cease to surprise me."

I ignored his comment, keeping my eyes ahead. "We're here to find the prophecy. That's all that matters."

He let out a harsh breath, bubbles trailing upward. "Right. Because suddenly, none of it matters to you anymore."

I forced my features into a mask. My heart hammered against the words I couldn't say: *Did you kill her? Did you take my grandmother from me?*

"I never said it didn't matter," I replied, my tone cold. "I said I no longer cared for you."

Finn's jaw tightened. His strokes grew harder, tail flicking in sharp bursts. "If you think I wanted any of this—"

That cracked something in me. The ache. The anger. The unbearable weight of suspicion. "What, Finn? What is it that you're not saying?"

"I—It's nothing." Finn shook his head quickly.

"Let's just get this done. I'll meet you at Santorini. I see no need to travel together." I veered off, cutting to the right beneath an outcropping of rock.

"Morgana—"

But I was already on the other side of the rock face, slicing through the water as fast as I could, my muscles burning as I kicked into the gloom. At this moment, I didn't care where I was going—only that it was away from him.

I didn't slow until the burn in my chest became unbearable and my muscles screamed for relief. Releasing a frustrated breath, I took in my surroundings. The moonlit waters seemed darker without a companion by my side, but I kept going, moving through schools of pale fish as the seafloor fanned out beneath me.

Something caught my eye in the sand, and I slowed. It looked purposeful, man-made. Goosebumps formed on my fur-covered arms, and I rubbed them, kicking forward and almost colliding with a gleaming blue marble rock half-buried in sand.

I jerked backward, spinning around to take in my surroundings. In the dim light, I could still see the sapphire-colored stones and painted tiles scattered across the seabed, their cobalt patterns breaking through ribbons of sand. Once-grand columns were now fractured and leaning, and an altar at their center lay broken in two.

I drew in a sharp breath, drifting forward to trail my webbed fingers along the nearest blue pillar, its base scattered with fallen stones. A scream tore through my mind as my skin met the cold marble. I whipped around, clutching my temples with trembling hands.

What the hell?

I nearly gagged on my panic as curls of crimson mist wound through the ruins and snaked around my legs.

Is that blood?

I tried to shake the red substance from me, but it was everywhere, twisting through the water and hanging like claret shrouds over the crumbling temple before me.

An eerie silence clung to the place, and a chill raced over my skin, raising the fur on my arms. I hugged myself, exhaled slowly, and closed my eyes as a haunting cry seeped from the ruins, swelling around me.

Manannán, as I'd seen him in my visions, emerged in my mind, his brown skin streaked with blood as he carved through bodies with a crimson-soaked blade. His olive eyes were narrowed on a figure in the distance—Mer Prince Kyano, crowned in glittering gold, with a vibrant green tail, his dark eyes burning with fury. Around them, the sea bloomed red. My blood. Siana's blood. I inhaled sharply as I noticed the lifeless body of a seal drifting just beyond the shattered temple, unnoticed by either man, both too blinded by their rage to see what they'd lost.

A touch on my shoulder, and the images faded. I spun around. Finn was floating behind me, his face pale with worry. Pháos hovered next to him, angling his head and chirping softly.

"What is this place?" I gasped, realizing that it had been a vision. *Only a vision.*

"These are the ruins of Ceruleus Templum." Finn gestured over the waters, his silver bracers gleaming in the turquoise gloom. "It was once a temple dedicated to the gods, until—"

"The battle," I finished for him, rubbing the goosebumps that remained on my arms.

Ceruleus Templum. This was the site of the Battle of the Blue Temple. Here, Prince Kyano, with his legion of Sirens and Mer, had clashed with Manannán, who commanded an army of the dead and sea beasts.

An icy grip tightened around my heart. This was where arrows from both sides had struck Siana, the woman they both loved. The woman who was my ancestor.

"Let's get out of here." I swallowed, forcing myself to speak steadily.

We continued in silence. Finn had returned to brooding, and my mind was filled with images of blood-soaked waters.

28.

MORGANA

As we neared the island of Santorini, the scenery began to change. Beneath us, massive stone terraces unfurled across the seafloor. They fanned out from the volcano's mouth like the ribs of a giant beast. Each was the height of a twenty-story building, stretching miles in every direction.

Finn's emerald tail flickered as he and Pháos dove closer to the terraces, and I followed. My mind whirred as Louisa's history lesson on the Minoans returned to me. These formations must have been created by the volcano that erupted over three thousand years ago, sending torrents of molten rock flooding outward.

I froze, the hairs on the back of my neck prickling. This very volcano was said to be the one that had seen the fall of the Minoan kingdom—Manannán's people.

We slipped into the opening of the vast horseshoe-shaped crater that made up the island of Santorini. Pháos chirped as the wall of the caldera rose beside us. Finn nodded, and the dolphin vanished into the blue with a flick of his gray tail.

"He will meet us back at Thálassa." Finn motioned after the creature.

Santorini's volcanic wall loomed on our left, extending a thousand feet below sea level. It curved around, framing a sunken basin—the hollowed-out heart of a once-mighty volcano—and we followed the curving rock face.

"I'm curious." Finn stared at my profile, his gaze burning into my cheek. "What did you dream of at the ceremony? What is it you desire most?"

My spine went rigid. "It's none of your business." I kicked away from him, toward the surface. After so many days in the deep, I was relieved we would soon be making our way to land.

My chest swelled with wonder as I lifted my head above the waves to see the sun rising over the island. Jagged cliffs towered above a gorgeous natural harbor. The sunrises over Ruadán's Port had been beautiful, but this . . . this was something else.

The waters around me shimmered with streaks of pink and purple, while the sky blazed a vibrant orange above the cluster of whitewashed houses and blue-domed churches perched high on the cliffs. Each one glowed beneath the sun's morning embrace.

The magic of my transition began to hum beneath my skin, and I exhaled, centering myself and allowing it to take hold. My furry body suit disintegrated, becoming my grandmother's fur coat.

"It's magnificent." I wiped the saltwater from my eyes.

Finn's features softened as he grinned back at me, sweeping his dark, wet hair from his forehead. The tattoos on his muscular forearms shifted as he kept his torso afloat above the waves. In that fleeting moment, I wished things could go back to how they'd been—wished I didn't know what Finn's family had done. But I did. And nothing could ever undo that.

From where we drifted in the water, my gaze fixed on the bay ahead.

Boats bobbed, and a crooked staircase led to the chalky houses high above. A pace of donkeys, draped in colorful saddle blankets, waited at the foot of the steps, ready to carry tourists up the winding ascent. I was glad the early hour meant no one was around.

So many stairs, up and up they wound. I assumed that was how we'd reach the island. My fur coat drifted around my bare body in the waves, and heat flushed my neck at the thought: when Finn shifted into his human form, he'd be naked too. The two of us, half-nude, would be climbing out of the water and up those steps.

Finn snorted a hard laugh, tracking my gaze. "Sorry to disappoint you, but we are going through the caves."

"Get over yourself." I rolled my eyes. *Arrogant ass.*

Finn flicked his tail, diving beneath the waves, moving toward the rocky expanse of the island to the right of the bay. I followed him, albeit less gracefully now that I was human, doggy paddling and trying to keep my head above the surface. I was coughing up saltwater by the time we reached the sheer rock face rising from the ocean floor.

Finn traced the stone with his webbed fingers, murmuring the same incantations he'd used when warding my bedroom—the old tongue of the sea—and glowing runes twinkled to life beneath his touch. A hidden door cracked open, revealing a narrow tunnel glistening with trapped aquamarine seawater, swirling beneath light shafts that poured in from high above.

He slipped inside, and I followed, the rock walls pressing close as we swam through the submerged passage. The tunnel led us upward until the waterline met a stone ledge.

A hint of a smile ghosted Finn's lips, magic still dancing in his eyes as he turned to me. "We have a villa in Oia, and I have some clothes. Wait here, and I'll bring you something to wear." He hoisted himself out of the water, his back muscles rippling as the drops cascaded from them, and then his toned ass appeared as he swung one leg up onto the rock.

He looked over his shoulder at me. "Do you mind?"

"Hate to burst your bubble, but not everyone's lining up to ogle you," I spat, my cheeks heating as I turned away.

I kept my gaze averted until the sound of Finn's bare feet slapping on the slick stone plateau faded, suggesting he'd climbed the narrow staircase winding up through the cliff.

I glanced around the ocean cave as I waited for him to return, wishing that my Selkie ancestors had blessed me with the same invisibility from humans the Mer had. The doorway to the sea had sealed behind us, but faint light filtered down from the steps above, illuminating faded cave paintings of sea creatures and runes etched into the stone walls.

Finn soon reemerged on the slimy rock ledge. "Here you go." His nakedness had now been covered up by his usual attire: a white T-shirt, dark jeans, and boots. He had a leather cuff fastened on his right wrist.

I caught the package he tossed me, but his gaze stayed fixed on me as I trod water.

"Do *you* mind?" I raised a brow in his direction.

The corners of his mouth twitched upward, but he turned around.

I scrambled out of the water, shedding my fur coat as quickly as possible, and slipped into the clothes he had bought me. "Are you serious?" I eyed my outfit with disbelief.

Finn turned, took one look at me, and let out a snort of laughter.

The T-shirt said, "I heart Santorini," and in the heart was the face of one of those iconic donkeys. The pants were painted with paisleys and swirling designs, and they ballooned out like something a genie (or, in this case, an unfashionable tourist) would wear.

"You need one more thing." Finn tossed me a fanny pack and Velcro sandals from under his arm.

I shot him a smile laced with vitriol as I strapped them on. "Fanny packs are making a comeback."

"Consider this payback for your granddad's nightgown," he said, still chuckling.

I followed him up the winding shaft carved organically into the cliffside, drawn toward the sliver of light above. We ascended in silence, spiraling higher along the weathered stairs. They opened onto a plateau, and beyond that, another set of stone steps led up toward the villa, perched high above the sea.

The villa was nestled into a dark stone terrace framed by whitewashed walls, where a turquoise pool glistened.

I turned in awe. Below us, a trail of chalky houses and pools tumbled down the cliff all the way to the glittering ocean, which was speckled with luxury yachts and cruise ships.

I followed Finn inside. The space had low ceilings and was fluid in its design, the arched doorways and smooth contours evoking a sunlit sea cave. Its decor was a mix of whites, beiges, and warm woods.

I scrunched my nose as Finn poured two glasses of wine. "Really, in the morning?"

"What's that saying . . . when in Rome?" He swilled his glass and took a sip. The corner of his mouth quirked as he surveyed me. His eyes danced with something almost hopeful.

"My mother owns a club here." He sipped with feigned nonchalance, eyes watching me over the rim. "Well, she owned one—it's my father's now. Do you want to see it?"

"The club?" I left my wine untouched and surveyed the views, lips pursed in displeasure.

"Yes, it's called The Aegean, after yours truly, but she used the Greek spelling, of course."

I turned back to Finn and found the shadows had lifted from his face. His features had softened, and the silver flecks in his eyes were pronounced. It was as if he were truly happy to be here on this island with me.

This prodded something inside me, and my rage flared in response. I folded my arms across my chest. "We are not here to go clubbing and drink. We are here to find the prophecy, so if you don't mind, I'd rather do that."

Finn's face fell, the hopeful look disintegrating, then he masked it with an arrogant smirk and shrugged. "Suit yourself. You aren't dressed for clubbing anyway."

"You can talk. What's with the leather cuff?"

He ignored my question and moved to open the far door of the villa for me. "After you, shifter."

I followed him up another flight of stairs, which opened onto a stone path carved into the cliffside. On our right, houses spilled down toward the ocean, and to our left, shops stretched into the distance.

"Welcome to Oia," Finn said, sweeping his hand toward the view.

As we walked along, the path came alive with color and movement. Boutiques offering high-end wares sat beside eclectic souvenir stalls—no doubt where Finn had picked out my outfit.

But soon, he veered away from the bustle, guiding me down a rocky hillside blanketed in brittle, desert-like grasses. A crumbling church rose ahead, framed by half-collapsed red brick walls and an overgrown path.

"This is where the dream led you?" I asked, raising a hand to shield my eyes from the sun as I surveyed the weathered structure.

Finn didn't answer. He simply kept walking.

I cast my eyes across the ruins as we moved into the old church's shadow. Made entirely of rust-colored bricks, it had a domed roof and a simple bell tower. Behind it, a steep, barren hillside loomed, enhancing its secluded, almost ancient feel.

An old man sat hunched on a wooden chair by the front door, his white hair falling over a bowed head. A loose tunic hung from his frail frame, paired with worn jeans and bare, weathered feet that looked like they'd never known shoes. His sun-browned skin was creased with time.

As we approached, he lifted his gaze to meet us. "Son of Poseidon. I have been waiting for you," he croaked as he fell under Finn's shadow.

"You're related to Poseidon?" My mouth went dry.

Finn nodded.

Of course he is.

"I am here for Poseidon's Box," Finn commanded, adopting his princely tone.

"Ah," the old man crooned. "But are you worthy?"

Finn rolled back his shoulders and stood tall. "Yes," he said through gritted teeth.

"We shall see about that. And who are you?" The old man's eyes traveled from my ugly Velcro sandals to the floral parachute pants and donkey on my T-shirt.

"We're here about the prophecy. Is that what's in the box?" I nudged Finn out of the way to stand before the old man, remembering Finn's shared glance with Pisceon.

"My dear, only the gods know what's in that box."

Finn drew himself into his princely persona. "War is coming, and we believe Poseidon has left us answers. As his direct descendant, Prince Aigéan Neptūnus, I command that you give me the box."

"You demand it, do you?" The old man chuckled, shaking his head.

"I will give it to you, Prince Aigéan Neptūnus, but first, you must earn it—if you can."

"By doing what?" My stomach dropped, and the man turned back to me.

"Do you two think you are the first to come here and request the box? I can only hand it to one who passes three tasks and proves their worthiness."

My stomach plummeted. "And no one's passed these tasks before?"

"Would I be sitting here, on this desolate hill, if they had? Once I relinquish the box, I will be free."

"What are these tasks?" Finn growled.

"Task one is designed to test your cunning and strength, task two the infallibility of your mind, and task three generosity." The old man raised his head, and his dark eyes glittered.

Great, just great. Now, I would have to stay on this island for however long it took to complete these tasks with Finn. Unless . . . A cold breath caught in my throat as an idea came to me . . . Unless I finished the first task on my own and returned to the old man without Finn.

"There is a nightclub on Perivolos Beach, the Aqua Inferno. Stavros Eliades, an ancient Siren, owns it. He has something of Poseidon's. You will find that item and return it. When you succeed, I will give you your next task," the old man rasped.

"Seriously? That's all you're going to tell us?" I blew out a frustrated breath.

"Come on, I know the place." Finn reached for my hand, but I tore my palm from his grasp.

He shrugged and turned away.

Following him up the crumbling track, I bit my lip to stifle a conspiratory grin. I'd use Finn to uncover everything he knew about the nightclub and its owner, then I would find whatever belonged to Poseidon, bring it back to the old man, and claim the second task for myself.

I hurried to catch up. "So, where exactly is this nightclub?"

"Near The Aegean." Finn turned, giving me a once-over, laughter dancing in his dark eyes. "But first we'll need to find you something more suitable to wear."

An angry breath escaped my nose, but I followed him back toward the shops of Oia, my step a little lighter now that I had a plan.

29.

I hefted the cool box of haddock onto my shoulder as the pale winter sun climbed over the dark, restless waves. I'd started this day the same way I began most others: up before the sun rose to train at my uncle's gym. Then, I'd joined my dad and my uncle on the seas.

Williamson Industries held an unassuming grip over much of Ruadán's Port and the Hebrides. My parents owned Saltmarsh Row—the bookstore, the Port House, and everything in between—while my aunt and uncle ran the fishery, the Bayside café, the local gym, and a whisky distillery. Most of my days were spent pitching in, drifting from one family business to the next.

Dad tossed our tackle into the back of my Ranger, his brown arms flexing beneath his sweater and fisherman's overalls. His long hair, tied in a bun, was still mostly dark but now streaked with silver.

My uncle, Angus, clapped him on the back. "Bright and early tomorrow then, Dylan?"

Dad nodded, and my uncle waved goodbye before stalking to his adjacent truck. He had the same brown skin, dark hair, and eyes as the rest of my family, but he was older and more worn.

Our interbreeding with humans meant we aged differently, and our powers manifested unpredictably. Some, like my father and I, were born with the gifts of High Sirens—wings and all. Others, like my uncle, barely possessed any magic. Unlike other Siren families that had dwindled, there were hundreds of Lughs across Scotland, but not all of us carried abilities.

Dad folded his arms across his broad chest, leaning back onto my truck, observing me with eyes the same amber as mine. "What are you doing today, son?"

"I'll drop these fish at Bayside, then watch the bookstore until Mom returns."

"Aye, where was she this time? I can't keep track."

"Venice."

"Why don't you stick around and join us for dinner tonight?"

I nodded, shoving my cold hands into the pockets of my jacket.

"The Neptūnus boy was here to see me a few days back . . . Pisceon."

I went still, my throat constricting. "And?"

"He wanted us to attend the summit in Okeanós."

"What did you say?"

My father exhaled. "I said we would go. You know how I hate these things, but our people deserve a voice."

"I'll join you."

He clapped me on the back, then turned and trudged up Croy Street's slick curve toward Saltmarsh Row and the Port House.

I drove the fish to Bayside, helped my aunt set the tables, and prepared the place for the day. Then, I headed across the clifftop to Parker's house.

When I arrived, the realtor was already waiting out front, her power suit a clear sign she wasn't from around here. She unlocked the front door, and my breath faltered as memories of what had happened inside washed over me like a flood.

"The Stewarts are selling it fully furnished, as . . . they suffered a personal tragedy here." The woman waved a hand over the space.

I followed her up the hallway from the open-plan living area to the bedroom, where Skye's things still hung.

"We would get all this stuff removed, of course." She gestured to the clothing, and my heart twanged as I saw her array of neatly arranged shoes.

"I'll take the house," I said through gritted teeth. "But I want to keep all the clothes. Please ensure they are left untouched."

"Great, I'll draw up the paperwork." The realtor's eyes lit up with glee. It was a wee town, and everyone had heard that the Stewart lad had thrown himself from the cliff, so I imagined she hadn't been having much luck with sales.

I had money—more than enough. I'd worked for my parents since I was a lad, but material things had never mattered to me until now. I set up a shell company under a different name and quietly bought the place. No need to draw attention. Skye probably hated that house and would never want to enter it again. But I bought it anyway. Just in case she ever wanted her clothes back.

It would also piss Finn off, as we were now neighbors, and the thought made the corners of my mouth twitch upward.

A few hours later, I cracked open the door to the bookstore and switched on the dim lights. We rarely had customers, so it didn't matter when I opened.

I missed those mornings training Morgana and Skye—it had given my life a sense of purpose.

I pulled my stack of books and notes from the shelf. If I wasn't going with them to Thálassa, the least I could do was keep digging into my research and see if I could find something that might help: information on the prophecy, Manannán, and now my new passion, Agápē.

Every morning, I woke up drenched in sweat, the Tidescar pulling at my heart with a relentless ache, urging me to go to Skye. I longed to take her hands in mine, gaze into her dark eyes . . . sink onto my knees in the sand at her feet and swear my never-dying love to her, pledging my allegiance. But I wouldn't. I wouldn't surrender to the part of my nature that made you daft and urged possessiveness. I would give her space to process and make a choice. And I would see her at the summit.

I exhaled, pulling the worn leather-bound tome I'd last been reading toward me.

I knew Skye was okay. I'd feel it if something happened to her. I'd felt it before. It rushed through you like the tide had receded from your heart, leaving it parched and broken. It was a feeling you never forgot—when your Tidescar died.

The Trials of Thera

30.

MORGANA

For the first task, we were going to Aqua Inferno, which, according to Finn, was one of Santorini's most fashionable nightclubs. That meant I needed to look the part.

Evening had fallen as I surveyed myself in the mirror on the villa's bathroom wall. The dress was definitely a step up from the "I love Santorini" shirt with the donkey on it, though it wasn't something I'd ever have chosen for myself. Beige patent leather clung to my frame, the corset pushing my little cleavage up to my chin. It squeaked every time I moved to tong my hair into a sleek, straight curtain.

I'd paired it with gold earrings, red lipstick, and strappy gold heels with laces that ran up my legs. Finn had dropped a small fortune at one of the high-end boutiques, and the sales assistant had made eyes at him the entire time.

The dress—if you could even call it that—was more like a shirt, barely covering my ass. I'd grown used to showing skin after so much time in my seal form, but at least that let me move. This? Completely impractical.

Finn's dream had led him to the Box of Poseidon, which was promising. After all, the old gods had created the prophecy.

But the look Pisceon had given Finn lingered in my mind. I didn't trust him, but I trusted his father even less. And if Finn was here, carrying out this mission without invoking his father's wrath, it could only mean one thing: the king supported it. It made my stomach turn.

I finished straightening my hair, swept on mascara, and batted my lashes at the mirror, grounding myself in the plan: find whatever belonged to Poseidon in that club and get it back to the old man before Finn did. After one final look in the mirror, I stepped out of the bathroom.

"Wow." Finn bit his knuckle in reverence as I entered the villa's living area.

He was lounging splay-legged at the kitchen table with a glass of wine in his hand. His jeans were rolled up at the ankles, his bare feet crossed lazily, and his hand-cut tank top revealed the ink that traced his arms, though he'd kept the leather cuff on his right wrist. Behind him, the open doors framed the aquamarine pool and the setting sun, dipping slowly toward the ocean on the horizon.

"I'm stuck doing these tasks with you. *The least* you could do is try to act somewhat professional." My nostrils flared as I folded my arms.

Finn's brows kicked up, and he snorted out a laugh. "You're stuck? Need I remind you that you begged to be here?"

I scoffed in his face as I tossed my sleek hair over my shoulder. His affection wasn't real; I had to remember that. I swallowed hard, grounding myself in my plan.

"Liquid courage?" Finn pushed a glass toward me. "They have some of the best white wine in the world on Santorini."

I took in his relaxed posture as I accepted my glass. He was enjoying this freedom, I realized. "Is your father also a descendant of Poseidon?"

Finn shook his head. "It's my mother's side. The Thálassians are descended from the survivors of Ătlanticus. I am a distant relative of Kyano, one of Poseidon's sons. My father has always been envious of me for this."

Wait, what? I almost choked on my wine.

"You're related to Kyano? Why didn't you tell me earlier?"

Finn shrugged. "My relation to Kyano and Poseidon spans thousands of years, and the gods were fond of . . . fucking."

"I just find it strange, is all. I'm related to Siana, Skye is descended from Agápē, and Manannán has returned . . ."

Could the Fisherman with the tentacled arm be the reincarnation of Cetus, the God of Beasts and Sea Life?

Finn studied me with dark, unreadable eyes before pulling a silver cigarette case from his pocket. He slipped one between his lips, smirking. "Let's just focus on the task at hand."

I tucked my hair behind my ears, biting my lip as I willed my expression into one of impassiveness. "So . . . tell me more about the nightclub and its owner."

"Aqua Inferno sits on Perivolos Beach, right next to my mother's club, The Aegean. Stavros, the owner, is an ancient Siren with a penchant for rare and priceless items, which makes this job challenging. He keeps his treasures locked away in a private suite above the nightclub, accessible only to high rollers—celebrities, tycoons . . . You get the picture?" Finn's cheeks caved as he drew on his cigarette.

"So, how are we going to get in there? Don't tell me you're a celebrity here in Greece?"

"No." Smoke plumed from Finn's nostrils. "But I thought we could go there tonight and see if we could scope out a way in." His dark eyes twinkled as they raked over my tight leather dress.

My lip curled, but I composed myself, batting my lashes and giving him my sweetest smile. The way Finn had been looking at me had given me an idea about how I could get the item without him.

Night had well and truly fallen as we strode up Perivolos Beach. Thatched umbrellas dotted the sand in front of Aqua Inferno, the music pumping from inside wrapping around us as we made our way between them to the indoor area.

I peeked at Finn from the corner of my eye. He had changed into a dress shirt and pants, his dark hair immaculately gelled, but a strand had fallen out in the sea breeze. He looked good. *Damn it.*

The bouncers nodded admission, and as we stepped inside, we were immediately enveloped in a vibrant atmosphere. Aquariums lined the walls, casting a shimmering glow throughout the venue. The sleek modern tanks stretched from floor to ceiling, housing exotic fish that moved through the water.

Aqua Inferno, indeed.

Music thudded through the space, blending with the hum of the tanks, making it feel like we were submerged in a dreamlike aquatic world. Finn took my hand and guided me through the throng of bodies, the beat of the DJ's rhythm pounding in the air. My skimpy dress blended in perfectly here.

"We'll have two of your best whiskies," Finn said to the bartender, then he leaned both his elbows on the bar to survey the partygoers.

I mustered a casual tone as I dragged my eyes across the space. "So, where is this room where he keeps his collection?"

"Stavros's high rollers' area is up there." Finn jerked his chin at the glass area above the aquariums. "We need to sneak in without him noticing."

I spun around, searching the venue. It was time to set my plan to get the artifact on my own into motion. I just needed to find Stavros.

"Don't make it obvious," Finn snapped, the muscle in his jaw flickering as my gaze lingered on the windows high above.

I sipped my drink and pretended to appreciate the fish tanks, tracking the space until I spotted him. Stavros. He was sitting on a gilded velvet chair in a shaded VIP area cordoned off by black-knotted ropes with two surly-looking henchmen at the entrance. The area lay directly beneath the tanks and the high rollers' room, so the entrance had to be somewhere behind him.

The eerie light reflecting off the aquariums illuminated Stavros's striking Siren features. He exuded a magnetic presence, effortlessly capturing the attention of everyone nearby, though his gaze remained aloof. Draped in a tailored black shirt that hugged his sculpted frame, he leaned back in the plush seat.

Behind him, a group of pretty girls sat on couches, laughing and drinking champagne. He cradled a glass, the amber liquid swirling as he sipped. His sea-green eyes swept over the room, taking in the revelry until they landed on me.

It was time to implement my plan.

With a slow breath, I closed my eyes, letting the world fade into the background. My body relaxed, sinking into the moment as I opened my heart to my power and cleared my thoughts, focusing only on the energy within.

I reached for the silver orb to activate my Selkie's allure as Aranare had taught me. Grasping that ancient, shimmering power, I concentrated on letting it radiate outward.

When I opened my eyes, the transformation was subtle. A faint glow had settled over my skin, like moonlight twinkling on a calm sea. I allowed myself to meet Stavros's eyes. If my plan worked, he would sense that the allure I radiated wasn't that of the Mers or Sirens. It was something else, something extinct—and that meant something worth collecting.

Stavros's lips parted as he took me in, and for the first time since I'd laid eyes on him, he seemed alive, his expression shifting from indifferent to fascinated. The club's noise faded into the background as his gaze locked onto me. His eyes darkened, and the hint of a smirk curled the edges of his mouth.

"What are you doing?" Finn hissed, and the allure I had conjured disintegrated.

"Improvising," I bit back.

He gripped my arm, but I shook him off.

Across the club, I watched Stavros nod to his bouncer, who unhooked the rope, and he began prowling through the crowd toward me. I became hyper-aware of my limbs, unsure how to position them. As Stavros approached, I settled a hand on my hip but instantly regretted it; the faux leather made my palm sweat. The Siren was tall—my gaze barely reached his chest.

"Care to join me in the VIP area?" he purred, his green eyes glowing gold.

"You flatter me." I batted my lashes, and Finn choked on his drink at the bar.

Stavros offered his arm, and I looped mine through it as he guided me across the dance floor toward the cordoned-off space. He gestured to the seat beside his velvet throne, the party girls casting jealous glances my way.

As I sat, my eyes swept my surroundings, and there, tucked behind another velvet rope, was the staircase that must lead to his private collection upstairs.

"Tell me." Stavros raised a large, ringed hand and ran it down my cheek. "What on earth *are* you?"

"I'm just a girl." I smiled coyly. What the hell was I doing?

He chuckled, low and dark, and I sensed his deep desire. I forced down the lump in my throat. My plan was working.

"I enjoy precious things like you." The Siren's eyes lit up with wicked delight.

I let my hand glide along his muscled forearm, which was resting on the arm of his gilded chair. "Surely I pale in comparison to the wonderful things a man like yourself would own."

Flattery was working, so I was going to roll with it.

He leaned forward, so close I could feel his breath. "Do you like precious things?"

"Yes." I walked my fingers daintily back up his arm, glancing at him from under my lashes. "But I like quiet spaces more."

I could almost feel Finn's hardened jaw and burning eyes across the room. Fear coiled like a snake in my gut, but I shoved it deep down. Stavros's fascination with rare things gave me an edge. It allowed me to get into the high rollers' room without Finn and find whatever this Siren had that belonged to Poseidon.

The Siren man stood, his mouth twisting into a devilish grin. "Come with me. I'll show you something."

He offered his arm once more, and again I slipped mine through it, letting him guide me past the now-seething girls.

This was it. He was going to take me to his room of treasures.

The shadowed staircase opened into a vast space, where floor-to-ceiling windows overlooked the glittering chaos of the nightclub below. A poker table dominated the center, its velvet top cluttered with chips, cards, and half-empty tumblers. A private bar stood at one end of the room, and at the other was Stavros's collection. The wall of objects was displayed under soft light—blades, chalices, scrolls, ceremonial masks, and crowns.

"This room is normally reserved for high-end guests. I suppose you could say I collect them, too. Elon Musk is arriving tomorrow with his friends, but tonight it is the perfect quiet space for us."

The patent leather of my minidress squeaked as Stavros pulled me against him and burrowed his face into my neck. "What are you?" he asked again, inhaling my scent.

"I'm just a girl," I repeated, pushing him away playfully and moving toward his collection. "These are some fine artifacts you have here . . ."

"I like a woman who can see the value in precious things." Stavros's scent—a mixture of bourbon and cologne—washed over me as he approached me from behind, wrapping his strong arms around my waist.

"Which is your most valued?" I asked, my voice wavering as he thrust against me and the length of him pressed into my back. My stomach turned, but I exhaled, forcing the feeling away. All I had to do was find out which item I needed to steal, and then I could get out of there.

"The Scepter of Tutankhamun." Stavros nuzzled into my neck, groaning as he pushed himself against me again.

I tore myself from his grasp. My eyes scanned the shelves until I spotted it: a gleam of gilded bronze and blue stripes, the long staff curling elegantly into a hook. The Scepter of Tutankhamun—why would Poseidon want that?

"Where do you think you're going?" Stavros grabbed me by the wrist and pulled me back into him.

"Boss?"

I exhaled in relief as we were interrupted by one of his burly guards.

"Can't you see I'm busy?" Stavros swung toward the man, letting my wrist fall free.

"It's Prince Aigéan. We apprehended him trying to get up to this room. There can only be one reason why he's here."

"Poseidon's Box," Stavros cried. "*You!*" He turned back to me, his face contorted with rage.

Oh fuck.

The world moved in slow motion for a moment as a wave of fear crashed over me. The room pulsed with the club's muffled bass, and a muscle in Stavros's jaw twitched as he glared at me, the beat from below vibrating through the soles of my heels.

Shit. Crap. Fuck. A barrage of expletives exploded in my brain.

The Siren's smile became serpentine as he circled me. Black scales burst from his flesh, glittering on his cheeks. Behind him, his brute security guard cracked his knuckles and blocked the door.

"You are going to look *so nice* in my collection," he hissed, eyes gleaming.

Cursing my tight leather outfit, I dropped into a ready stance. My pulse thrummed as I recalled everything I had learned on the cliff with Aranare. Stavros paused, eyes sweeping over me, and I realized how ridiculous I must look, poised to fight in this dress. He let out a dark chuckle, then he lunged.

I ducked, pivoting low, and drove my elbow into his gut before twisting to send a sharp knee into his ribs. He grunted, stumbling backward.

"Oh, I like you." The Siren grinned, brushing his dark hair from his forehead before rushing at me again.

His movements were fast, a blur of limbs. I parried with my forearm, but he knocked me toward the wall of artifacts. He faltered momentarily, worried about his precious collection. My hand found a blade from the wall—a ceremonial dagger crusted with black pearls—and I slashed upward, grazing his shoulder.

Blood spurted to the floor, and Stavros snarled, more beast than man now.

With the Siren regrouping and his bodyguard ready to join, I scanned for a way out. My gaze landed on the window, which overlooked the nightclub below.

Breath sharp in my throat, I grabbed Tutankhamun's staff from the shelf and hurled it full force at the glass. With a crash, it shattered in a glorious spray, shards catching the light like drops of crystalline rain as they poured down onto the dance floor below.

Stavros roared, and the guard surged forward.

I ran toward the broken window and leaped.

Wind and music rushed around me, and for one breathless second, I flew. Then I tumbled into a throng of people, and limbs began flying as fights ensued all around me.

In the chaos of my fall, Finn broke free from the guards holding him near the dance floor and pushed through the haze of strobes and smoke.

"Are you okay?" His dark hair was damp, lips parted like he'd run through hell to find me.

"I think so."

"Did you get the artifact?" he asked, eyes sharp as he pulled me up.

"I–I threw it at the window." I gestured to the brawling nightclubbers, a mess of body parts and grunts under the aquamarine glow.

Shit, my plan was unraveling. I'd lost the staff.

A patron stumbled from the chaos, striking Finn in the jaw.

Finn grinned wickedly as he rolled up the sleeves of his dress shirt. "Oh, I do love a good bar brawl."

The man swung again at Finn, who dodged it and punched him back.

My heart began to race. I couldn't have asked for a better distraction while I slipped out with the staff. My eyes darted across the flying limbs until I saw it, gleaming blue and gold amid the shattered glass on the floor. I ducked around the brawlers and grasped it.

Finn's fists were still flying left and right. He stopped momentarily to wipe blood from his lip and sweep his hair from his face, and then he was back into it.

Clutching the staff, I began to run, shoving through the heaving crowd, the bass pounding my skull. Sweat-slick bodies closed in around me, but I held the staff against my chest.

I caught a glimpse of the exit ahead just as a hand seized me and an arm clamped around my waist. Stavros's burly henchman blocked my path, sneering down at me, while a new man dragged me back into the throng. I thrashed, twisting against his grip, still holding the staff. My magic hummed in response, but I shoved it down. I couldn't risk it; there were too many innocent people in this club.

Across the room, Finn broke free from the brawl, blood streaking across his jaw, fists still clenched as his gaze locked on mine.

"No!" I gasped as one henchman yanked the staff from my grasp, and then Finn was there, slamming into the guard holding me with the force of a crashing wave.

The man dropped me to the floor and joined the fray.

The chaos of the nightclub throbbed around us—screaming patrons, blood, and flashing lights. But for a heartbeat, everything slowed, and a realization washed over me. "Wait." I grabbed Finn's forearm. "It's not the staff."

He froze, his fist cocked above the security guard he was about to pummel. "Are you sure?"

"It's the tanks." I dragged my gaze across the aquariums lining the space. "The fish. *They* belong to Poseidon."

A muscle tightened in Finn's brow, and then he grinned. "You astound me, shifter."

"Don't let them get away!" Two more burly security guards were pushing through the chaos toward us.

Cold amusement frosted Finn's dark features, and with a flick of his wrist, he sent lightning shimmering along his forearms, arcing in threads of pale silver. He raised both hands, and the aquariums began to glow.

An ominous weight settled over me. I'd never seen him do anything like this—I hadn't known it was possible. I hadn't realized the full extent of Finn's power until now. *Lightning.*

One by one, the glass tanks trembled and shattered, as if melting away from the walls. Water burst forth, hovering in midair in great spheres that shimmered with fish and drifting seaweed. Patrons gasped and ducked for cover, but the floating orbs moved above them, guided by Finn's outstretched arms.

He turned and conducted them toward the open door. The club's panic faded into hushed awe as the fish glided into the cool night. One by one, they returned to the sea. And when the final glowing drop vanished into the swell, Finn's hands fell to his sides, his body spent, yet his eyes remained intent on mine.

A cry rang out. The guards, who had been momentarily distracted by the fish, were charging toward us again.

"We need to move," Finn shouted, grabbing my hand and pulling me with him.

My lungs burned, and my feet ached in my heels, but I kept pace as we sprinted past the beach umbrellas and slipped into the safety of the shadows beyond. Only then did I allow myself to breathe.

"The patrons . . . they saw you . . ." I panted.

"Stavros will use his mind magic to erase their memories. He won't want this becoming a PR nightmare that deters his high rollers."

"He will be furious."

"I doubt we've seen the last of him." Finn shook his head.

I ran a hand through my tangled hair, part of me elated. We had completed the task, yet my insides were twisting. I had not managed to do it alone, which meant I would receive the next one with Finn. It was the first time I'd seen him wield lightning. I had hoped—prayed—that was a power only his father possessed.

The police officer had said my grandmother's heart stopped, and Finn once told me that *lightning can stop a heart with a single prod.*

I still didn't know for sure if he had killed my grandmother, but now, I knew he had the power to do it.

I was silent during the ride back in the black Mercedes van. Finn had a personal driver on the island, of course. I rolled my eyes, arms folded tight across my chest, and stared out as flickering lights streaked past the window.

When we arrived in Oia, I threw open the car door, pushed through the throngs of tourists crowding the bustling shopping street, and stormed down the stone steps. I flung open the door to the villa, Finn right behind me.

I swung to him as he closed the door in our wake. "What was that?"

"What?" He tipped his head, studying me.

"The lightning. Why have you never used it until now?" My breathing came in ragged gasps, but I fought to keep it in check.

"It's not a power I . . . enjoy using." He raked a hand through his hair, the muscles in his arms flexing beneath the snug sleeves of his black dress shirt.

My jaw was stiff as I glared at him. Several moments of silence passed between us as I took in his furrowed brows and what seemed to be pain in his eyes.

"I'm going to bed," I finally snapped, stalking away from Finn down the hallway.

"Morgana." I froze at the sound of my name, turning slowly to see him still standing where I'd left him.

"What?"

"Just so you know, only an heir of Poseidon can claim the box," he called after me.

Heat surged up my neck, but I said nothing. I continued down the hall, past the bathroom to where two bedrooms waited on either side. Each one was curved and sun bleached, with blue-and-white duvets and framed photographs of Santorini hung above the beds.

I took the room on the right and slammed the door, leaning against it with a sharp exhale. Thank the gods the villa had two bedrooms.

I climbed into the comfy bed and pulled the cover up to my chin. My feelings were a tangled mess.

Only an heir of Poseidon could claim the box, which I was not, but Finn was. That meant I had to work with him if I wanted to find out what was in that box.

Rage roiled inside me, and a harsh breath escaped my nose. Smug prick. He must have realized I'd been trying to work against him and escape with the artifact.

At least we'd completed the first task—there were only two more. I massaged my forehead. After we'd claimed the box, and read the second half of the prophecy it contained, I'd never have to see Finn again. Bit by bit, my pinched eyes and clenched fists loosened, and sleep washed over me.

I had just drifted off when I jolted upright. The soft sheets fell from my shoulders as my ears strained and I rubbed sleep from my eyes. I was sure I'd heard something—a cry of pain.

I whipped my head left to right, scanning the darkness, but the room was still, save for the distant sighing of the sea through the open window. A shadow flickered in the corner, and my breath hitched, but it was only the curtains swaying in the moonlight.

I must have imagined it, or perhaps it was a dream.

I yawned, rubbing a hand down my face, then eased back against the pillows. The tension ebbed from my limbs as my eyes fluttered shut again, sleep reclaiming me.

31.

SKYE

There seemed to be a party every night in the Kingdom of Thálassa, and tonight was no exception.

I adorned my wrists with golden bangles and pinned my dark curls into the new Grecian style I was embracing, littering the strands with glittering embellishments.

A knock sounded at my door, and I flung it open to find Alexandros floating there, waiting to escort me.

Tonight's soiree was in the gardens, and we drifted there together. Pillars draped in bioluminescent flowers lined the dining space, which was suspended beneath a stone roof. Beyond them, gardens with every color of coral stretched for miles into the aquamarine waters.

At the center of the dining pavilion hung a marble table heaped with delicacies, giant abalone-shell cradles dangled from golden chains around it, anchored high in the ornate roof above.

King Proteus and Queen Peisinoe sat at the head, their tails drifting beneath their cradles, which swayed with the water's movement. Beside them, seated along one side of the lavish table, were the Neptūnus Mer: Princess Glacies and Pisceon. Next to them sat Princess Porphura and her wife, Layla. Across from them, Edward and Alexandros's twin, Damon, had already taken their places, and we slipped into the swing-like seats beside them. Someone must have helped lift Edward into his.

Alexandros squeezed my thigh, and arousal coursed through me, tingling in the space below my navel. "Bella." He kept his purple-flecked eyes on me as he poured me a glass of wine, and I bit my lip at the thought of what we would engage in after dinner.

Alexandros had spent the night in my chambers after the pleasure party, and then again the night that followed, beginning my education in the erotic arts of those born with tails. I knew he had other lovers—he was very open about it in the glances he exchanged with passing mermaids and mermen—but it didn't bother me. This wasn't love; it was an arrangement of the flesh, and I was savoring every moment of it.

When Alexandros was pleasuring me, the thoughts of my lost humanity, Parker's severed throat oozing warm blood across my thighs, and his rough hands around my neck faded from my mind. With each moment lost to the ocean's pleasures, acceptance came more easily, and I learned how to let go. I was grateful to Alexandros for this mercy, for offering me a reprieve from the endless wars waged in my mind.

Pisceon slammed his fist down on the table, rattling our cutlery and causing the vats of Thálassian wine to teeter precariously as the chains that held the floating structure creaked. "Will you insist on engaging in this blatant revelry when our people are dying?"

A hush fell over the group. All eyes drifted to Pisceon, his muscular chest taut as his fierce eyes cut between us.

King Proteus threw up his hands. "My sons will gather our army, and we will attend the summit in Okeanós. What more would you have me do?"

"People need to know what we've seen. They need to be ready," Pisceon snarled. Glacies placed a calming hand on his arm, but he shook her off. "Tell them!" He glared at her.

"We saw unspeakable horrors, Your Majesty. The Drowned were stronger from using Mer blood, and the Fisherman holds some other magic," she told the king.

Pisceon cracked his neck muscles in frustration. "I can't laze around getting pleasured and drinking wine. I must do something while we wait for my cousin to return."

An angry breath shot out of the king. "I won't go around scaremongering and taking away what last enjoyment my people have!"

"Let me train them, then." Irritation flashed across Pisceon's face, but he kept his gaze locked on the king.

"Train them?" King Proteus's brows shot up.

"The Drowned won't die until they've served their sentence to the gods. Let Pisceon and me train your people to contain them," Glacies offered, and Pisceon nodded, his jaw so tight it seemed he could no longer speak.

The king rubbed his chin in thought while Queen Peisinoe ran her fingers through his purple hair. "Training isn't a bad idea, my love," she said. "Let them teach our people the art of warfare, and I will train the Siren girl in mastering her dream weaving." She smiled at me.

I was halfway through popping a peeled prawn into my mouth, but I paused to return the gesture.

Proteus sighed and took a deep gulp of wine. "Yes, you're welcome to hold training sessions for anyone who wants to join."

"Thank you," Pisceon grunted, but his tone remained curt.

"I'd like to train." Layla's golden bangles gleamed as she looked to Porphura, who nodded in agreement.

"I-I'll come to training, too," Edward piped up from his corner. "I've always quite fancied learning how to use a blade."

"I'm not training *you*." Pisceon's eyes flashed as he surveyed Edward. "I'll teach you how to use it, and you'll stab me in the back."

"Must you be so completely blind?" Edward folded his arms, his seat swinging with the sharp movement.

"Enough." Peisinoe raised a hand. "I have seen the boy's innermost desires, and trust me, Pisceon, he will not stab you with a blade."

"The Drowned boy can train with us." Glacies blew out a breath, reaching for the nearest vat of wine. "So can the Siren girl."

She hadn't used our names, but it was a start.

Pisceon snarled, gliding up from his swaying chair, his cobalt tail flicking sharply as he disappeared into the gardens. Damon excused himself and followed. I toyed with the seaweed salad on my plate as I watched him go.

"Don't worry, my brother will relieve him," Alexandros whispered into my neck, trailing one hand up my thigh to rest on the space where the heat was building.

I put down my fork and drained my glass of wine. "I think I'm ready to retire." I stifled a mock yawn, which turned into a little gasp as Alexandros intensified his gentle stroking between my legs.

"Each Mer kingdom can draw unique powers from the ocean within which it stands," Alexandros said, his hands on my hips, as he hovered before me on his fuchsia tail in my expansive stone-hewn chambers. "Those powers will also be channeled into lovemaking."

I angled my chin up at him. "If you breed with another kingdom, do you get both kingdoms' powers?"

Alexandros let out a low chuckle. "You'd like that, wouldn't you?"

I flushed.

The merman shook his head. "Sadly, no, that is rare. One kingdom's power normally manifests as the strongest. When my hair turned purple, I knew I would have the powers of Thálassa."

"Why *is* your hair purple?" I asked, reaching up and twirling a strand between my webbed fingers.

"Long ago, our ancestors used the hypobranchial glands of murex sea snails to create a purple dye for their hair. Over time, the color became part of our genetics. Now, where were we?" Alexandros slipped his hands around my lower back, drawing me close against him. "While my cousins in the Neptūnus Kingdom can manipulate the waters to offer pleasure..."

A flutter danced in my throat. No wonder Morgana was hooked on that merman.

"Our skills are different," he said. "We can manipulate the saltwater of the Mediterranean for healing and store magic within ancient artifacts, but above all, we are the keepers of pleasure. Pleasure is our magic." Keeping one hand on my back, he ran his fingers lightly up and down my arm, and I felt it—a tingling rush, unlike anything I'd ever known. "I haven't used this on you yet because it would have overwhelmed you, but I think you are ready now."

"How does it work?" I asked as he continued to trace his fingers down my arm, my skin quivering beneath his touch.

"Lie on the bed," he ordered, releasing me and gliding backward as he gestured to the ornate bed in the corner of my room.

I crossed the space, swallowing against the heat already pooling between my thighs from the lingering sensation of his touch.

He drifted toward me. "Now, close your eyes."

I let them flutter shut as Alexandros floated on his magnificent purple tail beside the bed.

"Take my hand," he said, guiding my palm to his wrist and curling my fingers around it. His skin vibrated beneath mine, radiating with the same pleasure-laced power he'd shown me before. "Place it where it feels good."

I bit my lip, slowly guiding his vibrating hand toward the area between my legs where the arousal was pooling. Unfurling one of his fingers, I pressed it into the space, whimpering immediately as its quivering magic pulsed into my flesh.

"That's it, bella, use me," he breathed.

I thrust his vibrating hand deeper, writhing and moaning with his touch. I'd never felt anything like this; the sensations traveled through my body in waves as I thrashed on the spongy bed, under his spell. I lost all my inhibitions, shoving his hand lower and letting his webbed fingers enter me as my hips rocked with the pleasure.

Heat surged from the space below my navel, wrapping around me, snaking up my back to culminate in the space above my shoulder blades.

My wings.

Tears bled from my eyes as I screwed them shut, forcing those monstrous things away.

"Are you okay?" Alexandros's voice was etched with concern.

I nodded through clenched teeth, pushing his hand further into me as the burn of skin stretching faded and my wings retreated.

My breathing steadied as I focused on Alexandros's touch and the pleasure coursing through me.

I pushed his fingers deeper and deeper still, until a gasp escaped my lips. I cried out, more tears streaming down my cheeks as the sensations compounded into a burst of oblivion.

Chest heaving, I opened my eyes to find Alexandros floating over me, his lavender hair drifting in the swell. He pulled his webbed fingers from inside me and sucked on them, a grin tugging at the corners of his mouth.

"And that," he said, "is how it's done in Thálassa."

32.

MORGANA

The rising sun was decorating the Mediterranean in pink and lilac hues as we picked our way over the arid grasses and scattered terracotta bricks to the crumbling church.

The old man lifted his head as we approached, his eyes alight. "You freed Poseidon's most prized possessions. Well done—you have proved your cunning and strength. Many before you have failed, assuming he wanted riches."

"Yes, well, I'm not many men." Finn gave a hard laugh, adjusting his stance.

I rolled my eyes. Something about this old man seemed to bring out the prince in him.

"But can you prove the strength of your mind?" The man rubbed his leathery hands together, looking between us, and my stomach hollowed out. If the dream ceremony had taught me anything, it was that I had no control over my own mind.

"There's a cave carved into the stone at the caldera's edge. Enter and bring me what lies within the chest to determine if you are truly a descendant of the god."

I pulled myself upright, chin high. "Do you *have* to be related to Poseidon to claim this box?"

The old man's eyes darted between us. "Yes, my dear, that is correct."

Great. Just great.

I crossed my arms, eyes flicking to Finn, who was watching me with a smug grin. Gods, I wanted to smack him.

Stavros's touch still clung to my skin as we wove through the crush of tourists back toward the villa, but so did the memory of Finn's lightning forking through the club as chaos ensued.I glanced sideways at him, and my insides tangled.

"We'll need to wait until sundown to look for the cave so you can use your Selkie coat." Finn shaded his eyes, gazing past the whitewashed houses to the glistening aquamarine sea beyond. "What do you want to do until then?"

My jaw flexed, words caught behind my teeth. "I'd prefer to do something on my own. I'll meet you at the villa before sundown."

Finn observed me for a moment, brows drawn. He was wearing a tank top and jeans but still had the leather cuff on one wrist. Then he shrugged. "Suit yourself, shifter. Just try not to get into trouble."

I left him by the stone path that wound down to our villa from Oia's bustling shop-lined strip and set off alone, the winter sun still blazing against the back of my neck.

I clenched my fists as anxiety seeped through me. Two tasks remained, and I was trapped working with this man who'd done unspeakable things. I hated how his smirk made my body run hot and cold, those stupid cuffs he'd taken to wearing everywhere, the way he called me shifter. I didn't trust him. I needed to clear my head, shake off the anger of my foiled plans, and refocus on the task ahead.

Soon, I found myself in one of the gift shops. It was a sea of blues and whites. Dream catchers hung from the roof. Paintings of the iconic Santorini houses leaned against the floor and littered the walls. There were snow globes with donkeys in them, and little bottles of ouzo. I grimaced, glancing down at the donkey tee and parachute pants Finn had bought me—my only option when I got dressed this morning. I looked the part in this store.

An old woman with gray-streaked hair and deep smile lines around her eyes appeared. "Protection from mati?"

"Excuse me?"

"Mati—the evil eye." She held up a silver bracelet, its bands threaded with tiny crystal eyes. The irises were blue stones, and the pupils were black.

I spun on the spot, startled to see the same design everywhere. The eyes stared at me from dreamcatchers, glinted in jewelry, shimmered in blown glass, and were painted into canvases.

"To ward off jealousy." She rattled the bracelet in my face. "I'm sure a pretty girl like you could use it."

"I don't know if I have any money." I unzipped the hideous fanny pack and found it stuffed with cash. Guilt flickered at the edges of my conscience—part of me hated accepting anything from Finn. But another part, colder, whispered that if he had killed my grandmother, then bleeding him dry was the least I could do.

"I'll take it, and can I grab a few of those sundresses?" I nodded at some pretty bohemian garments hanging from the ceiling.

She eyed me, chewing on her cheek before gathering a few dresses and the bracelet into a crinkling white plastic bag.

As I fastened the protection bracelet around my wrist, my thoughts drifted to the Battle of Ceruleus Templum—a war born of jealousy, a venom that spared no side. Perhaps the Greeks were right: jealousy was a slow poison, deadly to both the giver and the one it touched.

"Thank you." I smiled at the woman and then wandered out of the store.

"Efcharistó," she called after me.

Walking down the strip of shops, I toyed with my new bracelet. I passed a travel agency, its window lined with glossy posters—scuba diving, buggy hire, wine tours—until something caught my eye. *Akrotiri Tour.* The photo showed sun-bleached ruins and towering, dust-caked vases. I ran my fingers over it, and a flash of imagery consumed me.

The ruins vanished. In their place, vibrant terracotta buildings rose around a smiling Minoan sailor, his wife and young son at his side as they strolled through the thriving settlement. My breath hitched, and pain pounded my temples.

I winced, pressing a hand to my head—another vision. My empathic sight was strengthening, but for reasons I couldn't explain, it only ever showed me him—Manannán.

A bell tinkled as I strode into the store and forked out more of Finn's money from my atrocious fanny pack for the tour and a bus ticket.

A thirty-minute bus ride later, I stepped into the sheltering structure that now housed the ruins of Akrotiri, rubbing the goose bumps that had formed on my arms.

The entire site was tucked beneath a modern, light-filled roof to protect the ancient remains from the elements. It cast an eerie glow over this city that was frozen in time. Raised wooden walkways crisscrossed the dig site, allowing me to peer down into the layout of a once-thriving Minoan town.

"Around 1625 BC, the eruption suffocated the whole island in a thick layer of debris, around the same time the Minoans began to disappear from the pages of history . . ." a tour guide was saying.

As I walked along the tourist platform, a searing pain forked through my temple. I gripped the railing as the ruins disintegrated, and a vision unfolded. Manannán was dining with his human wife and child in a vibrantly painted house. Perhaps he had resided here thousands of years ago.

Another sharp twinge seared my mind, and the scene shifted. Manannán was in the tumultuous ocean as his son was torn from his arms, and then Manannán sank into the depths, his olive eyes burning red as he transformed into the God of the Drowned.

I stiffened, my heart pounding as the images faded, and soon I was back at the ruins of Akrotiri. Below me, crumbled buildings rose from the ash-packed earth. Ceramic jars rested in corners, cracked and half-buried, and the outline of staircases spiraled upward into vanished floors.

I had barely centered myself when, with another jolt of pain, the world swam out of focus, replaced by new visions of Manannán. This time, he sat slumped on an algae-covered throne within a towering stone fortress beneath the sea. His once-kind eyes burned with hatred, narrowed beneath drifting strands of dark hair. The golden hue of his skin had faded to a sickly pallor, and a sea monster twined its tentacles around the base of his throne.

I sucked in a breath as the vision morphed into Manannán on land with a beautiful dark-haired woman, and I knew immediately that it was Siana. Shivers prickled my skin as I watched them embrace on the windswept grass, teetering at the edge of a cliff above a churning sea. Perhaps somewhere in Scotland.

"I wish we could stay like this forever, amor meus." Manannán gently traced his fingers along the curve of her chin as they lay entwined. His dark hair was messy, as if her hands had just been tangled in it, and he wore a loose white linen shirt and black pants that clung to him in the sea breeze.

"This time with you is enough," Siana replied.

"Samhain, the equinoxes, the solstices—none of it will ever be enough. I curse the gods and their celestial games." Manannán raked a hand through his hair and pulled away from her embrace to settle splay legged in the grass, his eyes narrowing on the restless sea.

"Are you going to ruin what little time we have together as man and woman?" Siana wrapped her hands around his neck, kissing him until he softened and pulled her onto him.

My heart ached as the realization washed over me: Siana and Manannán had only been able to be together as man and woman when the veil between the living and the dead was at its thinnest.

The vision swirled to a glittering turquoise ocean and a dark rocky beach, presumably somewhere in the Mediterranean.

"You're spoiling our time together," Siana cried, reaching for her seal skin and holding it against her naked body.

Manannán strode up and down the beach, his brow furrowed. He was shirtless, wearing only black pants, and his bronzed muscles tensed as he moved. "It's killing me that Kyano is Mer royalty and the two of you can go to land whenever you like."

"I've told you we are only friends. It is you who is tearing us apart with this insane jealousy."

"Insane, am I? You try rotting in that bleak, joyless castle day after day, every bone in my body aching to be with you as a man. And all the while, you're up here, doing gods know what, while I wait . . . helpless until the veils finally let me walk above the seas."

"I spend time with you in my seal form."

"It's not the same, amor meus!" He rushed to her, running his hands down her curvaceous womanly form, taking in her full, dark-nippled breasts and then tangling his fingers in her ebony hair. "I just wish I could have this always."

Siana cupped Manannán's face in her hands, and his olive eyes softened as he looked down at her. Then they were tearing at each other, panting and gasping. She tore at his pants so his cock sprang free, and the two of them fell to the ground in a heated embrace.

There was a strange quietness in the air as the ruins materialized again, broken only by the murmur of other visitors. I leaned over a railing, drawing shuddering breaths and feeling oddly aroused.

Part of me felt guilty. My mind magic was still unrefined, and I could only summon visions of Manannán. Yet another part of me knew it mattered. I needed to understand what had driven the God of the Drowned to such jealousy—jealousy so all-consuming he'd waged war against Kyano, the Mer Prince of Ătlanticus.

But Kyano had been no different; he'd met Manannán in that battle with equal fury. So blinded were they by rage that neither had noticed Siana's lifeless seal form drifting above the bloodstained battlefield until it was too late.

I fingered the bracelet clasped around my wrist. *Protection from the evil eye.*

33.

MORGANA

Finn was pacing the villa when I returned, and he swung to me, exhaling in relief as I opened the door. "Where have you been?"

"Sorry—I got inspired to be a tourist."

"Well, I'm glad you bought some new clothes." He observed the bag of dresses in my hand, laughter dancing in his dark eyes as he scanned my donkey shirt.

"This lovely outfit you bought me will vanish when I put on my Selkie coat, and I'm not complaining."

He shook his head, still chuckling. "The shirt has kind of grown on me."

"I'll go get my things," I muttered, glancing at the sky, which had deepened with the shades of early evening.

A moment later, I stepped out in my fur coat, fastening my dagger over the atrocious parachute pants.

I followed Finn down the stone steps from our villa to his family's secret sea cave, and we slipped into the water. As we moved through the submerged passage, the water beside me thrummed as he dove, clothes shredding and disappearing, revealing his merman form. I watched the muscles in his back flex as he ran his hands along the rock face that opened to the sea, whispering his command.

My jaw began to tremble as I looked at him. Had anything between us ever been real? Or had it all been about doing his duty to the king? I guess it didn't matter now, because what his family had done was unforgivable. But once we'd claimed the box, I would confront him and get my answers. If he'd done what I'd suspected . . . then . . . then I'd kill him. I released a shaky breath, the thought sending a shiver down my spine as I paddled to catch up with Finn.

A gasp escaped my lips as the rock face shifted and the open sea unfolded before us, awash in pink and purple as the sun dipped below the horizon. The magic of my transition vibrated through my skin, and I slipped beneath the waves. My hideous outfit vanished, replaced by the sensation of magic twisting around me, revealing my sleek seal suit.

I dove beneath the crystalline waters alongside Finn, and we surfaced together just as the sun's final rays vanished. The sky had deepened to a dusky mauve, with the evening star gleaming against its velvet backdrop. We turned in the water, scanning the dark rocky cliffs of Santorini's caldera.

"All the old man said was that the cave was in the caldera. It runs the length of the island—it could take all night to find. Maybe even days." I let out a frustrated breath.

Finn rubbed his chin, water droplets falling from his muscular arm. "Yes, it does present a problem."

"Do you think magic calls to magic, like your family's sea cave and the runes?"

"It's worth a try." Finn swam to the closest wall of rock with a flick of his tail and swept his hands along the stone.

I followed suit, pressing my palms to the jagged rock of the caldera, concentrating on the spot where the sea met stone.

Nothing. I felt nothing.

We worked in silence. My insides were still twisted as I chewed over everything we'd been through in my head. Finn was brooding too, because that's what the merman seemed to do best.

After what felt like hours, night had deepened around us. My hands were raw from scraping rock, and my legs were aching from treading water. I chewed my lip, eyes trailing the endless caldera. "I wonder," I murmured.

"What?" Finn snapped his head to me, a muscle tightening in his brow. His mood had grown increasingly darker, suggesting he found this just as monotonous as I did.

"Well, when I visited Akrotiri today—"

"You did?" He shot me a quizzical look, but I waved him off.

"There was a sign for a beach *called* Caldera. Could it be that instead? If we've learned anything so far, it's that the old man likes to mess with us."

He pushed the hair out of his face. "The caldera *of* Caldera . . . It's worth a try. Nice work, shifter."

"Don't call me that."

"You never used to mind."

"Well, that was *before*—"

"Before what?"

"Forget it." I shot him a glare. "Let's go."

Caldera Beach lay on the opposite end of the island from Oia, but we made our way along the rocky wall, palms pressed to stone until we reached it. The bay was composed of ochre sand and framed by small cliffs that rose on either side, as if someone had bitten into the earth.

"Let's take a side each," I suggested, and Finn nodded.

The water lapped at my waist, a deep cerulean under the moonlight, as I pressed my hands into the cliffs on the left side of the beach. In the silver light, the rock glowed a deep, rust-red.

I pushed my aching palms into the stone over and over again. Nothing. I didn't even know what I was supposed to be feeling.

I reached a section where the rock face thickened and curved inward. Goosebumps prickled along my arms as I moved into the hollow, water sloshing at my waist. Pressing my hands to its rim, I eased forward, and a vibration began to radiate beneath my palms. I paused at what looked like solid stone until my webbed fingers brushed its surface, and my breath caught in my throat as the Runes of the Ocean shimmered to life.

"Over here," I called.

A splash sounded behind me, and Finn surfaced, diving in and out of the waves until he reached my side, slicking dark hair from his eyes as he took in the glowing runes.

"What do they say?" I asked, throat tight.

"To pass, you must face the shadow within," he said gravely. "Un intras asphere skios intos."

A chill skittered down my spine as he repeated the passage in the old tongue of the sea and the dark rock face shifted, parting slowly to reveal a gaping crevice.

"How do the runes work?" I wondered aloud as I watched the glowing symbols fade.

"When they were carved, they were imbued with magic. Reading the words in the old tongue of the sea awakens it."

My thoughts were interrupted by a melodic hum rising like a seductive Siren's song from within the dark cave, drifting out to swirl around us as if carried on the swell.

"That can't be good." I brushed my sopping wet hair from my face and felt for my dagger, now strapped against my hip.

"Remember, it's a test of the mind," Finn said, his brows furrowed as he observed the dark crevice before us.

"Right." I released my dagger and swam toward the doorway.

We moved cautiously into the cave, the water lapping against our torsos and emanating a low, whirring sound as if whispering. The entrance vanished behind us, swallowed by the rock, and we were alone in the darkness.

"You okay?" Finn's webbed fingers grazed the small of my back, but I flinched away from his touch.

"Look at the sea," I yelped as the dark, swirling waters ignited with bioluminescence. Whooshes and flickers of light hissed through the cave, dancing across the stone.

"Just keep moving." Finn's shaky voice came from beside me. The murky water shifted, becoming crystalline, the calm surface reflecting our likeness.

"*Finn.*" I froze as my reflection warped and a vision twisted to life around me. A version of myself appeared in the mirrorlike waters. My eyes glowed silver, arms outstretched, and I unleashed a torrent of magic across Drowned, Sirens, and Mer alike, turning them all to dust.

Fear rooted me in place as Skye and Edward disintegrated before my eyes. Edward's maroon uniform was all that remained after they'd dissolved into salt and sea. I had killed my friends . . . turned them to dust.

"No," I choked. "No!"

Then my grandmother emerged from the water before me, her once-beautiful eyes hollow and her face gaunt and gray. My chest tightened as I met the empty gaze of her lifeless sockets. The air caught in my throat. I couldn't breathe—

"It's not real," Finn whispered, shaking his head. "Don't let it consume you."

I squeezed my eyes shut and pushed forward through the water. When I opened them, my grandmother's face had vanished and we were once again moving through the dark cave, the churning ocean lapping at our sides.

I jolted as Finn cried out, recoiling as the waves around him shifted, swirling into the same reflective mirror that had taunted me. There he floated in his father's crown, a sinister smile curving his lips as bloodied Mer were dragged before him. His eyes were empty, his jaw set. When I appeared in chains at his feet, he didn't flinch as he commanded my death.

Finn lost his composure and shot water magic at the vision. "I will never become my father," he snarled, his beastly form overtaking his face and claws shooting from his hands.

The sighing tides swelled as more visions slammed into us like breakers.

My pulse hammered in my ears, and the ocean blackened before me, rot threading through coral and kelp. The Captain rose from the seafloor, his face mutilated by the Fisherman's mark. One eye socket gaped empty, the sea snake that had once filled it now gone. Whispers wound around me. *The girl who failed us all.*

I screwed my eyes shut and pushed through the dark waters. When I opened them, the vision had faded, but a new one was unfurling.

Finn, just a boy, tending to a menagerie in a seaweed glade. He'd patched a dolphin's eye, wrapped kelp bandages around an injured seahorse, and healed turtles, fish, and starfish in soft sponge beds. His expression held none of the darkness it carried now; it was alight with happiness as he sent a now-healthy stingray on its way.

A lump rose in my throat as King Neptūnus appeared. "What is this?" he thundered, lightning flashing in his eyes as he surveyed the glade.

"They were dying. I saved them," young Finn stammered. His boyish face was hopeful for a minute, as if his father might have been proud.

"You're a pathetic excuse for a son," the king spat. Lightning licked his arms, and with a sweeping motion, the glade ignited in white radiance. When the magic cleared, Finn's healing work floated lifelessly, belly-up in the current.

Finn was trembling now in the waters beside me as the vision morphed into the limp body of a purple-haired mermaid brought into the palace in his father's arms.

Abalone. Her throat had been slit, and silvery crimson blood drifted into the water from the wound.

"No," Finn rasped. "Mother."

The lifeless Abalone sat up, blood still streaming from her severed neck. "You failed me, son," she rasped.

Finn dry retched, his body convulsing in the water beside me. Tears ran down his cheeks as he summoned another surge of water magic to shatter the vision.

The more Finn fought the visions, the fiercer they became.

They were breaking him.

The imagery shifted to a new scene. Finn, a bit older now, was chained to the wall in a dungeon. I recognized it as the same one Edward and I had suffered in. His body was covered in welts—lightning welts. His father emerged in the doorway, a dark figure.

"You're weak, boy," he snarled, moving further into the chamber, surveying his son, his golden tail rippling in the lamplight. "You're the reason your mother is dead. You're always reading books, tending to your animals. If you'd been stronger, you might have protected her." Lighting erupted from the king, and fern-like red marks ruptured on Finn's body, opening into raw wounds as his father struck him again and again.

Finn roared at the vision. He was weeping now, his muscular chest shaking with each breath. The cave trembled as he sent lightning skittering across its walls.

My stomach tightened. I had to do something.

I grasped Finn's clawed hand beneath the dark water. "This isn't real," I whispered, but my voice cracked.

Finn couldn't hear me. He continued to cry out, lashing at the water around him.

"Finn!" I cupped his chin in both my hands, drawing his eyes to mine. His skin was pale, the jagged teeth of his beastly form still bared.

"Look at me." I cradled his face, searching the depths of his fear-stricken eyes.

Finn met my gaze, brows furrowed, damp strands of dark hair clinging to his forehead as he placed his clawed hands on my shoulders. I wrapped my legs around him to keep from drifting in the swell, locking eyes with him, anchoring us both and ignoring the visions hissing around us.

Finn's breathing began to steady as he stared back at me, his tail sweeping slowly beneath the waves. Gradually, the churning waters calmed, his claws and beastly form faded, and the visions and whispers dissolved into silence.

"Thank you," he said with a rough laugh as I unwrapped my legs. "I'd lost myself."

"Behind you," I cried as a slick round rock podium rose from the water, encircled by the swirling sea.

At its center sat a chest carved from barnacle-crusted oak and inlaid with gleaming brass. It shone wetly under the shifting light now filtering through from somewhere high above.

I reached for one of the handles, but as my skin met its metal searing pain lanced up my arm. A cry tore from me as I snatched it back. Dark blisters appeared where my palm had made contact with the box.

Heart pounding, I jolted away in the water, as black rot bloomed from my fingertips and spread up my wrist. An agony like nothing I'd ever experienced before shot through me, and angry welts blistered my skin, peeling back to reveal raw flesh beneath.

"W-what's happening to me?" I gasped, tears of pain bursting from my eyes as the disease traveled further up my arm.

"It must be cursed. You touched it, and you're not Poseidon's heir." Finn's expression was taut with fear.

"What?" That was all I could manage before I crumpled in pain. My heart rammed against my ribcage as terror curled in my gut.

The rot had made it to my shoulder and was creeping across my chest. It was going to consume me. I was going to die here, in this cave.

"Give me your hand." Finn lunged for me in a spray of water, grabbing my cursed palm in both of his. My mouth went dry as the disease began to spread across his skin.

He screwed his eyes shut, whispering in the old tongue of the sea. "Sōzō hos ti fractos."

"Wait, no. What are you doing?" I tried to pull my arm away, but he held me tight.

His magic flared as he kept my decaying hand clasped tightly in his. I'd seen him use this same power on the injured dolphin, but this was different—this time, he was fighting a curse.

Finn grunted, buckling with pain, as the rot began to abandon my skin, and crept into his.

"No," I yelled as Finn's jaw clenched. The veins in his neck bulged as he took it into himself, and his arm became blistered like mine.

Fear stole the air from my chest as all the black and violet corruption bled into him, leaving my arm clear. Only then did he let go of my hand, gazing at me with the same expression he'd worn after healing the dolphin, he let his magic erupt. It poured from his palms in threads of gold, swirling around the curse and battling with it.

A strangled sound escaped me. The curse was winning. He wasn't strong enough—

I reached for him, pulling him close despite the rot. As our eyes met, light wove through the darkness, unraveling the disease into dust, and with it, the silver cuff on Finn's wrist cracked open.

He recoiled, his bare underarm exposed for the first time. His dark eyes darted to mine, flickering with fear. Black veins snaked their way down the underside of his wrist.

My breath faltered. "The curse is still there?"

Finn's breathing was ragged. He shook his head. "No, it's gone, but I didn't mean for you to see this."

An ominous weight settled over me. I didn't want to accept its truth, but Finn shook off my gaze, reaching for the box. He unsheathed his dagger and raised it above the chest as he flung back the lid.

It was empty.

"Fuck," he snapped, shaking the box before hurling it against the cave wall. It ricocheted and floated beside us in the water. "Someone got here first."

34.

MORGANA

It was still dark when we emerged from the cave of visions, though dawn's first glow tinged the horizon. We'd been in that cave the whole night, yet it had only felt like a few hours.

We swam silently toward the passage leading back to Finn's villa, the chest floating between us. Its emptiness weighed on my mind like a stone.

The darkness the visions had evoked remained with Finn. His brows were drawn, and his jaw was tight, muscles standing out as his tail beat against the water.

I observed him from my peripheral vision, everything I'd learned in that cave burning in my chest.

As the whitewashed villas of Santorini rose from the towering rock face above us, Finn ran his hands over the stone, chanting under his breath in the ancient tongue of the sea. The Runes of the Ocean glowed, revealing the hidden doorway to the cave that led to the villa. He left it open so we could still see the sky and waters beyond, waiting for the moment I would change back.

Exhaling slowly, he swept his dark hair from his forehead as he pressed his back against the cave wall. His tail flicked beneath the surface, keeping him afloat. I leaned into the wall beside him, my webbed feet treading water beneath me.

"What are those veins on your wrist?" My chest constricted as I asked the question that had been plaguing me since the cave. I feared the worst, but I didn't want to believe it.

Finn was silent for a moment before he blew out a shaky breath. "I think you already know."

"The Shadow?"

He nodded.

Icy hands gripped my heart as the weight of the realization bent the world around me. "But the prophecy. If it's in Poseidon's Box, it can save you, and we only have one task left."

"If the old man accepts the empty chest."

"And if the prophecy—or some other cure—is not found . . . how long will you have?"

"Maybe a year. If I'm lucky, two." He blew out another breath. "But as the disease progresses, I would need to stay in the Sānitātem just to remain alive, and frankly, I'd rather take my own life."

Biting the inside of my cheek, trying to stifle the lump in my throat, I glanced sideways at Finn, his dark, soaked hair slicked back and the tattoos across his chest stark against his skin. An unexpected ache bloomed in my chest, but I quickly shoved it down. This man was my sworn enemy.

Through the cave entrance, I could see the milky glow of dawn spreading across the horizon, and the magic of my transition susurrated across my body.

The moment my human form returned, I spun to face Finn. "Don't worry, we will find the prophecy." I rested my hand on his inked forearm, my gaze tracking the pale scars beneath the designs. The wounds his father left him for being a boy with a heart who cared about animals.

"Yes." He put his hand on mine and gripped it, but his eyes were filled with sadness.

I quickly pulled back, lowering my gaze from his. It found his sculpted chest, and I noticed the heart tattoo that he'd gotten just after I'd fled the Neptūnus castle.

"What's that tattoo about anyway?"

"My true love for you?" He deflected with a sarcastic eye roll.

I gave him a playful shove, grateful for the chance to lighten the mood, which had grown so heavy. But not before I caught it—a flicker of something darker crossing his face, the same shadow I'd seen when my eyes landed on his scars. It made me wonder if the new tattoo had something to do with his father.

My damp coat hung heavy as I climbed out of the water and turned away, allowing Finn to transform and slip into the clothes he'd left at the water's edge.

The sky was blushed with the deep purples of early morning as we hauled the empty chest up the winding stone steps to the villa.

"Let's get a few hours' sleep, then take it to the old man," Finn said as we entered.

We set the empty chest on the floor and stood silently for a moment, watching as water pooled around it. Both of us were lost in dark contemplation. Finally, Finn sighed and strode down the hallway to his room. He paused at the door. "Good night, shifter," he murmured.

"Good night," I said, offering a small smile. For reasons I was too tired to try to understand, I didn't mind him calling me that anymore.

Exhaustion settled deep in my bones, and my eyes were heavy as I tossed my damp coat onto the bedroom floor. The moment my body hit the soft bed, I was asleep.

A muffled cry echoed through the villa, and I sat bolt upright in bed. This time, I knew I'd heard something.

Finn.

I sprang up, tossing the sheets aside. Pale morning light was filtering in through the curtains. I couldn't have been asleep long.

I swung to the door, then, realizing I was naked, scrambled on the floor for my sheet, which I wrapped around myself. The sound came again, filled with pain and terror.

I tore across the hall and flung open Finn's bedroom door. He lay writhing on the bed. The curtains had been drawn to block out the daylight, but the lamp cast a soft glow across his body. He was stripped to his jeans, his chest slick with sweat as he clutched his bare wrist to his chest.

"Finn?"

"Go back to bed," he tried to say casually, but his face was distorted in unmistakable pain. He writhed again, tossing his arm outward, and I saw the veins clearly; they were alive, snaking up his forearm.

"The Shadow!" My stomach hollowed out as I rushed to kneel beside him.

He nodded through clenched teeth, a shudder of pain contorting his features. His eyes rolled back as he arched off the bed, every muscle rippling with the tension of agony.

"Does this happen often?"

He shook his head, sweat beading on his brow. "Only when the veins grow. It usually happens when I'm run down or have been drawing upon a lot of magic."

"Because you siphoned the curse from my arm," I breathed, my face blanching as I brushed my fingers across his forehead. He'd known it would cause the veins to grow, yet he'd used his magic to save me.

"It doesn't last long. You should get some more sleep." The tattoos in Finn's chest flexed as he drew sharp breaths, his body convulsing with another wave of pain.

"I'll stay." I settled on the floor, leaning over to push his damp hair from his forehead.

Finn sank back into the pillows, one jean-clad leg cocked and the other straight, his abs rising and falling with rapid breaths.

"May I?" I reached for his wrist, and he tilted his chin in assent.

His hand trembled in mine, but his pain seemed to ease as I traced the veins with gentle fingers. Three main arteries branched like roots beneath his skin, each sending out thinner lines that darkened before fading into flesh.

The ache that had been gnawing at my chest since I'd realized he was dying flared, and all the feelings that had been twisting in my gut the entire journey burst free in a single, shuddering breath. "Finn, did you kill my grandmother?"

Pain, fear, and something like sympathy flickered across his face. "No," he said quietly.

"I-I don't believe you." My lower lip trembled.

He said nothing, just continued to survey me with a sad expression.

"Show me!" Tears blurred in my eyes as I squeezed his hand, willing a vision to come. But there was only darkness—the same swirling shadows that always met me when he released his shields. I let go of his hand, my brow furrowing with emotion.

"This . . . this is why you told me you hated me?" Finn stilled and his dark gaze swept my face.

I nodded, chewing on my lip. "When I touched the box and the rot spread through me, why didn't you just take it and let me die? Then you could have had the prophecy all to yourself."

His brows hiked up, and he opened his mouth and then shut it. "Honestly, is that what you think of me?"

I didn't reply, forcing down the lump in my throat.

"I would have let that rot consume me if it meant keeping you safe." His face had a light sheen of sweat, and then he buckled, another agonizing cry tearing out of him.

I leaned closer to him, brushing my hand across his forehead.

His voice cracked as he whispered, "I'm so sorry you lost your grandmother."

Tears sprung from my eyes, and he reached for me, wiping them off my cheeks with his thumb.

"I'm sorry about everything." He shook his head, onyx eyes reflecting the lamp light.

I gripped his hand, holding it tight as his frame tensed with another wave of pain. Eventually, his breathing steadied, eyes fluttering shut.

After some time, his gentle exhale alerted me that he'd drifted off. I was still holding his hand, so I laid it across his chest, which was rising and falling with each breath.

I stood, surveying the sleeping man, his dark hair strewn across the pillow, lips slightly parted. Untangling the twisted sheets, I pulled them over him.

As I crept back to my room, something buried deep within me stirred. Finn hadn't killed my grandmother. I exhaled. Still, I had the distinct impression he was withholding information about other things. Were the veins creeping up his wrist punishment enough to excuse the secrets he kept? Maybe. I wasn't sure.

One thing I knew for certain—he loved me. He'd used his magic to save me instead of taking the chest for himself, even though it was killing him.

I wanted to trust him despite not having all the answers. But maybe that's what trust really was: choosing someone, even in the dark.

My heart clamored as I climbed back into bed. I hoped the empty chest would be enough to fulfill the second task and grant the third.

35.

SKYE

There was a soft knock on my chamber door, and I flung it open, biting my lip, expecting to see Alexandros. Instead, I found Layla and Porphura.

"We are taking you to the market to get everything you need for dream weaving." Porphura giggled, grabbing me by the wrist and pulling me from the doorway.

"Everything I need?" My brows kicked up as I followed the two of them down the stone steps to the throne room.

"Yes." Layla waved a hand, her gold bracelets jangling. "You can't practice a dream weaving ceremony without the proper priestess attire."

"Wait." I stopped in my tracks, and both mermaids swung toward me. "That all sounds very serious. I'm curious about dream weaving, but I don't know if I want to be a . . . a priestess."

Porphura gave a sharp snort, her indigo tresses rippling with the motion. "Don't get ahead of yourself, honey. Becoming a priestess takes rigorous training, but at least you can start by looking the part."

I remained frozen, my stomach knotting as her lips curled into a devious grin. "If you're worried you will no longer be able to stroke my brother's tail, Agápē is the goddess of love. Her priestesses are encouraged to be sexually adventurous."

I flushed but trailed Layla and Porphura across the patio, its waters lit by sunlight from high above, where the king and queen sat breakfasting with Edward.

"Good, my girls have found you." Queen Peisinoe surveyed me from her abalone swinging chair. "They will help you get everything you need for tomorrow's practice ceremony."

I nodded, then drew my gaze to Edward. "Do you want to come?"

"I'd rather spend the day in the library. Only if that's okay?" A blush crept up his neck as he looked at the king and queen.

"My boy," King Proteus boomed. "You are our esteemed guest. Our library and its books are yours to visit when you wish."

"You'll love our village. It is the most beautiful of all the Mer shopping quarters." Layla laced her fingers through mine and gently squeezed as she pulled me after Porphura's flickering purple tail.

I waved over my shoulder at Edward, who was still beaming from ear to ear.

Layla hadn't been lying: the Thálassian shopping village was a wondrous place. Nestled in shallower sun-dappled waters close to the eastern coast of Sicily, the stalls bloomed around a central piazza. Mer eateries crafted from pale limestone lined the edges of the square, their balconies adorned with potted sea plants. Winding streets snaked between them, forming an intricate network of shops. Each street was marked with a blue-and-white tile signed with the Runes of the Ocean. Above all, the piazza's bell tower stood watch, chiming every hour, its toll echoing through the waters.

"Let's do something fun first." Porphura swung toward us with a flick of her purple tail, hazel eyes gleaming.

I shifted nervously from foot to foot, dragging my eyes over the bustling space, where Mer moved in colorful droves.

Layla raised her brows. "Have you ever been to a high-end Mer boutique?"

I shook my head.

"You're going to love it," Porphura cried, yanking me toward one of the lanes.

Elegant shops with smoothed sand façades lined the path, each with an arched doorway framed in gold. Algae and small sea plants still clung to the rock in places, but it was well groomed.

"We enjoyed the human shops on Taormina and Santorini so much that we replicated them in our kingdom. Perhaps this will help you feel less homesick." Porphura grinned, waving a webbed hand at the stores.

An ache thickened in my chest as I surveyed the high-end Mer boutiques. There was glimmering signage—etched in Runes of the Ocean— above each entrance, and in front of some stores, lilac-tailed Thálassian guards paced.

"And we can put things on the palace tab . . ." Layla hooked her arm through mine. "One of the perks of us both being princesses."

She and Porphura pulled me toward one of the fanciest stores. The Mer guard at the door bowed his head and opened it, allowing us to drift inside. Behind the crystal-clear glass, mermaid mannequins spun slowly in the current, modeling the latest jewelry, headdresses, and chains that could be draped across the hips to hang down over the tail.

Beautiful harp music floated through the boutique as a young mermaid attendant drifted forward, gesturing for us to sit on pale sponge couches before a table laid with goblets of wine.

Porphura pulled me down beside her, her purple tail curling along the edge of the couch. On my other side, Layla lounged on her belly, propped on her elbows, her long braids rippling down her back.

"Look." Porphura wrapped her fingers around my wrist and used her free hand to point to the back of the store, where Mer tailors and jewelers were crafting new designs before our eyes.

My mind slipped into a memory of pacing back and forth before Parker's house—how I'd almost gone back to a man who had cheated on me and tried to kill me, all because he had bought me designer clothes. A guilty nausea formed in the pit of my stomach, and I shrugged off Porphura's gentle touch.

"I don't think I need anything." I shook my head. "I have enough jewels in my room."

"But that's no fun." Porphura crossed her arms, lips pursed in mock displeasure.

"Let's have a wine at least." With a swish of her golden tail, Layla shifted into a seated position, her fins curling around the couch as a grin played on her lips. She handed each of us a chalice. "To enjoying freedom before war."

My insides remained in knots, but I raised my glass to the two beautiful mermaids sitting on either side of me.

A few hours later, arms stuffed with shopping bags, cheeks glowing, and mouths sticky with Mer candy and wine, we finally found ourselves back in the piazza before the laneway of shops dedicated to the Agápē, the Goddess of Love. The lane unfurled before us like a ribbon of rose-hued sand, winding through an alcove hung with pink bioluminescent lanterns. The water here was warmer, tinged with a scent of sweet salt.

My mouth fell open as I surveyed the shops, perfumeries, Mer jewelers, tailors, silk-weavers, and poetry scroll shops, all trades dedicated to the art of love.

"Wait, is that a . . ." I caught Porphura's wrist as we passed a store, its windows lined with glowing potions and coral items of different shapes. Inside, the walls were decorated with artists' impressions of Mer and Sirens engaged in what seemed to be acts of lovemaking.

Porphura bubbled with laughter. "It's a store for pleasure items, yes. But I doubt you'll need anything from their shelves when my brother is warming your bed."

I felt a blush bloom across my skin.

Layla gestured to the next shop, where mermaids and mermen sat at round tables, throwing each other nervous smiles. "A dating cafe."

"Okay, I think I like this Agápē." A smile toyed on my mouth.

We reached the end of the lane, where a templelike structure loomed, nestled in an alcove tiled with rose-colored stone. Ribbed pillars rose to meet a square roof, a domed crown behind them. The magnificent building glowed with a pinkish hue, as if bioluminescent algae dwelled in all its crevices.

"The priestess store." Porphura drew me to a stop before it. "Well, it's not technically a store, because you don't *buy* the clothes—you must be worthy."

My breathing quickened. "You never said anything about that."

"We'll meet you back out here." Porphura pushed me toward the entrance before letting Layla pull her away, the two of them drifting hand in hand back down the lane of lovers.

Inside the temple, translucent cloaks hung from Mer and Siren mannequins crafted from stone. There were deeper-toned garments as well, dusky blues, inky purples, and stormy grays adorned with the Runes of the Ocean, scalloped hems, and veils that drifted in the swell.

Shelves of accessories glistened: coral circlets, bunches of bioluminescent flowers, bracelets of what looked like bone, as well as an assortment of balms and elixirs. A blessing area at the back of the temple allowed priestesses to pray or meditate beside a pool of pearlescent water on sponge cushions.

My spine went rigid as I took in the space, heat rising at the back of my neck as a wave of unworthiness washed over me, making me want to flee.

"Daughter of Agápē, I have been expecting you." A priestess in a flowing cloak, her silver-painted lips and dark eyes serene, glided forward and took my hands in hers. Her aquamarine scales matched mine, though where I stood on legs, she drifted forward on a tail.

I flushed, casting my eyes over the nearest priestess mannequins, tall and elegant, carved into marble. "Queen Peisinoe . . . erm . . . sent me here to get some things for dream weaving."

"Do you need to accommodate wings?" The priestess raised her brows.

"What do you mean?" I asked, the tightness in my gut strengthening its hold.

"Some of us are blessed with tails, others with legs, and a few with wings. Wings are rare, though—they manifest only in the most powerful High Sirens." She surveyed me thoughtfully.

A throb pulsed down my spine, a reminder of the skin-splitting agony I'd felt as those feathered structures tore free from my back. I chewed the inside of my cheek and shook my head. "No, I don't have any wings."

The assistant leveled me with a long stare, and my heart climbed into my throat, but after a moment she flicked her tail and retreated to find my items.

While waiting for her to return, I dragged my gaze to the vaulted frescoes on the ceiling, artwork spanning the inside of the temple's domed roof. Sealife clung here and there in places, but I could still make out the imagery. A woman with dark cascading hair was fleeing down the curve of a golden beach. Her body twisted in motion, hips torqued, one arm flung forward while the other curled to shield her ribs. Her skin was streaked with blood, and from her shoulder blades, two jagged stumps glistened where her wings had been torn away.

Behind her, a man draped in darkness lurked. His face—half in light, half in shadow—wore an expression of remorse. In his outstretched hands, he held her wings, aqua and white feathers tinged with smears of crimson.

The background swirled with divine allegory: clouds shaped with faces of sorrow or indifference watched from the heavens. In the lower corners, cherubs with hollow eyes fluttered, and on the sea's edge, the tide curled in like hands, reaching for the woman.

The fabric of the priestess attendant's cloak brushed my arm, drawing my attention from the painting. "When you tear away a creature's wings, do not be surprised if they never return to you," she murmured, gazing at the roof.

"I-is it the story of Agápē?" A lump lodged in my throat.

The priestess nodded. "She fell in love with a human king, but he began to resent the Siren goddess because she had more power than he ever would. One day, he saw her bathing at the beach, her wings splayed, and it was more than he could handle. He took his dagger and carved them from her back, and she fled back to the ocean."

Power vibrated through me, the space between my shoulder blades burning with the ache of wings longing to break free, but I forced it down.

"What about her wings? Did they ever grow back?"

The priestess shook her head. "No, they never did."

"And what about the king? Did she ever seek her vengeance?"

"She didn't need to. When the man's rage subsided and he realized what he'd done, he cried out for her, begging her forgiveness and asking her to return. He went mad with the pain of it all and slit his own throat. They found him sprawled on the floor, the wings of the goddess laid out on either side of him, a bloodied knife in one hand and a deadly cut across his neck."

I clenched my jaw to stop it from trembling.

"Lying between her broken wings was the closest he'd ever come to touching the power of the love goddess who had once offered him her heart."

I rubbed shivers from my scaled arms and clutched my new priestess's cloak against my chest. The fabric was translucent, as if made from large stretched kelp fronds dyed purple.

"Thank you for this," I murmured.

"No need to thank me, child of Agápē. You earned it when she chose you."

I grabbed the rest of my bags from the doorway, carefully stowed the cloak in one of them, and stepped back into the laneway of love. I was ready to go back to the Thálassian palace, share a glass of wine with Alexandros, and then later . . . later, I would use his hands, his body, and his lips to push everything that had bubbled to the surface in the temple back down deep inside me.

Layla and Porphura emerged from the pleasure store, giggling and clutching more bags. I forced a smile as they looped their arms through mine, but as we drifted back to the palace, my mind was elsewhere, filled with the image of the Goddess of Love fleeing toward the sea, away from the man she'd given her heart to, the same goddess who had granted me a second chance.

36.

Searing pain rippled through my back as wings burst from my skin. I cried out, my body twisting to make room for them. Magic twined up my spine, and the urge to fly gripped me, but something was anchoring me to the ground. Glancing over my shoulder, I saw him—the man from the painting of Agápē—clutching my wings. My breath hitched. His face . . . his face was that of Parker, and his expression was laced with smarmy vindication.

My eyes snapped open, and I drew a shuddering breath. It had been a dream. Only a dream.

Alexandros lay on his stomach across my stone bed, his powerful back rising and falling in sleep. I was curled against him, my arms wrapped across the ridges of his spine. My cheek rested between his shoulder blades, and one of my scale-covered legs was draped over his tail.

I lifted my face from the merman's body, tracing a finger down his back muscles, which looked like they'd been sculpted by the sea, as the watery light of morning filtered into my chambers.

"Bella." Alexandros stirred, his purple hair drifting with the current. His fuchsia tail, curled to one side, rested just over the edge of the bed.

"Good morning," I purred as he shifted, turning to pull me into his arms.

The mattress had just enough give to cradle our bodies, the soft, porous sponge anchored to the stone frame so it wouldn't drift with the swell.

I trailed kisses down his sculpted chest, the fine dark hairs scattered along it teasing my lips. Heat built between my thighs as I reached the seam where his torso met the indigo scales of his tail. Wicked thoughts unfurled in my mind, visions of what we were about to do.

"I can't today, bella." He cupped my chin, guiding me away from his sensitive spot, his eyes searching mine.

"Why not?" My expression shifted into a teasing sulk.

"Damon and I must go to Italy and raise the Thálassian army." Alexandros rose from the bed and glided to the stone table at the room's center. He grabbed a seaweed tie, looping his indigo hair into a topknot, the muscles in his shoulders flexing with the motion.

I wrapped my arms about myself, chewing on my lower lip. "Will you be gone long?"

"I suspect a few days."

"Oh." My lip quivered. With him gone, I'd be left alone with my thoughts each night.

"Don't cry, bella." The merman drifted over, running his thumb across my chin and tilting my head back so my eyes met his.

"I'm sorry." I wiped a tear from my eye with my fingers . . . my *webbed* fingers. I would have nothing to distract me from this new body, these unfamiliar hands, and the things they'd done. "It's just, you've been a good diversion. I find myself not wanting to be alone."

"Hey," he murmured, threading his fingers through my hair before letting them drift to my shoulders. "You're a powerful Siren of Agápē. Don't ever forget that. I think training with my mother will be beneficial for you. As fun as it is"—he gave me a wicked grin—"you can't keep hiding behind pleasure and wine."

I sniffed back my tears and nodded, dragging my gaze to my new priestess's cloak, hanging from a hook beside the door.

"When I get back, we'll celebrate." Alexandros pressed a quick kiss to my lips, then glided to the door, throwing me a wink before slipping out and closing it behind him.

Fastening my new translucent cloak around my shoulders, I made my way to the temple of Agápē, where I was to meet Queen Peisinoe for my lesson in dream weaving.

Mer priestesses moved about the space, their hooded cloaks hooked about their shoulders. They billowed in the water as the mermaids went about their business, ensuring that bioluminescent offerings were placed in all the right spots.

I padded warily past statues of stone-eyed gods to the four basins in the temple's center, where a mosaic stretched across the platform—a beautiful Siren woman, presumably Agápē, rendered in many shades of blue.

Queen Peisinoe emerged from a cluster of priestesses, tossing back the hood of her purple cloak, which was identical to mine. Her dark hair floated behind her as she drifted to join me by the pool.

"Take a seat, my child." She gestured toward the stone steps leading to the pools, then sat herself, stretching out her long pearlescent-scaled legs, which glittered in the light.

"This place is so beautiful," I whispered, dragging my eyes over the stone pillars of the temple.

Peisinoe's expression held the trace of a smile. "Agápē valued beauty."

I gasped as another group of priestesses glided into the temple, carrying the lifeless body of a mermaid between them, a soft chant echoing from their lips.

"Do not be afraid," Peisinoe said, following my gaze. "Sirens are escorts between this world and the next. They brought this mermaid to me so I could help guide her onward. So few of us remain that a blessing into the afterlife has become a luxury."

Swallowing a gulp, I watched the priestesses place the body on an altar at the far end of the temple and begin to arrange glowing flowers around her.

"Come, I will show you." Peisinoe threaded her fingers through mine, leading me to where the dead mermaid lay.

The mermaid's hair was dark, her eyes haunted by purple, and her skin ashen in death. All around her, Mer priestesses were anointing her body with balms. An ache thickened in my throat. They'd hidden the black veins that laced every inch of her torso. This mermaid had died from the Shadow, and they were concealing the marks before sending her to rest.

One of the priestesses stepped forward, meeting Peisinoe's eyes. She nodded before moving silently away with the rest of her sisters.

Peisinoe let go of my hand, allowing her magic to radiate. "We ask Agápē to give our sister a peaceful passage to the afterlife." There was a sadness behind the Siren queen's eyes as she lowered her hands, still emanating power.

I caught my breath as the body before us disintegrated into the water with what sounded like a long exhale. Peisinoe kept her head bowed for a moment longer before retaking my hand and leading me back to the dais and the pools.

"What was that?" I asked, my throat still burning.

"She will be at peace now." Peisinoe stared at me thoughtfully before reaching over to lift my chin to better study my face. "Oh, the dream magic is strong in you."

"What will it allow me to do?"

"It allows you to grant dreams to others, as we did for Aigéan and Morgana, but it also lets you see their memories once you've been put to sleep."

"Like slip into their minds?"

"Yes, you can slip into the memories, desires, or dreams of others with intention." Peisinoe blew out a heavy breath.

"Is that how you saw Edward's mind?"

The Siren queen nodded. "But remember, this process is sacred and must not be undertaken lightly. Using your dream magic will leave you exhausted—mind, body, and soul—and you must always remember to call upon the goddess herself and offer your thanks afterward."

"What will we do today?" I asked, dipping my finger into the crystalline pool beside me, where the liquid curled around it.

Peisinoe plucked my hand away. "We won't be using the pools today. Instead, I'll show you how to access a memory. We'll perform the ceremony, and I will gift you one of mine."

I crossed my arms over my chest and nodded.

"First, you must make a blood vow." She took my hand, drawing a knife from a chest beside one of the pools and slicing a clean line across my palm.

I winced as crimson spilled from the cut.

Peisinoe dragged the blade across her own palm. "A blood vow cannot be broken, and you must ask the dreamer to make one to ensure the memory is uncorrupted and true."

She pressed her bleeding wound to mine, and a finely hewn tattoo appeared on the backs of our hands—a small heart.

I gasped, pulling my hand back.

Peisinoe smiled. "It will fade once I have given you my true memory and the blood oath is fulfilled."

With that, she pressed her bleeding palm to her mind, and a faint light radiated from it. "I'm going to place my palms on your temples. Keep your gaze locked with mine."

I nodded, and she knelt beside me, her scaled legs gleaming as she placed her hands gently on either side of my head.

"Now, you must call upon Agápē, asking her blessing to use the sacred art of dream weaving to access my memory, freely given."

"Please, Agápē." My voice wavered, and Peisinoe nodded in encouragement, her hands still on my temples. "Please allow me to access the memory Peisinoe wants to give me."

"Good. Now close your eyes," the queen purred.

I closed my eyes, and no sooner had I done so than a vision swam before them. A memory. Peisinoe's memory.

King Proteus, younger, smiled at her from across an opulent ballroom—somewhere in Thálassa, judging by the architecture. Merfolk danced and drank, a blur of scales and colors swirling through the room, but Peisinoe saw only the purple-haired man drifting before her.

The memory faded, the temple and Peisinoe, still kneeling before me, swimming back into view.

"And that was the first time I saw my husband." She smiled sadly, and my heart clenched as I thought of the veins on Proteus's neck, which had darkened in the short time we'd been here.

I thrust my hand to my eyeline and gasped. "The tattoo has gone."

She nodded. "Our bargain of ink and blood has been fulfilled because the memory I showed you was true."

My eyelids drooped, and I raised a hand to my temple. "I'm so tired."

"Yes," Peisinoe breathed. "You will have exhausted yourself."

Good. I wanted the magic to drain me, to tear through every aching part of me until I was so spent that, when I returned to my room alone, I would collapse into bed. No thoughts, no dreams, no feelings at all.

Peisinoe's eyes held the weight of understanding as she looked at me. "One of my priestesses will take you back to your room. But first, we must offer thanks to Agápē."

"H-how do we do that?" I stammered.

She took my hands in hers and met my eyes. "Thank you, Agápē, for granting us a dream."

"It's that simple? You just say it?" I scrunched up my nose.

Peisinoe squeezed my hand. "Do not underestimate the power of gratitude."

37.

SKYE

I didn't know how long I'd slept when I awoke in my chambers. Perhaps only a few hours, judging by the watery light about me, suggesting it was still day. I sat up, bringing a hand to my temple, then sank back down.

Weariness clung to me from the dream weaving, a heavy shroud that had settled deep in my bones. I stared at the ceiling, and thoughts began to creep in. Parker's blood on my hands . . . I shoved the sponge pillow over my face, but they kept coming. Aranare's grief-stricken face . . . the grotesque wings that had torn from my back before, I'd sliced into the flesh of Parker's throat.

I threw myself out of bed and grabbed the vat of Thálassian wine—refilled daily and left out for guests—turning it over in my hands. With an exhale, I set it back down.

No more hiding behind drink.

My breaths came ragged as I flung open the door to my chambers and rushed to Edward's room. I found him at his mirror, carefully combing his copper hair into its usual immaculate quaff. Relief coursed through me at the sight of his familiar face, a fleeting refuge from the storm of thoughts tearing through my mind like a flock of raging blackbirds.

He grinned, moving from his bathing chambers into the main space. "I'm just off to combat training."

"Oh." My face fell.

"Why not come along?"

I'd always hated sparring with Aranare, and the exhaustion from dream weaving still hung over me. Still, the alternative was to stay here alone with . . . with . . .

"I'll come," I said quickly. "But you know your hair will only get messed up during training, right?" I plastered on a grin, rifling through the items in Edward's bathroom to find a strand of seaweed to secure my ponytail.

We descended the expansive stone steps and entered the throne room, moving beneath the arch that led to the gardens.

"How are you doing with all this?" Edward asked, waving a hand over the carefully curated corals blooming in beds on either side of us.

Had he seen something in my expression? I bit the inside of my cheek as the thoughts I'd been avoiding surged forward, but I mastered a quiet laugh. "Now, *this* I don't mind." I gestured to the gardens.

"You know what I mean. Coming to terms with this new life can be awfully difficult. I know Morgana found it a struggle."

"It doesn't seem like it," I mused, thinking of the strength that seemed permanently etched onto her features.

"She endured quite a lot." Edward's brow furrowed. "Not only with Finn, but with the Drowned, and the mystery surrounding her missing father."

I exhaled a sea of bubbles. "Right, and I'm all torn up because I killed one lousy asshole who deserved it. Is that what you're saying?"

"Of course not. What I'm saying is you're not alone. Morgana and I were thrust into this world, albeit in different ways. We may feel lost and bewildered, but at least we have each other."

"Thanks, Edward." My voice softened as I leaned in, gripping his wrist. "Do you think you'll be any good in combat?"

"I'd rather spend my time in the magnificent library, but I suppose I'll give it a go."

I chuckled, looping my arm through his, the darkness retreating to the periphery of my mind.

Around fifty Thálassians had turned up for Pisceon's combat training, which was being held in an expansive open area not far from the castle, where the sand was arranged in turrets and drifts and hemmed by flowing bushes of seaweed.

"Pair up," Pisceon called as more Mer drifted into the glade. Glacies supported him from the sidelines, wearing her silver breastplates.

We lined up in pairs along the sandy seabed, and Edward and I became a team.

"Face your opponent!" Pisceon's cry carried down the line of Mer as he hovered at the far end.

I tightened my ponytail and turned to Edward.

When we were in position, I glanced along the row of Mer and a few Sirens. Many were wearing the purple sheen of the Thálassian army, their tails gleaming in uniform brilliance. Others were nobles and royals, Porphura and Layla among them. The purple-haired mermaid wore her ponytail like mine, while Laya's dark braids were knotted into a bun. Both gave me a friendly wave and a wink.

Pisceon swam up and down the line of pairs, his muscular brown arms folded over his torso, cobalt tail swishing. "These Drowned are not like anything you will have encountered. Mer blood fuels them."

A hissing and muttering traveled through the group.

"Mer drained of blood, floating lifeless in the Atlantic, while darkness spreads from Port Royal like a sickness. The Drowned march in silver-stained groups, rallying more to Manannán's cause and collecting our blood wherever possible." Pisceon's head was cocked in a beast-like tilt as he scanned us from end to end.

I glanced down at Layla and Porphura's faces, now grave and devoid of color.

Pisceon continued swimming up and down the line. Glacies remained to the side, arms folded over her breastplate, pale eyes narrowed.

"Regardless of their strength, the Drowned are ignorant and brutish." Pisceon's eyes flicked to Edward. "We can outsmart them."

"But how?" cried a young boy. He didn't look older than sixteen in human years.

"Our powers may be stunted, but we can contain them. We Neptūnus Mer can harness the currents, disorientating or trapping them in whirlpools of water. Thálassians' magic is less practical in combat, but the salt you draw from the Mediterranean can be used to blind them momentarily."

"Blind them?" A Mer somewhere down the line sniggered.

Pisceon swung to him. "Do not underestimate being prepared and resourceful, unless you want to end up drained and stamped with the Fisherman's seal." At this, he beckoned Glacies. "As you know, our friends in the Kingdom of Krumos in the Southern Ocean can draw steel from ice. When we visited them, we forged these."

Glacies came forward. Her long pale hair streamed in the water as she held up a crossbow and quiver filled with barbed arrows. Their metal tips shone in the watery surroundings as if forged from ice.

"We have a bag of these. Krumos will forge more and bring them to the summit. Today, we will teach you how to shoot. These arrowheads will be difficult for the Drowned to remove."

Glacies glided back, grabbed a woven seaweed bag full of weapons, and dumped them on the sand beside Pisceon.

"Porphura." Pisceon nodded at the princess. "Have all your skilled weavers make nets from kelp and bring them to the next training session."

She nodded.

He picked up the seaweed bag and began handing quivers and cross-bows to each pair.

"Can you be trusted, Drowned boy?" He held the weapon against his chest when he reached Edward and me. "We shall see," he said, handing it to me before moving on with a flick of his cobalt tail.

Glacies followed Pisceon, handing each of us a roughly-hewn metal breast plate.

"Remember, the goal is to hinder." Pisceon floated before us, just above the sandy training ground. His chest was tensed as he gripped his ice-hewn arrow and fitted it to the bow. "Your target is the Drowned, slippery and savage." Eyes flicking in Edward's direction again. "They won't fall from a single blow. You aim to pierce them with as many arrows as possible. I will demonstrate."

A guilty lump formed in my throat, and I swallowed it down. I hadn't mastered a single combat skill with Aranare; mostly, I'd sat pouting on the sidelines while he and Morgana clashed sticks.

Pisceon motioned Porphura forward and held a large dummy piece of sea sponge out beneath his arm. Porphura readied her bow, purple ponytail swirling, the hooked arrow left the weapon with a twang, shooting into the sponge between his chest and bicep.

"Excellent. One of you will act as the Drowned," Pisceon said, glancing between us, "while the other shoots the weapon."

My brows kicked up. "Isn't this a bit dangerous?"

"All the more incentive for you to get it right." Pisceon's lip curled as his gaze whipped to me.

Edward and I helped each other into the heavy breastplates and positioned ourselves as Pisceon and Porphura had, Edward with the weapon and me holding the target. Maroon uniform billowing in the swell, Edward cocked his bow. I stiffened, heart pounding, fighting the urge to run as the arrow hurtled toward me, but it pierced the sponge beneath my arm.

"You're good at this." I blew out a relieved breath.

Edward nodded at me. "Your turn."

I lifted the weapon to eye level, the breastplate was too large, and it creaked as I adjusted my stance, fingers fumbling for the trigger. My ankles knocked against each other, stirring up a cloud of sand as they shifted for leverage, and I toppled face-first onto the seabed.

"Again," Pisceon yelled. His fists were clenched, and veins rippled up his forearm as he swam from pair to pair, surveying us.

He drilled us repeatedly, moving through the formations. We shot the sharp instruments until every muscle in my body was stiff and my temples throbbed with a relentless headache. All along the line of Mer, arrows flashed and cries rang out when someone missed the target and nearly nicked their partner, but thankfully, the sponge cushions were large enough that no serious injury had occurred.

As the training wore on, Pisceon became increasingly manic as he recounted his battles with the Drowned. He glided back and forth before us, clenching and unclenching his fist.

"Let's go again," I panted, lifting the heavy weapon and handing it to Edward with a hiss as a ripple of pain tore through my aching limbs.

Edward released the arrow; this time, his aim was off, and it shot past me, landing with a thud in the sand before Pisceon. "Oh, bollocks." He turned crimson as Pisceon's head swiveled in our direction.

The merman surged forward, gripping Edward by the wrist and dragging him before the group. "Know your enemy," he cried.

Edward's eyes blazed. "Kindly get off me at once."

"Pisceon." Glacies rushed over, unfurling her friend's clenched fists from Edward's arm. "I think that's enough for today.

38.

MORGANA

Iawoke to warm sun streaming through my window; it must have been around midday. I rubbed my eyes, blinking through my exhaustion as everything that had happened the night before clawed back into my head.

Finn had saved me from a cursed death, only for the chest to be empty. I'd learned he hadn't killed my grandmother, but also that the deadly Shadow was slowly consuming him.

As we got ready and began the trek to the crumbling church, carrying the chest from the sea cave of horrors between us, we remained silent and solemn, both still weary.

When we arrived, Finn dumped the chest at the old man's feet, sending ochre dust flying. "It was empty!"

The man laughed, low and deep. "You faced the fear of fear itself and proved your mind unbreakable."

"Right," Finn grunted, raising a hand to shield his eyes from the bright sun.

My shoulders sagged in relief. We hadn't failed.

"Now for your final task." The old man clapped his hands. "A riddle."

I raised my brows. "Seriously?"

"Do not mock the power of words." He pressed his weathered fingertips together and surveyed me. "Words are the most powerful weapon on earth. They can make you feel invincible or destroy you, and sometimes they change the course of history."

My insides wound tight, and the prophecy swam into my mind. The sun had climbed higher, now beating down on us with blinding intensity, and drops of sweat ran down my spine.

"Let's hear it then." Finn crossed his arms. He had replaced the leather cuff, hiding the inky veins of the Shadow.

"I am born in pain, pressed and torn, my essence is crimson when I am drawn. I thrive in darkness, the aftermath of strife. I give men courage; I give men life. Solve the riddle and make a generous offering," the old man crooned, his eyes gleaming as he glanced between us. "You have until sundown." He threw back his head in laughter. His rickety chair groaned under the movement, and a stray black cat slinked out from the ruins, brushing against his legs.

"Let's go back to the villa and brainstorm. I can't think in this heat." I grabbed Finn by the wrist, tugging him away as the man continued to laugh.

On our walk back to the villa, we began sharing ideas. Finn strode beside me, his muscular arms on full display as he rubbed his chin in thought.

"'I am born in pain and thrive in darkness . . .'" I muttered, my new sundress brushing against my legs. "Perhaps it is some kind of demon."

"Yes, but it also gives men life."

"Wait a minute!" A manic chuckle escaped my lips as I stopped in the middle of the tourist strip, people jostling past. "It's blood."

Finn spun to me, his eyes widening with excitement. "Yes, *yes*! That works."

I hurled myself into his arms without thinking. "Of course—it was so obvious."

Heat crept up my neck as I realized this was the first moment of real affection I'd shown him on this trip. We stilled, caught in each other's gaze until he tangled his fingers in my hair and rested my forehead against his chest, the rest of the world fading away around us.

We had solved it. We were about to claim the box. Poseidon's Box. If it held the second half of the prophecy, I had kept my vow to the Captain and my grandmother. We would be able to stop the war and cure the oceans of the Shadow, restoring everything to its original state, as it had been before the curse.

I practically skipped over the barren land that led back to the ancient crumbling church where the old man sat with his skinny black cat.

"I'm sure he will be happy to be released," I said breathlessly.

"Wait a minute." Finn gripped my wrist, pulling me to a halt. "He said to make an offering, and the task was about generosity. Did you bring that dagger?"

I nodded, patting my hip.

"That was quick," the old man said, eyes alight with a hungry glint as we approached.

I reached for my blade, but Finn was faster. His hand slipped beneath my dress, retrieving it and slicing it across his left palm. Silver-streaked crimson dripped onto the cracked earth between the man's bare feet.

"The answer is blood, and here is your generous offering," Finn drawled, wiping my knife on the dry grass beside us before handing it back to me.

The small kitten crept forward, sniffing at the blood, but the man nudged the creature away.

"Can we have the box now?" I asked, squinting against the sun's glare, my sundress fluttering in the sea breeze.

"You may have the box," the old man croaked, "*if* you solve the riddle, and you have not yet done that."

My throat went dry. "It's not blood?"

"If it were, you would have the box, and I would be free. You have until sundown to try again." He sighed, and his little cat mewed in unison.

I squinted at the sun, which was now low over the ocean. At best, we only had a couple of hours left.

"Should we go back to the villa?" Finn asked, pressing his fingers against his wound to stem the blood.

"No, let's walk. I need to clear my head."

Instead of returning to the bustling tourist drive, I led us down the winding stone staircase, away from the path we'd taken before. Down and down we went, the afternoon sun glaring on the back of my neck as I replayed the riddle in my mind. Over and over again, I ran through the words. Each answer I came up with seemed logical at first, but it didn't tick all the boxes when scrutinized.

By the time we reached the water and the cluster of venues at the cliff's base, the sun had sunk lower still, and my ideas were becoming more and more far-fetched.

I scrunched up my nose and swung to Finn. "Do tomatoes grow in darkness?"

"Seriously?" He rasped out a chuckle.

"We have to solve it," I cried, my voice breaking. "We can't have gone through all of this not to."

"Let's sit down a moment, and get something to eat." He gestured to the closest venue, Dimitri's Taverna. Nestled along the water's edge, it had a wooden decking area sheltered from the sun, littered with white wooden chairs and tables with blue tablecloths.

"Ah, I love Greece almost as much as I love that sundress." Finn's dark gaze dragged over me as we sat down at one of the tables overlooking the ocean.

I turned my attention to the sea so he wouldn't notice my smile. Since I'd hugged him, something had shifted. He seemed lighter, the shadows gone from his expression.

Finn leaned forward onto his elbows and grinned. "What's better than ordering seafood while the salt of the Mediterranean embellishes our forearms?"

I squinted at the sea, hoping it could provide some answers, while he ordered fresh oysters, urchin caviar, and a tankard of wine.

"Do you want anything else?" He raised a dark brow at me.

"Just some of that Greek cheese . . . What's it called again?"

"And Saganaki." Finn threw an arm over the back of his chair as he addressed the waiter.

Once the man had left, I brushed my hair behind my ears and met Finn's gaze. "Okay, we need to focus."

"Focus isn't getting us anywhere. Let's drink." He lifted the carafe from the table and filled both our glasses.

"Really?" My brows flickered. "Have you given up?"

"I haven't given up, I'm just not going to let some old power tripper of the gods stop me from enjoying being in Santorini with a pretty girl."

Heat crept into my cheeks and ears as Finn tossed back his glass.

"War is coming, and I'm dying. The least you can do is have a drink with me."

I sighed and took a sip, my eyes narrowing. "As long as you don't stop brainstorming. We only have a few hours, and that box might contain a way to save your life."

"Yes, yes." He waved a hand, turning to call to the waiter, "We'll have another carafe of this red and ouzo shots for everyone in the house." The patrons around us cheered as he yelled the last bit.

My mouth popped open as I watched Finn. Gone was the moody, brooding merman with the furrowed brows. Maybe it was the relief of my discovering the truth about the Shadow that had done it. Or perhaps it was knowing this was his last taste of freedom before we returned to Thálassa, and then the summit, where he'd have to face his father and play the prince once more.

His dark eyes flicked to mine, and something inside me flared as I realized I still loved him. I'd told myself I didn't, that it was only hate I felt, but when I saw the Shadow's veins twisting under his skin like harbingers of death, I knew that wasn't true. I threw back another mouthful of wine.

One hour and four carafes later, Finn had embroiled the surrounding patrons in our revelry by buying wine and ouzo for the crowd.

"Dimitri, turn this up, would you?" he cried, edging out of his seat. He began to clap his hands slowly to the rhythm of the bouzouki, his fringe falling across his forehead.

I'd seen people dancing to this tune at weddings in movies and recognized it as "Zorba the Greek."

A devious grin appeared on Finn's face as he grabbed the nearest patron by the elbow, spinning the elderly woman into a circle. She flushed as he held her hand. The infectious beat filled the tavern, and the silver flecks in Finn's eyes sparkled with the music.

He drew the diners in one by one—young and old, tourists and locals alike—until a line of dancers snaked through the narrow space, arms slung over each other's shoulders.

Ba-da doom, ba-da doom, ba-da doom-doom.

The tune echoed through the space as the line of dancers swayed.

"How do you even know this dance?" I called over the music, clapping my hands to the beat.

"My mother was Thálassian, remember? And I've lived a long 116 years!"

Under Finn and Dimitri's tutelage, the group moved to the left in unison, a small, deliberate side step, the soles of their shoes barely touching the worn stone floor.

Releasing the patron at his side, Finn swept over and seized my hand, brushing his thumb over mine. A smile flirted with his lips as he pulled me to my feet. My protests dissolved into laughter as I stumbled into step beside him, my arm looping over his shoulders and then around the tourist who was jigging on my left.

Ba-da doom, ba-da doom, ba-da doom-doom!

The tempo quickened. Our fumbling feet grew bolder, stomping harder as the melody spiraled, and I floundered along to the rhythm.

The glow of the setting sun caught my eye, painting the waves beneath it in a rosy blush. It was almost sundown, and we hadn't solved the riddle. I looked over at Finn, who grinned back, his dark hair falling across his face as his slow side steps turned into quick bouncing hops with the heightening music.

Ba-da-doom, ba-da-doom, ba-da-doom-doom!

I let out a breathy laugh and surrendered to the rhythm, taking in the beauty of Santorini's famous sunset, the water glistening under its golden glow.

Who cared if we didn't get the box? We'd find another way.

The world had that blurry, magical feeling from just the right amount of wine mixed with sundown.

I froze, pulling my hands free from Finn's and the tourist beside me as a realization crashed over me.

"Morgana?" Finn stopped dancing, his brows furrowing with concern.

"Wine," I gasped.

"You heard the girl—more wine over here," he yelled over his shoulder to Dimitri.

"No, the *answer* is wine."

39.

MORGANA

The sun had almost set as we rushed back up the stone steps toward the church. I had a pitcher of red wine clutched against my chest, and Finn was on my heels. Despite the severity of the situation, I kept giggling when I stopped to catch my breath, unable to believe we'd solved it.

I was also drunk—very drunk.

Now that we were out of the frantic atmosphere of the tavern, the world was not only sparkling with the glow of liquor but also swaying. The sun sank lower, its last rays decorating the skyline, and Finn took me by the hand, dragging me up the terracotta cliff face.

"It's so beautiful." I hiccuped, sucking in air to calm my burning lungs and surveying the setting sun.

Finn blew out an exasperated breath. "Your new job is to do everything you can not to spill that tankard."

"Why is that my new job?"

"Because *this* is my new job," he grunted, slinging his arms around me and lifting me against his chest. His muscles tensed as he began the climb up the mountain.

"Don't drink it!" he scolded as I lifted the glass vat to my lips. "This test was about generosity."

I choked on a chuckle, and he rolled his eyes. "Luckily, I've had good practice carrying you."

There was only a speck of light on the horizon, and the world was seconds away from sinking into night when we reached the plateau on which the crumbling church stood. The old man raised his head and smiled as Finn put me down before him.

"The answer is wine," I slurred, setting the tankard on the dry earth at his feet.

The man licked his cracked lips as he raised the carafe. "I've been parched for so long," he rasped, before throwing back his head and drinking deeply of the crimson liquid.

The sun dipped below the horizon as the stray cat crept forward, weaving between our ankles with a soft purr. The man dropped the empty tankard, which shattered at his feet, and with a sigh of relief, vanished in a cloud of swirling dark smoke. It coiled around our ankles, wrapped itself around his old wooden chair, and condensed into a trembling black mass on the seat. It shifted and took form, solidifying into a silver box. Its metal surface was etched with raised spirals, and an opaque heart-shaped stone sat on the lid. Something about the design evoked a strange familiarity.

"The question remains: can you do what needs to be done to open it?" the old man's voice echoed from the ruins, followed by a laugh. Then the black smoke disappeared, and there was only the box on the chair and the crumbling structure behind it, now bathed in the evening's shades of indigo.

We'd done it.

I flung myself into Finn's arms, and he spun me around. When he released me, we both turned back to the box. I grabbed it from the chair and attempted to open it, but it was locked. "What did he mean by do what we need to do?"

I thought I caught a flicker of discomfort on Finn's face, but his lips tugged into a grin. "We need a key. Luckily, we've already found it. Inegar is bringing it to the summit."

That was it—the key with the matching design. I'd seen it before, in the pawnshop.

Mr. Inegar was King Neptūnus's most trusted advisor. A knot of unease formed in my stomach at the thought of his involvement, but I swallowed it down. My grandmother had spent her life chasing the prophecy that could save the Mer from the Shadow and perhaps even bring peace to the oceans. We had to see this through.

Walking side by side, we picked our way back up the uneven path toward the hustle and bustle of Oia, now a glittering mass of lights in the distance. I had the box tucked under my arm, my sundress rippling in the tepid evening air.

Finn rubbed the back of his neck and then met my stare. "It's our last night here. What would you like to do?"

"Why don't you show me your mother's nightclub?"

His whole face lit up, and my belly fluttered as he placed his hand on the small of my back.

40.

MORGANA

The Aegean club was on Perivolos Beach, and a wave of fear washed over me as the black Mercedes van pulled up and the thatched umbrellas of Aqua Inferno came into view. But Finn and I kept to the shadows, walking alongside the sighing ocean to avoid Stavros or any of his henchmen.

All the clubs along this beach had umbrellas, but The Aegean had white, decadent structures, while the rest were thatched. The wide parasols shaded luxurious daybeds, and behind them rose a tasteful ivory structure designed to echo the island's iconic windmills. Between two sleek bars, an indoor pool glittered under mood lighting. Quieter than Aqua Inferno, The Aegean seemed tailored to a wealthier, more refined crowd.

"After you." Finn unhooked a turquoise rope from one of the daybeds and gestured for me to sit.

I bit my lip, hesitating. "Shouldn't we ask first? Places like this usually have a minimum spend."

Finn's brows pulled together, and he gave me an exasperated look that said *I am a Mer prince, and I own this place.*

"Right." A grin tugged at the corners of my mouth.

I slipped into the daybed, which was also white, settling back against its cushions and taking in the dark ocean stretching and sighing before me, and above it, the twinkling stars. Finn left to get us drinks, and for the first time on this trip, I let myself absorb the beauty around me—the midnight waves, the silver sickle of the moon in the sky.

He returned with a bottle of rosé and two glasses. Kicking off his boots and rolling up his jeans, he dropped onto the sunbed beside me. He pulled his knees up, wedged the bottle between them, and handed me a glass.

"To wine," he said, smirking as he poured our drinks.

I giggled, clinking my glass against his.

"She used to love this place." Finn sighed, gazing out at the sea as he sipped.

"Your mother?"

He nodded.

"It's beautiful," I breathed, taking in the salty air and swilling my drink.

"I should come here more often." Finn leaned back. "But my father keeps me busy."

My stomach knotted at the mention of the king, but I pushed the thought away. I'd chosen to trust him. I turned onto my side and studied him. Lying there with the ocean breeze stirring his dark hair, he looked more at ease than I'd ever seen him before.

"So you never wanted to be . . ." I hesitated, picking my words with care—Finn always tensed when his past came up. "You never wanted to be . . ." I trailed off again. I didn't really know what I was trying to say. A mercenary, perhaps?

Finn tilted his head, eyes meeting mine. "With the animals?"

I exhaled a relieved breath. "Yes."

"When I was younger, I'd sneak off to that ocean glade and heal them—dolphins, turtles, whatever I could find. I used to have this strange gift, a way of connecting with them that other Mer didn't. They were my friends." He let out a hard laugh. "Then my father found out, and as you saw, he killed them all. After that, my gift went away, but it seems it's back now." He looked to the moon and back to me, the silver flecks in his irises alight under its pale glow.

We were silent for a moment as we both sipped our wine, and everything I had witnessed in Finn's visions wove its way into my thoughts. The kind boy he'd once been with his animals, and then Finn, a little bit older, seeing the body of his lifeless mother. I pictured the purple-haired Abalone in human form walking along this same beach many years ago when she was still alive. Perhaps my grandmother had come here with her.

"A-and you knew my grandmother?" My chin quivered as I turned back to Finn.

"Yes. Not well, but I knew her. Only in seal form. She left the Neptūnus Kingdom right before my mother's death."

"It must've been hard, seeing your mother like that," I murmured, the vision from the cave lingering in my mind. "Just hearing about my father—someone I never even knew—was painful. I can't imagine what you went through." I reached over and ran my hand along his forearm.

"My father always blamed me for her death. If I hadn't been so soft, I could have protected her. He made me into the warrior I am, but I guess it was too late." He sucked his teeth and smiled grimly.

"Finn . . ."

He turned to me, dark eyes searching my face, as the wind played with his ebony hair and tugged at his T-shirt.

"Your mother's death wasn't your fault." I slid my hand from his arm to his cheek.

Lines marred his forehead as he blew out a harsh breath. "My father was right about one thing. There is no room for emotions in a world so dark."

The sadness in his gaze cleaved my heart in two. "Don't say stuff like that . . . There is always light. Just look at the moon and the stars above us."

"It becomes hard to see beauty when I've spent a lifetime watching pollution spread like rot through my people, once vibrant reefs wither and die, and oil spills clog the lungs of sealife."

Tears filled my eyes as I stared up at him. "That's why we have to find the prophecy . . . I want to help."

"*You* are my light." His gaze dragged over my face.

I dropped my chin to my drink as my cheeks heated. "See, there you go, you're not unfeeling after all."

"I might be cruel to others . . ." He put his drink aside, taking my face in his hands, and dropping his forehead to mine. "but never to you."

We stayed like this, in charged silence our breathing quick and mingling as his thumb traced my cheek. Tingles exploded on my skin and I pulled away from him, focusing on the inky waves to gather my thoughts.

He gripped my hand, reclaiming my attention.

"I—" His expression was gentle, but a sadness moved through it.

My eyes darted between his but he said nothing, the moon light dripped into his gaze like mercury. My heart pounded as I waited for him to finish whatever he was trying to say. I waited and waited, but he didn't speak.

Finally, he released me, rubbing a hand over his jaw. "It's getting late. We should go back to the villa."

41.

MORGANA

It must have been almost midnight by the time we returned to the villa. We'd soaked up some of the wine with a souvlaki along the way, the silver box tucked securely under my arm.

Finn opened the glass doors leading in from the patio, and the pool glistened like polished polished jade under the golden nightlights.

I set the box on the kitchen bench, pulled a bottle of white wine from the fridge, and popped the cork. Grabbing two elegant glasses from a shelf, I joined Finn at the table by the pool.

"Tomorrow we return to Thálassa, and then we'll travel to Okeanós for the summit," he said, taking the drink I handed him. His dark brows were drawn as he looked out over the ocean.

The summit meant he would have to see his father, and so would I.

The air had chilled with the deepening of night, and goosebumps formed across my forearms.

Finn slipped inside and returned with the box, placing it between us on the glass table.

"Really?" I shot him an incredulous stare.

"We just secured the most valuable item in all the oceans. We should keep it close."

"I suppose." I rubbed more shivers from my arms.

Still standing, Finn took a long sip of wine and stretched, his back muscles rippling beneath his T-shirt before he yanked it over his head and tossed it onto the ground. He set his glass on the table, keeping his black jeans on as he dove into the pool.

"Come on, it's heated!" He pushed his wet hair from his forehead.

I grabbed the glasses and bottle of wine, placing them next to the pool before settling beside them and letting my legs dangle off the edge. As the heated water caressed my skin, the shivers began to fade.

Finn swam over, propping his elbows up beside me, his jean-clad legs stirring the water below. Droplets glistened on his neck and shoulders in the glow of the underwater lights.

I sipped my wine, observing him with curiosity. "You didn't grow a tail?"

He snorted out a laugh. "I can control my transformation—I don't go sprouting a tail whenever I touch the water."

My cheeks flushed.

He edged closer to me, his dripping left hand sliding up my right thigh, stopping at the hem of my sundress. "Did I mention how much I like this dress?"

Heat pooled above my navel and spread to the space between my thighs as my mind was consumed with images of the muscles in his body pressing against mine, the perfect length of him, and how good it would feel to have him slide inside me again. I swallowed hard as I met his dark gaze.

"Did you know the moon was once a planet called Theia?" Finn gestured to the sky, then let his other damp hand rest on my left thigh.

I shook my head, glancing at the gleaming sickle above us. He increased the pressure of his touch, digging his thumbs into the soft skin on the insides of both my thighs.

"Theia and Earth collided, and after that cosmic collision, the moon was ripped from the debris, a heart plucked from the chest of two unified beings." Finn circled his thumbs in wider arcs, and my skin prickled as he positioned my legs on either side of his torso.

"Do you know how hard it is to be around you without kissing you, without *touching* you? It is as the moon aches each night, gazing down upon the earth that was once part of its own heart."

I focused on his eyes for a beat, but then his gaze trailed to the space between my legs.

Fuck.

He gently pushed my right leg further aside, glancing up at me. "Look at me." His voice was low and rough as I drew my eyes to his. "Is this okay?"

I nodded, and the muscles in his tattooed arms flexed as he gripped both my thighs, slowly sliding his hands upward. He pressed his wet face against the fabric of my dress between my legs, the pool sloshing around his waist with the movement, and I let out a gasp as the indent of his mouth brushed the sensitive parts of me. Finn took the noise as an invitation, nuzzling deeper.

I whimpered, my body telling me that it wanted this more than anything, so I spread my legs wider to let him know that he was welcome.

He pushed my skirt up and brought his hands to the area between my thighs, tracing his fingers over the lacy front of my panties as he surveyed the space. My back arched under his teasing caress.

"I've never been a pious man . . . but you will always bring me to my knees," he whispered, and tingles formed across my skin as his lips brushed my leg.

He began kissing his way down the inside of my right thigh, and arousal consumed me as he brought his tongue to my sex, licking it slowly. His hot breath mingled with the heat of my desire, and I gasped as he pulled my panties aside, his tongue flicking faster.

I thrust myself forward to feed his appetite, and he feasted on me with the hunger and urgency of a starving beast. My mind was clouded with drink, with need, the intoxicating light of the moon, and the desperate ache in my chest that reminded me we didn't know how long Finn had left. So I lay back on the damp concrete, crying out in pleasure as I let him claim the space between my legs with his tongue.

Just as I was about to break for him, he swept me over the edge and into the pool. We stood there, momentarily breathless, chests heaving, the crystalline water lapping against our waists before we rushed to one another.

He slipped his hands around my ass, drawing me into him as my legs wrapped around his hips. I felt the length of him, rock hard beneath his jeans, and I scrambled beneath the surface to undo them. A gasp of excitement escaped my lips as his cock sprung free, and I held the stiff length of it in my palm.

I guided him toward my entrance in a frantic movement, my breathing ragged as he slid inside.

"Fuck," he rasped as I began to rock against him.

Still moving up and down, I drew him into a heated kiss, nipping his lower lip. His body felt so good beneath me, and I arched my back, my long, wet hair shaking against my spine.

I met Finn's gaze, and he was looking up at me as if I were a goddess. His expression only fueled my desire, and I let out a whimpering moan.

He pressed his thumb against my sex and began moving it in circles as I rocked harder on his length.

"You feel so good." I bit my lip as another gasp of pleasure escaped me.

"*I'm yours*," he whispered as his cock slipped in and out of me. "Whether you hate or love me, I will always be yours."

With these words, the length of him throbbed inside me, and I bit my lip as the feeling of his body against my sensitive parts intensified.

"Whatever destiny awaits us, I am yours. Our souls are twin currents, forever twining beneath the waves." His dark gaze scorched through me as his body stiffened, the muscles in his arms standing out beneath his tattooed skin.

I gasped as my climax made its way from my lips. Finn pulled my hips into him for a few final thrusts before he let out a low groan.

Swallowing a gulp, I leveled my gaze to his, my legs still wrapped tightly around his muscular hips.

The corners of his mouth twitched. "You never fail to surprise me, little shifter."

I threaded my fingers through his ebony hair, resting my cheek against his. Above us, the stars glittered in the night sky, and the silver box on the table by the door seemed to shimmer with its own light.

We both startled when a crash echoed through the villa. The front door slammed open under a heavy kick. I untangled myself from Finn's embrace as Stavros and two of his henchmen strode into the outdoor area.

"Well, well, well," Stavros crooned. "Thanks for getting her ready for me."

"Don't touch her," Finn growled, hastily buckling his jeans and swinging himself from the pool to face the three men.

I clambered out beside him in my wet sundress.

"You made a real mess of my establishment, princeling." Stavros folded his arms across his chest. He was wearing another immaculate black suit.

One of his burly security guards gestured to Poseidon's Box on the table. "It's here."

"Grab it and go," Stavros barked. "Then we will pay the staff at The Aegean a visit. That was Mummy Dearest's nightclub, wasn't it?"

A vein in Finn's temple throbbed, and he rushed forward, swinging his fist at Stavros's head. Stavros caught his wrist, and they stared each other down.

Finn grunted as the man drove an uppercut into his gut. A low growl escaped Finn as he charged the Siren, and the two of them landed on the ground in a tangle of fists and snarls.

One of the burly security guards came toward me, while the other tucked the box under his arm.

"No!" I cried. We hadn't come all this way just to lose the box now.

I reached for my dagger, still strapped to my hip beneath my sundress, but my trembling hands could barely grip the hilt. There were three of them and only two of us. We'd lose the box while we fought them off unless . . . unless I used my powers.

The rough fingers of one of the henchmen closed around my arm as I searched for the silver orb of power. Heart thudding, I let it fill me.

Stun, not end. Stun, not end. I repeated the mantra to myself. I didn't want to kill these men, but we needed to get out of this.

My heart pounded, driving power through every vein as the henchman yanked me into a headlock. The magic burned like wildfire beneath my skin, threatening to consume me if I didn't offer it release. With a frantic breath, I unleashed it.

42.

MORGANA

I floated in a bubble of calm. Some part of my subconscious knew I had failed to master my magic, stunning myself and leaving Finn alone with Stavros, his henchmen, and the box. But it was so peaceful here in this stupor. Before my eyes, a pale, blinding nothingness bloomed. As I hovered in a trance, it slowly warped, colors bleeding into the void until a vision began to take shape.

Manannán's blood-smeared face was heavy with anguish, and his eyes were bloodshot from tears. He collapsed to his knees in the sand, clutching the lifeless body of a seal, while all around him, Drowned men clashed with Mer in brutal combat beneath the waves.

Manannán rose unsteadily, still holding Siana's body to his chest.

"No!" A heart-wrenching cry echoed across the battlefield. Mer Prince Kyano had spotted them. Devastation distorted his handsome face as he pushed through the carnage to Manannán's side.

"What have we done?" Manannán turned to Kyano as the merman ran a trembling hand across the seal's limp body.

The two men's swords lay forgotten in the sand.

"Please, save her." Manannán tilted his face to the waters above. He stood, cradling Siana against his chest. Kyano raked a hand through his brown hair, eyes shining with agony as he hovered beside them, his viridescent tail flicking through the bloodstained water.

Then, the vision shifted, and the fighting was over. Lifeless Mer, Sirens, and sea monsters floated in the crimson undercurrent. The booming voice I now recognized as Poseidon's echoed around the two men, still standing together and holding Siana's lifeless form.

A merman emerged from the water, hair so dark blue it bordered on black. His muscular torso was etched with ancient Runes of the Ocean, and his eyes blazed with the azure brilliance of the sea. Poseidon.

At his side appeared a beautiful woman with cascading black hair and skin adorned with aquamarine scales. Her full lips were set in a pout of displeasure, and her deep brown eyes burned with emotion. Agápē. A seal appeared behind her, its eyes shining with heartbreak. My heart clenched. It was Síocháin, Siana's mother.

Then came a monstrous figure. Glistening tentacles spilled down his back. Though fiercely handsome, the man's face had a greenish hue, and a slick, scale-like suit clung to his powerful form. Cetus.

The gods of old were coming together to pass judgment.

Poseidon glided forward, his gaze filled with scorn. "Manannán, for your part in this battle and Siana's death, we sentence you to an eternity in the shadows."

Manannán bowed his head, and his form began to curl and twist, unraveling into wisps of darkness. It slithered into the ocean's gloom and was swallowed by the deep.

"Kyano, my son, you disappoint me. Because of you, we strip the Mer of their full strength and curse you to live as a broken man. You will only be free when three become one."

Kyano burst into a blinding white orb of energy and vanished into the ripping waters. The four gods surveyed the scene in heavy silence. Then Síocháin gathered Siana's lifeless body into her flippers, and with a final glance, they vanished, leaving behind only blood-drenched waves and the drifting corpses of their people.

In a flash of light, the images faded, replaced by a new scene: a roiling, dark sea and a cave carved out of a black cliff face. A handsome young merman followed a watery passage into the cave, a glowing ball of light held high in his hand. I recognized his pale hair and chiseled jawline. Taranis.

The merman plunged beneath the waters at the back of the cave, following the slick rock as it descended into darkness. Something curled around bleached bones littering a slimy plateau. As Taranis reached out, it slipped down his throat. His eyes darkened and then flashed red.

He swam from the cave, emerging in the tossing ocean, pushing his pale hair back from his forehead. His jaw clenched, his gaze burning red, the shadow of Manannán moving within him.

The vision disintegrated as I hit the wet concrete beside the pool with a gasp.

Finn was leaning over me, his dark hair astray, as he helped me into a sitting position.

"What happened?" I snapped my head around, scanning for Stavros and his henchmen.

"They're gone," Finn said gravely.

My shoulders sagged in relief when I noticed Poseidon's Box was back on the table. "Did you kill them?" I blinked hard, trying to steady myself.

"No." He shook his head slowly. "You did, when you turned them to dust."

The world tilted beneath me, my breath coming in sharp bursts as Finn hauled me to my feet. A cold shiver crawled down my spine as I spotted the three piles of silvery powder by the pool.

My Selkie ancestors had been gods of peace, and some of that power lived within me. However, it had curdled, tainted by my father's Drowned blood. And that made me a weapon.

Tears filled my eyes, and I shook my head as my top lip trembled. "I-I didn't mean to."

"Hey, it's okay." Finn wrapped an arm around me, scooping me into his chest.

I pulled back, looking up at him through damp lashes. "I'm a killer."

"No," he whispered. "You are a warrior. There's a difference."

Part Four

The Summit

43.

SKYE

We were gathered for our usual indulgent breakfast on the outdoor patio, where the hanging table surrounded by shell cradles swayed in the current.

Alexandros and Damon had not yet returned from rallying the Italian army, but King Proteus and Queen Peisinoe were already seated at the head of the table. Porphura and Layla sat hand in hand on one side, with Pisceon and Glacies on the other.

I helped Edward into a swinging chair beside Layla, and Pisceon let out a callous snort. Edward responded by giving him the finger, and I bit back a smile.

I had just begun tucking into my plate of oysters when Elias, the herald, floated into the area, making a sweeping bow. "Your Highness, I present Princess Aarna Okeanós."

He gestured to the palace, and I stifled a gasp as the most beautiful mermaid I had ever seen emerged. Her crimson tail swished gracefully as she glided up the garden path toward the dining patio. Her brown skin shone in the aquamarine light, jet black hair falling in long, lustrous tresses down her back. Golden bangles adorned her arms, necklaces were piled above a gleaming warrior's breastplate, and a delicate golden nose ring caught the light as she moved.

Princess Aarna dipped her head at the king and queen. "I am here to escort you to the summit in my kingdom." Her brown eyes flicked to Glacies.

"Aarna, join us!" Proteus gestured at the vacant swinging chairs, and Aarna slid in beside Glacies, her tail curling underneath the cradle.

"I've missed you, sister." Layla leaned forward, shooting Aarna a grin. This morning, her dark braids were wrapped around her head in an elegant topknot adorned with gold.

The women in Okeanós sure knew how to dress.

"Does everyone go to this summit?" I asked, popping a piece of clam meat into my mouth.

"Only the most powerful members of each house. Our armies remain on standby until a decision is made." Proteus piled caviar onto his plate.

Was Aranare the most powerful member of his house? I stiffened, heart pounding, as images of his amber eyes swam into my mind. I had tried not to think of him, and I managed most days between training, the parties, and Alexandros. But sometimes, when my guard slipped, the thought of him returned, and with it, a surge of fresh rage curled my fists tight. *If he hadn't been there . . .*

Other times, different things would drift into my thoughts—the way his cheeks would flush when he looked at me, his shaky hands as he instructed me in training—and these thoughts were worse . . . much worse. So I locked them away.

Aarna interrupted my reveries, craning her neck to look at Pisceon. "Cousin, I hear you've been training the Thálassians to contain the Drowned."

"Cousin? I thought you were *Finn's* cousin," I blurted, eyeing Pisceon's dark brows—so like Finn's—but now I noticed his skin was the warm brown of the two Okeanós mermaids.

"My father was King Neptūnus's brother, and my mother was Aarna and Layla's mother's sister." Pisceon's eyebrows came together in exasperation.

"*Was?*" I said before I could stop myself.

Pisceon's expression was hard as he stared back at me. "Both my parents died from the Shadow."

My gaze shifted to King Proteus, and I noticed the Siren queen squeeze his hand.

"So you two are sisters." I quickly changed the subject, glancing between Aarna and Layla. I could see it now: they had the same brown, amber-flecked eyes. Yet Layla had darker skin and thick hair, whereas Aarna's fell in midnight tresses.

"Yes." Laya laughed softly. "Our parents are king and queen of Okeanós. You will meet them at the summit."

I smiled like I understood, but my head was spinning.

"I will join your training today." Aarna's grin this time was for Glacies, and I caught a faint flush rising in the pale-haired mermaid's cheeks.

Side by side, they looked like two warrior women who could take on any Drowned and did not need to toil with us.

"Great." Proteus clapped his hands. "Tonight, my sons return from Italy, and we will make merry."

My stomach fluttered, heat pooling below my navel. I had missed the gorgeous purple-haired merman warming my bed.

After breakfast, I found Edward in the Thálassian library. My breath caught in my throat as I cast my eyes over the space. Vaulted stone ceilings painted with colorful frescoes met white marble shelves that wound down to the floor, each packed with an array of books.

The Mer could swim and browse the higher shelves, but the librarian had made Edward a ladder of kelp. She moved it along for him so he could peruse each section.

His cheeks were flushed as he climbed down the slick ladder, cradling a stack of ancient books. "Can you believe this place?"

"It's magnificent," I breathed, turning on the spot to take it in.

"Never would I have believed that any Mer could treat me so kindly," Edward said, shaking his head. "The Thálassians have well and truly proved me wrong."

I trailed after him as he made his way to a cozy curved alcove in one of the stone walls and started organizing his books on the table there.

"What are you reading?" I asked, picking up a worn tome wrapped in dark leather, its gilded front cover featuring a symbol of a shell.

"The Thálassians are distant kin of the Ătlanticus Mer, so they've preserved some of the original texts. Did you know the Ătlanticans could store power in objects? They passed that ability down to the Thálassians."

"Like that necklace I almost bought at the Sunken Bazaar?" I lifted my chin in thought.

"Exactly," Edward said, his throat working with excitement. "It's quite fascinating, and look at this." He thrust forward an ancient leather-bound book, its yellowed parchment worn thin with age.

My brows flickered. "What am I looking at?"

Edward exhaled in exasperation, pulling the book back and running a freckled finger down the page. "It's a poem by an ancient Mer poet of Ătlanticus."

He rolled his shoulders, adopting a regal tone as he read aloud. "'Quaking with rage, Poseidon's voice doth boom. Manannán, you are sentenced to a life of shadows and gloom. Destined forever to walk beneath the sea, your fate is tied to prophecy.

"'But the God of Seas and Skies was sly when he decreed: When my artifacts are united in holy trinity, my people will reclaim their power, and my son, Mer Prince Kyano, will be free.'"

He leaned toward me over the table. "Do you think this has anything to do with the prophecy?"

I made a face. "Deciphering the prophecy is more Morgana's thing."

"You're right." Edward rubbed his chin, eyes distant with thought.

"As much as I'd like to stay here and read ancient poetry with you, we'd better get to training. Pisceon may be chiseled like a god, but he's a moody prick who will have our heads if we're late."

Edward chuckled, neatly stacking his books before following me out of the library.

Pisceon hovered before the line of Mer and Siren trainees, a thick coil of green seaweed net bundled in his hands. We slipped quietly into place at the end of the queue.

"Some of you may not have the skill of combat." His voice rumbled like a distant storm. He unfurled the net with a wrist snap, and the strands whispered through the water like a living thing. "This," he said, "will give you just as much power over the Drowned as a seasoned warrior like me."

"One could scarcely imagine him more arrogant," Edward huffed.

I stifled a giggle. "He's totally hot, though."

Edward made a noise of indignation, earning a sharp glare from Pisceon.

"One motion," the merman instructed. "One clean throw. Hesitate, and the Drowned will tear it from your grasp."

I gathered up the net as Edward stepped into the role of a Drowned, facing me head-on. I bit my lip as I bundled the slimy weed into my chest. "I apologize in advance for my clumsiness."

Pisceon glided behind me, his cobalt tail stirring the water as he brushed his thumb over my hip. "Now throw—from here," he said.

With a twist of my body, I hurled the net outward, where it curled over Edward, weighted down by shells and stones woven into its edges. It settled on the seafloor while Edward struggled beneath it. I pulled the draw line tight, trapping him within a web of seaweed.

"Good." Pisceon let out a dry laugh as Edward writhed like a cat caught in a sack.

"Always a fan of a *captive* audience, weren't you, cousin?" a deep and amused voice said from behind us.

I spun around. Finn hovered nearby, his emerald tail glittering as it flicked behind him. Dark hair drifted around his face, and a smile tugged at his mouth as he watched Pisceon instruct us.

Beside him stood Morgana, sleek fur clinging to every curve of her toned body. Her long red hair flowed down her back, and her face lit up when she spotted me. She was clutching a silver box tightly under her arm.

I squealed, sand kicking up behind me as I ran to throw my arms around her.

"Excuse me, but aren't you forgetting something?" Edward's grumbling reminded me that he was still caught in the net.

Morgana and I rushed forward, giggling as we freed him. He surfaced, rosy-cheeked and muttering under his breath.

Finn rested a hand on Morgana's lower back, then gestured toward the castle. "We'd better report to the king and queen."

I winked at Morgana, who flushed and quickly pulled away from Finn. She cast a nervous glance toward Glacies, and I followed her gaze, but Glacies and Aarna were too busy laughing and tossing the net between them to notice Finn and Morgana's arrival.

"I'll accompany you, cousin," Pisceon grunted. "Keep practicing," he yelled at his line of Mer.

"We'll come too." I followed behind the group, dragging Edward with me. I needed to know everything that had happened on that trip.

We trailed them into the throne room, where King Proteus and Queen Peisinoe awaited us.

"Welcome back!" King Proteus threw open his arms, gliding from his throne to embrace his nephew. "Was your trip successful?"

"It was." Finn dipped his chin at his uncle, then locked eyes with Pisceon and nodded, and it seemed Pisceon's shoulders sagged with relief.

My eyes narrowed into slits, and I turned to Morgana to see if she'd noticed, but she wasn't watching them; her eyes were tracking the darkened veins in Proteus's neck, and pain flickered across her face.

"So you found the prophecy?" Proteus asked, absentmindedly touching the dark tendrils.

"Not yet, uncle, but we believe this box could hold the answers, and Inegar is bringing the key to the summit." Finn gestured to the silver treasure cradled in Morgana's hands as he ran a finger along her arm.

Edward's eyes narrowed, and he let out a noise of disapproval beside me.

I raised my brows. "What did you have to do to get it?"

"Don't ask." Morgana's lips pressed into a thin line, a shadow lingering across her expression.

Something had happened on that journey that had darkened her and drawn her and Finn closer. Whatever it was, they were no longer enemies.

But could they ever be lovers after what Finn's family had done? Perhaps they were destined to remain in a gray area, I thought, watching the heat fade from Morgana's neck and chest now that she had moved away from his grasp.

"We will head to the summit tomorrow, but tonight, we celebrate!" Proteus clapped an arm around Finn's back.

44.

MORGANA

The evening's celebration had been set up in the Thálassian gardens. The songs of Mer musicians rose from below, drifting through my balcony's open doors, mingling with the sounds of laughter and revelry from early guests.

I lay on my sponge bed and stared at the colorful frescoes on the ceiling. I didn't feel like celebrating. My mind was still spinning, and the bitter taste of bile lingered at the back of my throat.

I had killed three men. Yes, they'd meant to kill us and steal the box, but still, I had ended their lives. And I hadn't meant to.

Or perhaps I had, my mind whispered, and the thought turned the nausea in my throat to a slow, rising burn.

You are a killer. The words echoed in my mind.

Killer, killer, killer. The chant drifted in through my window, becoming a part of the Thálassian minstrel's song.

I had no control over my powers.

I had made an internal vow to my grandmother and the Captain, who had died for me, that I would find the prophecy, and I had killed three men in that search. Not Drowned silver-stained men already on a path to the Garden of Mortimer from blood-use, but an ancient Siren and two mortals.

Killer, killer, killer. The words curled in from my balcony, strummed on a Thálassian harp.

Finn had let me keep the box, which now sat on my bedside table, taunting me with its secrets and the price I had paid to possess it.

There was a soft knock on my door, and Skye entered. She was draped in Thálassian gold, her dark hair artfully pinned. She looked more comfortable in her Siren's form, making her all the more beautiful.

She chewed on her cheek as she stood in the doorway. "I thought I'd come and do your hair."

I sat up and patted the bed beside me, glad for the distraction from my thoughts.

"So," Skye asked in a would-be casual voice as she began braiding my hair, "did you and Finn have fun?"

I blinked hard, trying to steady myself. "He's dying."

"What?" Skye gasped, letting my hair fall and moving around to hold my hands in hers.

"The Shadow." I tried to shrug off her concerned gaze. "I guess the thought of losing him became a bit of an aphrodisiac."

"Maybe it's my new Siren senses, but I understand love now, and I see it all over that merman's face every time he looks at you. Why don't you just ask him about your grandmother? Then you two can move forward." She moved behind me to fasten a golden choker around my neck.

"He said he didn't kill her . . ." I forced down the lump in my throat.

"Do you believe him?"

"I think so. I want to trust him."

Skye gave me a knowing look but chose not to press further. "I have to ask you something . . ." She let out a shaky chuckle, as if wanting to change the subject.

"What?" I arched a wary brow.

"Does Finn use the water to . . . you know . . . pleasure you?" She adjusted my hair, biting on her lip to stop a grin.

Heat spread to my cheeks, ears, and neck, but I nodded.

"Oh, dear lord." Skye sank back onto the bed beside me.

There was another rap on the door, and Edward entered. "What is it you're discussing?" he asked, sliding onto the end of the spongy bed, his gold necklace glinting.

"Oh, you know." Skye looked at her nails. "All the Mer pleasure Morgana's been getting."

"Skye!" I shoved her.

"You haven't!" An angry breath shot out of Edward, and he folded his arms. "We can't trust him."

Skye giggled. "You don't need to trust someone to ride their twelve-packed body like the world is ending."

"Am I the only one here with a shred of sense remaining?" Edward's brows lowered as he pursed his lips.

"You could use some Mer pleasure." Skye stood and let a sultry hand glide through Edward's copper hair.

He swatted her off. "I will never love again."

"*So* dramatic." She stared at him, lips set in a teasing sulk.

"What's so dramatic?" Edward exhaled sharply. "That I grew close to Donahue and Daniel, and now they're both dead?"

"It was a coincidence." I rubbed his knee, and he lifted his chin, not looking at me.

"Let's have some fun tonight." Skye twirled playfully and grabbed a carafe of wine from the stone table. She poured the crimson liquid into conch shells and passed them around with a grin. "To sexual reawakening." She held her drink up.

"I shan't drink to that." Edward's cheeks flamed.

"I'll drink to it." I raised my conch and winked at Skye.

"As you wish." Edward rolled his eyes and lifted his conch.

As I tipped my head back and let the scarlet liquid slide down my throat, it whispered *killer* with every gulp. A desperate urge rose within me to drain the entire vat, to silence the whispers once and for all.

No expense had been spared getting the Thálassian gardens ready for the soirée. The coral glowed in deeper colors beneath moonlight that filtered down from the surface, casting silver shadows across the array of carefully curated plants.

"Wow," Edward murmured as he, Skye, and I made our way down the steps leading from the palace between the pillars of the outdoor breakfast area into the gardens beyond.

My breath caught as I took in the beauty before me, and for a fleeting moment, all the turmoil within me fell silent. Coral clusters blossomed in hues of violet, soft pink, and jade. Anemones and iridescent seahorses flitted between them, and glowing orbs had been laid along the sandy tracks between the flowery beds, drawing guests toward a clearing.

In the central glade, revelry unfolded. Mer took partners to the dance floor or lounged on decorative stone benches, sipping from conch shells. Laughter rang through the currents, mingling with the haunting tunes of the Mer minstrels in one corner.

Stone tables heaped with oceanic delicacies had been placed around the space, and at the garden's center, two thrones built from a collective of dried coral pieces housed King Proteus and Queen Peisinoe.

"It's like *The Little Mermaid*. But in this one, there are sex scenes." Skye exhaled as Alexandros approached, his muscled torso rippling with each swish of his tail.

"May I have this dance?" he asked, extending his arm toward her as we reached the entrance to the sandy glade. His violet hair was tied in a topknot, and a golden crown gleamed atop his head.

Skye nodded and offered him her dainty arm.

Damon drifted forward and held his arm out to Edward. A blush bloomed across my friend's freckled skin, but he let the dark-haired, dark-scaled Siren lead him onto the dance floor.

Once they left me alone, awkwardness crept in, and I was about to make my way over to the king and queen when a familiar, deep voice caressed the back of my neck.

"Care to dance?"

I turned. Finn was floating behind me; he had golden cuffs on both wrists, and they glinted as he tucked a stray curl behind my ear.

My lips parted, but nothing came out, so I nodded.

As the music swelled, he drew me to his chest, and my fingers wandered over the inked patterns on his arm.

"I can't stop thinking about our time by the pool." Finn's voice was low and rough against my neck. "Do you know how much I ache for you, I ache for *this* . . . It is as a storm swelling upon the horizon, desperate to break."

I chewed on my lower lip, heat engulfing the place between my legs. I scanned the dance floor to distract myself from the feeling. Finn's powerful tail swept in controlled arcs, guiding us through the water.

Glacies and Aarna leaned into each other at one of the tables, sharing a vat of wine.

"This is the happiest I've seen her, spending so much time away from our castle," Finn murmured, following my gaze.

I watched as Aarna took Glacies's hand, guiding her to the dance floor. They locked eyes, then shared a kiss.

Layla and Porphura twirled nearby, as did Skye with Alexandros, and Edward with Damon. Pisceon was drifting alone, arms crossed, brows furrowed, his eyes tracking Damon and Edward.

"Are Pisceon and Damon . . . ?" I asked Finn as we spun, my hair swirling around me.

"For tonight or this week, maybe." He twirled me away from him. "Pisceon never gets attached. Before he left our castle, he was dallying with a mermaid. She fell completely in love with him, and he pushed her away."

"But why?"

"Pisceon lost his family to the Shadow. He is scared to let himself fall in love, since he might lose them too." Finn's fingers wove through mine as we danced face-to-face again.

My throat burned as I watched Pisceon pace, his cobalt tail swishing in agitation while he tossed back gulps of wine. Damon had pulled Edward closer, and Pisceon's eyes were narrowed on the pair.

"Damon will be using the Drowned boy to make Pisceon jealous." Finn rolled his eyes, holding my body against his.

"Poor Edward. He has sworn off love, just like Pisceon. Perhaps they would make a better pair."

Finn let out a hard laugh. "Yeah, right, a Mer and a Drowned."

"Can we go somewhere quiet? I-I need to talk to you about what happened with Stavros."

Finn's eyes searched mine, filling with concern. He nodded and didn't let go of my hand as he guided me through the crowd, weaving between vibrant corals until we reached a quiet clearing. Here, the reef gave way to long, swaying seaweed surrounding a secluded patch of sandy glade.

He turned to face me, running his hands up and down my arms. "Gods, you in this Selkie suit."

When I stayed silent, he pulled back, searching my eyes. I couldn't meet his gaze, so I looked away. "I can't control my powers. I turned those men into dust, and it's all I can think about."

"They were no loss." Finn waved a hand. "Good riddance, if you ask me."

"He was a Siren, and they're almost extinct." Tears welled in my eyes. "I feel sick about it. I'm supposed to be here to fix things, not break them."

"Sometimes, the only way to fix something is to break it first."

"Spoken like a typical prince." My throat burned with the threat of tears, so I changed the subject. "Why do you always speak like that—in poetry?"

Finn's eyes were intent on mine. "I've always loved poetry, the way it paints a beautiful picture of dark, messy things. Bukowski, Plath, and my favorite, Byron—"

I snorted a laugh.

"What?" A dimple appeared at the curve of his mouth.

"It's just ironic, as you *are* the Byronic Hero . . . dark . . . brooding . . . tortured."

Finn knocked his shoulder into me, but then his eyes glazed over. "Books were always an escape for me."

"Me too," I said quietly. "I liked that I couldn't sense the emotions of the characters, but that was before all of this. Now I'm living in a book, and I'm not sure if it's a fairy tale or a horror."

Finn tilted my chin so my eyes met his. "Do not resent the power coursing through your veins, little shifter. You are more powerful than I'll ever be. You are the tidal force that reshapes coastlines, the tempest that commands the sea, the Siren song, and the shipwreck that follows. Any creature who does anything less than worship you *deserves* to become dust."

"And what about you? Do *you* worship me?"

"Yes." He purred the word. "Let me show you how much."

Water caressed my ankles and wound its way upward, brushing the insides of my thighs. I swallowed as it curled between my legs, stroking the sensitive parts of me.

Finn moved back so he could survey me. I liked seeing his expression as he watched me—it made me feel beautiful. My blood was zipping, and the space between my legs throbbed at the thought of being with him as a merman. His dark eyes continued to drink me in, and my breasts grew heavy, my nipples peaking as if begging for his touch.

With a flick of his tail, he closed the distance between us, and my pulse jumped as his hand curled around my lower back, pulling my fur-lined stomach against the sculpted indents of his hips and the smooth scales of his tail.

"I never thanked you for what you did—saving me from Stavros and his men. If you hadn't used your magic, I might not be here," he whispered into my neck, planting a soft kiss there.

His hand slid into my hair, and I gasped as the water pushed deeper into me. I pressed my lips to his in a desperate kiss, the shadows that had haunted me dissolving beneath the warmth of his touch. He met me with equal force, our tongues circling one another slowly as his hands trailed down my back, fingers brushing between my legs.

I inhaled sharply as his fingers moved inside me, and the water pressure worked with them.

A wicked idea came to me, and I pulled back from his embrace with a cheeky grin, then dragged my lips along the hollows of his collarbone.

I kissed my way down his chest, over his new heart tattoo and the indents of his stomach muscles until my knees were pressed into the sand and my face was against the sensitive part of his tail, where his manhood would have been. Acting purely on instinct, I licked the area slowly, his scales grating against my tongue.

"Fucking hell," he growled, and his tail stiffened, showing me that I was doing something right.

Tracing the same space, I moved my tongue back down, circling slowly, stopping to apply extra pressure. Finn let out another low groan, tangling his fingers in my hair, the muscles rippling in his chest as he threw his head back.

A soft gasp escaped me as he sent water pressure shooting back up my legs and caressing between them as I licked and stroked the sensitive space on his tail.

"I want to taste you." His voice was like gravel as he reached for me.

With a flick of his fins, he swept me into his embrace, and we were suspended horizontally in the water. He held me beneath him, tattooed arms cradling my body as he kissed me fiercely. His tail beat against the water, keeping us afloat. I whimpered into the kiss, and he pulled back, surveying my face, a smile flirting with the corners of his mouth.

A delighted yelp escaped me as he flipped me with ease so that the space between my legs was at his mouth. He wrapped both his muscular arms around my ass, lifting my hips so he could lick me with long, slow strokes.

Pleasure shot through my body in wavelike throbs as Finn flicked his tongue faster, aided by his water magic, and I moaned with the sensation. I hooked my arms around his emerald tail and began to do the same to the sensitive parts of him. He shuddered beneath me, and feeling him tremble at my touch only heightened my arousal.

We were suspended like this, my long red hair flowing out beneath me, as he stiffened further, and his muffled groans from between my thighs deepened. Heat surged through me, and I cried out as my orgasm crashed over me like a wave. Finn shuddered in my arms, unraveling in perfect time with me.

We slowly released each other, breathing heavily. I landed on the sand, pushing my strands from my face, my emotions a churning vortex of guilt and satisfaction.

Finn raked a hand through his dark hair and surveyed me, his golden cuffs glinting in the aquamarine light, a reminder of the disease consuming him.

"Do you feel any better?" He cupped my cheek bringing my gaze to his.

I shook my head as everything I'd suppressed swam back. "I can't just ignore what I did."

"I'm not suggesting you forget it," he said softly, his hands gliding down my arms to rest at the crooks of my elbows.

A blood-curdling scream sliced through the water.

"Hold that thought . . ." Finn let go of me, and we pushed our way back through the coral beds to the dance floor.

Finn and I emerged at the edge of the coral clearing. The music continued to weave through the water, but the Mer on the dance floor had stilled.

The cry had come from a beautiful mermaid whose armor stood out among the crowd. She was dark-skinned and dark-haired, and a black breastplate gleamed over her torso. Her amber eyes were fierce despite the distress shadowing her face.

"It's Asherah," Finn hissed beside me, "the warrior queen of the Kingdom of Mors."

"Mors? As in the guardians of the Garden of Mortimer?" I hissed, my stomach twisting.

Finn gave a grim nod, grasping my hand and guiding me forward. We weaved through the gathering as we followed Asherah. Her shoulders were trembling, but she held them high as she made her way to the coral thrones where Peisinoe and Proteus sat.

We stopped at her side, the three of us now standing before the king and queen.

"I came to warn you," Asherah cried, a black metal sword strapped to her back. Her tail was jet black, but the scales shimmered with hints of green.

Queen Peisinoe stiffened, stepping down from her throne to take Asherah's hands in her own.

"Warn us?" Finn's brow creased as he turned to the warrior mermaid.

"All the Protectors have fallen. Manannán's forces have taken back the Kingdom of Mors, and he's granted the title to the Fisherman."

"What do you mean he's taken back?" My heart began to race.

"The Mors Kingdom was Manannán's palace before the gods stripped him of it." Finn pursed his lips, looking ill at ease.

The throne I'd seen him on in my visions. The hairs in the back of my neck stood on end.

King Proteus paled as he rose to stand. "And the Garden?"

"The Garden of Mortimer and all its wicked souls are now answering to Manannán."

Queen Peisinoe placed a webbed hand on Asherah's arm. "Your people?"

"They fought bravely, but there were too many Drowned, and they don't die. Those who escaped scattered as emissaries, hoping to reach the kingdoms in time."

"And your husband, the king consort?" Finn asked, his throat tight.

Asherah's shoulders trembled, but she stood tall, steadying her breath. "He's gone."

Other partygoers had been listening, and a swell of chaos erupted, their conversations breaking into screams and shouts.

"Silence," Pisceon yelled, drifting to the king and queen's side from where he'd been pacing the dance floor. "There's no time to waste—we must go to the summit immediately." He looked to Proteus, who nodded his assent.

I swung to face Finn. "If the Mors Kingdom has fallen . . . what does that mean?"

"I don't know," he said, his voice grave, but he threaded his fingers through mine in reassurance.

45.

MORGANA

Finn guided me away from the chaos and back to the palace, where we found Alexandros and Damon seated on their thrones in the echoing chamber. Pisceon was drifting to and fro before them, his muscles on full attention as he mused, and he threw a grateful look in Finn's direction as we swam over to join them.

Aarna swept into the room behind us, her dark tresses trailing like ink in the water as she tugged Glacies along by the hand.

"What's going on?" Glacies asked as they reached us.

"All the Protectors have fallen; Manannán now controls the Kingdom of the Drowned." Pisceon's eyes flicked like a predator's from one person to the next.

Alexandros leaned one elbow on the armrest of his throne, the other hand tracing a crack in the stone. "The king and queen have gone to ready themselves. We will leave immediately."

"Manannán will expect us to head to the summit; he will be ready." Finn pinched the bridge of his nose.

Pisceon ran his tongue over his teeth. "A procession will attract attention—"

"Let's split up." Finn interrupted him. "The Thálassians leave tonight, and we follow at first light."

"Our route takes us past Port Royal . . . under the shadow of *his* fortress." Glacies' features were strung taut. It was the first time I'd seen the mermaid lack composure.

"She's right." Pisceon's whole body stilled as if he were remembering. "Silver-stained Drowned march in armed cohorts through those waters."

A silence settled over the group, and my stomach hollowed out as I glanced between them. Aarna was clutching Glacies's hand, Pisceon still drifted back and forth, and the twins exchanged tense looks.

"What if we take the Tunnel of Hēracleion?" Finn finally said, a dangerous edge to his voice.

"But no one uses it anymore. Who knows what ancient horrors lurk in its shadows?" The color drained from Aarna's face.

"The tunnel leads straight into the Red Sea—we could reach Okeanós in just over a day," Damon said, rubbing his chin. "Or we take the longer route through the Atlantic, past Port Royal, and it'll take three, maybe more."

"We don't have time for this. Let's put it to a vote," Alexandros interrupted. "All in favor of the tunnel?"

All of the Mer except Aarna raised their hands. I rubbed at my chest. I had no idea which one to vote for, but with the majority choosing the tunnel, it looked like that would be the route. My insides knotted when I noticed the fearful expression on Aarna's face as she realized this, too.

"It is settled." Damon lounged back in his chair.

Aarna released Glacies's hand, lifting her own to her chin in concern.

"Where's Skye and Edward?" I whipped my head around, realizing they had not joined us.

"Skye's taken the Drowned boy to their chambers." Alexandros drummed his fingers against the arm of his throne. "I will return there to say . . . farewell before we leave." A flicker of pain crossed his face, and I wondered if he'd grown more attached to Skye than he meant to.

"What of the army?" Pisceon's gills flared as he turned to the twins.

Damon waved a webbed hand. "One thousand warriors are on standby, awaiting the decision from the summit."

"Take a cohort of guards for your travels," Alexandros told Finn.

"The guards stay with you. We already have some of the Deep's most powerful warriors traveling with us." Finn smiled grimly, his eyes trailing over Glacies and Aarna.

A cry rang out as Porphura and Layla entered the room. Both their faces were pale as they looked between us, and Aarna broke from Glacies's side to throw her arms around her sister.

"You are to leave immediately," Aarna said, gripping Layla's hands in hers. "We are taking the Tunnel of Hēracleion,"

Layla's face blanched. "Is that wise? I've heard dark stories of that path."

Aarna cupped her sister's chin. "I would feel better if I were traveling with you."

"We both know I'm better with a sword." Layla masked her fear with a grin as she pulled away.

Aarna rolled her eyes and gave her a playful shove.

"She won't be alone." Porphura clasped Layla's hand in hers, and Aarna offered her a grateful smile.

"You must travel lightly," Finn said, addressing the twins on their thrones.

Damon nodded. "We will take our herald and a cohort of six guards. Plus the king, queen, and the princesses." He smiled at Porphura and Layla.

My stomach turned as I took in the grim faces of the twins and Pisceon.

"There are crossbows and nets for everyone." Glacies toyed with the silver necklace she was wearing. "Make sure your people take them."

"Try not to show off too much." Aarna elbowed Layla in the ribs in an attempt to lighten the mood.

"Please. You're the flashy one." Layla snorted, adjusting her golden bangles.

Aarna's face was shadowed as she turned back to her sister. "Unless you do something stupid."

But Layla's face broke into a cheeky grin. "Like saving your ass?"

"Too much time has already been wasted," Porphura said, her purple tail flicking as she retook Layla's hand.

Aarna pulled her sister into a swift, tight embrace. Then, with a final glance, Layla and Porphura swept out of the room.

Alexandros drifted up from his throne. "We will see you on the other side, cousin." His expression was grave as he inclined his chin toward Finn before turning to leave with Damon.

46.

ARANARE

Mom pulled a leather-bound tome from her satchel and dropped it on the table in front of me. I was sitting hunched over other texts in the bookstore's dim back room.

Leaning back in my chair, I surveyed her. "Venice went well, then?"

"My contact at the Marciana National Library uncovered a recent shipment of books from a secluded monastery on the island once known as Cythera."

I opened the tome she had placed before me, gently examining its worn parchment pages, which were inscribed with the Runes of the Ocean.

"Translating this could take weeks. Are we sure that whatever's in here will be useful?"

Mom shut the title, wrapping her knuckles against the insignia scratched into the leather. "See this?"

"Aye, it's the Insignia of the Ocean." I rubbed a hand down my face.

"Look closer," she urged, tucking a strand of gray hair behind her ear, her eyes alight with excitement.

I examined the insignia again, noting a Siren, sea beast, seal, and a mermaid.

"There's no Drowned!"

"Precisely." My mother observed me with folded arms. "This is the story of the four eldest gods, before the God of the Drowned was made. We must understand each god's role and how they once upheld the balance of the seas, because that knowledge might be the key to preserving peace."

I drew the tome to me, standing to rifle through the shelves until I found our rune key, then returning with it to the table.

"Let me know what you find. I'm going to see your father," my mother said, closing the door and leaving me alone with the ancient book. Its scent was a mix of old paper and aged leather.

I ran my palms over its cover. We hadn't had much luck with our research so far, so I didn't have high hopes for this text. I expelled a weary breath as I turned to the first page, and soon, I was lost in a world of gods and fables.

I hadn't slept.

The rune key lay open beside me, the ancient tome spread wide. Papers, sketches, and books I'd drawn for reference littered the table in front of me. I stretched back in my chair, raking both hands through my hair. What time was it? I wasn't sure.

I lifted my coffee cup. It was stained, cold, and empty.

Damn it.

How many had I drunk?

My notepad was filled with frantic scrawls, story after story I'd copied from the tome and pressed into paper. From these, a larger tale was beginning to unfold . . .

"You look like shite." Mom appeared in the doorway, chuckling as she surveyed the chaos. "Have you been here all night?"

I nodded, a weary grin tugging at my lips as I raised my eyes to hers.

"From the Port House." She held out a large takeaway coffee, and I accepted it gratefully.

She leaned over, rifling through my notes and drawings, then pulled one out and examined it—charcoal sketches of the planets. "What is this?"

"The tome held the story of creation—the Siren's creation. *My* creation." My eyes glowed with excitement.

"I suspected as much." Mom's brow creased. "Tell me what you've found."

I riffled through my notes, selecting the leatherbound pad where I'd compiled all the stories into one narrative, and began to read. "The Earth was born from dust and gas swirling around the young sun, shaped by collisions with countless celestial bodies. Among them was a fateful impact that formed the moon."

"Yes, yes." Mom folded her arms. "This matches the world's creation as we know it. Interesting."

I shot her an exasperated look, and she waved a hand, motioning for me to continue.

"One of these collisions brought the Star-Walkers. Celestial beings of immense power, each carried a different gift."

I stopped to haul a breath and suck back some more of my coffee. "When they struck the Earth, they did not perish. Instead, they remained, shaping the molten world, cooling its surface, crafting the skies, and calling forth the oceans. As the earth evolved, so did they, becoming stewards of its forces.

"Four of the Star-Walkers became guardians of the sea. Enchanted by the beauty they had wrought, they chose to dwell within it, reshaping their forms to reflect their creations.

"Cetus, proud of the beasts he had summoned from the deep, gave himself the form of a man fused with a giant squid.

"Poseidon, ruler of tides and skies, adorned himself with a powerful tail, becoming one with the currents he commanded.

"Síocháin, guardian of peace, became a Selkie, able to walk as a seal or a woman and keep balance between land and sea.

"Agápē, the goddess of love and death, took a seductive and winged body to tenderly guide the souls of ocean creatures to the afterlife."

I paused, heart aching at the thought of Skye and the beautiful aquamarine-scaled body that frightened her too deeply for her to see its magnificence. Maybe sharing these stories of Agápē with her could help her finally see what I did.

Mom was looking at me expectantly, so I continued.

"But even gods grew lonely."

I leaned back in my chair as I thumbed a new page in my notepad and read aloud: "Each fashioned a super race in their image. These divine children—Mer, Sirens, Selkies, and Seabeasts—flourished. They interbred, even with the gods themselves, and demigods were born.

"But this star-forged world was powerful, and its creatures evolved on their own. From the tides, man emerged. He rose, and he ruled. But man was fragile. He drowned. Again and again, his body sank, and his soul wandered the depths, lost and unseen, for Agápē's light did not reach him, as she was only the caretaker of the ocean's creatures.

"So Poseidon forged a new god, the God of the Drowned, to gather the forgotten and rule the restless dead."

I snapped the notepad shut, taking a long sip of my now lukewarm coffee.

My mother stood silently, her arms crossed and her brow furrowed, as she took it all in. At last, she exhaled and gripped the back of the vacant chair. "So there was no mention of the prophecy or what it might contain?"

"No." I shook my head. "The book is all about the old gods, finishing with the creation of the Drowned god."

"Keep this in mind when you go to the summit and observe." Mom tapped a finger to her temple. "With Manannán's rise, the shadows of the old gods are stirring again, pulling those tied to them into unknowingly reenacting the past."

47.

MORGANA

The Thálassians and Queen Asherah had departed with a cohort of guards. This meant that Skye, Edward, Finn, Pisceon, Glacies, Aarna, and I would travel together.

We were set to leave at dawn, but it was still dark when I slipped through the aquamarine waters to replenish my oxygen, the moonlight tinting the sea with silver. I broke the surface and drew in crisp air, brushing wet hair from my face as I gazed at the glittering night sky.

It was happening—a war.

Manannán had reclaimed Mortimer and had his army of the Drowned. But we had the box, and Inegar was bringing the key to the summit. If the prophecy was inside, we could stop all of this.

The water rippled beside me, and Skye emerged, grinning. "It's not safe to swim alone," she said, flicking her head back, water cascading in a glittering arc.

"I need air. I wasn't blessed with gills."

"Oh, right, I forgot." She ran a hand over the tears on the side of her neck, a sadness emanating from her.

I reached for her hand beneath the waves and squeezed it.

"I hope Alexandros and the others make it to Okeanós." Worry lines creased Skye's forehead as she swiped at her dripping lashes.

"They're skilled fighters." I gave her a reassuring smile, but my stomach churned as I recalled the fear etched across all the Mer's faces last night.

"Come on." Skye's eyes lit up with relief, and she grasped my hand, pulling me back beneath the waves.

As the wondrous Kingdom of Thálassa stretched out beneath me, I thought of the wars I'd seen on the news, cities reduced to rubble. I hoped we'd find a way to spare these ancient halls from Manannán's wrath.

Poseidon had stolen his son long ago, when Manannán was still a man. Then Kyano had taken Siana. At the heart of all this hatred . . . was *love*.

A sliver of hope ignited in my chest. Maybe—just maybe—there was still a way to end this without bloodshed.

The rest of the group was waiting in the throne room. Glacies, Pisceon, Finn, and Aarna wore Mer armor with daggers strapped to their backs. Aarna had chosen gold, while the Neptūnus Mer and Glacies were adorned in silver.

I strapped on my knife and put Poseidon's box in Edward's string sack, which was filled with the last of his rum.

"Guard it with your life," I muttered as it clinked against the bottles.

Glacies and Aarna had slung satchels of provisions across their chests, and Pisceon gripped a coiled seaweed net. A pile of crossbows and quivers, which we could strap on alongside our blades, lay on the floor beside him, his cobalt tail flicking as he hovered above them.

"Here." His muscles flexed as he tossed one to each of us.

He neglected to throw one to Edward, but Finn rolled his eyes and handed Edward the last bow.

"Per solane et pallipoia." Glacies nodded to each of us, murmuring something in the ancient tongue of the sea—words I couldn't understand, but somehow felt.

We moved through the Thálassian Kingdom in a procession. Glacies and Aarna led the way, with Pisceon, Finn, and his dolphin Pháos guarding the rear. Skye and I held the middle, carrying Edward between us, Pisceon snorting with laughter when we picked him up.

An arch of Corinthian pillars, speckled with algae, marked the edge of the vibrant Kingdom of Thálassa. After we passed them, we entered the Mediterranean wilderness. Seaweed still swayed, and rock formations bloomed with color, but the landscape beyond grew untamed, less tended. Ancient ruins and sunken shipwrecks lay scattered along our path, remnants of forgotten human wars and lost empires.

My stomach tightened as I turned to Finn and Pisceon. "Will we pass the Mediterranean's Drowned ship?"

"*The Icarus* lies between Egypt and Turkey, but we will veer inland at Abu Qir Bay to avoid those waters."

The sea seemed still and quiet, as if the ocean were holding its breath, waiting for the impending battle. We moved in equal silence, all on high alert, our eyes sweeping the surroundings for even the faintest glint of silver.

As we veered toward the Egyptian coast, the sea grew warmer, flecked with pale sand. The seabed blushed a deep desert red in places, and the water shifted to a luminous aquamarine.

We passed between bulbous masses of red rock, their surfaces veined with algae, until we emerged into an eerie glade where streaks of crimson sand fanned out like spilled pigment across the ocean floor.

"Stop." Glacies threw up a hand, her blonde hair rippling in the swell.

There were Mer ahead, and they seemed motionless. *Suspended.* My whole body began to tremble. Silver. There was silver in the water.

A wave of dread washed over me. I couldn't breathe; everything that had happened in the Atlantic Ocean came flooding back as the lifeless bodies before me grew clearer.

"They're Thálassians," Aarna cried, rushing forward.

Skye and I alighted, placing Edward beside us. Shadows from the crossbars pooled about us, and nausea rolled through me as I raised my eyes to the corpses strung up above us. Edward swayed as he took them in, his face paling to a sickly shade.

There were four of them hanging from the crossbars. Their arms stretched out eerily, tails wrapping mournfully around the bases of the driftwood poles. Two Thálassian guards—I recognized their lilac tails. Elias the herald, and . . .

"Layla!" Aarna's gut-wrenching cry sliced through the water as she rushed to the fourth figure, wrapping her arms around her lifeless sister.

Pisceon tightened his fists into balls. "They must have been set upon last night."

Pháos swam in circles, clicking angrily.

"Oh, my sweet sister." Aarna sobbed as she unpierced Layla's wrists, cradling the mermaid's limp body in her arms.

Edward retched, and Skye began crying beside me.

Pisceon's shoulder muscles rippled as he turned to us. His features all closed off, as if a shutter had fallen across his face. "Retch all you like, Drowned boy. Your people did this."

Finn put his hand on Pisceon's arm, but his eyes were also filled with something dark.

Aarna continued to wail, clutching Layla's body to her chest. My throat was tight as I thought of Porphura.

"The others must have escaped through the tunnel." Pisceon's dark brows lowered. "It's imbued with ancient magic. The Drowned won't be able to enter once the door is sealed."

I breast-stroked toward the remaining crossbars, gently touching Elias's cheek. His eyes were shut within bruised hollows, skin pale as bone. Jagged holes marked his wrists where the blood-hungry Drowned had pierced and drained him. And there was something else—a mark on his cheek.

"I think you guys should come and see this," I called.

Pisceon and Finn appeared at my side as I ran my finger across a spiraling imprint, slick and glistening like a wet burn, on the boy's right cheek. The shape resembled a coiled tentacle wrapping inward.

"The Fisherman's mark," Pisceon growled, breathing out sharply.

"I've seen this before." My insides knotted.

Finn's jaw clenched, muscles flexing beneath his tattooed skin as he folded his arms across his chest. "We cannot linger. We must reach the Tunnel of Hērákleion before night falls on these waters."

"I'm not leaving her!" Aarna choked back a sob as she brushed Layla's dark hair from her forehead. The mermaid's once coffee-colored skin had faded to a pale caramel in death.

"I might be able to help," Skye said softly.

Silence fell over the group as every gaze shifted to her.

48.

SKYE

I flushed under everybody's stares. *What the hell am I doing?*

My mind slipped into images of Layla smiling as she chose jewels with Porphura and me at the Thálassian village . . . Layla offering me a goblet of wine in the fancy Mer boutique . . . Layla, her golden tail flicking through the piazza as she gazed at the purple-haired mermaid she loved.

Now, Layla was gone.

Aarna let out another gut-wrenching sob, awakening something in me. "Peisinoe told me that Sirens can grant the souls of those who have left us a blessed passage to the afterlife," I said. "I thought perhaps . . . I could . . ."

Aarna glared up at me with bloodshot eyes. Her sleek, dark curls were a mess, and the kohl that usually rimmed her lashes was smudged. "Peisinoe is one of the last ancient Sirens. You're half-human. What can you possibly do?"

"Layla was kind to me. I'd like to try at least." I pursed my lips to stop the tremble.

Glacies put her hand on Aarna's back. "Let her try to help, my love."

Aarna nodded slowly, and I glided over to them. She released Layla into my arms before throwing herself into Glacies's embrace and sobbing furiously.

I couldn't help but glance at Finn. His brow was furrowed, and his eyes were dark, but his face showed only pain for his wife-to-be and her lover, not jealousy.

"Let's do this properly." I blew out a breath. "Lay the Mer beside Layla—and someone gather coral and shells for Agápē."

Aarna helped me ease Layla onto her back so she could float in the current. Her long, dark plaits, matted with blood, drifted sadly in the swell. Pisceon and Finn rested the Thálassian guards and Elias beside her, their lilac tails now faded to gray.

I motioned for Aarna to join me beside the floating Mer, and I began to arrange their clothes and hair with care, as one would before a funeral on land. Aarna understood. She moved to her sister, drawing fresh kohl from the satchel on her back to repaint Layla's eyes. She removed her own jewelry and placed it on her sister, adorning her for her journey to the afterlife.

Morgana and Edward returned with corals and shells. Guided by instinct, I placed a shell over each of the floating Mer's eyelids, then clasped their lifeless webbed hands around bundles of coral and seaweed, pressing them to their chests.

When we were done, the four Mer drifted in the aquamarine water, their tails sweeping downward, and beautiful faces serene in rest, the flowers and seaweed adorning their bodies rippling in the swell.

Something about the scene before me reminded me of the pyres Vikings used to build to send their kings off on burning ships. But these Mer had no pyres or boats beneath them, just the current that had been with them all their lives, which would now take them to the afterlife if I did this correctly.

An ominous weight settled over me. The operative word being *if*.

"Say your goodbyes," I said softly, looking at Aarna.

She buried her face in her hands as her long, dark hair trembled down her back. One final shuddering sob escaped her before she wiped her eyes and clasped Layla's limp hand.

Glacies touched the small of Aarna's back. "I will make them pay," she whispered into the neck of her lover.

Pisceon and Finn stood back, arms folded, dark brows drawn. Pháos hovered beside them, clicking softly. Morgana and Edward stood together on the other side of the four floating Mer.

I exhaled a deep breath and stepped forward.

Morgana's eyes flicked up to meet mine. "I-I would like to help."

I nodded, and she moved to my side.

Calling on my powers had never been as difficult for me as it was for Morgana. She had described hers as a silver orb deep within her, but mine operated somewhat differently. It was a light that encompassed my being.

I drew a slow breath and then released it.

A sharp inhale from Glacies told me my power was spilling outward. I glided toward the three floating Mer, placing a palm on each of their foreheads, letting the light pour from my touch.

My Siren wings pressed against the skin between my shoulder blades, straining to break free beneath the rising seep of power. I held those awful, monstrous things back, gritting my teeth as pain tore through me.

Glancing at Morgana, I saw her radiating something silver that snaked through the waves. I smiled encouragingly at her to show that it was working—the power of peace.

Glacies began to sing, words I did not recognize, and then Aarna, Finn, and Pisceon joined in. The tune was soft and haunting, yet achingly beautiful, as all the Mer's music was. It rose around us as I continued to channel my powers into each of the dead, silently asking Agápē to grant them safe passage to the afterlife. It moved through us like a gust of wind would on land, but it was a wave down here. It swept around our bodies like a sigh, rushing over the floating Mer, twirling and dancing around them in a final, tender embrace. Then, with a sound like an exhale, the whirlpool stilled, leaving only glittering foam in its wake, humming with a song of freedom.

Aarna let out a strangled sob and threw herself into Glacies's arms. Morgana withdrew her powers, and I did the same.

"Thank you, Agápē, for granting this passage." I bowed my head, which seemed appropriate. A final searing line of pain burned the space between my shoulder blades.

No. I shook my head, and the sensation faded.

Thoughts of Porphura and Layla, their arms linked through mine, emerged in my memory, and a sob curled in my throat as I imagined what Porphura must be going through—if she was even alive.

Finn toyed with the dagger slung across his back, motioning us to follow him with a sweep of his tattooed arm. "Darkness is falling. Take a moment to gather yourselves, but we need to hurry if we're to reach the tunnel."

As we moved into the darkening ocean, I trailed behind the group, exhaling a stream of bubbles as my gills quivered. Some fragment of the turmoil that had been living within me had stilled.

49.

MORGANA

As we reached the shallower water of Abu Qir Bay off the Egyptian coast, the ocean around us deepened with the shades of night. Tumbled limestone blocks emerged from the seafloor, their square shapes unmistakably carved by human hands. Rounded time-worn ship anchors, pocked with holes, told stories of a once-thriving port, and now and then, I glimpsed the eroded granite eyes of some forgotten pharaoh gazing up at me from beneath drifting sand.

"Here," Finn said, holding his palm over a jumble of red granite rocks.

"But it's just ruins." I rested a hand on his tattooed forearm, brows furrowed as I scanned the tumbled blocks.

"This tunnel was built when there were still alliances between man and Mer." Pisceon explained, then he glided forward, sweeping his webbed palm over the rubble, and whispering in the old language of the sea. "Per archaos hudos apergo." The rocks glowed with the Runes of the Ocean and ancient hieroglyphics.

"The Mer needed a trading route from the Mediterranean to the Red

Sea. That's why this underwater tunnel was built, but it is said to have fallen into darkness." Pisceon gestured to the shimmering symbols, and my eyes widened as more began to bloom across the ruins.

Finn started chanting, and Pisceon joined him. As their haunting tune swept through the ocean, the tumbled stones began shifting and knitting themselves together to reveal a doorway between two tall rectangular pillars. The tops of the pillars were etched with more intricate hieroglyphics and Runes of the Ocean, flanked by paintings—a merman on one side, the sun god Ra on the other. Between them, a staircase descended into watery darkness. On either side, two granite sphinxes stood.

Pisceon nodded at the sphinxes. "For protection. This doorway originally stood in the port of Thonis-Heracleion, but we relocated the entrance here when the city sank. Once archaeologists began poking around and excavating the ruins, we had to enchant it to make it look like rubble."

I brushed the ancient stone frame, and the Runes of the Ocean glowed beneath my touch. A chill crept through the water as I pulled back my hand, raising the fur on my arms. The darkness seemed to have thickened.

Fear stole the air in my chest as I heard it: a drumlike echo.

Thrum. Thrum. Thrum.

Beside me, Finn tensed, claws unsheathing as his jagged teeth and beastly eyes overtook his face. I swung out from the doorway, hand flying to the dagger at my hip, gaze locked on the shadowy figures approaching through the gloom.

Drowned. Manannán's two henchmen—Teachie and Rackham.

Teachie's right eye socket was hollow, skin peeling from his cheek. Rackham followed behind him, cracking his knuckles. A cohort of silver-stained Drowned flanked them.

Teachie's mouth curved into a wicked grin. "I have been looking forward to getting my revenge, princeling. Maybe I'll drag you to the dungeons of Port Royal and see how you like it."

My eyes darted across the group. They had at least double our numbers, and Mer-blood fueled them.

"We cannot win this. Fend them off and close the door behind us," Finn growled, motioning us to spread out across the doorway.

The Drowned didn't give us time to plan or think. The water blurred as they rushed forward, moving like tattered puppets. Rackham lunged for me, but remembering my training, I dropped low. I spun and caught his wrist midstrike, twisting until I heard bones snapping. His weapon clattered into the sand.

For the Captain . . . and for . . . I gritted my teeth as I slashed his stomach with my dagger, and he staggered backward, nursing the wound. Causing this pirate pain felt damn good after what he'd done to me.

Beside me, to the right of the tunnel, Finn clashed with Teachie. His water blade had materialized and was locked with the pirate's barnacle-ridden sword. Pháos fought at his side, lashing out at the Drowned with swift strikes of his tail.

Pisceon moved away from the doorway, throwing himself into the Drowned with brute force. They screeched as he slashed them, bodies crumpling and then knitting themselves back together. A grunt echoed as he drove his blade into a Drowned pirate's chest. I cried out as another tackled him from behind, dragging him toward the seabed.

Rackham had picked himself up, bones snapping back into place, his stomach already healed. He glared at me as I stood braced, guarding the tunnel's mouth. Then, blinded by rage, he charged. I pivoted, using the water's resistance to my advantage, and struck him with an open palm to the chest, just as Aranare had taught me. My strength pushed him back, and I followed through with another slash of my dagger, sending him staggering away from the doorway.

I brushed my hair out of my eyes, a grin splitting my face. The smile faded as more Drowned crept toward us out of the gloom. In my periphery, I could see Glacies fighting with eerie grace, holding the tunnel's left, ice forming at her fingertips as she sent razor shards slicing through the current. Even with her jagged teeth and claws, she remained beautiful, like a fearsome queen carved from frost. Aarna protected her flank, spinning a twin-bladed staff like a steel cyclone.

Skye was hovering behind the sphinxes to the left of the entrance, and Edward fought in front of it, holding his own with his crossbow, but the Drowned were advancing. I reached for my magic, but it flickered, unstable as I remembered Stavros.

Shit. I couldn't risk it.

"Get into the doorway," Finn yelled, backing toward the tunnel as he parried Teachie. "Pisceon and I will hold them off."

The shadows thickened, like ink unfurling through water. My blood turned cold as a man emerged, dark tendrils snaking around him like writhing smoke—the Fisherman.

I froze, panic licking at my ribs as his tentacled arm wound tight against his chest. More Drowned spilled out from the gloom behind him.

No. There were too many of them, and they were advancing too fast. We'd never win, never contain them.

The monstrous arm of the Fisherman hurled toward Edward.

"Look out!" I cried.

He barely managed to roll away behind a limestone outcropping before the tentacle smashed into the wall on one side of the stairs, where he had been a moment before, splintering it into sand.

Aarna and Glacies grabbed Skye and ushered her into the safety of the descending stairs. I had turned to follow when a cry cut through the dark waters.

Pisceon. He was pinned to the ground, a Drowned's blade pressed to his throat. Finn was locked in battle with Teachie, but he swung his head toward the sound. He was too far. He'd be too late.

My stomach became leaden as I reached for the silver orb inside me, but Edward pulled himself out from behind the jagged rocks before I could grasp it. He loaded his crossbow, aimed, and fired. The barbed tip sliced through the water and struck the Drowned through the side of the head.

Pisceon shoved the body off. "You saved my life," he rasped, eyes wide with surprise as his beastly form faded.

"Thank me later," Edward muttered, reloading with shaking hands.

"*Now!*" Finn roared. Black-festering blood smeared his chest as he struck Teachie down with a brutal twist of his watery blade.

I raced to the tunnel entrance with Finn, Pháos, and Pisceon on my heels.

Edward! He didn't have fins or webs, and he'd fallen behind. A snarl tore through the water as three Drowned lunged from the shadows, silver-streaked limbs glinting as they reached for him.

Edward twisted to look at us, and his eyes . . . his eyes were filled with a fear that broke my heart. It was as if I were watching the scene unfold in slow motion. One Drowned clamped a clawed hand around Edward's ankle, and another slammed into his shoulder, knocking him off balance. He hit the ground, and a puff of sand burst up around him. A scream tore from my lips, echoing through the water, and I paused on the steps between Finn and Pisceon.

Finn turned to his cousin. "If I don't make it back, close the gate."

Pisceon nodded.

With a flick of his tail, Finn shot away from us, back out of the shaft toward where the hungry Drowned were pawing at Edward.

"Come on." Pisceon grabbed me by the wrist and pulled me down the stairs to the watery darkness of the tunnel, where the others were waiting. The three Mer started chanting "per archaos hudos klos," and the rocks began to knit themselves back together, closing the entrance to the shelter.

Shaking off Pisceon, I scrambled up the stairs again to peer through the closing rocks. Edward was lashing out at the Drowned surrounding him with his crossbow, catching one in the gut, but they kept coming. Bubbles escaped his mouth as he screamed. Finn was swimming through the water, his emerald tail beating against the current as he raced toward Edward.

My stomach hollowed out as the tunnel door edged shut, the Mer continuing to chant their haunting melody. The gate was almost closed now.

I let out a strangled sob. "I'm going out there."

"No!" Glacies jetted forward, grabbing my wrist.

Just then, lightning erupted from Finn as he reached Edward, scattering the Drowned with a clawed fist. He seized Edward by the collar of his uniform and pulled him close. I exhaled in relief, but then an icy laugh sliced through the darkening waters—a rattling, desolate sound.

The Fisherman. He coiled his grotesque tentacle inward, winding tight in preparation to strike.

The tunnel was almost sealed off; only a small rectangle remained, and I watched in horror through it. They'd never make it.

My heart pounded, and my chest felt like it might burst with the severity of its rhythm. I had to go, had to help—

A sob tore from my throat as I shook Glacies off, kicking toward the opening, but Finn emerged first, muscles straining as he held the final rocks apart with one arm. He slipped through, dragging Edward behind him.

Just as they cleared the gap, the stones slammed shut, seconds before the Fisherman's tentacle cracked against the tumbled limestone rocks above.

Silence fell, dust curling at the seams of the doorway. Only our shared, ragged breaths echoed through the space.

I threw my arms around Edward, then pulled back to see he was unharmed. "You're okay." I exhaled in relief.

"Yes." He flushed, untangling himself from me and straightening as if he didn't want the powerful Mer to see me making a fuss.

I held back a smile as I asked, "Have you got the box?"

He nodded, tapping the bag still slung across his back.

The corner of my mouth turned up. "You've gotten good with that bow."

"After what happened with Donahue, I felt the need to train." Edward shook his head, then turned to Finn. "And thank you."

Finn was still breathless, but a grin tugged at his lips. "No problem, Drowned boy. Maybe now you'll start trusting me."

Edward folded his arms, chin angled high. "That is yet to be seen."

With a whisper in the old tongue of the sea from Pisceon, oil lamps lit up along the "tunnel"—if you could call it that. It was vast and cathedral-like, its walls carved with intricate hieroglyphs brought to life by the lamplight. The entrances were flanked by gigantic carvings, a pharaoh on one side and a mermaid on the other.

"Wicked." Edward blew out a bubbly breath at my side.

An agonizing grunt cut through the darkness. Finn was doubled over, clutching his wrist.

A wrinkle deepened between Pisceon's brows. "Did you get hurt, cousin?"

"Just a stitch," Finn muttered, exhaling sharply. One hand waved dismissively while the other stayed pressed to his chest, his silver bracer glinting in the dim light.

My stomach dropped, heart thudding in my chest as I dragged my eyes to him. His face was pale and drawn in tight lines. When his eyes met mine, they were filled with fear.

50.

SKYE

I was shaking. What the hell was that thing with the tentacles? The Fisherman? First he had killed the Captain, and then Layla, and now he was chasing us. And he wasn't even the true villain . . .

I didn't want to imagine what it would be like to face Manannán, the one these monstrous Drowned served.

I scanned the dark tunnel, goosebumps prickling the bare patches of skin across my breasts and neck. It gave me the creeps.

"Let's split ranks," Pisceon commanded. "Who knows what long-forgotten evils lurk in these ancient places."

With a flick of her obsidian tail, Glacies swam forward. "Aarna, the Siren girl, and I will take the front. The rest of you take the back."

Aarna summoned a sphere of silvery light, gripping my arm, then pulled me after her. We moved cautiously, leading the way along with Glacies while the others followed with Pháos. We kept our pace slow enough for Edward to walk with us.

Tall walls of stone and packed mudbrick loomed on either side of us, crumbling in places where time had taken its toll. Carvings of Mer, sphinxes, and crocodilian sea beasts watched us with jeweled eyes that flickered to life as the pearlescent light Aarna held aloft moved past them.

My eyes widened as I observed the glowing orb. "Your light is changing color."

"The Indian Ocean is abundant in pearl farms. We draw this from them." Aarna brought both hands to the ball, and it swirled between her fingers in shades of silver, rose gold, and pale blue, like a glowing pearl.

"Before the curse, what was your power like?" I asked.

"No living Mer was there to witness it, but the old accounts say the gods and sea creatures were once one. We held divine knowledge, shared immortality, and drew power not in fragments but as part of a great, unified whole. Gods, nature, magic, and even mankind were all connected. But man grew greedy, and that greed rippled through us. In time, everything changed."

My throat constricted. "And this tunnel was built back then, in the Days of the Gods?"

"No one knows exactly." Aarna blew out a breath. "But it was constructed long before the city of Thonis-Heracleion was built around it. It is a very ancient place."

I reached out, my fingers trailing over a hieroglyph, which gleamed at my touch. A hollow note reverberated through the stone, and I snatched my hand back.

"Still think this place abandoned?" I asked, a cold chill snaking down my spine as I hurried back to swim alongside the two warrior mermaids and the glow ahead.

"We will soon find out," Aarna muttered.

A lump formed in my throat. "I'm so sorry about Layla. She took me to the Thálassian village once. It was one of the best days I've ever had," I gushed.

"Thank you for saying that." Aarna sent a long sigh into the darkness. "I'm sorry I doubted your Siren's magic."

We fell into silence after that, each of us lost to our shadowed thoughts, the dark waters of the tunnel pressing in on either side of us. On and on we went, following the light of Aarna's pearl.

Sometimes, the passage narrowed into a tightly packed mudbrick tunnel, then widened into expansive halls fit for kings. Statues of pharaohs loomed in the shadows, and hieroglyphs adorned every inch of stone. Fish darted between the effigies, and seaweed grew along the tunnel's edges.

We passed through a room lined with square pillars, each of which was decorated with carvings. Aarna's pearlescent light swept across more primordial paintings dotted with scum and corrosion. I could make out images of fish-bodied gods, winged Sirens, and a priestess wearing a seal-headed robe.

Glacies swam just ahead, silent, her tail a streak of obsidian in the gloom. Her fingers often returned to brush the hilt of the blade strapped across her back. "This darkness feels unnatural," she murmured. "I will be glad to be free of this place."

"I would rather be in this darkness with you than at the summit watching you and *him* play husband and wife." Aarna jerked a thumb over her shoulder to where Finn drifted behind us.

"You know that's how it has to be, and now is not the time to discuss it." Glacies exhaled sharply, but her shoulders soon slackened. She slowed, letting her fingers interlock with Aarna's.

"Layla and Porphura were so happy together. Why can't you two be like that?" I blurted.

Glacies let out a furious huff, her gills flaring with irritation.

"Sorry if I overstepped," I added quickly, my face warming.

"The Niveus and Neptūnus families are different from the Thálassians. They are the largest, have the most dangerous powers, and control the majority of military might, which makes them more . . . conservative," Glacies explained.

Finn snorted from the darkness behind us. "Conservative is an understatement."

"What about your family, the Okeanós?" I stared at Aarna, deep in thought.

"They would like nothing more than to see me happy with the woman I love," she said stiffly.

I turned to Glacies, whose jaw was tight in the dim light. "Can't you just defy your family?"

"It's not that simple," the warrior mermaid hissed. Her eyes gleamed beneath the shadows, and jagged teeth flashed in the lamplight.

"If not for the humans and the Drowned, perhaps we wouldn't be fighting the Shadow—and the strongest of our houses wouldn't be forced to marry," Finn ground out from behind us.

"Could you refrain from slandering the Drowned for a few hours? I dare say I ought to have traveled with the Thálassians," Edward snapped.

A harsh laugh escaped Pisceon. "Bit difficult when we just put four of our own to rest . . . Oh wait—and then more Drowned tried to kill us."

"Let's just get through this tunnel without killing *each other*." Glacies rubbed an exasperated hand down her face.

Something soft brushed against my bare ankle, and I squealed in fright. Aarna guided her light to the stone floor, picking up a purple flag emblazoned with a murex snail shell. "The symbol of Thálassa," she breathed.

"They must have passed through here." Glacies reached for the dagger at her back again.

Did the torn flag mean Alexandros, Porphura, and the other Thálassians had made it through the tunnel? I didn't even want to consider the alternative. Unease twisted deep within me, and I stumbled into the damp wall. As my skin made contact, a ripple of sighs wound through the corridor—soft at first, then sharper, like pleas, as if the stones themselves remembered too much.

"Do you hear that?" Aarna whispered.

Glacies's eyes darted around. "It's not coming from ahead."

"No," Aarna said, her voice tight. "It's coming from *inside*."

My blood chilled as a hiss echoed through the tunnel, and the dim wall lamps blinked out one by one. Another rush, like wind slicing through water, and Aarna's light flickered out, leaving only darkness.

"That can't be good," came Pisceon's voice from somewhere behind us.

Aarna's pearly orb flickered back into being, but the shadows seemed thicker now. They danced across the walls and crawled along the tunnel floor. I turned on the spot, scanning the space, and a chill crept into my marrow when my eyes landed on a painting. It was worn by salt and time, but I could still make out the image chiseled into the rock and colored with pigments of yellow, inky blue, and red: a serpent of cosmic scale, its body looping through the heavens and underworld.

Another hiss echoed through the place, and Aarna's light extinguished once more. "Shit," she cursed, spluttering it back into being.

"It's Apep," Edward whispered as he moved to my side to survey the painted serpent. A single red jewel, or perhaps paint too rich to fade, formed its eye. It seemed to be . . . gleaming. "The great chaos bringer. The enemy of Ra, the sun god."

"Verrrrrry gooooood, Drowned boy." The hiss echoed through the chamber. And then, the red eye blinked.

"And here I thought we were going to have a nice stroll through an ancient tunnel," Pisceon joked, steel ringing as he unsheathed his blade.

The painting shivered, and dust trickled from the ceiling as the serpent uncoiled. Its head emerged from the wall. No longer bound by limestone, it cocked to survey us.

"Don't look into its eyes!" Glacies shouted, shielding her face as the snake's gaze sought hers.

"Whhhhy not, princess? Are you scared of a bit of chaos, a little darkness?" Apep's voice was like the sweetest poison, a seductive vortex tugging at the edges of my mind inviting madness.

Pháos shot forward, hitting the serpent with its snout. Apep hissed, recoiling as dark smoke poured like ink from its mouth.

The tunnel dimmed, and all heat drained from the water. Stone cracked, and Aarna's light sputtered out again. We could no longer see the ancient snake, but I could feel it slithering between our ankles in the dark.

"Form a defensive ring," Pisceon barked.

Edward and I edged together. Aarna's shoulder was pressed on my other side, and Glacies, Finn, Pisceon, and Morgana must have been making up the rest of the circle, with Pháos in the middle. The dolphin was letting out short, sharp clicks.

"Yesss, that's it. Panic . . . I thriiiiiive on your elated heartbeat, the pulse thudding in your throat, your quivering gills. Give me chaos . . . Give me fear."

Glacies let out a scream that split through the darkness. "I-it's showing me things!"

The snake's scaly body brushed against my leg, and I shrieked. A vision started to form in my mind, even though my eyes were open.

No! I scrunched up my nose, squeezing my eyes shut, but it made no difference.

There was Parker, his eyes lifeless and his throat gaping . . . gaping from the cut that I had made. My hands, clasped in Aarna's and Edward's, suddenly felt hot and slippery . . . Blood. They were covered in blood.

My stomach churned as Parker smiled, a cruel smile, which turned into a wicked laugh, and the movement tore the slit in his neck further, dark blood belching out.

I vomited. Gasping with terror, my breathing came in short, sharp bursts.

"Layla," Aarna cried. "My sweet sister, it is all my fault. I should have traveled with you."

"Apep, also known as Apophis," Edward was muttering beside me, his cold hand clammy in mine. "As the solar deity and bringer of light, Ra upheld Maat, the cosmic order. In opposition, Apophis was his greatest adversary, earning the title Lord of Chaos . . . and Ra was the Sun God."

"Would you be quiet, Drowned boy!" Pisceon snarled.

"I've got it," Edward cried. "We need light. Bright and pure. Now."

"Sssssoooooo smart, Drowned boy." The voice reverberated through the tunnel. "But I grow stronger with every frantic breath you take."

"We need to calm ourselves," Finn thundered.

"Yessss, Prince Aigéan Neptūnus. I see the darkness that lives within you. Like calls to like."

"Don't listen to it," Finn growled.

I tried to calm my breathing as Parker's cold face appeared again. This time, he was holding something white-and-aqua-feathered and matted with blood. It was a wing.

"No, I will not let you affect my mind, " I whispered, and the image faded.

Edward began writhing and crying out beside me as Apep's tail flicked past his calf, and I squeezed his hand until his breathing steadied. We stayed with our backs to each other, facing the dark water as it stirred around us.

Aarna's pearlescent light flared, then sputtered and blinked out like a dying star.

"We need lightning! The pearl isn't strong enough," Morgana cried.

"We've got this, cousin," Pisceon shouted. "The rest of you, focus on calming yourselves and not giving the creature anything to feed off."

Lightning flickered from the two Neptūnus Mer, but shadows curled around the light, deepening until it extinguished. The serpent laughed from somewhere in the shadows, the sound chilling and hollow. As darkness twisted like ink through the tunnel, swallowing us, a cold knot formed in my stomach. I couldn't see. It was too thick. Too close. I focused on my breathing, in and out. In and out—

Light flared, and I looked over my shoulder to see Finn raise his arm, lightning coiling around his tattooed skin. Beside him, Pisceon bared his teeth, summoning his own crackling current. But each strike was devoured—snuffed out when it formed, lost in the churning black.

"Again!" Finn grunted. The lightning sparked, then faltered.

I craned my head, looking over both my shoulders, searching for Apep, but I could no longer see the snake.

"It's no use," Pisceon groaned from somewhere in the gloom. "The darkness is too heavy, and our powers aren't strong enough."

A gleeful hiss sliced through the darkness, and Aarna screamed. "It's going to drive us mad, and we'll die here in this tunnel," she sobbed.

"Wh-what if we do it together?" I asked, my voice wavering. "I mean, if it thrives on chaos, surely we can fight it united."

"The Siren girl's right, it's worth a try," Glacies called.

I let the warmth of my power pulse into Edward's cold hand, and from my other side, Aarna's energy flowed through him to meet mine. Pisceon grunted, as our magic merged—peace, love, the cold icy power of the Arctic, monsoon tides of the Indian Ocean, and the might of the Atlantic.

As warm power cascaded through my body, my wings pressed against my back, their desire to break free so great it felt as if a hot poker was stabbing my skin.

A cry tore from my lips, tears leaking from my eyes as I fought to keep those shameful things hidden. With a final jab, they retreated, the sensation like fiery coals crumbling through my insides.

I squinted as the tunnel was lit a brilliant silver white, our shared power threading upward in a spiral of elemental force. The darkness reeled, the serpent hissing and striking as if it had been engulfed in flames.

Finn drew a sharp breath and raised his arm. Lightning surged up it this time, flooding the corridor with more blinding radiance. The shadows cracked and scattered, recoiling into the walls like smoke being blown by the wind.

Light again exploded outward in a sudden blaze as Pisceon's lightning joined Finn's, a great lance of brilliance arcing through the shadows. Apep recoiled, once more becoming a moving mural on the wall, its body writhing and shuddering as if burned by the memory of the sun.

"Was that a god?" I asked, my voice trembling.

"I don't know." Aarna shook her head, her webbed hand still clasped tight in mine. "Perhaps it was some essence of one. As Manannán's presence grows and evil spreads through the waters, we shouldn't be surprised if more long-forgotten things rise from shadows."

51.

MORGANA

The tunnel returned to silence, and the mural on the wall remained still. Only our ragged breaths permeated the watery darkness.

Aarna rekindled her orb, and her face blanched behind its pearly glow.

"Let's get out of here. I'll carry the Drowned Boy," Pisceon muttered, scooping Edward up under his muscled arm. Edward didn't complain. His face remained pale, his freckles stark against his skin.

We picked up speed, swimming in tight formation through the tunnel. Pháos led the way, his pale belly moving through the dark like a guiding light. My legs were still trembling, and goosebumps prickled beneath the fur on my forearms, but the water felt lighter, and my senses told me we would soon emerge in the Red Sea.

An agonizing cry cut through the darkness, and Finn doubled over at my side, his tail flicking sharply. Dread curled within me—*the Shadow.* He had been using too much magic, and it was growing.

"Finn," I said softly, placing a hand on his back, hoping to soothe him before the others noticed, as he didn't seem to want them to know.

His muscles clenched, veins pulsing in his neck as he fought to steady his breath and mask the pain, but another tortured cry tore free, and Pisceon spun around.

"Cousin?" Pisceon's eyes were filled with fear.

Finn grunted again, and he clasped his silver-cuffed right wrist to his chest. His body shook with effort, and a trickle of blood leaked from his nose before the ocean cleaned it.

"I know those cries. I hear them in my nightmares," Pisceon said. His tail swished as devastation, anger, and pain all exploded on his face, and his fingers curled at his sides. "Fuck!" He swung his fist at the tunnel wall.

The others had stopped. Skye's and Edward's faces were etched with confusion, but Aarna and Glacies were taut with worry.

Pháos swam to Finn's side, nuzzling him gently with his snout.

"You go ahead." Finn waved a hand. "I need a moment, and we shouldn't linger."

"We will stay," Glacies said gently, and Aarna nodded.

Finn grunted again, his hair sweeping across his forehead with the movement. "Look on the bright side—you'll be free of our engagement sooner than expected." He managed a grin at Glacies between ragged breaths.

There was a pained look in her eyes, as if she were trying to hold back tears. "Don't for a moment think I'm not truly sorry this has happened to you."

"Fuck," Pisceon said again through gritted teeth, his muscles all standing at attention as his hand tugged into his hair.

"Let's carry on." Finn managed to glide forward, still clutching his wrist to his chest.

The rest of us moved after him. Pháos led the way, clicking softly beside Finn, who reached out to pat the dolphin.

We moved quickly, the tunnel walls blurring. A heavy silence had settled upon us, and my mind wandered into dark thoughts. The Shadow was taking its toll on Finn, and Proteus must be suffering the same agony. *While the disease spreads and the Mer weaken, Manannán's strength grows.*

But the prophecy in the box Edward was carrying could end all this. A flicker of unease curled in my chest. No one knew what was written in the second half of the prophecy.

A line of red granite sphinxes, half-eroded and littered with spots of sea life, appeared on either side of our path, and we slowed. Fish darted around the statues, and seaweed rippled between the creatures' paws.

Glacies's shoulders sagged. "We have reached the Red Sea."

Aarna held up her pearl light, which flickered across an expansive door carved with rows and rows of hieroglyphics and Runes of the Ocean.

"You're sitting this one out," Pisceon said, throwing out a muscled arm to block Finn from advancing toward it.

Finn grunted in assent as the other Mer pressed their hands to the door, chanting in the old tongue of the sea. The carvings shimmered, and then the entire structure dissolved into watery aquamarine light.

Aarna and Glacies surged ahead, and we followed them into the blue. The Mer resumed their chant, and the doorway melted into a jumbled mass of algae-covered rocks and rubble.

The Red Sea was a sprawling rainforest. Brain-like structures blossomed in pinks, greens, and various earthy hues. They clustered to form bulbous masses of color where fish swarmed.

Pisceon, still pressing Edward to his chest, rolled his eyes at the Drowned boy's breathless gasps. Skye and I weren't much better, tugging each other excitedly toward intricate anemones, beautiful starfish, and eels tucked into rock crevices.

"The Red Sea possesses the world's only climate-resistant corals. Even with the Shadow creeping in, they've managed to survive," Pisceon explained after Edward let out his tenth dramatic gasp. I was drifting slowly above the reef like a snorkeler, delaying the group.

"It is wondrous." Edward sighed. "I've no idea why I spent a hundred years toiling away in the Atlantic."

Glacies swung to us, exasperated, her pale blonde hair curling in the swell. "We have to pick up the pace."

We began moving quickly again, the vibrant coral becoming a colorful blur as we swam over it. Soon, it thinned and gave way to the open ocean. Occasionally, larger sea life passed us—whales in the distance and dolphins gliding through the depths. Pháos veered off again, vanishing into the blue. No doubt he'd return when he was ready.

I fell back, momentarily marveling at the group swimming before me—my friends. We hadn't started that way, but that's what we'd become somewhere along this journey.

"We'll set up camp here." Finn stopped, and the others pulled up abruptly around him. He gestured to a sunken ship half-submerged in drifts of sand. "Okeanós is not far away, but we've been traveling for two days straight, and we need rest."

No one disagreed; we all heard the words that Finn was too proud to say, that *he* needed rest.

Evening was filtering through the water in deeper shades as we alighted beside the boat. My shoulders drooped with exhaustion after all the magic we had used in the tunnel, and I was glad to make camp.

"At least I'll get one more night with you." Aarna's face lit up as she took Glacies's hand and pulled her towards the mottled vessel.

I dragged my eyes over the ship. It had split in half when it hit the ocean floor, and its hull pointed skywards. The rear stern and poop deck had toppled to one side, not far away. Sails hung in tattered strips from the masts, their once-white material ghostly against the aquamarine glow of the water. And there, on the very tip of the largest mast pole in the ship's middle, I saw it: a small black flag emblazoned with a skull.

"It's a pirate ship." I hesitated, as memories of what Teachie and Rackham had done to me came flooding back.

Finn noticed and drifted closer, linking his fingers with mine. "Not all ships are Drowned portals. By the state of this one, it hasn't been inhabited in a long time."

"Well then, enough gaping—let's set up camp." Pisceon eyed me and Finn, cobalt tail flicking. "And don't get any ideas just because it's our last night before we see our families." He paused, then smirked. "Actually, I take that back. I *do* like to watch."

"You're sick." I flipped him an obscene gesture.

Pisceon grinned wickedly, and then, with a flick of his tail, he shot to one of the masts and ripped away a large piece of sail.

"What are you doing?" Skye gasped from where she and Edward stood beside me. She looked over her shoulder like the pirates might return from the dead and reprimand us.

A real possibility down here.

"Making hammocks." Pisceon grinned. "Come on, I'll show you . . . Or you could share mine."

Skye's cheeks flushed crimson, but she kicked off from the seafloor, puffs of sand scattering in her wake, to follow Pisceon and gather sheets.

"Drowned boy." Finn nodded at Edward. "Help the princesses find us a place to sleep, as I presume you know your way around the bowels of a ship."

Edward straightened proudly. "Did you know the 1960s were considered the golden age of piracy in the Indian Ocean? I rather suspect that's where this vessel hails from—"

"Save the history lessons for later, please." Finn held up a webbed hand, but dimples shone in his cheeks from fighting a grin.

I followed Finn away from the shadow of the old ship's elevated hull until we found a rocky area where waving seaweed and fish swarmed.

"Dinner." Finn gestured to the plants.

I ripped at a patch of the drifting weed, and Finn snorted a laugh behind me. He shot forward and put his hand on mine. "We must find the edible strains." He brushed his webbed fingers gently over the patch, identifying a red plant with thin, vein-like leaves. "Gracilaria." He pulled away a small bunch, then continued riffling through the foliage, finding a brown weed. "Sargassum." He plucked some and handed them to me. "And we never rip it, we just take what we need."

"Got it." I nodded, caressing the weed with the same tenderness as Finn, but I had no idea what I was looking for.

I liked seeing him like this, the care and consideration he took toward the environment. He said his healing powers hadn't returned until he met me, but he'd been picking up rubbish long before that. It proved he'd always had this shred of compassion, the part that cared for animals and the sea.

"How's your wrist?" I asked as he selected more plants and handed them to me, his ornate bracers shining in the watery light

"I will be glad of some rest."

"The sooner we get to the summit, the better. If the rest of the prophecy is in the box, you will no longer have to suffer."

"Yes." Finn stilled, his eyes looking anywhere but mine. I studied his face, desperately trying to read the words he wasn't saying. Finn noticed and blew out a bubbly breath. He caught my chin, tilting my head so our eyes met, and running his thumb down the side of my cheek. "Let's not talk about the summit or my father, and just enjoy our time together."

When we returned to the ship, the others had strung up tattered cloth hammocks for each of us inside the hull. They'd artfully tied them between old pieces of the boat, so they formed a circle of beds. Around the hammocks and in their middle, they'd lit an eclectic mix of rusty lamps, which must have been gathered from around the ship. Their trembling light bathed the space with a milky glow. No doubt, Pisceon had used a spark of Neptūnus lightning.

Glacies and Aarna were lying in a hammock together, hands linked. It was wide enough for two, but just barely.

Edward sat on the floor beside one of the beds, trousers hitched above his leather boots, eyes gleaming, and a barnacle-ridden glass bottle in one hand. He'd found a rum stash and refilled his sack.

Skye lounged in the next hammock over from the princesses, and Pisceon rushed forward to collect the food from us.

"We didn't know if you two would like to share." He jerked his head at the hanging beds.

My cheeks heated, and I glanced nervously at Glacies, who pulled herself from Aarna's embrace and smiled at me. "It's okay, you know. Aigéan, and I have never been . . ."

"Oh." I swallowed and cast my eyes over the hammocks. There were only five, so it looked like they had chosen for us, and Finn would be sharing with me.

"If you don't want to, I can always share with the Siren girl." The corners of Pisceon's mouth quirked.

Edward scoffed.

"In your dreams." Skye crossed her arms over her chest, her bed wobbling as she threw him a scowl.

I was too tired to care, so I crawled into the hammock and nibbled on the medley of seaweed Pisceon handed me. I preferred fish.

Finn and Pisceon began warding the ship, their beautiful voices echoing through the dusky sea. When they had finished, Finn moved toward our hammock, his tattooed chest flexing in the lamplight.

I climbed out so he could get in first and accommodate his broad torso. The bed sagged between the wood, and Finn settled in, his tail curling up the length of the bed. I hesitated, eyeing the space beside him, then I climbed back in—awkwardly—my legs tangled with the curve of his tail, and the hammock wobbled precariously.

"Sorry," I mumbled as I elbowed him in the chin for the third time in thirty seconds.

After a few more agonizing moments, I twisted sideways, resting my arm and torso across his chest. One leg was cocked where his hips met a tail. I burrowed into his chest, breathing him in, and his thumb stroked my knee.

Edward and Pisceon climbed into their swinging beds. Edward took a few bottles of rum with him.

The gentle glow of the lamps was comforting, and my eyes drooped as the current moved the hammock, Finn's chest rising and falling beneath me.

"Let's take a moment to remember before we go to sleep," Aarna said, sitting up, and Glacies stirring beside her.

"Whatever do you mean?" Edward asked, still wide awake. As the Drowned didn't sleep, he was our dedicated watchman.

"Let's go around the circle and share one memory of those we have lost," Aarna whispered, her ebony tresses fell over her shoulders, and the lamplight was reflected in her eyes.

"Layla and I were only a year apart in age, so when we were younger, we always pretended to be twins. We were competitive to a fault—" Aarna giggled. "Layla never wanted to be a warrior; she wanted to be a princess and wear lovely jewels, but then I started training, and she made it her business to get better than me. I never told her, but I think she achieved it." Aarna smiled at the memory. "I can't help but feel this makes her death my fault."

"It's not your fault." Glacies clasped her hand.

"Your turn." Aarna shook away the shadows, the light making her golden skin glow as she turned to Edward.

"Well, there was a Drowned man by the name of Donahue." Edward took a long swig of rum. "He's gone now. We were intimate once, and after that, he became dark and dangerous, so I shunned him. But the truth is—one I never told him, nor cared to admit even to myself—I was attracted to him, like that, too."

"So, the Drowned boy likes a bit of danger in his men . . ." Pisceon rolled over onto his stomach to survey Edward over the side of his hammock, his cerulean tail fanning behind.

Edward flushed.

"You can go next, Pisceon." Aarna's mouth flattened.

"Hmm." Pisceon paused, flipping onto his back again. "There was once a little merman who lost his whole family to the Shadow, then he became an orphan, but luckily, his big, bad uncle took him in." When no one spoke, Pisceon looked to Skye. "Perhaps you'll pity me enough to warm my hammock now. Or how about you, Drowned boy, I *am* a bad man."

Edward hmphed.

"Would you take this seriously?" Glacies interjected, looking down at Aarna, the hammock wobbling with her sudden shift. "She is trying to help us heal. Who's next?" She swung her head to Finn.

Finn's torso tensed, and my heart lurched as I remembered the visions we'd seen of his mother, Abalone—her blood flowing into the water.

Finn cleared his throat as if he were trying to find the words, then his body tightened, and I knew he was shutting down to avoid the emotions Aarna's probing had brought to the surface. "Continue to be sentimental all you wish, but I'm getting some rest."

I slipped my fingers through his webbed hand. He squeezed.

The others went quiet, and my mind slipped into images of my grandmother and the war we were on the brink of. How many more lives would be lost before the end?

Even though Pisceon had joked and Finn refused to participate, I knew that everyone was thinking of those who were no longer with us as they closed their eyes.

Sleep soon claimed me, soothed by the rise and fall of Finn's chest and the hammock swaying in the current.

52.

MORGANA

Pisceon roused us at dawn, and after much mumbling and grumbling, we were swimming again. The seafloor beneath us rose and dropped in elevations and depressions, occasionally falling away into deep trench-like structures. Then, the sand turned to turrets and dunes. On and on they stretched beneath us, becoming so monotonous that I was glad for our aquatic superspeed.

After what felt like hours, the dunes thinned, and a towering wall of red sandstone appeared on their outskirts. Algae darkened its crevices, and at its center was a gate.

Someone whispered my name, soft and gentle, as if carried to me on the current. Finn. He dropped back from the group to swim beside me, grazing a finger up my arm.

"The walls of Okeanós." He gestured at the gates. The color had returned to his handsome face, his dark hair rippling in the swell, and the silver flecks in his eyes were alight again.

"I need to surface for air before we go in there," I told him. The tightness in my lungs had begun, and I knew I only had a short supply left.

"I'll come up with you." He grinned, and his gills flared. "We'll meet you guys back at the gate," he called to the others.

I yelped in delight as we moved together through the aquamarine depths. Up and up we went.

We swum fast, testing our speed. My powerful Selkie form spiraled upward as I kicked with my webbed feet and parted the waters with my webbed hands. Beside me, Finn shot toward the surface, a blur of torso and tail.

Joy spread through me as I shed my inhibitions, letting the wild sea creature within take over as I rose higher and higher. A gleeful whoop escaped me when we broke the surface, waves lapping at my chest. A blue sky streaked with white clouds stretched overhead.

Finn emerged, too, gills flaring as he brushed his fringe back from his forehead.

"Santorini could've been like this for us." I squeezed the ends of my hair, chest heaving as I drew deep breaths, replenishing my oxygen. "I'm sorry I didn't trust you."

Finn looked away, his throat working as if he was going to say something, but instead he pulled me into his arms, hands cradling my face as he kissed me.

I responded by wrapping my legs around him. My heartbeat increased as his hands slid down my lower back to the curve of my ass.

"We have this time now." A wicked grin curved his lips as he hoisted me up until my breasts crested the water. His dark gaze lingered, eyes hungry as if he were seeing them for the first time. I reached across and touched his face, my fingers tracing his cheekbone.

Pressing his lips to my neck, he dragged them slowly across my skin. Heat exploded below my navel, and I raked my fingers through his hair, tilting his chin up. I held his gaze for a moment before I kissed him again.

His tongue slid into my mouth, tasting of sweet seawater as we kissed each other deeply.

I ground my body against his muscular torso, and his grip tightened beneath my ass as his water magic snaked around my thighs and between my legs. Arousal shuddered through my body, and my fingernails dug into his arms.

I reached one hand beneath the waves to touch his tail, but he caught it.

"I want to watch you." His thumb drifted to my mouth, tracing my lower lip, and he increased the water pressure.

Oh, holy gods.

We stared into each other's eyes as I moved up and down on his toned abs, my breathing heavy as the feeling of the water intensified. I bit my lip against the pleasure, stifling a gasp.

"That's it, baby. You're fucking beautiful." Finn's dark eyes were half-lidded as he tipped his head to study me.

I lost myself in the hardness of his body pressing against mine, the sensation between my legs, and his hands pulling me into him. I surrendered to the feeling, a cry escaping me as I came undone.

He rested his forehead against mine, keeping me close as we rose and fell with the waves, our breath coming in shared, ragged inhales.

"Your magic." I swallowed my pleasure, which was quickly replaced by a wave of guilt. "You shouldn't be using it." I unhooked my legs from his hips, my stomach churning.

"It's fine," he said, eyes aglow with a mischievous glint. "The water manipulation doesn't take much exertion."

"We'd better rejoin the others," I muttered, moving away in the tossing waves.

He caught my wrist. "Wait."

I let him pull me back against him.

"Morgana," he whispered. His mouth was right over my ear, and goosebumps ran down my neck at the sound of my name. " I . . . I love you. I had to say it before we go in there." He pulled back from me, eyes intent on mine as he cupped my chin, his thumb gently grazing my cheek as he sighed, "three simple words that encompass both my salvation and my ruin."

My pulse stuttered as I gazed up at him, searching those dark eyes. It was the first time he'd said those words to me so plainly, without hiding behind poetic sentiments. I stared at the drops of water running down his cheeks as my heart went into overdrive, thudding at my chest, as did my mind. "Finn . . . this thing between us . . . and you being a descendant of Kyano . . . I can't help but wonder if it's real or simply the hands of fate."

"Does it matter?" Finn's dark eyes flicked back and forth, searching mine. "What is love but a feeling you've known someone in a past life? A sense of *home*. Sometimes you feel it right away; sometimes it takes time to develop. But once it settles in your heart, you realize it was there from the moment you first saw them. Tell me you don't feel that when we're together."

My mind fought for control, but I let my heart lead, glancing up at him through wet lashes. "I feel that," I whispered, warmth blooming across my cheeks and neck.

"In Okeanós, Glacies and I will have to be . . ." He paused, a shadow dancing over his face. "With all the kingdoms here, we'll have too . . ."

I chewed on my lip. "But Aarna's parents are okay with it?"

"They are different from our families. You'll see. Even though Aarna's family is supportive, and this is their palace, they will honor my father's wishes while he's here."

"I understand," I said, despite the sour taste on my tongue.

"Thank you." Finn let out a relieved exhale, but his gaze was weighted with sadness, and he kept his hand on my wrist. "If Neptūnus and Niveus hadn't united through marriage, we likely would've ended up at war. Glacies and I honor our parents' wishes for the sake of our people. But things won't stay this way when we succeed them."

I nodded and looked away, steadying my emotions. When I turned back, my face was composed, chin tilted. "Race you to the gate?"

A devilish grin split Finn's face, and then he went under. I plunged after him, slicing through the current with my webbed hands and kicking furiously. But I was no match for the mighty sweep of his crimson-tipped tail, which kept him just ahead until he arched into an elegant dive, gliding to a stop where the others waited thirty feet from the gate. I alighted beside him, my feet sinking into the soft sand.

"You're back? I lost the bet—you lasted longer than I thought." Pisceon shot Finn a conspiratory wink, and my cheeks flamed.

"No one entered into a wager with this man." Edward folded his arms and rolled his eyes. "His bet was with himself."

Glacies blew out a breath as we all started moving toward the towering rust-colored gate. "Well, here goes."

Finn kept his hand on my lower back as we approached, but he let go just as we reached it.

I turned back to him. "Wait. The box?"

"Keep it in your room. I will get the key from Inegar and find you."

I dragged my gaze to Edward. He still had the string bag across his back, the silver box glinting inside it.

At the center of the wall stood an arched doorway, its stone frame intricately carved. Flanking it were elegant minarets, where two Mer guards watched from above, their saffron tails flickering in the current.

Aarna lifted a hand to one of the guards. He gave a curt nod but remained rigid, shoulders squared and spear crossed firmly over his chest.

As we passed under the intricate archway, the door creaked open, and the gardens appeared. Groomed ribbons of sand led the way to the palace, flanked by rows of carefully curated seaweed that rippled with the current. At the center, a glistening pool mirrored the palace's grandeur in its still surface.

My breath hitched as I lifted my eyes from the palace's reflection to the structure itself. No sea life clung to its walls, which were constructed from white marble. It shimmered in the water, its minarets, vast domes, and graceful arches rendered in a pale mother-of-pearl.

We had reached the Kingdom of Okeanós.

53.

ARANARE

Smack. The punching bag swayed with the force of my fists. I grunted as I threw in an uppercut. Sweat was dripping from my shirtless back and chest as I pounded the bag again and again.

Smack, smack, whack. I threw in a roundhouse kick.

The summit. That's what was consuming my mind. The chain rattled as I threw in another uppercut. All the pompous pureblood Mer and some Siren houses would be there, houses that looked down on my family. On my clan.

Smack, smack, whack.

Then, of course, there was *her.* Skye. My heart quickened, heat rising to my cheeks as she swam into my thoughts—the idea of seeing her again, meeting her mahogany eyes once more. The Tidescar on my heart purred at the thought.

Smack, smack, whack.

I had so many burning questions. Questions that kept me awake night after night, tossing and turning or staring at the dark ceiling, since she left. How had she changed? How would she receive me? And most of all, could I face her without letting these all-consuming feelings take hold?

I grabbed my towel and dabbed the sweat from my brow and heaving abs. Then I reached for my water bottle, gulping down the cool liquid before squirting some onto my face, shaking my head as the droplets scattered.

My mind remained turbulent as I showered and tossed my gym bag into the back of my truck. Damp hair clung to my neck, leaving droplets on my jersey as I climbed into the driver's seat.

I exhaled, my hands tapping anxiously at the wheel. My shoulder had healed where her blade had sliced through my flesh, but a pale scar remained, like moonlight slipping through a closed curtain. The disfigured flesh posed another question: would the mark linger, signifying the beginning of something, or would it always be a reminder of its end?

My parents' house was a simple stone cottage at the end of Saltmarsh Row. As I pulled into the drive, the Ranger's headlights wavered across the tightly packed gray bricks, casting them in flickering light.

Dad and I would be diving beneath the waves tonight for the summit, but first, we'd all share a meal as a family.

Mom turned from the bubbling pot on the stove and beamed as I pushed open the front door. A fire was crackling in the stone hearth, filling the cottage with a comforting warmth. Dad sat at the roughly hewn wooden table, his brown hair tied up in its usual topknot, peeling carrots.

My father was the epitome of salt of the earth. Though gifted with High Siren powers, he rarely used them, preferring to fish, mend what was broken across the family's businesses, and spend time with those he loved. He adored my mortal mother, even as her hair turned silver and time etched itself into her face while he remained less touched by age.

He didn't see any of that; he only saw her. There was no doubt he carried a Tidescar on his heart bearing her name, but in his case, it was something wondrous: a lifetime of love that still burned as if it were new, for someone who loved him just as fiercely. I could only hope to have something like that one day.

"Will Skye and Morgana be at the summit?" Mom asked, watching me with that all-knowing gaze only a mother could give, like she could see exactly what was churning in my mind.

At the sound of Skye's name, the Tidescar scrawled across my heart throbbed, burning beneath my skin. "I hope they make it there." I slid into the seat beside Dad and pulled some carrots toward me, setting to work chopping them.

"They're strong girls." Mom leaned over, scooping up the peeled carrots and dropping them into the pot.

"Aye." I nodded in agreement.

She stirred the pot, then set the lid in place before sweeping over to sit beside Dad, slipping her fingers into his calloused hand. "Just try not to get too caught up in the politics of it all."

I raised my brows. "What, that we're half-breeds, less worthy than the rest?"

"Well, that, and everything else . . ." Mom sighed.

"I know the Lugh Sirens have traditionally stayed out of these matters, but with the research I've been doing, and the girls,"—my throat tightened—"I think it's time we got involved."

My father regarded me thoughtfully. "Only the most powerful members of each clan are invited to the summit. That's you and me. With power comes both choice and responsibility." He squeezed Mom's hand. "My allegiance is here—with your mother. But your path is yours to choose, son. And if you opt to fight, I'm certain many in the Lugh clan will stand with you."

I nodded.

"Let's eat," Mom said, clapping her hands as she rose to fetch the pot from the stove.

Dad had stood too and was already slicing and buttering a loaf of bread at the counter.

I glanced at Mom as she slid back into her seat and began ladling food into our bowls. "What will you do while we're gone?"

"The family businesses won't run themselves. And I'd like to continue reviewing the research we've been working on."

We ate, laughed, and talked until the soup was half-gone, the bread reduced to crumbs, and the fire faded to glowing embers. Only then did my father rise and kiss my mother goodbye.

Cold sliced at my skin as we stepped outside, the wind sweeping off the distant cliffs and roaring into the bay. But the sky was clear, stars scattered around a pale moon. The waves sighed as we walked the slick street past Morgana's grandfather's house, and my Tidescar ached.

Isla, that was her name—the girl I'd loved ten years ago. My boots slapping on the wet tar made me think of her now. We'd been walking to the beach from Saltmarsh Row, on this very same street, on a misty evening. She was laughing, her hand clasped in mine. Then she let go and stepped into the road, where a car burst through the mist, its headlights fierce like the putrid yellow eyes of a death-born demon. And I was too slow. She died in my arms.

I rubbed the space on my chest where my faded Tidescar burned as I followed my father over the rocks to the cool, moonlit sand. Casting my eyes to the stars, I whispered the apology I always made when I thought of her.

The waves crashed louder, and my Siren form stirred beneath my skin, aching to be released. I waded into the surf, the dark swell lapping at my hips, scales shimmering across my torso, arms, and back. Then, I dove beneath the water, my mind consumed by a single thought.

I'm going to see Skye again.

54.

MORGANA

Two guards with orange tails as bright as goldfish stopped us at the palace's front door, an open archway in a carved marble wall lined with mosaics. Both had dark skin, striking features, and toned physiques, standing sentinel with their long spears crossed over the entrance.

Aarna swept us aside, moving to the front of the group.

"Princess." The guards bowed their heads. "We didn't see you there." Their spears remained across the door. "Can we ask what *he* is doing with you?" They were staring at Edward.

Aarna gestured a webbed hand at him, her gold bangles jangling. "That Drowned boy saved Pisceon's life. He should be treated as a guest of honor."

"And what about *this*?" The guard turned his dark eyes on me.

"This—" Finn shot forward, drawing himself up to his full height and scowling at the Mer guard. "*This* is the last of the ancient Selkies. You will speak to her like you'd speak to a queen."

"Finn." I grabbed him by the elbow as heat spread to my cheeks and ears.

"Prince Aigéan is right. This seal girl is also a guest of honor. Now move aside, or I'll tell my father you barred me from entering my own home." Aarna stiffened, her dark tresses swaying with the swell.

The Okeanós guards moved out of our way, and we swam through the arched ogival entrance into vast open-air chambers. The airy room was constructed from marble, but every inch of its walls was painted with intricate designs.

Aarna guided us into another grand room, where a colorful and growing crowd, made up of Mer and a few Sirens, had begun to gather around a decadent table spread with delicacies. At the far end, five thrones stood watch, empty for now. I presumed the Okeanós family was somewhere among the guests.

Aarna must have spotted them, because she left us and rushed to a stunning woman with dark hair and gold jewelry, presumably her mother. Beside her, a dark-skinned merman with a blue mohawk and a sapphire tail to match pulled the princess into his embrace.

"Oh, my sweet daughter." The Okeanós Mer queen wailed as Aarna collapsed into her arms, trembling with sobs. A younger merman—striking, with coffee-toned skin, sweeping blue hair like his father's, and a neatly groomed mustache—rested a comforting hand on Aarna's back.

"That's Aarna's brother, Prince Salil, Queen Samudra, and King Ali." Glacies's voice was tight as she watched the family grieve Princess Layla.

My gaze swept the room for the Thálassians, and my stomach dropped when I couldn't see them. My eyes landed on King Neptūnus, and my teeth ground together. He watched us from beside the table of food, dark eyes narrowed, and his long, black hair drifting in the swell.

Rage simmered in me as his mouth curled into a sneer, eyes sweeping our group with disdain. I glanced sideways at Finn. Every muscle in his body was taut, his jaw clenched as he gave his father a curt nod.

The king flicked his golden tail in response, and my fingers hovered over the hilt of my dagger. The fury coursing through me lured my power to the surface. His cold gaze lingered on me, and my mind was consumed by all he'd done—the death of my grandmother, the dungeons he'd thrown me into, and the scars he'd left on Finn.

The king's eyes darted to my blade, and for a heartbeat, I thought I saw fear. But his sneer quickly returned as he moved away into the crowd with a sweep of his gilded tail. Finn remained rigid beside me, a muscle twitching in his jaw as he watched his father draw King Ali into conversation.

"Come on." Glacies took Finn by the elbow and pulled him from the space, beckoning the rest of us to follow. "Let's go find our chambers." She guided us from the meeting room back into the vast high-ceilinged space. Staircases rose in three directions, and above them, rows and rows of intricately carved archways with pointed crowns lined each level.

Aarna emerged behind us, wiping her kohl-stained eyes.

"I couldn't see the Thálassians," Skye said, her voice trembling, and I knew she was thinking of Alexandros.

Aarna's lower lip quivered, but she pulled herself together with a shaky exhale. "The rest of them made it. They are here and safe."

"Can you show us to our rooms, my love?" Glacies asked gently.

"You'll be on the third floor," Aarna snapped. "With *him.*" She glared at Finn, and Glacies reached for her, but Aarna shook her off.

My heart clenched for both of them—for *all* of us.

"I need to get cleaned up." Glacies sighed. "Someone grab the Drowned boy."

With a grin, Pisceon swept Edward into his muscular arms. "Hold on tight." He gave a low chuckle.

Edward let out a resigned huff.

We alighted on the third floor, and Skye grabbed my arm, guiding me to the door beside hers.

Glacies offered us a kind smile as she and Finn moved to a doorway on my left. "See you later for the soiree."

"Can I have the box?" I asked Edward, who was taking the room on Skye's other side. He fumbled with the bag across his back and handed me the beautiful silver object.

"Come to my room once you've freshened up," Skye said, looking between us. There was an ache in her eyes, which pleaded not to be left alone.

The rooms of Okeanós were equally beautiful to those in Thálassa. They had walls of gleaming white marble and domed ceilings crafted from something resembling abalone shell, stretching out like a mimicry of moonlight hitting the sea.

I unbuckled my dagger and placed it beside the silver box on the elegant low stone table, which was the room's centerpiece. Kicking off with my webs, I breaststroked upward and flung myself into the floating bed, a seaweed cradle suspended midchamber by thick kelp. I let my legs stretch out, sinking into the silky hammock and dragging a hand over my face.

The rage King Neptūnus stirred in me had ignited my power, and my elated heartbeat spread it through every inch of my skin, itching to erupt and reduce the merman to dust.

I exhaled. I needed to avoid confrontation with the king at all costs, especially when I was tired—too tired to harness my shields. Every muscle in my being was aching from our travels, and my eyes drooped with fatigue. I didn't feel like going to the soiree. I'd spent the last of my strength holding my power back, and all I wanted now was to curl into this soft cradle and drift to sleep, rocked by the gentle ebb and flow of the surrounding waters.

But I couldn't. We had to finish this.

I sat up, my long tresses falling over my shoulders as I surveyed the box on the table below. It glinted under the glow of the pearl lamps on the walls, taunting me, a reminder of the blood now on my hands, the blood I had spilled to claim it.

We'd done it. We'd faced Thera's trials to bring Poseidon's Box to the summit, but I'd become a killer in the process.

Finn would find me at some point with the key. Maybe then, all of this could finally end. The thought sparked enough resolve for me to swing my legs over the hammock's edge and drop to the floor.

I padded into the adjacent bathing area. The walls were adorned with a mosaic of tiles. On them, coral shelves displayed body glitters, golden jewelry, and sea flowers that could be pinned into your hair, whilst schools of cleaner fish flitted through the space.

Above the shelves, there was a mirror. The glass had been cut into the shape of an onion dome, and around the edges was a frame woven with intricate engravings. I didn't recognize the weary face staring back at me. Purple rings rimmed my eyes, and my cheeks were gaunt. There was so much going on that I'd forgotten to eat most days. I supposed going to the soiree would do me good, as I could use some decadent Mer delicacies.

I blew out a breath, reaching for a sea flower and trying to pin it into my hair, but my hands still trembled from my encounter with the king. It kept slipping free and wafting away on the swell.

I rifled through the jewelry: intricate earrings, stacks of bangles, broad collars, and rings with colorful stones lined a lacquered tray on one of the shelves.

They were all beautiful—too beautiful. I didn't even know where to begin. With a frustrated sigh, I left the jewelry behind, raked my fingers through my hair in a half-hearted attempt at grooming, and made my way to Skye's room.

Her chambers turned out to be identical to mine: an elegant bathroom, a stone table, a hanging bed, and a cluster of sea sponge couches for reclining. Edward was already seated on one of them, while Skye swanned between the bathroom and the central area as she adorned herself in the jewels of Okeanós.

Edward motioned to the empty spot beside him. "Ah, good, you're here. I've been meaning to have a word with you. Skye doesn't share my fascination with ancient poems." Skye snorted from the bathroom.

"What is it?" I asked as I sank down next to him.

"Whilst I was in Thálassa, I spent a good deal of time in the library, reading about the prophecy and Kyano, who was, in fact, a distant relative of the Thálassians." Edward rested his elbows on his knees, studying me closely.

"He's related to Finn." I massaged my forehead.

"I came across a poem that suggests Poseidon laid down a curse on Kyano as he did on Manannán, and I cannot help but feel it plays a part in all of this."

I nodded, chewing on my lip. "Yes, I saw it."

Edward's copper brows kicked up. "Whatever do you mean?"

"I've been having visions of Manannán—of his life as a man, his rise to God of the Drowned, and the fate that followed."

Skye swooped over and started pinning flowers into my hair.

"Did the visions reveal what became of Kyano?" Edward leaned forward.

I shook my head. "He just disappeared in a flash of light."

"How curious." Edward's brow furrowed.

Skye chuckled as she linked a necklace around my neck. "I saw how you looked at Finn's father. For a moment, I thought you might murder him in front of us all."

"Yes, my magic wanted to." I swallowed.

"I know he was behind your grandmother's death, but while we're here, you must keep it in check. It isn't safe." Edward wrung his freckled hands.

"It's not just that . . ." My voice cracked.

Skye paused, fingers tangled in my hair, and looked at me inquisitively.

"He burns Finn . . . with his lightning. Finn doesn't like to speak about it, but he's done it since he was a kid."

"The scars!" Skye exhaled.

"Good god," Edward muttered.

I nodded.

"When I last saw Finn—before I returned to Ruadán's Port—he met me in Therme Skótos for a sort of . . . date, and he'd just come from his father. The burns were fresh, and they were all over his body. Seeing the king brings all that back."

Skye observed me with understanding in her dark eyes.

"He also has this new tattoo . . ." My voice grew quieter.

"The heart upon his chest?" Edward chimed in. "I noticed it as well."

"I suspect it has something to do with his father, because when I mentioned it, the same shadows passed over his face as when I noticed the scars."

Skye's eyes filled with curiosity. "Did you say a heart?"

"Yes."

"When I did a dream ceremony with Peisinoe, we made a blood oath, and a heart tattoo appeared on our hands. When that blood oath was fulfilled, the heart disappeared."

"You think Finn's made a blood oath?" I stared at her, jaw slack and mind whirring.

"I'll examine his tattoo at the soiree and see if it matches the one that appeared on my hand."

Skye stepped back, and I moved to the mirror, letting out a small gasp. She had woven white sea flowers through my hair, and though the jewelry had overwhelmed me, her choice was perfect—a broad collar of hammered gold, delicately layered with filigree, and a pair of matching earrings.

"I don't care what anyone says—looking good can feel like armor. And tonight, I think we all need a little of that," she said with a grin, rubbing balm between her webbed hands before she used them to style Edward's copper hair.

"Such a Siren thing to say. I don't know how I never guessed it," I rasped with a chuckle. The others laughed, too, and for a minute, the darkness lifted in this simple moment with my two best friends.

55.

SKYE

My stomach tightened as we made our way back downstairs. I had been smiling and joking with Edward and Morgana, but my heart was thudding against my chest, and it had taken all my willpower to stop my hands from trembling as I pinned Morgana's hair. *Aranare.* Would he be here? Only the most powerful members of each house were invited. Surely that wasn't him, I exhaled, shaking the thoughts away.

The soiree rooms mirrored the palace's grandeur, with high ceilings and intricate archways, but here, every surface was adorned in elaborate tile mosaics. The space was alive with color and movement as Mer and Sirens filled the hall, each dressed in their finest displays of oceanic elegance. Edward gasped as he and Morgana stepped in behind me, the three of us freezing in place as we entered the space.

Princess Aarna hovered beside her family, radiant in golden jewelry, her crimson tail gleaming as they spoke in hushed tones. King Neptūnus drifted nearby, deep in conversation with a stunning pale-haired woman whose icy-blue tail shimmered like frost. Beside her loomed a towering merman with a chest twice the breadth of Neptūnus's and a tail of glittering obsidian. A jagged crown of icicles rested on his head, glinting in the light.

"Bit of a tail-measuring contest all this, if you ask me," a voice with a rich accent crooned behind me. I spun around. Alexandros was floating there, his bronzed chest flexing as he grinned lazily.

I threw myself into his arms. "You're okay." I pulled back, observing his face.

His playful expression grew grave. "Layla stayed behind to fight, giving us the chance to reach the tunnel. She gave her life for us."

I glanced over at Aarna and her family again. A shadow hung over their faces while the other partygoers made merry around them.

"Where's Porphura?" I scanned the crowd for the lavender-haired mermaid.

"She hasn't left her room." Alexandros's shoulders curled, and I noticed the weariness behind his smile.

"We sent Layla to a peaceful afterlife," I whispered past the lump in my throat. Beside me, Morgana nodded, her eyes reflecting the same sorrow.

Alexandros thumbed my cheek. "I am glad you are coming into your own, bella."

I flushed and looked away.

"And the tunnel?" I pulled my gaze back to his, searching those purple-flecked eyes.

"The darkness we faced there will haunt me for all eternity." Alexandros shook his head. "But come now, let's not speak of such things," he said, straightening as he swept an arm around Morgana and me, flashing a wink at Edward. "Let's get some drinks, and I will point everyone in the room out to you. You can try to guess which ones I've made love to."

I nudged his chest playfully with my shoulder, letting him keep Morgana and me tucked in his muscular embrace as he guided us through the gathered Mer toward a table piled high with food and drink. Edward trailed behind.

Alexandros released us, his back muscles rippling and his lilac tail swishing as he leaned over the decadent spread. He filled three golden goblets with wine and handed one to each of us before pouring his own.

"Now, where were we . . ." The purple-haired merman slipped an arm around my lower back as he drifted between Morgana and me again. Sipping from his glass, he surveyed the crowd.

"That's Queen Drifa Niveus and King Väinö Niveus—Glacies's parents—talking to King Neptūnus. They rule the Arctic Ocean." Alexandros pointed to the large merman with the crown of icicles and his stunning wife, whom we'd seen on entering.

Alexandros took another long swig of wine, then swept his gaze across the room. "That magnificent creature over there with Glacies and Finn is Glacies's brother, Jökull."

"Wow," Morgana mumbled, flushing, and I turned to see a muscular merman with sweeping blonde hair, an icy-blue tail, and shards of frost-like armor gleaming across his chest.

I narrowed my eyes, watching Finn's flexing torso as he spoke with Glacies and her brother. His golden dress cuffs were in place; now I knew they hid the veins of the Shadow. The heart tattoo on his chest resembled the one that had formed on my hand during the dream ceremony, but his had two concentric bands, whereas mine just had a single line.

I turned to the others, and Morgana leaned around Alexandros, eyes questioning. "I can't be sure," I whispered.

Alexandros gestured to a beautiful dark-skinned Mer-couple. "King Kaiholo Pācificus and Queen Moana Pācificus rule the Pacific. Beside them, the Sundara Sirens from the Indian Ocean, Mai and Malik." I followed his gaze to another striking dark-haired Siren—this one with a tail—and beside her, a long-limbed male Siren with scaled legs and wavy hair swept into a bun.

"I can't keep up," Morgana muttered.

Alexandros ran a hand through his amethyst hair. "I find drinking helps."

She looked to Finn and Glacies, then King Neptūnus. "I think I'll stay off the wine tonight."

"And who else . . . Ah yes, the House of Krumos from the Southern Ocean," Alexandros said, gesturing toward a burly man with a bronzed chest clad in gleaming steel. Beside him stood a queen, regal and pale as ice, with sweeping red hair that floated like fire in the water. "And their son's here somewhere. Ah, yes." He pointed to a handsome merman with auburn hair and pale skin like his mother's. "Prince Hurley. Now, I wouldn't mind sleeping with him."

"Is that everyone?" I asked, my throat tightening as I scanned the room.

Alexandros rubbed the dark stubble on his cleft chin thoughtfully. "Yes, we've got Neptūnus, Okeanós, Krumos, Niveus, Pācificus, and Thálassa Mer representatives. "And Agápē, Sundara, and Kaimana Siren representatives, as well as Queen Asherah and the other Mors survivors. We're just missing—"

"The Lugh Sirens," a voice said from behind us. Smooth as honey, sweet with temptation, yet tightening something deep within me like a drawn bowstring.

Aranare.

I turned, and my stomach knotted as I took him in—caramel skin, golden eyes, and a bronzed chest with a smattering of dark, glistening scales that matched his inky tail. He looked utterly at home in his Siren form.

Beside him was an older, yet equally handsome, man with shoulder-length brown hair and a chiseled chest adorned with the same black scales.

"My father, Dylan." Aranare waved a hand to the man.

"Nice to meet you." Dylan's kind eyes lingered on me, then he turned to Morgana. "It's lovely to see you like this." He grinned broadly at us while Aranare's face stayed tense, a faint flush in his cheeks as if he were struggling to keep his expression composed.

My gaze slipped to Aranare's right arm, and my mouth went dry. There, between bronzed skin and glinting scales, was a pale scar, the one I'd left when I slashed him moments after taking Parker's life.

I glanced at him from under my lashes, wondering if he'd read my thoughts—if he was thinking the same thing. But he stared straight ahead as if determined to look anywhere but at me.

So, that's how it was now? I'd told him I hated him—that I'd never forgive him—and I meant it. But I hadn't expected it to feel like this. Like a knife in my chest was being twisted. I pressed my lips together to stop the sudden unwelcome tremble, placing a hand on Alexandros's forearm.

"More wine, bella?" he asked, reaching behind me to grab the vat and top up my glass.

"Father, we must go and say hello to the Sundara Sirens," Aranare said coolly. Dylan shot us a final friendly smile before his son led him away.

"You okay?" Morgana whispered as Aranare and his father greeted the stunning Sundara Siren, Alexandros had called Mai. She adjusted her hair casually as she spoke with Aranare, her attention fixed on him.

"Yes, of course." I brushed off her comment, watching Aranare again. He was still speaking with Mai, with not even the hint of a glance in my direction.

I turned back to the others to find Alexandros's eyes darting between me and Aranare.

"Perhaps I should guess who *you've* slept with here." His indigo-flecked eyes twinkled.

"We haven't slept together," I snapped.

"No, but you want to, don't you, bella?"

A few hours later, after too much Mer wine, I found myself wandering the gardens. I seated myself at the edge of the crystalline pool, trailing my fingers across its glistening surface. As I moved, bioluminescence clung to my skin, lighting my hands. The water had to be magic—there was no other explanation for how a pool like this could exist beneath the ocean. I'd heard of brine pools deep in the sea, but this wasn't like those. It was clear, reflective . . . almost otherworldly. Maybe they had bewitched a brine pool.

I chuckled and tipped back more wine, my curls brushing against my back. I tried not to dwell on the logistics; it made my head spin. Thankfully, I'd never been much of a science enthusiast, so accepting the mechanics of this world came easily enough. I stretched my scaled legs into the pool, letting them drift through the water as bioluminescence glittered in the ripples they stirred.

Edward had stayed inside with the Thálassian Mer, and Morgana had already excused herself, claiming she needed rest, but we both knew the truth: her eyes hadn't left Finn or King Neptūnus all night. Something had warred behind her expression. The merman was under her skin, coursing through her like a drug, sweet in small doses, but I feared the darkness within him meant too much could be fatal.

I stood, sipping from my intricate golden goblet as I paced beside the pool. My mind filled with images of Aranare and the beautiful Siren he was still inside talking to—Mai. When I left, she was biting her lip and looking up at him as he laughed at something she'd said.

Guilt flushed my cheeks; I couldn't believe how badly I'd wanted to throttle her, especially when she'd done nothing to deserve it.

Why should I care? I hated him. *Hated* him.

I tossed back more of my wine. If it hadn't been for him . . . I shook my head angrily.

Stop blaming him. You killed Parker. You're the monster, an unwanted voice in my subconscious hissed.

But if he hadn't been there, I would have . . . What would I have done?

I sensed a presence behind me, and I spun around.

There he floated, tail gleaming like an oil spill, bronzed abs tensing under a scattering of scales, and amber eyes shining with emotion as they met mine. Something about those eyes was so familiar, so comforting after everything we'd been through, but I shoved the feeling deep down, locking my shields to ensure the guy wasn't using any of his allure on me.

"What do you want?" I snapped, planting my hands on my hips.

Aranare reached for me as if to take my hand, then hesitated and pulled back.

"Are we going to talk about what happened?" he asked softly, a flush rising in his cheeks as he crossed his arms over his chest.

"You didn't seem so keen to talk inside," I bit out, my spine stiffening.

He ran a hand through his dark curls with a weary sigh. "I didn't expect seeing you again to be so hard."

Something tightened in my heart, but I tossed my hair over my shoulder and turned away from him. "There's nothing to talk about. What's done is done."

"I thought maybe with some time . . . with some space . . . you might see things differently."

Tears stung my eyes as I swung back to him. "And how might that be?"

"He hurt you in the name of love—but that's not love."

"And what about you going to his house? What did you hurt me in the name of?"

"That's different," Aranare breathed. His expression changed, and a sadness seeped out.

"How?"

"I went there to protect you, not wound you."

A sob tore from my chest as I hurled my goblet into the pool. The last crimson liquid bled into the clear water, reminding me of spilled blood. Parker's blood. On my hands.

Tears streamed down my face as I rushed forward, pounding my fist against Aranare's solid form. "I hate you for doing this to me. You made me a monster. If I hadn't killed Parker, I wouldn't have been forced into this scaly, freakish body. I could have . . . things could have been different . . ."

"You're not a monster," he whispered, catching my wrists as his eyes locked with mine. He was staring so hard I felt it pinching in my chest.

I glared up at him through teary lashes. "Oh, yeah? What am I then?"

"Aye, you are no longer human. But you are the most captivating creature I have ever seen. I've thought this since I first saw you at my uncle's cafe. This form, all of it . . . It's still you. And I think you're perfect. Not in spite of this. With it. Because of it."

"Don't talk to me like this. Don't you *ever* talk to me like this," I cried, struggling to wrench free of his grasp. "Do you know what I have been living with after that night?"

"Skye," he said softly, and the way he said my name wrapped around my heart and squeezed.

"Let go of me!"

He released my wrists, and I yanked myself free, stepping back with a glare. "I told you I'll never forgive you."

His eyes lingered on me for a moment, but he said nothing. I held his gaze, fuming, hating the silence and whatever thoughts hid behind it. When he still said nothing, my cheeks began to burn, so I stalked away with a sharp wave of my arm.

I stormed through the garden, wiping at my eyes as the ache in my throat swelled. Pushing it down, I slipped back into the glittering mosaic chamber, past the mingling Mer.

My eyes scanned the crowd until they landed on Alexandros. Without a word, I grabbed his wrist and pulled him through the grand archway. As we left, I glanced back. Aranare drifted in the doorway behind me, his face etched with grief as he watched us go.

Something ached in my chest, but I pushed it down, down, down, keeping my arm linked with Alexandros's as he led me to his chambers.

56.

MORGANA

A fanfare of trumpets announced the summit, their sound drifting through the palace. I hadn't slept well, my mind consumed with images of King Neptūnus's dark eyes and the silver box. I stepped from my chambers just as Edward and Skye emerged on either side of me.

"Here goes. Soon, we'll know if the Mer will go to war." I choked back a rising tide of emotion as I looked between my friends.

Skye rubbed both her temples. "My head hurts."

"Someone had a good night." I giggled.

"I don't want to talk about it." She shook her head. "Where is this thing supposed to be held?" She dragged her gaze along the upper floors of the palace.

"I guess we follow the obnoxious trumpets. How very typical." Edward rolled his eyes.

The horns echoed from a central point in the palace, and he'd had the right idea. Mer and Sirens were emerging along the curved corridors, all making their way toward a grand marble staircase where the two passageways converged and descended. We allowed ourselves to be swept along with the crowd.

A glittering black tail and familiar muscular back caught my attention. "Aranare," I called, and he turned, bronze chest tensing with the movement. His eyes glowed topaz down here, alight with a wildness they never had on land. His smile fell into an expression of disapproval, bordering on abhorrence, as his eyes traveled over us, and Skye stiffened beside me.

"I-I'm sorry, I've got to find my father." Aranare's mouth flattened. With a flick of his midnight tail, he shot into the crowd as if he couldn't get away fast enough.

"What happened last night?" My eyes sprang wide, and I gripped Skye's wrist.

"Don't ask," she mumbled, her cheeks staining red.

We continued moving along with the throng. A webbed hand seized my arm, and my breath hitched as it pulled me back from the others, but it was only Finn. "I need to talk to you—now," he hissed, brow furrowed and face pale.

"What is it?" I asked as he yanked me from the crush of bodies and pressed me against the wall.

"I—" Finn raked a hand through his hair, biting his lip as if the words were lost somewhere he couldn't reach.

I tilted my head when he made eye contact, studying his expression.

Then behind him, I heard someone say, "Well, if it isn't the little Selkie." The voice sent a chill through me, cold as the deepest parts of the Atlantic. My magic surged to the surface, and I knew who it was before I raised my eyes.

King Neptūnus emerged from the crowd, gliding toward his son. His dark hair billowed around his shoulders, and the tattoos above his brows tightened with the same fierce expression that was carved across his face. He wore gleaming silver armor and a matching coronet.

"Father." Finn stiffened.

"Come now, Aigéan, we must find our seats." The king dragged his black eyes over me, radiating distaste. "I'd ask your Selkie friend to join us, but the Neptūnus seats are reserved for purebloods. I don't know what would happen if we let such riffraff under our banners; she might very well implode."

My heart smashed my rib cage with angry fists, and my power rose in response. I gritted my teeth as it hummed beneath my skin, and my eyes burned, alerting me that the power was shining in them, too.

The king noticed and let out a dark chuckle.

He's baiting me. This is what he wants.

I took a steadying breath, feeling the magic retreating as I offered a calm smile.

"Let's go before the little beastie loses her temper," the king said, followed by a cold, manic laugh that quickly faded as he crossed his muscular arms, eyeing his son expectantly.

Finn looked like he wanted to speak, but his father was waiting, watching. He gave me a look that I felt somewhere in my chest, then turned and followed King Neptūnus and the rest of the Mer.

I waited until they vanished into the crowd, then trailed behind the last of the lingerers toward the doorway at the base of the grand marble stairs.

Inside, the summit chamber stretched like a vast, domed sanctum carved from the sea's heart. Its walls of white stone were inlaid with runes etched in glimmering silver. Overhead, a soaring central ceiling of translucent pearl refracted the bioluminescent light from enchanted orbs suspended in the current.

I stopped, my heart lodged in my throat, awestruck by the grandeur before us.

Edward and Skye stood frozen by the doorway to my right, and I rushed to join them, my mouth falling open as I took in the rest of the space. The floor was a great circular mosaic depicting the Insignia of the Ocean and its houses. Around the edge, what must have been the unique brand of each great household was carved into stone, the etchings glowing like the runes on the walls above. A hollow ring of clear crystal—the speaker's circle—was in the chamber's center.

Elevated platforms of polished stone, arranged in tiers around the speaker's platform, housed different royal families. Silk banners hung vertically along the walls, depicting each house's lineages. Their colors were vibrant, and they waved and shifted with the current.

"Where should we sit?" Edward asked nervously.

I scanned the space and the radiant banners. I understood his hesitation. None of us had a "house" here.

"Come on, let's sit with the Kingdom of Thálassa." Skye pushed forward, taking us both by the hand and leading us to where the Thálassians were gathered, a space adorned with purple banners depicting the Insignia of the Ocean and a murex snail shell.

Queen Peisinoe and King Proteus offered warm smiles, and I couldn't help but grin in return. If I'd had to choose a house, it would have been Thálassa, especially knowing my grandmother had once lived among them.

Skye slid onto the platform on the king and queen's left, beside Damon, Alexandros, and Porphura. Alexandros's purple hair was tied up in a bun, and Damon's dark curls drifted about his face as he turned to wink at me.

Porphura offered us a weak smile, and my heart clenched. Her features were pale, her hair disheveled, and her posture weighed down by grief.

Edward and I slipped onto the podium, which placed me beside Queen

Peisinoe. Her dark hair, adorned with golden jewels, cascaded down her back, glinting against the aquamarine shimmer of her scaled body.

I scanned the chamber, eyes searching for Finn. He sat beside his father with Glacies on his other side, Pisceon and Inegar sitting to the king's left. Behind them, a trio of pearl-tailed guards hovered, and something in my gut twisted as memories of Neptūnus's cold, dark dungeons came rushing back.

Their deep-emerald banners were emblazoned with the ocean's shared insignia and crowned by a dark wave tipped with pearlescent foam.

Mr. Inegar peeled away from the king's side and glided toward the central podium.

You've got to be kidding me. He's running this show. I shot Edward a look, which he returned.

"We are gathered here to discuss Manannán's imposing threat," Inegar began. "As you all know, the God of the Drowned has returned." A ripple of anger coursed through the crowd, and he paused, waiting for it to subside. "With his blood-fueled henchmen, he has reclaimed the Garden of Mortimer and overthrown the seven Drowned Protectors."

I dragged my gaze to Queen Asherah seated with the remaining Mer of Mors on a dais beneath the Neptūnus delegation. Behind them hung a black banner emblazoned with a gnarled sea flower.

"We have called you here to decide whether we will go to war," Mr. Inegar boomed, then fell silent, clasping his webbed hands over his chest as he surveyed the crowd, inviting them to respond.

"If Manannán has reclaimed Mortimer, what does that mean?" The question came from the dark-haired and striking Mai of the Sundara Sirens.

Mr. Inegar's face was grave. "We do not know. The gods never expected the Mors Kingdom to fall."

A ripple passed through the crowd again.

"I say we go to war!" The cry came from King Väinö, Glacies's father, from where her family sat beside the Neptūnus Mer under banners of ice blue, each adorned with a snowflake.

"Agreed," boomed King of Krumos from the next dais over. He sat beneath silver banners marked with a shard of ice, flanked by his red-haired queen and their son, Prince Hurley. "We've already forged barbed arrows and crossbows for everyone, as instructed by the Neptūnus ward," he declared, leaning forward against the stone railing. He glanced at Pisceon, who gave a slight, encouraging nod.

"But there are so few of us left," wailed Mai, her dark eyes wide with fear.

"Yes," Aarna's mother, Queen Samudra, cried from underneath orange banners. "The Shadow has made us vulnerable."

"So you would cower like weaklings?" King Väinö rumbled. "We still have *some* powers."

My gaze landed on King Neptūnus, silently observing the chaos, his eyes gleaming as he stroked his chin.

"It's easy for you, Niveus Mer, with your icy weapons, but what about us Sirens, whose powers lie only in the mind?" Mai called from her podium.

"*We* will fight with you."

I turned to see who had spoken. Aranare was standing tall, his voice steady. Beside him was his father, beneath black banners emblazoned with a Celtic triskele.

"You survived the Shadow by breeding with humans," Malak shouted from Mai's side, eyes blazing as he glared at Aranare, whose podium was beside his own.

The room erupted into a frenzy of frantic conversations, voices rising and blurring in a tangled crescendo. I whipped my gaze from one house to the next, trying to follow the storm of clashing words.

"This is chaos," I muttered under my breath.

"Happens every time." Queen Peisinoe turned her dark eyes on me. "We will go to war in the end, as the stronger houses like Niveus and Neptūnus support it, but first we must sit through this charade." She sighed and reached for her husband's hand.

My stomach clenched as I noticed the dark veins had crept further down the king's neck. My eyes shot to Finn, who was wearing his silver arm cuffs. When his dark gaze met mine across the room, it seemed filled with something—fear and . . . *sadness.*

"Silence!" King Neptūnus's cry rumbled through the room like a crashing wave. His dark hair rippled behind him, and his golden tail glittered as he glided to the stage, holding a silver box.

My stomach dropped to the soles of my feet as my gaze snapped back to Finn. He had left his seat to follow his father to the circular stage, his eyes carefully avoiding mine.

No—it couldn't be.

My breathing turned ragged. It had been in my room . . . We were supposed to open it together.

"Isn't that your box?" Edward gripped my arm as King Neptūnus raised it into the air. On its lid was the opaque black stone, a heart.

I nodded, my stomach too nauseated for words.

"My people, there is hope." King Neptūnus kept the box held high above his head for all to see, and Peisinoe, recognizing it, shot me a quizzical glance.

Panic clogged my mind as I watched the man who had caused my grandmother's death present the box to the son whom I was now sure had helped him. I gripped the edge of our dais, afraid that if I didn't hold on, I might collapse.

"My son has found one of the items of Poseidon's Trinity."

King Neptūnus handed the box to Mr. Inegar, and he produced the silver key I remembered from the pawnshop. "He is a descendant of the god and will release the fragment of power."

I swallowed. "Fragment of power." I turned to Peisinoe. "What does he mean?"

"There's an old legend," Peisinoe whispered hurriedly. "When Poseidon stripped the Mer of their powers, he left a chance for them to reclaim them, using Ătlanticus magic to store fragments of them in three items: a ring, a box, and a necklace. It's said that when all three are reunited, the Mer's full power will be restored."

"Some of you have been whispering about me, saying I may not be of sound mind." A smile twitched King Neptūnus's lips as he scanned the room. "But just remember, when one-third of your powers are returned to you, the Neptūnus Kingdom and *my* son were responsible."

"The poem," Edward gasped from my other side. "'When my artifacts are united in holy trinity, my people will reclaim their power, and my son, Mer Prince Kyano, will be free.' But what does this have to do with Kyano?"

I didn't care about the poem, Kyano, or this trinity. My world was fading in and out of focus as a dark mist consumed my subconscious. Finn had lied to me . . . and I'd let myself fall for him again.

On the speaker's circle far below, Mr. Inegar handed Finn the key. He slid it into the box, which trembled in King Neptūnus's webbed hands. With a sudden jolt, a ripple of power erupted, undulating through the chamber like a shockwave. The force rolled through the water before sweeping into each Mer like a tide returning home.

The Mer in the room glowed beautifully for a moment, as if remembering something long forgotten. I leaned forward, mouth agape, as Proteus gasped, the fragment of magic pouring into his being. He slumped forward, then shot upright, shoulders thrown back.

A stillness hung over the chamber. The light faded, but something had changed. Power. The air was charged with it.

"Finn dragged me around the ocean looking for this . . . this box, when I could have been searching for the prophecy?" My throat was so dry that the words would barely come.

Peisinoe turned to me, kindness softening her dark eyes. "He needed you. He couldn't have opened it without you. The legend says the box can only be unlocked when two descendants of the gods make love before it—a symbol of unity."

The old man's words from the church swam into my mind. *The question remains: Can you do what needs to be done to open it?*

Edward grabbed my hand. "Please don't tell me you lay with him in front of the box?"

I clutched the stone dais, drawing breath after shuddering breath as my heart fractured into a million tiny pieces, each sharp and slicing as they cascaded through my veins.

"Oh, good lord. You did, didn't you?"

I ignored him, a storm of nausea, grief, and rage erupting inside me as the black mist rose to consume me. I fled from the chamber, shoving past Edward and the other Mer, the world a mess of blurry outlines in an all-consuming nothingness.

Behind me, a swell of movement and noise erupted as the crowd rose in cheers for the Neptūnus royals still standing on the stage.

57.

MORGANA

I stumbled toward my chambers, the world passing in a warped haze of colors, shapes, and sounds obscured by the pain and confusion clouding my being. I collided with people and objects, but I didn't care.

Tears blurred my vision as I grabbed my dagger from the stone table in the center of my chambers, where it had sat beside the box.

The box. Finn—or one of the Neptūnus Mer—must have slipped back to retrieve it. The thought ignited a ribbon of rage that curled through me, kindling the power slumbering at my core. I clenched my fists, trying to contain it.

Then the door to my room swung open, and there was Finn. His ebony hair was disheveled, his chest rising and falling with quick, ragged breaths. His emerald tail flicked behind him, and his expression was twisted by fear.

My power stirred, purring in response to the rage that burned through me as I met his dark gaze. "*You . . .*" My heart was pounding as I glared at him. "You dragged me across the ocean chasing this box when I could've been searching for the prophecy? We made a promise to Peisinoe and Proteus."

"Having a third of the Mer's power will help Proteus and my people. It won't stop the Shadow, but its effect will lessen," Finn said quickly.

"So this was for your own selfish gain? You used me. You slept with me in front of the box just to cure yourself. If you'd been honest, I—I would've helped you willingly."

"That's not it at all. You don't . . . You can't understand."

"What don't I understand? You distracted me just now in the hall so Mr. Inegar could slink into my chambers and retrieve the box!" My power raced through my veins, pulsing with my elated heartbeat, begging to be unleashed, to annihilate the merman who had hurt me this deeply.

Finn's black eyes shone with agony. "I stopped you to tell you everything, but my father . . ."

"The Captain died hoping I would find the prophecy!" I ground out. "It was his final wish."

Finn moved toward me with a flick of his tail, reaching for my face, but I reared backward. "I'm sorry," he whispered. "This was only to protect you."

"You *lied* to me, and I don't understand why, because the prophecy could save you, too."

He drifted back and forth in silence for a moment, a muscle ticking in his jaw. At last, he turned to me, his expression unreadable, his voice cold as ice. "I will never help you find the prophecy. In fact, I will do everything I can to ensure you never find it. If that means lying to you, I'll do it again. If it means letting this insidious disease claim me, I'll do that, too."

Silver power crackled through my clenched, trembling fists. "I'm going to ask you again . . . *Did you kill my grandmother?*"

Pain flickered across Finn's face, his anger giving way to something desperate. "Morgana," he said softly, almost a plea.

I stifled a sob. "Did you?"

"No, I didn't kill her." He sighed.

A sliver of something quivered inside of me: relief.

"But I may as well have . . ."

The relief vanished, swallowed by a silver fireball of angry power burning in my chest. "What do you mean?" I could barely eject the words, my body taut and trembling, staring straight into the jet-black eyes of the man I'd thought I loved.

Finn sighed, brows furrowed, eyes pinched. "I was the one who tracked her down for my father."

The world flashed silver as my power consumed me. I barreled into Finn, smashing him against the wall, my forearm pinned to his throat. He caught my wrist as I reached for my dagger, but my free hand struck his face with full force.

I didn't know what I was doing—I didn't know anything anymore, not even my own name or why I was here. Only rage. Blinding rage. The love and hate for this man that once battled within me had burned away, replaced by a searing silver-coated fury.

I clawed at him, teeth bared like the beast King Neptūnus had dubbed me. Finn grunted as I slammed him further into the stone wall. Ripping my dagger hand free, I drove it to his throat, surrendering to the dark side of my smoldering power, letting it consume me the way it craved.

Finn's eyes widened, fear and disbelief shining in them, reflecting the creature I had become. "No, stop," he choked as I pushed the blade closer, allowing it to nick skin.

But I couldn't stop. Wouldn't stop. I would turn him into dust like the others. The dark depths of my power purred with anticipation, feeding off my rage, eager to be unleashed.

He locked eyes with me, refusing to look away. "I-I didn't know what my father would do to Iona, I swear."

"But if you had known, you would have done it anyway. What Daddy Neptūnus says goes, right?"

"I-I don't know." Finn shook his head.

"Liar!" I held his gaze, breath quickening as my power coiled inside me like a serpent of silver shadows, poised to strike the moment I gave it leave.

"Morgana, no." Skye's voice sliced through the darkness roiling inside me.

I didn't release Finn, but gentle hands—hers and Edward's—pulled me back. I fought against them, eyes locked on the dark-eyed merman I'd once loved.

I shook my friends away, chest rising and falling as I stared Finn down. My knuckles were white from the force I was gripping my dagger. The metal pulsed beneath my skin, encouraging me, and I lunged.

"No!" Skye screamed.

Finn grunted as my blade pierced his abdomen, and silver-streaked blood dripped around the hilt as I dragged the knife down. His eyes pulled wide as they locked with mine. I retrieved the blade, and he inhaled sharply, blood spraying into the water and twisting around us. My features remained composed as I met his stare, refusing to shrink from the devastation on his face. Crimson globules belched down Finn's stomach and trickled over his emerald tail, flowing between his fingers as he brought them to the wound.

"If I ever see you again, I will kill you." I spat the words like venom before racing from the room.

"Morgana, wait," Skye called. I could hear footsteps slapping on the marble floor behind me, but I was already swimming, stowing my dagger in the scabbard at my waist as I wiped angry tears from my eyes.

I burst through the arched palace entrance, slicing through the water faster than I'd ever swum. There were two saffron-tailed guards at the gate.

They crossed their spears over the entrance. "We can't let you leave until a decision has been reached from the summit." My eyes flicked between them, then up to the minarets where two more guards stood sentinel.

I ignored their command, surging forward. Spears shifted in my direction, teeth bared as their faces dissolved into beastly forms.

"P-please, I can't stay here."

They answered me with a thrust of their weapons.

My fingers twitched over the hilt of my blade, and the Mer guards clacked their teeth, advancing.

No, I couldn't, I wouldn't remain trapped in another palace on the orders of Mer.

My blood screamed in my ears, and my power, which remained slithering at the surface of my being like quicksilver, answered. With a cold flick of my wrist, the guards' bodies went slack, spears falling to the seabed as they disintegrated into dust.

Shouts from above alerted me that the sentinels on the tower had seen, but I was already shooting through the gates.

I didn't slow until the Okeanós Kingdom had disappeared; only then did I spiral upwards. Up and up I went until I broke the surface, gasping for air as my lungs sucked hungrily at the oxygen.

It was daytime, and the sun was high in the sky. The waves glittered under its caress. Each sparkle was a fresh jab to my chest, a cruel reminder not to trust beautiful things or the heart.

I filled my lungs with air and dove back down to the seafloor, gliding over the desert of dunes with steady strokes, my hair streaming in the swell. I didn't know where to go, but I couldn't stop. Maybe if I just kept swimming, I could outrun the ache in my heart.

On and on I swam, until my bones ached and the tightness in my chest threatened to shut off my airways. When I couldn't swim anymore, I crumpled into a sobbing heap on the sand.

It was all too much.

Finn had tracked my grandmother down—and that made him responsible, even if the final blow wasn't his. He had lied to me. Lied, and still slept with me . . . All to open the box, following his father's command.

And his father—his father was the one who had taken my grandmother's life.

Now that the Mer had a third of their power back, and the Drowned had reclaimed Mortimer, we were closer to war, and I had failed. I'd failed the Captain and my grandmother, all because I'd given my heart to a man I shouldn't have. I was a damned fool, but I wouldn't be a fool anymore.

More tears spilled from my eyes as I doubled over, sobbing and gasping. I wept until the cries gave way to silence.

When the shuddering ceased, something inside me shifted—hardened. And I welcomed it. I settled into that darkness, letting it seal away the innocent, naive part of me that had repeatedly given my heart, only to have it torn apart.

I'd killed two Mer guards in my anger and stabbed Finn. Nausea swirled in my gut, clawing up my throat as Louisa's words swam into my mind. *You need to stay in the realm of peace and light. Don't let the darker side of your power take hold.* I pushed them away, shoving them down until they were buried deep, and then I let my inner light go out.

"Well, well, well." A raspy voice ghosted my neck as silver-stained fingers clamped around my arms, pulling me against a broad chest.

Drowned.

I squirmed, kicking and clawing, but the man held me against his chest. I knew those rough hands and their foul stench; they still visited me in my nightmares. Teachie and Rackham.

"Get your fucking hands off me!" I cried, my breath coming in sharp, ragged bursts as memories of Teachie's hands on my legs as he pried them apart flooded my mind.

"Now, now." He tsked into my neck, continuing to hold me tight against his chest. "As much as I would like to take what was denied me last time, we have a job to do."

"Oh yeah, and what's that?" I spat, my eyes narrowing on Rackham, as he moved before me, arms crossed over his tattered tunic.

My smile was feral as I reached for my power. I was going to enjoy turning these two assholes to dust.

"Delivering you to the Lord of the Drowned." Teachie pulled something from his pocket and stabbed me in the neck—a syringe. I bit back a cry as pain lanced from the wound, radiating through my body.

"What did you inject me with?"

"Blue-ringed octopus venom." Rackham's lip curled as Teachie continued to hold me fast. "Acts as a neurotoxin, because we can't have you using your seal bitch powers, now can we?"

"No," I gasped as a tingling numbness consumed my body and the periphery of my mind.

"We may not be able to fuck you, but doing this will feel just as good," Rackham grunted, and with that, his fist collided with my face.

The world went black.

58.

SKYE

Edward dashed after Morgana, his urgent footsteps echoing through the Okeanós halls. Finn made to follow, but I threw out an arm to block him. "Give her space."

He retreated into Morgana's chambers, clutching his stomach, blood still wept between his fingers, but a light radiated from his palm, which was quelling the flow. It looked like the same healing magic he'd used on the dolphin.

"What the hell was that?" I pounded my fist into his chest. His crimson-stained hands flew up, and I saw that the wound had almost knit itself back together. "Answer me." I shoved him again.

Pain flickered in his eyes as the force of my push sent him drifting backward. He rubbed a hand down his face and began drifting to and fro in front of me. "It's not what you think," he finally said, shaking his head.

"Really? Because it sounds like you betrayed her when she'd just started trusting you again."

"I was protecting her!" Finn's voice cracked with fury, his black eyes blazing as he swung around to me. For a heartbeat, the shadow of a long-toothed beast flickered across his face, then vanished, replaced by a raw mix of pain and desperation.

"From what?" I crossed my arms as I glowered at him.

"It doesn't matter. You wouldn't believe me." Finn resumed gliding back and forth, muscles taut beneath his inked skin, the torment in his mind visible in his features.

It was time for Morgana to get the answers she needed.

"Why don't you show me?" I moved forward, reaching around Finn to draw the dagger from the sheath slung across his back.

He went still, his dark gaze narrowing with interest. "What?"

"Make a blood oath with me and give me a true dream that explains all of this." I angled my chin in challenge. "If you were protecting her, it shouldn't be a problem."

Finn said nothing, but he stopped moving, and every muscle in his body tensed. I eyed him expectantly, but he stayed silent. It was so awkward that I found myself hoping he would say something after a few seconds. Finally, he raked both hands through his hair, a line deepening between his brows.

I drew a sharp breath, taming my growing fury. "Well?"

He raised his dark eyes to mine, the shadows falling from his face, his expression becoming almost hopeful. "Yes, I'll show you a dream of what happened after Morgana stunned my father and left our castle. Then you can know my intentions were true."

"That depends on what I see. Give me your hand," I ordered, holding the dagger ready. I was going to enjoy this.

Finn extended his tattooed right arm, and I took his hand in mine. As

I cut, I flashed a wicked grin, but he didn't flinch, even as crimson blood, laced with silver, spilled across his skin.

I winced as I sliced my own palm, but I pressed it against his like Peisinoe had shown me. "Do you swear that the memory you offer me as a dream is uncorrupted and true?"

Finn nodded, his eyes were intent on mine.

"Say it," I growled.

"I swear a blood oath that the memory I give you is uncorrupted and the absolute truth." He kept his bleeding palm against mine, and a finely hewn heart tattoo appeared on our hands.

Finn held my gaze as I forced his bloodstained palm to his forehead. Just as it had with Peisinoe, a faint light bloomed from the contact.

"Please, Agápē, grant me a dream of the memory Finn has chosen for me." I pressed his hands on either side of my temples, taking one last look into his eyes.

Morgana's marble chambers blurred and swam out of focus, replaced by a blinding flash of brightness. Shapes emerged out of the luminosity and sharpened as the dream vision took hold.

King Neptūnus, Princess Glacies, Pisceon, and two guards were passed out, floating motionless in the water around a stone table, beneath a wall adorned with a stained-glass mosaic glinting with filtered light. Finn hovered nearby, his fist unclenched and poised above his father's throat. But after a tense beat, he let it fall, turned, and drifted from the room.

"Aigéan," King Neptūnus bellowed, waking up from his stupor and righting himself with a swish of his golden tail.

Finn reappeared in the doorway, and his father's dark eyes narrowed on him.

"That little shifter bitch." Pisceon rubbed his temple, chuckling as he righted himself.

With a beat of her black tail, Glacies spiraled upward, smoothing her hair before crossing her arms, pale eyes flashing. "Did that seal girl just stun us?" Her brows flickered as she looked at the king.

"Get out!" King Neptūnus roared, his voice laced with venom. "I need to speak to my son."

Finn squared his shoulders and straightened, holding the king's gaze.

Pisceon and Glacies glided from the room, and as he passed, Pisceon brushed Finn's shoulder and mouthed, "Sorry."

"Father . . ." Finn began. He seemed to be pulling himself together and mastering some kind of neutral expression.

"Where is the girl?" the king snarled.

"She escaped with the Drowned boy while we were unconscious."

"So you've fallen in love with the half-breed." King Neptūnus rubbed his chin, casting a scornful gaze over his son.

"N-no." Finn stumbled over his words, but then he braced himself. "I am doing my duty to you—to the realm. I only want to use her to help us find the prophecy."

The flush in his cheeks and the tremble in his hands made it clear he was acting, and the king noticed. "Lies!" he hissed. "I saw the way you looked at each other." He moved closer, eyes gleaming, golden tail flicking. "What if I told you that to *use* her, she would have to die? Would you still be so eager then, Aigéan?" The king arched a dark brow and then let out a low, cruel laugh.

"No." The reply slipped from Finn's lips in a whisper.

His father's malicious smile grew as he took in the shock and grief distorting his son's handsome face. "Perhaps you need a reminder of where your loyalties lie." The king's lips curled, and his dark eyes grew feral. In a crack like a splitting sky, lightning shot from his wrists, pinning Finn against the stone wall. His mouth parted to speak, but his body was jolted with its force.

"You're pathetic, boy," the king spat. "I thought you could fight me off by now. How can I pass my throne on to you when you can't even withstand a bit of lightning?"

With that, he struck Finn again. The fire of it zigzagged up his body, forming blistering welts as it receded and hit again.

Finn seemed to be trying to summon his power, to strike back, but the force of his father's lightning trident kept his magic suppressed, held at bay like a storm sealed behind glass.

"I send you to do a simple task of gathering information, and you fall in love with the girl. Pathetic weakling . . . you will hang in the cells until you remember your duty to the realm. Guards, take him to the place where he used to hang as a boy!"

The king's expression was void of emotion as two pearl-tailed guards surged in, seizing the now barely conscious Finn and hooking their arms beneath his limp frame. They dragged his welt-covered body down to the lowest level of the castle, along a dark, narrow passage that led to the dungeons. There, they shackled him to the slick, sea-worn walls.

The cells were dark, lit only by the pale light of a small lantern. Without a word to Finn, the guards vanished up the gloomy corridor, leaving him suspended, his skin scorched in a jagged network of blisters from his father's lightning.

After hours of silence and darkness, Finn's head lolling as he drifted in and out of consciousness, a figure appeared at the bottom of the stairs: an older merman with a weathered face and a lilac tail that glinted in the lamplight. Mr. Inegar.

"Just like old times, huh, Inegar?" Finn croaked, cracking open a bloodshot eye to meet the man's gaze.

The old merman drifted forward, kelp coil in one hand, a whiskey decanter and a glass in the other. He poured a measure of amber liquid, then set the decanter on the stone floor.

Finn sipped from the glass Inegar held to his cracked lips, then blinked his eyes open as the older merman brushed back Finn's hair and touched his clammy forehead.

"What did I tell you? The girl is making you reckless," Inegar grumbled as he wiped the kelp coil across Finn's blistered chest.

Finn spat silvery crimson blood, which twisted in the water like a ribbon. "I will never help him. I am done doing his duty."

"It's true. She has to die, you know . . ."

An echoing silence passed between them, Finn's chest rising and falling quickly. "What does that mean?" he said finally, opening a bruised eye.

"The girl has to die to fulfill the prophecy, and she needs to die *willingly*."

"You're lying," Finn hissed. "Father told you to tell me this."

"I wish I were," Inegar said, shaking his head sadly. "We found another line of the prophecy. We planned to recapture the girl and keep her in the dungeons until we could persuade her to give herself up, but then you two had to act out . . . and now the king's keeping you down here until he can use you to convince her to sacrifice herself. He wants to leverage the feelings you have for each other."

"I will never do that!"

"Suit yourself, but he will hang you here until you do or until you die. Then he will find another way to pursue her. The girl's got a soft heart." Inegar sighed. "It won't be hard to get her to give herself up to save others."

Finn spat more silver-stained blood. Inegar only observed him sadly, before drifting back up the dark stairwell, leaving Finn shackled to the slick dungeon wall, tears tracing down his cheeks before the ocean claimed them.

"Please," he whispered into the empty cell. "Please . . . I'll do anything."

But Inegar was gone, and there was only darkness, and the weak light of the single lamp. Shadows festered in the slick corners of the dungeon, gathering mass and creeping along the floor. They coiled around Finn, whispering as they moved, snaking over his body like they had a mind of their own. He whipped his head around, eyes scanning the growing blackness as if questioning whether he was losing his grip on reality.

"Little prince." A voice echoed through the chamber.

Finn moved his head from side to side, squinting into the darkness through bloodshot eyes, but no one was there. Only shadows. Only the silence of the dark.

The voice sounded again—male, smooth and seductive, laced with a hint of mischief. "Why are we so sad, little prince?"

Finn scanned the cell, but nothing was there.

"You cannot see me, but you can feel me." The shadows caressed his torso, his shackled wrists, and wrapped around his tail as a shiver of cold rippled through the water.

"Who are you?" Finn demanded.

"Why, I am you . . ."

"Show yourself!"

"That now nameless and timeless cannot be seen, but I know the prophecy's words, and the herald tells it true."

Finn blinked and blinked, shaking his head as if worried the same madness consumed him as his father. The darkness crept closer, its icy presence seeping into every corner. Its breath, cold as the deep, brushed against him as it whispered the complete prophecy:

"Evil begets evil. Sin begets sin. All love will be lost, and you'll know no peace.

In shadowed depths where silence reigns, a curse was cast, eternal chains.

The spirits of Manannán and Siana must return, for only then shall the clans truly learn.

The blood of both Drowned and Selkie line is the answer, the curse's sign.

When stars align in stormy skies, and tempest waves start to rise. Siana's spirit, with purpose clear, shall face the curse without fear. With a willing heart and sacrifice, blood is the key to breaking the ice. Only with blood that need not be taken is the curse shaken."

"No," Finn hissed.

"If Father Neptūnus knows all this, the girl is not safe." The voice warned.

"There has to be another way!" Finn braced against his shackles, the clatter of metal echoing through the chamber.

"There might be." The darkness pulled back from him, and a hint of mischief returned to its tone.

"Tell me," Finn roared, muscles straining, a vein pulsing in his neck as he fought the restraints, shaking with fury. He tried to summon his lightning, but it only sparked and sputtered out.

"What will you give me?" The darkness's voice had become sly.

"Anything," he rasped, his rage quieting.

"Would you give me your heart and soul?"

"Yes."

"Good." The voice was a purr now. "Then a bargain is struck."

Finn's expression buckled in agony as he slammed his head against the prison wall, the shadows curling tighter around every inch of his body. They crept up his arms, slithering over the shackles, then recoiled as a ripple of magic burst from him, reverberating through the dungeons. Through slitted, bruised eyes, he looked down, catching sight of the heart-shaped tattoo now carved into his chest and a fresh weeping gash on his palm.

"Poseidon's Trinity exists, and your father is looking for it." The voice purred. "Make him promise to forget the girl, and you will find the three items and reclaim the Mer's power."

"But no one has ever found any of the Trinity. They believe it is only a legend," Finn cried, his voice hoarse with the intensity of the magic that had just burned a brand on his chest.

"Your father has the key to Poseidon's Box, and I know how you can find it."

"You do?"

The darkness caressed Finn's body. "The Sirens have always stayed out of the feud. But ask your aunt, Queen Peisinoe, for a dream of what you desire most—tell her it's to save the Mer from the Shadow—and she will grant it. Use it to find the box."

As he listened, Finn's bruised face lit up with hope.

The shadows pulled back, skittering to the room's corners, but the voice echoed through the room. "I have kept my end of the bargain. When the time is right, you must keep yours."

"Who are you?" Finn asked again.

"That, I think you know." The shadows returned, creeping back across the floor.

"Kyano? But you disappeared. Why has no one found you until now?"

"You also know the answer to that, little prince. I can only reveal myself to my reincarnation."

"No!" Finn clenched his fists, a muscle ticking in his jaw.

Cruel laughter echoed from the shadows, and then they were gone.

"Wait, how do you know the Trinity exists?"

"Because the Trinity is me, and I am the Trinity." Kyano's voice whispered from the gloom.

"Poseidon made the Trinity out of you?"

"Yes," Kyano purred. "He used the Ătlanticus magic to store me in three objects. If you find all three items and restore the Mer's power, I will be free."

Finn bared his teeth. "And if I don't?"

"Well, I will take your heart and soul. A bargain is a bargain, after all." The wicked laughter sounded again, and the newly cut tattoo on Finn's chest seared. Then the shadows and the voice disappeared.

Finn hung there, limp and breathing heavily, until Mr. Inegar reappeared. He raised his chin to meet Inegar's eyes. "Are you and my father looking for the Trinity?"

"We might be." Inegar clucked as he dabbed a fresh seaweed coil against Finn's welts.

"That's why you've kept the pawn store all these years? In the hope the Trinity will pass through its doors?"

"Yes." Inegar blew out a weary breath. "But we haven't had such luck . . ."

"Tell my father I will help him find the Trinity if he promises to forget about the prophecy and the girl."

Inegar chuckled. "I highly doubt he will do that."

"The prophecy is said to benefit all, and no one knows exactly what will happen if it is fulfilled, but the Trinity only benefits the Mer."

Mr. Inegar was silent as he continued to tend to the prince's welts.

"Tell him I made a blood bargain with the spirit of Kyano," Finn pressed.

Inegar pulled back from Finn and raised both bushy white brows. "Kyano?"

"Yes," Finn ground out. "He has told me how to find the first item."

Inegar's expression filled with excitement, and with a flick of his lilac tail, he disappeared up the stairs, then reemerged moments later. "The king is willing to make a deal. You find the Trinity, and he will forget about the prophecy and the girl."

Finn's eyes flashed. "Will he make a blood bargain?"

"Yes, he said that he will." Inegar unhooked the shackles holding Finn and helped the merman up the dark passage.

The dream faded into a thick black fog. A light appeared, and I blinked through my contracting vision as the beautiful marble chambers of Okeanós swam back into view. Finn was hovering before me, his chiseled jaw tight, dark eyes searching mine, and his hands still pressed to each of my temples.

I raised the hand I had cut to eye level, inspecting the skin. The heart tattoo had vanished. Grabbing Finn's hands from my temples, I saw his mark had faded too.

Peisinoe's words swam into my mind: *The tattoos fade if the dream is true.* Finn had given me an actual memory, but my stomach hollowed out as everything I had seen flooded my being.

"This," Finn said, gesturing to the heart tattoo on his chest, "is the bargain I made with Kyano. The small second line, inside the heart, is the one I made with my father. As long as I help him find the Trinity, Morgana will be safe, and he will not try to use her to fulfill the prophecy."

I exhaled, "And if you don't find this Trinity, you must give up your heart and soul to Kyano?"

"Yes," Finn whispered. "But I would willingly give up my heart and soul a thousand times over if it meant keeping her safe."

I ran a hand through my hair, scrunching my nose in thought. Morgana had described the welt-like burns she'd seen on Finn's body when she met him in Therme Skótos, and the new tattoo on his chest. It was there that he'd asked her to come to Thálassa. All of it led back to this. My mind spun beneath the weight of it all.

"Do you understand why I can't help her find it?" Finn's lips pursed, his features strung taut. "Why I had to lie to her and get her to help me find the box?"

"'Blood taken when it need not be taken' means she needs to die willingly," I whispered, inhaling sharply as I continued to process everything I had seen. "So at the Thálassian dream ceremony, you dreamed of what you desired most, and that was to protect Morgana from the prophecy?" I chewed on the words carefully as I processed everything.

Finn nodded, but then his eyes pinched together with fear. "You can't tell her. You can't *ever* tell her."

"I understand why you did it," I said slowly, though my mind was racing. "But this isn't our choice to make for her."

"No," Finn shouted, slamming his fist into the table as his claws protracted. The marble cracked beneath the force. "I did all this because I love her . . . and I don't want to lose her, even if it means I don't get to have her."

"Oh, honey." My eyes softened as I observed his pained expression. "I don't doubt that you love her, but I fear that after everything you've endured with your father, you don't know how."

"Guys," Edward's voice called from the doorway, pulling my attention from Finn. "Morgana's gone."

I rushed toward the door, but a wave of exhaustion crashed over me, and my body buckled. The dream magic was taking its toll.

"Are you okay?" Edward's eyes widened.

"Just give me a moment." I waved a hand, fighting against the bubble of fatigue clouding my vision. "Thank you, Agápē, for granting me this dream," I whispered under my breath.

I'd almost forgotten to thank the goddess, but the overwhelming exhaustion had served as a reminder.

59.

"The Okeanós scouts saw the Drowned take her, but she was too far for aid, and after she turned two of our own to dust, they weren't very motivated to help." Pisceon's jaw was tight, arms crossed over his muscular chest as he swooped into Morgana's chambers, his cobalt tail slicing through the water.

The mood in the room was somber. Edward and I sat slumped on the spongy couches while Pisceon and Finn drifted back and forth on their tails. Finn had told Edward everything he'd confided in me, and as it turned out, Pisceon already knew about it.

My brows flickered. "But the Mer are so much faster than the Drowned. Couldn't the guards go after them?"

Pisceon rubbed a webbed hand down his face. "The Drowned are using Mer blood, which means they can travel at our speed."

"They will be taking her to *him*. We need to leave now." Finn's shoulders were curled with the weight of a man on the edge of breaking.

"I think you've done enough," I snapped, resting my elbows on my scaled knees. I was still exhausted from the dream ceremony, and it was making me grumpy.

"This is all my fault," Edward spoke softly from beside me, absently rubbing his chin.

"How on earth would any of this be your fault?" I leaned over and asked in a low voice, careful that the two brooding mermen wouldn't overhear.

"Well." Edward rubbed his temple. "In the Thálassian library, I read that Siana and Kyano were supposed to be together—an arranged marriage. He held the power to heal; she carried the power of peace. Together, their magic could protect the ocean."

I nodded, chewing on my lip. "Like how Finn healed that dolphin and his wound."

"Exactly," Edward muttered. "But she didn't love him, she loved Manannán."

My eyes flicked between the two Mer, a severe frown wrinkled Finn's forehead, whilst Pisceon continued to pace.

"I didn't tell Morgana any of this because I didn't trust Finn . . . I *don't* trust him, but what if I was wrong and they are meant to be together?"

I massaged my forehead, closing my eyes as I let it sink in.

When I didn't answer, Edward continued, "After all, the poem about Kyano was accurate, wasn't it?"

Finn adjusted the straps securing the daggers across his back. "We have wasted too much time. I'm going after her."

Aarna and Glacies glided into the room, their drawn expressions suggesting they'd been informed of Morgana's capture.

"Wait," Pisceon cried, holding up a webbed hand. "You can't just go out there swinging your tail around alone. We need to be smart about this. War is coming, and you're the crown prince of Neptūnus. Our people need you. We just got a third of our power back, and if we're strategic, it gives us an edge."

"You're right," Finn grunted and rubbed his chin. "When the sun rises, I will address my people and tell them their queen"—he smiled at Glacies—"will prepare them for battle. She is just as skilled a warrior as I am."

Glacies nodded in assent, answering his silent question, confirming she was willing to take on this duty.

Aarna put her hand on Glacies's arm. "My brother Salil and I will train our warriors with yours."

Glacies drew her shoulders back. "When the army is ready, I'll lead them to the outskirts of Port Royal, where we will make camp."

"Great." Finn nodded. "Cousin, you can help me find the girl."

Pisceon grinned and flexed his arm muscles.

"I'm coming with you. Your dream may have been true, but I still don't trust you," I interjected, narrowing my eyes on the two dark-haired mermen.

Finn paused, running his tongue over his teeth. "As you wish."

Pisceon's eyes sparkled as they traveled over my Siren form. "The more the merrier."

"What of me?" Edward rose from where he'd been sitting beside me.

"I think I can speak for everyone when I say we're all sick of carrying you, Drowned boy." Pisceon cracked his neck.

I placed a hand on Edward's arm. "Why don't you return to Thálassa with the others? Use their library—see what you can uncover about the prophecy. Maybe there's a way Morgana doesn't have to die."

I glanced at Finn, his face drawn and eyes off somewhere else. "And," I said, a bit quieter. "See if you can find out where the rest of Poseidon's Trinity might be. Whatever Finn's done, I don't want to see him hand his heart over to the shadow of Kyano, and I don't think Morgana would either."

Edward grinned. "Seems a sound idea to me."

"Then it's settled." Pisceon clapped his hands together. "We leave at the rise of the sun."

I tossed restlessly in my seaweed cradle, a hand pressed to my forehead. Once or twice, the thought of seeking out Alexandros for a moment of distraction crossed my mind, but this wasn't a time to run from my feelings. It was time to face them.

Something was wrong. I could sense it in my bones. Finn loved Morgana; of that, there was no doubt. I felt it in my Siren blood, and the dream he'd shown me had been real. But take a man who's been tortured, forged into a weapon for his father, taught to bury his heart, and then give him one.

I sat up, shaking my head, the cradle swaying with the sudden movement. Yes, Finn loved Morgana—so much that he would lie to her, even sell his heart and soul to the shadows. But a love like that breeds foolish, reckless choices. And what else would he do? Burn cities of innocent people to the ground only to save her? Maybe.

He couldn't be trusted.

His love for Morgana was raw magic—a wildfire, fierce and unpredictable. It burned hot and dangerous, capable of consuming everything in its path, even the one he loved most.

Swinging out of the hammock, I drifted to the floor, quickly scanning my surroundings. I hadn't taken to wearing any weapons, but I did have my priestess of Agápē cloak, the crossbow, and the seaweed net from Pisceon.

I buckled the cloak around my throat, the light translucent material tumbling over my shoulders, and drew the hood, bundling my net and bow under one arm.

I had to go alone.

The gardens were draped in watery midnight shades. As I slipped toward the gates, my kelp cloak made blending into the shadows easy. The heavy silence pressed against my chest, wrapping me in the familiar dread of being alone. There would be no distractions on this journey—no diversions to help me forget the creature I'd become. No Alexandros and his pleasures to drown out the image of Parker's blood on my hands, his throat split wide. Nothing to shut out the shame and horror that churned inside me every time I looked at this new body.

Panic tore through me, accompanied by the urge to run back into the castle, curl up in bed beside Alexandros, or wait until morning and allow Finn and Pisceon to accompany me.

I screwed up my eyes. *Your friend needs you.*

Exhaling in a sea of bubbles, I continued through the dark gardens. *Your friend needs you.*

"Where are you going?" Four orange-tailed guards stood before the intricate arched doorway between me and the dunes. They must have heightened their security since Morgana's capture.

"I'm a priestess of Agápē." I met their eyes and let a little bit of my magic radiate. "I am doing the work of the Siren Goddess." I bowed my head, and to my surprise, the guards moved aside as though compelled, and the gate creaked open.

The desert of underwater dunes looked deep blue in the moonlit waters, and so much larger than it had been when I'd passed over them with the others, but I began my trek, breaststroking across the vast sandy wilderness below.

One stroke, then another. Just keep swimming.

We knew Manannán's lair was in the sunken city of Port Royal—the Wild West of the ocean. I swallowed. But where exactly was that? The Pacific . . . No, I was sure I'd heard them say Atlantic. *Damn it.* I wished I'd paid more attention in geography.

My brows pinched as I sank to the seabed, eyes sweeping the terrain. The soft dunes had given way to towering rocky canyons, their sides worn into jagged, organic shapes where the ocean had gnawed at them. Sea life flitted in and out of crevices like ghosts.

Morgana said she had some kind of aquatic sense of direction. Perhaps I had that too. I reached for my magic. I seemed to be able to sense vague directions, but I couldn't remember which ocean I was supposed to be heading to.

I spun around, taking in my surroundings, my dark hair swirling in the swell. The canyons loomed, high and misshapen, casting long shadows over the sandy floor below. I continued swimming through a narrow passage between them, the silence pressing around me. My cloak fluttered eerily around my shoulders, and I found my fingers twitching for the crossbow on my back.

Something skittered before me, and my pulse quickened, but when I peered into the darkness, I saw only the shadows at the base of the canyons. I exhaled and kept swimming. A light glowed momentarily before blinking out. A shiver ran down my spine as I squinted into the gloom.

This was a bad idea. I should turn back.

More lights flickered; they were beside me on the rock face: eyes, bulbous and silver.

I careened to the opposite side. The shadows stirred, and more glowing lights appeared. Eyes peering out at me from the crevices—so many eyes. They swarmed across the dark canyon walls looming on either side of me, creeping onto the path ahead and behind, cutting off any escape.

My breath grew short, and I raised my bow, fingers trembling. The pale-eyed creatures crept from the shadows, encircling me.

I spun, heart hammering. They looked distinctly human, yet their skin was stretched thin over gaunt faces, their bodies hunched, hair mostly gone, and their eyes . . . their eyes were like silver globes. Remembering my webs, I kicked upward, but they were all over the canyon, scuttling up the rock face on all fours, leering like starved hyenas at the first sight of prey.

My fingers trembled as I loaded the weapon, firing into the swarm below me, striking one, then another. I swung my seaweed net, which twisted around the rock and tangled.

Please! I yanked at it, and it ripped.

There were too many of them, and they were closing in on the sand below me and leaning off the rock face to stop me from swimming upward. I twirled on the spot, kicking hard with my webs, my breath coming in sharp inhales.

These must be Drowned, but they weren't like the ones we had fought at the tunnel of Hēracleion. They were something else—something worse.

And they kept coming, slipping out of hollows in the rocks.

Panic consumed me as I flew back, my grip faltering on my crossbow.

Magic—I needed to summon my magic. I reached inward for the spark of power, willing my breath to steady, but fear clawed at my chest, and it flickered just beyond my grasp.

Terror consumed me as cold, bony fingers closed around my ankles, and my magic extinguished. I screamed as more slimy hands seized me, rising from below, from the cliff face, dragging me down. Clawlike nails raked across my scales, yanking me toward the ocean floor. The stench was rancid, a sickening blend of rot and salt, as they kicked and shoved each other in a frenzy to reach me. I couldn't get out. There were too many of them.

This was it—I was going to die.

I closed my eyes and surrendered to the putrid Drowned. They tore at my cloak, sniffing greedily at my hair and neck, their breath sour against my skin.

Light erupted. A blindingly beautiful radiance filled the canyon shaft, and the Drowned squealed and squawked under its brilliance. A growl rumbled through the space, and the last few creatures scuttled from me. I looked up, holding a hand over my eyes to shield them from the glow. I caught a familiar scent—heather, wood, and honey—just before Aranare yanked me against him, drawing us into a deep crevice in the side of the canyon. His magic stirred around us, willing the space to become a shelter.

"You're here." I breathed in his scent like the sweetest poison.

"We have to fly out," he hissed, his chest rising and falling as it pressed against mine. "They are all over, and they'll jump for us."

"What are those things?" I glanced up at the jagged rock above, where silver eyes gleamed in the shadows, rotten teeth snapping and snarling.

"Drowned who have used Mer blood for too long. They've become rabid and starved, and that makes them lethal."

My bottom lip quivered. "Can't you just use that light again?"

"That was only a light, and I had the element of surprise."

"I can't use my wings." I lied, shaking my head. "I-I haven't been able to since I killed Parker."

"We fly out or we die." Aranare's whisper was an urgent command. His chest rose and fell in quick succession.

An icy grip tightened around my heart, and I trembled against him. "I-I can't . . ." Tears streamed down my face as I thought of those awful webbed and feathered things.

"It's okay, I will carry you." Aranare wiped a tear from my lashes, lifting my chin until my eyes met his. "A long time ago, I lost someone close to me. I was there. I saw it happen. I won't go through it again."

At that moment, a clawed hand reached into the crevice, only to recoil with a shriek as Aranare's magic seared the creature's flesh. Beyond our hiding place, the rock face teemed with them—hundreds of Drowned clinging to the stone, snarling and waiting.

"On the count of three." Aranare wove his fingers with mine, and I nodded.

We stepped into the canyon, and the waters oscillated as the rabid monsters swarmed toward us, scuttling across the seabed on all fours, reaching from the shadows with snapping teeth.

Aranare's wings flared like obsidian drapes, and his growl sent tremors through the canyon. The Drowned, clinging to the rocks on either side of us, faltered. I blinked through the brightness as he unleashed his power, momentarily scattering the creatures. He hovered above me on his midnight tail, eyes burning topaz, wings unfurled. Still holding my hand, he started to move upward, wings an inky shadow as they beat against the dark waters.

The rabid Drowned began advancing again, licking their rotten maws as they leaned off the rocks.

My power thrummed between my shoulders, and my wings were desperate to break free, but I screwed my eyes shut, suppressing their emergence.

More Drowned leered off the rock face, and then they began to leap. I let out a bubbly scream as one landed on Aranare's shoulders, wrapping its legs around his neck. He tossed it off, but more were already flying at him. They grabbed onto his wings and clung there as another landed on his shoulders, throwing its bony legs around his throat.

"Go." Aranare's voice trembled as he let go of my hand. I drifted back to the seabed, and my feet thudded into soft sand.

His wings were in shreds now, and he was sinking toward me as they pulled him to the ground. Panic froze my limbs as they descended on him in a frenzy, clawed fingers raking into flesh.

"Skye, get out of here." Aranare managed as their teeth sank into him and the water clouded red.

But I wouldn't run anymore.

Two of the creatures reached for my ankles, and I bared my teeth. Blood screamed in my ears as I went for the power slumbering within me, the darker one, the one that had slammed Aranare and Morgana against the wall that night in the lighthouse, the one that had killed Parker. My chest rose and fell in quick succession as it poured through my body, bright and blazing. Deadly as a scorned lover. Power drawn from heartbreak. My chest cleaved in two as it tore from my being, sending the decaying Drowned flying backward.

Pain seared the space behind my shoulder blades as my skin shifted and stretched. A cry ripped from my throat, and in another burning slice of agony, the wings burst free. Their feathers were laced with delicate, translucent webs that glimmered like moonlight reflected on the water. They unfurled above me, ethereal and powerful at the same time. The cloak of Agápē hung in tatters around me, shredded because I hadn't chosen the version made to accommodate wings.

I scooped Aranare into my arms, his muscular frame resting easily against my chest, supported by the strength of my wings as they brushed against the water. I moved swiftly, faster than I had ever swum with the Mer. Soon, the Drowned below were nothing more than distant, gleaming eyes, so far beneath us they could've been stars strewn across a midnight sky.

I kept gliding, arms wrapped tightly around Aranare, my wings splayed and beating against the water, until the jagged rocks of the canyons gave way to soft sand and the dunes rose to meet us once more. Only then did

I lower myself, wings not disappearing into my skin but draping neatly behind me as I alighted on the seafloor.

I stepped back from Aranare, sucking in a sharp breath as my eyes dragged over him. "Your wings." They hung in ragged strips at his back, and his body was covered in cuts where the rabid Drowned had clawed at him.

He ran gentle fingers down my arm, ebony tail flicking. "They will grow back."

I dropped my chin and turned away as shame crept through me at my monstrous form, but the hot, burning power still simmered beneath my skin, coating my pale chest in glittering luminescence. I threw back my shoulders, angling my chin high. I was a powerful Siren of Agápē. My friends needed me; I would not be meek, I would no longer hide from who I was becoming, and I would not let anyone take my wings.

There was too much darkness, too many terrifying creatures. And I'd already killed one of them, a grin curled my lips. Perhaps it took a monster to end another monster, and I'd made sure Parker would never hurt another woman, just as I'd saved Aranare from those horrid Drowned.

If I want to survive in this world, I can no longer be afraid of myself.

Aranare must have seen something in my expression because he cupped my face in both hands, midnight scales glinting along his forearms. His dark hair drifted in the current, and his topaz eyes were gentle as they found mine. "Your wings won't always be painful once you get used to them," he murmured, running his thumb across my cheek.

I nodded as his gaze dragged over my face.

"Thank you for saving my life." He brushed my hair over my shoulders with both hands and pressed his mouth against my forehead. He kissed me there, then pulled back, allowing our eyes to meet once more.

We held each other's gaze, his hands resting in the crooks of my elbows. The emotional charge between us deepened as we took each other in. But

I knew I couldn't kiss him. I'd spent years being submissive and small for Parker, just hoping for a scrap of his affection. Then I'd run straight to Alexandros, using his sensuous touch to forget . . . to *hide*. If I kissed Aranare now, I'd lose a part of myself I hadn't yet reclaimed. I needed to find that girl again—to know who I was—before I could give myself to anyone. Even though my heart was pounding, begging me to tell him I felt something, that I always had. Instead, I mastered a neutral expression and pulled away.

My throat worked several times before I could speak. "What were you doing out here?"

"After what happened at the summit, I needed to make sure you were okay. I saw you slip through the gates from the castle balcony." His eyes flared. "Why were you out here alone?"

"The Drowned have Morgana. I'm going to find her." A pang shot through my chest at the thought of what they might do to her. Was she already hanging on a crossbar somewhere?

Aranare's brows drew together in concern. He said nothing at first, lost in thought, then he unfurled his tattered wings, swishing his tail as he extended a hand to me. "Then let's find her together."

I drifted to join him. We began moving, his malachite wings splayed like dusky shawls, casting shadows across the ocean floor. Beside him, I moved like reflections in water on my aquamarine wings.

We swam side by side, slipping forward into the endless blue.

Together.

We'd find her together.

60.

MORGANA

Why was it so dark? I brought my hands, which had been bound together with rope, to my face. I was blindfolded, and someone was hauling me through the water, holding me beneath my arms. From the stench searing my nostrils—rum and rot—I knew it was Teachie and Rackham.

We were moving quickly, at a speed that would match my own or the Mer's. How far had we traveled whilst I'd been unconscious? My head throbbed where Rackham had struck me, and a dull ache weighed down every inch of my body.

"Where are you taking me?" I rasped, turning my blindfolded face from side to side, searching the dark for the pirates I knew were on either side of me.

No answer, just an awful chuckle and rummy breath.

I wriggled against their grip.

"I wouldn't do that if I were you," a voice warned. I suspected it was Teachie, from the husky tone.

A chill crept through the water, pebbling the skin on my arms as a mournful wail sounded, soft, like a distant breeze, but then intensifying into a wailing scream. The hairs on the back of my neck stood on end as the lament filled with grief and anguish. "W-what is this place?" My voice cracked as I shook my shoulders against the hands holding me.

"Those are the cries of the souls lost to the garden." Teachie's breath was warm against my neck.

The Garden of Mortimer. We must have been passing the outskirts of the Mors Kingdom.

We continued moving, and my insides knotted as the haunting cries drifted after us, like pleas of desperation. My throat was parched, and hunger twisted in my stomach. I battled to stay alert, but exhaustion crept in, and soon, my eyes fluttered shut.

I awoke to rough hands removing my blindfold. The ocean surrounding me was warmer here, its hue a blinding light aqua as the bandana slipped from my eyes. I thrashed against the two pirates' grip, but they held me fast, dragging me through the water.

"We thought you might like to see this mermaid lover," Teachie growled in my ear as they hauled me up a sandy bank.

My blood chilled as I took in the scene below me from its ridge. Tattered pavilions stretched out as far as the eye could see, and thousands of silver-stained Drowned moved between them. The pirates dragged me down the sandbank toward the waiting cavalry, then hauled me along a winding path of sand that snaked through the tents.

Terror clawed at my core as my gaze darted left and right. Awnings crowded the walkway on either side, their frayed cloth coverings crudely propped on driftwood poles and lashed together with rope, looking like they might have been salvaged remnants of torn sails.

There were Drowned all around us. Some were sharpening weapons, some sitting at makeshift tables sharing bottles of rum, others brawling or fucking. All of them were covered in the same silver-stained veins as Teachie and Rackham.

As we passed, the ones nearest the sandy track halted to leer at us. Some jeered and whooped as if I were a battle prize. My stomach turned when a Drowned man with a ripped cap and overalls licked his rotten teeth. "Can I have some of her once you're finished?"

He reached for me, and I let out a frightened yelp, but Rackham kicked him away.

Then I saw the Mer, and bile burned the back of my throat as my insides churned. They had been strung up on crossbars at regular intervals along the walkway. Most were wearing black armor, and I recognized it as the same design worn by Queen Asherah of Mors. These were the bodies from Manannán's most recent victory.

As we drew closer to the nearest crossbar and its shadow fell on my face, nausea eddied in my gut. I looked up, meeting the lifeless merman's cloudy eyes. His hair hung limp, dark tail faded, skin gray, and his body . . . his body was a husk of what it might've been, gaunt within his Mors armor.

I'm so sorry this happened to you. I silently prayed for him.

A long-clawed hand seized his tail, and I gasped as the slick, hairless head of a Drowned man appeared, sinking its rotting teeth into the merman's flesh.

"Get off him," I cried, trembling against Teachie and Rackham as the creature sank its teeth deeper, a revolting expression of bliss spreading across its face as it began to drink.

"You make me sick, all of you," I spat, tears blurring my vision as my shoulders shook.

Teachie and Rackham only laughed and continued dragging me between them.

At the end of the rows of tents lay a sunken galleon, half-buried in sand and listing to one side. Its bare masts jutted forward, casting long shadows across the seabed, its wood distorted by the presence of sea life. The pirates hauled me toward the towering deck, where a crudely fashioned hatch had been hewn.

"Put her blindfold back on," Teachie grunted. Rackham began refastening the bandana over my eyes as Teachie held me still.

"Wait, no," I pleaded, panic churning through me at the thought of being shrouded by darkness while heading into what seemed to be the heart of this awful place.

I tried to escape, squirming and tugging and kicking him in the shin. I reached for my magic, but it wasn't there. I scrunched up my eyes, but there wasn't even a flicker of silver. The blue-ringed octopus venom must still have been in my system, or perhaps they'd injected me with more while I'd been passed out.

"We can't have you seeing the layout of the lord's underground lair now, can we?" Teachie made a scoffing sound. "Not that you'd have much luck escaping. The maze of tunnels we've built travels beneath the Caribbean to the sunken city of Port Royal."

My world went dark again as Rackham finished fastening the tie around my eyes and grabbed my right arm again. The wooden door creaked open, and the two pirates hauled me through it. I could tell we had gone into the eroded ship's belly, and then we began traveling downward.

Down and down we went, and then across. The water was stuffier here, scents of rock and dank searing my nostrils. I had no sense of how long we'd been traveling—maybe half an hour, or many hours.

Hunger and exhaustion clouded my mind. When my fur-clad knees struck slimy rock, I collapsed forward, grasping at the slick floor with my webbed hands. There was a shuffling, grunting, and a swish in the waters surrounding me.

"Release her," said an authoritative voice, edged with darkness and death but also silky and seductive. I knew that voice—I'd heard it in my mind many times before.

The blindfold was yanked from my face.

From where I crouched on the floor, I saw I was in a dark stone chamber, candlelight flickering with the swell. Above me loomed a long dining table set for two, laden with food, and above it hung a massive oil painting.

"Untie her hands. Let her stand." That voice again.

Teachie leaned forward, grunting, and the stench of stale rum burned my nostrils once more. A meaty fist wrapped around my upper arm, drawing me to my feet.

"Why is her face bruised?" The voice had become a snarl as the shadowy speaker moved forward.

"S-she struggled, My Lord." Teachie's hands were trembling as he quickly released my arm and stepped away from me.

"I'll deal with you later. Now leave us."

The stink of rum faded with the shuffle of Teachie and Rackham's retreating footsteps. The room swayed before me, and I blinked and blinked through my exhaustion, willing my eyes to focus.

A merman hovered before me in the candlelit chambers, his pale white tail glittering in the gloom. I dragged my eyes upward. Sandy hair, dark brows and lashes, chiseled cheekbones, and a muscular chest.

Fear stole the air in my chest. I knew this man—I'd seen him before at Samhain, and in a cloud of darkness beneath the sea. I'd seen him in my visions, entering the dark cave where the shadow of Manannán had claimed him.

My breath caught in my throat; there, scrawled on his chest, was the tattoo my grandmother had described in her diary. *Amor perdot nos.* Love will destroy us.

Taranis. The hairs in the back of my neck prickled—Manannán in

Taranis's body. I stood before the merman responsible for all the drownings, Mer drained of blood, and the impending war.

"Hello, amor meus," the merman purred, and his dark eyes flashed red.

"*You.*" I curled my fists, eyes narrowing, but my pulse was pounding in my ears. "You killed the Captain and Abalone. The Mer strung up on crosses." My whole body trembled as I stared the pale-haired merman down.

He looked at his nails. "All is fair in love and war. The Captain had foreseen his death at my men's hands—he went willingly."

"That doesn't make it okay."

The merman rushed forward, cupping my cheek with his webbed hand, his dark eyes searching mine. "Oh, Siana, my love, I am so glad you haven't changed. I do love these little fights that we have, always about the same thing. You killed so and so . . . tortured this and that . . . but then we will be tangled together in no time, because some part of you likes this dangerous dance with death." His thumb traced the line of my bottom lip, and watery shadows curled around us both.

"Get off me!" I stumbled backward.

"Now, now, is that any way to treat your old lover?" He tsked as his eyes roved over my body.

I reached for my dagger, but it had been removed from my hip.

The merman noticed and let out a low, wicked chuckle. "You don't need that here, amor meus. If you behave like a good girl, I won't hurt you."

I continued to step backward, my eyes flicking across the slick stone chambers for a way out. There were two doors, a Drowned standing guard at each one.

That low chuckle again as he prowled toward me.

My fingers brushed cool stone. I'd backed myself into the far wall of the chamber.

"Thousands of years passed, and I waited for you. Time bent around your absence. Empires crumbled, and our love became a legend. I forgot the man I once was, but I remembered *you*." The merman's irises flashed red, and dusky tendrils of liquid shadow crept from him, curling around my waist, arms, and throat, pinning me against the wall. "Now you would deny me?"

My body threatened to tremble uncontrollably, but I cast the darkness from me with a rough sweep of my palm. A flicker of pain passed his face, as though I'd dealt him a blow.

I turned inward, searching for a speck of the silver power I'd grown used to, but there was nothing. My stomach sank, but I pushed back my shoulders and leveled him with a defiant glare. "Who are you? Taranis or Manannán?"

"Why, I am both. I have Taranis's body, humanity, and a shadow of the soul he left behind, but at my heart, I am Manannán." He rushed forward again, taking my webbed hands in his, and darkness curled around us as I recoiled into the wall. "Don't you recognize me, amor meus?"

I gazed into his dark eyes, and all the visions I'd seen came flooding back: Manannán, the Minoan sailor, losing his son to become God of the Drowned. Manannán, fighting with Kyano over Siana and being turned into shadows, only for Taranis to find him in a dark cave.

"No, I don't know you." I shook my head, hoping he couldn't feel the tremble in my hands. "I'm not Siana, but if you loved her, you'll let me go."

"That, I cannot do," his breath burned against my temple as he whispered the words, then he released me, drifting toward the grand dining table. But he turned back, dark eyes glittering. "I've been known to be rather . . . possessive." His tone had become deep and predatory, and a chill spread across my skin.

"I will spend every minute trying to escape this place, and if I get a chance to kill you, I will." I clenched my fists, standing taller as the hardened thing inside me nodded in approval.

That sinister laugh again. "Oh, please stop. If you keep talking like that, I'll have to have you right here and now."

"The prophecy will be found that can stop all this—can stop you."

"They're just words, amor meus. Their power is only what you choose to give them. Look around you—my army of the Drowned grows. Soon, we will defeat the Mer, and I will rule the ocean. The Mer are desperate, clutching at forgotten riddles and ancient whispers." With a flick of his pearlescent tail, he pulled out the gilded chair at the head of the stone table and slid into it, his fins curling around the side. "Sit . . . eat. You must be famished." He gestured to the seat beside him, and my stomach rumbled as I took in the decadent spread, but I shook my head.

Manannán clicked his webbed fingers, and the Drowned guard from the doorway advanced, seizing me and lifting me toward the table. I kicked and thrashed against his grip, but he hauled me over and forced me into the chair beside Manannán, who watched the scene unfold, dark eyes gleaming with amusement.

"So much spirit." The merman leaned back in his golden chair, running a hand through his pale hair. "It made my tail stiff when you broke my storm wheel."

"You're disgusting," I spat.

The Drowned man stepped behind me, pinning my shoulders against the chair's back. I writhed, shaking against his grip.

"Leave her." Manannán waved a lazy hand at his henchman, who let go of me and retreated to the doorway. Tendrils of dark water with shadowy faces of sea serpents slithered from him, wrapping around my torso, their pressure strapping me to the chair. I tried to break their bonds, scratching and yanking, but these shadows were different than the ones he had used before. Dangerous. I gasped as they wound around my throat.

"N-no," I managed as they pulled tighter.

"Are you going to be a good girl and dine with me?"

I didn't answer, and more dark tendrils poured from the merman, seeping from his skin and eye sockets, which had turned pitch black. They strengthened their grip, closing off my airway as if some sea monster had its tentacles around my neck.

"Sto—" Tears leaked from my eyes as I tried to speak, but the words wouldn't come, so I nodded.

"Good." Manannán's voice returned to a purr as he released his hold on me, and the shadowy serpents faded into the water. "Now that little spat is dealt with, let's talk business." He stretched in his chair again and surveyed me with dark eyes.

"Business?" My voice cracked as I brought my hands to my burning throat.

"You've not been able to control your powers, have you?" He plucked a golden dish filled with seaweed rolls from the table and thrust it toward me. "Siana, I must insist you eat."

Nausea now swirled in my belly alongside my hunger, but I lifted a shaky hand, grabbing a roll from the plate. I didn't want his shadow snakes to force feed me. "How do you know about my powers?"

"I've been watching." He leaned his elbows on the table, stabbing a golden knife into the stone.

My eyes flicked to the blade and then to my place setting, but I had not been given any sharp utensils.

He tilted his head to one side. "How about we make a deal? I'll teach you how to harness your magic—"

"I don't want your help. You're a monster!"

"Ah, yes, I thought you might say something like that." Manannán rubbed his chin. "But you possess ancient magic, and only someone of the gods can teach you to control it. I presume from your self-righteous attitude you don't want to turn any more innocents to dust." Shadows spilled from him, crawling across the table as the corners of his mouth quirked. "Or perhaps you do, and we are more alike than you care to admit."

"I'm nothing like you," I spat, swiping at the wisps of darkness caressing my cheek.

"That remains to be seen."

"And why would you want to help me?" I crossed my arms over my chest and held his gaze.

"Well, you possess the spirit of my long-lost lover who was slain in the battle of my creation." The merman plucked a prawn from one of the decadent seafood dishes and began peeling away the shell. "I suppose you could say I seek absolution, amor meus." He raised his brows before popping the prawn into his mouth.

I gritted my teeth. "Don't call me that."

"Sorry." He grinned lazily. "Amica mia."

I glared at him, knuckles white and mind whirring. "*If* I accepted your offer of training . . . what would I have to do in return?" My stomach constricted.

A devilish grin spread across the merman's face, and his dark lashes fluttered over even darker eyes. "Oh, I don't ask for much. Only that you dine with me here each night. I'm a lonely man, you see."

"If I do this—have dinner with you—will you stop killing Mer and draining their blood?"

He threw back his head and laughed, the muscles beneath his tattooed chest taut with the movement. "I do not think you are in a position to make such demands. But you always knew how to soften my heart. Perhaps after a few dinners, I could be persuaded to be more . . . merciful, but I will not make any promises."

"I will *never* make a deal with you when Mer are being strung up to be consumed by the Drowned," I snarled, letting the dark beast inside take control.

Manannán's jaw was hard as he stared back at me. My eyes darted from his silver hair, to his obsidian brows, and muscular chest—someone this evil should not be allowed to be so attractive. The thought pulled my scowl tighter. Several beats of silence passed between us, but then he chuckled. "There's the Siana I remember . . . I *could* force you." Watery darkness built around him, and panic rose in my chest as his grin turned feral. "But that wouldn't be any way to get you to forgive me now, would it?"

"I will never—"

Manannán held up a finger to silence me, the murky water wisps remaining poised at his sides. "Did you know I'm keeping the court of Mors alive in the dungeons? I bring out just one daily so my Drowned can feed on the freshest fare."

My stomach churned. "You make me sick."

"Yes, well, like I said—words. Now, my Drowned need sustenance. But this monster *might* be persuaded to free a Mer for every dinner you share with him." He leaned forward, and the tattooed words scrawled on his chest flexed.

My voice was mercilessly calm despite my thundering heart. "And if I refuse to make a deal with you?"

Manannán looked at his nails as if considering this. "We have an array of dungeons for you to choose from, and just think of all the Mer who will die simply because you turned me down."

My hands curled into fists on the stone table as I glowered at him.

"Should I ask the guards to drag you away, or do we have an agreement?" Manannán angled his chiseled jaw. "I think you might enjoy having your freedom in my court. After all, there is someone here whom I think you already know."

The room vaulted as my heart thundered. *My father.*

Epilogue

FINN

I positioned my seaweed coronet between my dark strands.

I hadn't lied to Morgana—I didn't know my father was planning to kill Iona when I tracked her down. But what tortured me was that, at the time, I hadn't cared. I'd been numb, doing his work, feeling nothing. He'd made sure of that.

Drawing myself to my full height, I strapped on my silver breastplate.

After my mother died, my father's mind deteriorated. He tortured me with his lightning over and over again. He blamed me, and I believed him. I still do.

I clenched my fists.

Perhaps I could have saved her if I'd been stronger.

I exhaled a shaky breath, reaching for my daggers and returning to the mirror to strap them across my chest.

Years passed, and the Shadow ravaged our kingdoms. I watched as the Mer around me withered and blackened. My people, my family. The Shadow was humanity's fault, and I despised them.

My father said the things he asked of me were meant to save our people from the Shadow, and I clung to that. It was what my mother would have wanted. Duty was important to her—*amor perdot nos.*

When Pisceon was brought into our kingdom as my father's ward, we carried out the work together. He'd known great pain, and it had hardened him—left him sharp, cynical. He became my friend, my ally.

Somewhere amid all the atrocities, I lost my way. We would drink, and smoke, and fuck humans, not thinking about the things we'd done. After years of carrying out the whims of a mad king, we no longer remembered what we were fighting for. I found a poetic kind of pleasure in the life of a cynic. Every day, I challenged the world to prove me wrong, and when it didn't, when it reaffirmed my derisive beliefs, it offered vindication.

Sometime after that, Glacies arrived. My betrothed, beautiful but cold. It was obvious she wanted nothing to do with me. I hated watching the engagement frost her over, hardening her more with each passing day. She'd lost family to the Shadow as well, and along with Pisceon, we found some kind of friendship in our bleak existence.

Then I met Morgana, and everything changed. Slowly, the world around me returned to color.

Looking in the mirror, I clicked my ornate bracers into place, pausing when I reached the right wrist. The creeping black veins were inky stains against my skin, but they hadn't grown since we'd been in Okeanós. Perhaps it was because I hadn't been using my magic, or it could be from the shred of power that had been returned to us.

Since she'd left, the darkness had consumed me. There was no horizon, no current beneath me. I was sinking. My heart was a ship with no compass, circling the same grief-dark seas. There was no moon or stars in these waters. No, they'd turned their backs; there was no light without *her.*

The door to my chambers flew open, and Pisceon emerged. He was also dressed in his silver armor, which clinked as he moved toward me. "The Siren girl left to find the seal girl without us." A muscle feathered in his jaw.

"So we follow her. She's got no training. She'll need us."

"The guards informed me that Aranare went after her."

Typical White Knight Williamson. My fists curled at my sides, and my gills flared, but I released them with a bubbly exhale. At least they had a better chance with him—I should be grateful.

I bared my teeth, lashing my emerald tail. "We leave now."

Pisceon threw out a muscled arm.

"What?" I growled.

"The scouts we sent to Mors have returned. The kingdom lies in ruins, overrun with silver-stained Drowned. With the Garden now under Manannán's control, it no longer claims their souls, not even those driven rabid by bloodlust."

"Oh, holy gods."

"There's something else." Every muscle in Pisceon's torso tensed.

"Tell me, cousin." I bit down so hard my teeth hurt, and he shifted uncomfortably before me.

"The scouts reported seeing two Drowned men escorting a red-haired woman into the war camp."

I drew a rough breath, taming the fury burning through my insides. "So he has her. I can't . . . I *won't* give up on her. If I have to tear down his kingdom on my own, so be it."

Pisceon nodded. "You know I'll always have your back, but we need to be strategic. Your father is with the other kings and queens. The armies are rallying here. We are going to march on Mortimer and then Port Royal."

I exhaled slowly. "Then I'll stay. We'll ready our armies and march them to the Lord of the Drowned's door. And when I face him—the man who killed my mother and stole the girl I love—he will meet my blade."

Pisceon cracked his neck, mouth twitching into a grin. "Oh, good, I'm ready for some bloodshed." He slapped me on the back, his silver breastplate clinking as he retreated, leaving me alone with my thoughts again.

I swung open the doors to my balcony and drifted out, pressing my palms into the cold stone railings as I surveyed the beautiful gardens below and the desert of dunes beyond the gate.

The Mer are going to war.

I breathed out, my gills flaring as I stared into the distance. Everything seemed so still, but only for a moment.

It started with a noise, like wind on land—the ripple of thousands of tails swishing in succession. My eyes flicked to the rolling expanse of the dunes. At their crests, dots of color appeared as that sound swelled around me.

The Mer armies were arriving.

As I leaned against the balcony railing, the specks of color gathered into a glimmering formation across the sands before the castle, the water swirling in rivulets around them. Each contingent bore its house's distinct colors and symbols, a rainbow of scales and banners unfurling before my eyes.

I was dying. Having a third of my power back would subdue the Shadow, but it wouldn't stop it. And I'd sold my soul to the spirit of Kyano to protect Morgana from my father and the prophecy. Would it all be for nothing?

No. I would make sure of it.

It won't matter if I'm gone . . . Ours is a story of almosts, and I'm the one who broke any hope we had. But I can't, I won't see her give herself up for the prophecy, not when there is a way to save her.

Doubt crept in, and I wondered if Skye was right. Should I have told

Morgana what was in the prophecy and let her decide? No, I'd made the right choice. If the Trinity was found, I could save my people from the Shadow, and Morgana wouldn't have to die.

Emotions strangled me as she slipped into my thoughts. When I first saw her sitting at the edge of that jetty—so innocent, so unguarded—something in my heart had awakened.

It hadn't mattered that my allure failed; she'd come to me willingly. She'd looked into my darkness and answered it with light.

But now I knew she had a darkness akin to mine that lived within her. I'd succumbed to mine, and she'd chosen to be good.

She was all that I wasn't. And I'd sworn I'd do everything to shield her from this dark, dangerous world, but I'd failed. I'd been unable to protect her from me. From *my* darkness. I'd broken her heart.

I turned away from the hordes of Mer growing ever greater on the dunes and rubbed a webbed hand down my face. I should have known my scars would extinguish her light, that I'd taint her with the shadows I carried. I should've walked away before my pain left its mark on her.

They say the broken only know how to break. Perhaps they're right.

I won't let what my father did to me compel my actions.

I will not let my love destroy her.

My knuckles cracked.

No.

I would lead my people into battle, and we would face my uncle—face Manannán. I would enjoy every second of ripping his throat out with my teeth.

I'd been better since she came into my life. My healing magic had returned, and I'd managed to keep the bloodlust at bay, but now . . . now I had nothing left to lose.

After Manannán was defeated, I would find the Trinity, and a new day would come. A day when my people would be free of the blood-hungry Drowned and the Shadow, a happy ending where she didn't have to die.

Then I would do what I should have done when I first saw her sitting at the end of that jetty and *walk away.*

Acknowledgments

Thank *you*, my reader, first and foremost.

If you're reading this book, I can presume it's because you took a chance on my debut, *Sea of Evil and Desire*, and I am so grateful for your support. Thank you to my New Zealand Street Team of Sirens, my ARC readers, BookTok and Bookstagram girlies, the South African girlies on BookTok who have all been so supportive, and my girlfriends who never read but made an exception for my book (then encouraged me to get even more unhinged with this one). Reading your messages was what pushed me to keep going and get this out when I wasn't sure if I could.

I also love seeing the passages that you highlight on Kindle. Your words influence me more than you may know. I might create an Easter egg just for you, or change the course of a character's future because of something you've said. For example, after laughing with my lovely reader, Tess, I incorporated some jokes about tail span.

Writer burnout is real, and I pushed myself extremely hard to deliver this book in the same year as *Sea of Evil and Desire,* and I couldn't have done it without your encouragement. I am beyond grateful that people relate to my crazy, weird world.

I'd also like to thank my amazing developmental editor (and sister), Eve Gailey. It is a dream come true to hire my talented sister for this. She is an editor in the film and television industry, and was always pulling me up and ensuring the characters felt what was happening, and that the stakes were as high as possible (at all times!). Sometimes I laugh about what a disaster the books could have been without her.

Thank you to my cover designer, Vivien Ries. I honestly didn't know how she could create a cover that I liked better than book one, but she did it!

My line editor, Jenny DePierre, who tightened up everything and is always a pleasure to work with.

To all the talented authors and filmmakers who have come before me, shaping my imagination and inspiring me.

And my dog, Diego, for being my fluffy support animal while I live the hermit life of an author and take him for long walks weeping over Sleep Token between writing sessions.

Chapter Six and Eight Synopsis

Your mental health matters. If you choose to skip chapters six and eight, here is an overview of these chapters, so missing them will not affect your experience.

Skye goes to Parker's and begins packing to return to Morgana's, but Parker comes home early and convinces her that he loves her. She decides to go on the yacht for his birthday after all.

On the yacht, Parker ignores her for most of the night, but when he sees her speaking to his work colleague, he confronts her in a jealous rage. They argue, and he punches her in the face, sending her flying overboard to be swallowed by the seas.